HEATHER

SHADOW
OF
TWILIGHT

FATED DARKNESS | BOOK 1

For Stefanie

For believing in me
even when I doubted myself,
for being my rock,
my confidant,
and the truest friend

PROLOGUE

ALL THE STORIES ARE REAL

Having a mate isn't all it's cracked up to be. It's a rare occurrence nowadays.

For most, it's just another fairytale. A story for mothers to tell their pups. Instilling the belief in true love and love at first sight.

Of course, everyone knows what a mate is. Each pup has heard the tales and could recognize the signs. The great bond of Ezekial and Rhea. The first mated pair that began the werewolf race is a legend.

Before words were written and Christianity ran rampant in the west, Ezekiel and Rhea were the werewolf race's founders. As neighboring tribes, they had been at war with each other for generations. Their parents arranged their marriage as a way to bring peace.

It is said, when Ezekial first saw his new bride, it was like the air was sucked right from his lungs. When they took hands for the handfasting, his skin burned where they touched, igniting something visceral within. That night they consummated their marriage, forging a bond like never before. Together, they created the mate bond. The connection allowed each other the ability to mind link and sense when the other was in danger.

The Moon Goddess watched from above as she witnessed the bond build and grow and took it as a sign. On the next full moon, the Moon Goddess blessed the couple. Ezekial and Rhea transformed into great wolves, becoming the first-ever Alpha and Luna. Given their bloodlines and their tribes' connection, every member of both clans transformed into wolves, becoming the first wolf pack.

Once they completed the transition, Ezekial and Rhea weren't only able to mind link one another, they were able to communicate with every member of their tribe, their pack. In wolf form, they found another part of themselves. Blessed by the Goddess, they were each given a spirit wolf. The other half of their soul that occupied the same mind and body.

As the first mated pair, Ezekial and Rhea felt compelled to mark one another. Biting into one another's flesh, leaving their mark and scent to remind the pack that they were taken, no longer free to other potential mates. Thus, sealing the mate bond forever.

Being a wolf meant more than just the pack and mate bond. It came with violent mood swings, extreme highs and lows, and temperamental, sometimes unstable personalities. The higher ranked a wolf was, the more prone they were to fits of rage. Especially if they felt challenged or threatened. The Alpha and Luna were positioned at the top of the pecking order. Their word was law.

It is believed that Ezekial and Rhea received special powers after completing the mating ritual. The ability to receive prophetic dreams, healing one's mate. Some even believe that Rhea was the real Alpha, her power greater than Ezekial's, but this has been shot down by the elders. Back in the day of Ezekial and Rhea, even if they were real at one time, lived in the age of man. Women were submissive and docile, obeying their husbands, always.

Nowadays, the story of Ezekial and Rhea is considered a fairytale. It's still their story of origins, but even the elders no longer hold the mate bond to a high standard. Of course, every girl's dream is to find the prince that will whisk her away to his castle. Where they'd live happily ever after. Where they'd find their mate, feeling complete and whole and loved.

But Amelia knew better. She lived in the real world.

CHAPTER 1

FATE'S A BITCH

"Amelia! Get your ass out of bed! Now!"

Amelia lifted her head off her pillow. Her eyes squinted at the light filtering in through the crack of her curtains. She grabbed her phone on the nightstand and turned it on to check the time. Nearly noon. Crap.

Throwing off the blankets, she attempted to sit up clutching her pounding head. Her stomach rolled as bile rose to the back of her throat.

Ugh. She should never have drunk so much last night.

Amelia and her brother had snuck out to a party. A bit of a pre-birthday celebration in their honor. Let's just say tequila and beer do *not* mix. She could barely remember what happened except that she broke up with her boyfriend shortly before puking all over his car. Not one of her finest moments.

She clutched her head even harder as the sound of someone banging on her door increased the pain exponentially. She staggered out of bed, flinging the door open, ready to punch the jerk when she caught sight of her brother. He looked almost as bad as she felt.

He looked like hell. Purple bruises ran down the side of his thin face. Dark circles rimmed his blood-shot, sea-green eyes. He was barely able to keep them open with the sunlight streaming through her windows.

"What do you want?" she gritted out through her teeth, trying to keep her voice low to avoid the throbbing in her brain.

"Dad is threatening to disinherit us if we don't get downstairs. The Alpha ceremony is tonight, and we promised to welcome the visiting packs. Some have already begun to arrive," Damon told her.

His hair was wet and combed back, wearing a clean black shirt and jeans. He was already showered, but she could still smell the alcohol on him as though it was seeping from his pores. She wrinkled her nose in disgust. "You reek, bro."

"I know," he lifted his shirt to his nose, sniffing the material, coming away looking like he was ready to vomit. "I showered twice."

"Come in," she whispered, gesturing for him to enter her room. She closed the door firmly behind him, locking it.

"Can we just do this already? *Before* dad kills us. We cannot go downstairs looking like death," he whined.

"Oh, shut up. He'd never kill his favorite son," she waved him off.

"I don't know about that. He's already linked me about a hundred times today. Threats have been made."

"That's weird. I haven't gotten any."

"That's because he would never threaten his princess," Damon said, making a wild gesture with his hand at her throne-like room that they stood in the middle of. With her canopy queen bed, the wall-to-wall book cases and a large vanity looking out over her bay window. She was definitely the spoiled one.

She rolled her eyes and punched him in the shoulder. "Please, he threatens me daily. He knows I'd kick his ass."

This made him chuckle as he tried not to wince at her punch. "Hurry up. He's yelling," he whined once again.

Amelia shook her head at him as they took each other's hands. Their arms hung between them as they started to relax. She focused on her wolf, Rey, as she connected with her twin's wolf, Zeke. Their wolves began to hum to one another, melding their minds and their powers. She could feel the tension in her shoulders dissipate, her headache receding and disappearing altogether, along with the lingering nausea.

Feeling like she'd gotten twenty-four hours of sleep, she opened her eyes to find her brother's face. His dark circles and black eyes were completely gone, revealing tan, olive skin with a light dusting of freckles. His emerald eyes no longer looked glazed over from the lingering effects of alcohol.

They had completely healed one another.

Ever since their first shift at age six, they had a different bond than most twins. No matter how far apart they were, they could always reach each other through the mind link. Even if they couldn't reach the rest of the pack. They also had the nifty ability to heal one another.

When they were twelve, Damon had fallen out of a tree. Tumbling thirty feet to the ground, resulting in compound fractures in both of his legs. Sure, his wolf could have healed him. He wouldn't have had to be in the hospital for more than a day, but Amelia was terrified as she watched her brother's blood stain the earth red. She could remember feeling like throwing up at the sight of the bone piercing through flesh. It was gruesome and horrifying to see. He wasn't just her brother. He was her best friend, her other half. When he hurt, she hurt.

She remembered rushing to his side and holding his hand, reassuring him that he was going to be fine. Their father was already running for the phone to call the pack doctor.

That was when her wolf spoke to her, telling her to close her eyes and follow along, humming a soothing melody. It was a quiet, soft little tune, and she obeyed her wolf instantly. When she opened her eyes again, his legs were completely healed. Their father had shown up in the backyard, frantically yelling at the pack doctor over the phone when he noticed his son was standing beside his daughter. Blood was soaked through his torn jeans, but the skin was completely smooth, as if nothing had happened.

Their father had made them swear on the Moon Goddess herself, to never speak a word of it to anyone.

Her brother's arms winding around her shoulders snapped her out of the past and back to the present.

"Thanks, Mia. You're the best," Damon said, taking her in for a hug.

Amelia squeezed him back, instantly comforted by his embrace and his wolf. She was nervous about leaving on her worldwide adventure. Nervous about leaving her twin. They had never been separated before at such a distance or length of time. The longest they had been apart was a week. He had stayed home over summer break and she went off to Jacksonville, Florida with her friends. The whole time she was gone, she felt homesick and completely isolated. She hated it.

She was terrified she would feel that way again once she left. That she wouldn't be able to last long on her own, but she was stubborn enough to try. Once her brother took over as Alpha, she felt she no longer had a place in their pack. Since her brother was without a mate, she *could* take over the Luna duties. Her pack had been without a Luna ever since her mother passed away over ten years ago, but she didn't want to be stuck in the same house she lived in all her life. She longed to be free.

She didn't care where she went. With no real destination in mind, all Amelia wanted to do was wander. Go wherever her feet carried her. Ride a train to the west coast, stow away on a boat to the Philippines, climb the West Andes. She wanted to see and do it all.

Amelia pushed him away, hearing her father's voice in her brother's head. "You better go before he names someone else Alpha."

Damon chuckled. "Do *not* take your time up here. Dad wants you downstairs ASAP. The next visiting pack is arriving in thirty minutes."

"Which pack?" Amelia asked, walking over to her dresser mirror.

Surprisingly, she didn't look too bad. The healing must have done something to her hair. It was no longer limp or lifeless and still retained some of the curls from last night's party. She could work with that.

"I think it's the Twilight Moon Pack," Damon informed her, pulling open the bedroom door.

"Oh, good. I haven't met their new Alpha yet. Old Alpha Demetry handed down the title just a few months ago to his only son. Every time I've ever met the old grump his son's been away," Amelia disappeared inside her walk-in closet, running her fingers along the rows of clothes, looking for the item she had in mind.

The Twilight Moon Pack were their closest neighbors. Residing about four hours away, their territory crossed over the border into New York. The pack was similar to theirs in terms of size and strength. They had been allies for generations, usually intermarrying to continue the peace. Amelia had visited the pack a few times over the last few years, making friends as she went. Although some just didn't appreciate the bond of a fist to the face. Strange.

"Twenty minutes, Mia," Damon warned her before shutting her bedroom door behind him.

Amelia quickly picked out a simple white lace, knee-length dress. The dress's top was a simple scoop neck, racerback, exposing her shoulders to the warm summer air and slipped on a simple pair of black flats. She was already tall and didn't need the added height from heels.

She quickly went into her adjoining bathroom. Brushing her teeth and running a comb through her hair, she touched up her make-up. Giving herself a last look in the mirror, she ran out of her room, slamming the door behind her.

Amelia Rhea Smoke! Where the hell are you? The Alpha is pulling up now! Her father's voice boomed in her head.

She hated it when he said her full name. *I'm coming! It's not my fault you have my room up on the fifth floor!* she snapped at him, earning her a warning growl in her head.

Ignoring him, she raced down the stairs as quickly as she could. Once she reached the second floor, she jumped over the banister, landing evenly on the balls of her feet. She pushed through the bustle of the Packhouse as members gathered around, awaiting the new arrivals.

Outside, the humid air washed over her, making her instantly grateful she decided on a dress and not jeans. Straightening out her dress and running her fingers through her hair, she stepped off the porch to stand beside her brother, who waited beside their father. At the head of the welcoming committee, she was one of the first to catch sight of three large, black SUV's driving up their driveway. She bounced anxiously on her toes, unable to keep from fidgeting.

"Will you relax?" Damon hissed at her.

Amelia huffed loudly, settling herself down. "I can't help it. I'm excited," she beamed, barely able to keep her voice even. "You're gonna be Alpha tonight. I'm so proud of you," she nudged him with her elbow, teasing him.

Damon glanced down at her, smiling. Even though she was taller than most girls, he still towered over her, and she loved it. She may be his older sister by mere minutes, but he had always taken on the role of dutiful protector and savior.

Not like she needed it.

She was glad she'd be by his side tonight. Standing by him as he became Alpha of their pack. Her stomach had been doing somersaults over the last few days every time she thought of leaving him behind. From their numerous conversations, she could tell he was nervous as well, but no matter what, he continuously supported her.

They all stood in silence as the vehicles finally pulled up the circle drive—the SUV in the middle parked in front of the awaiting welcoming committee. Amelia felt as if there was a hurricane of bats going off in her stomach.

Each SUV door automatically opened, letting out a dozen men and women from the Twilight Moon Pack. The men all looked like giants, typical for werewolves. Each pack trained differently, but they all had a vicious metabolism and daily training, making for some fit individuals.

She couldn't help but check out the males standing in front of her. Most of the men in her race were beefy and cut. Smooth planes of defined, rippling muscles that her fingers itched to touch. Color rose to her cheeks at the mere thought of being with a male. Luckily, she broke up with her boyfriend last night. Maybe she could have some fun before she left tomorrow.

You're disgusting.

Amelia couldn't help but smirk at her brother's remark. *Stay out of my head and we won't have a problem.*

It's not my fault we're connected. Stupid twin bond.

Amelia tried to hide the snicker trying to escape, earning her a steady glare from her father. She quickly shut up, throwing on her steely mask, otherwise known as resting bitch face.

A part of her wanted to make her brother squirm even more, possibly make him blush in the presence of the Twilight Moon Pack. Giving her plenty of ammo to embarrass him for all eternity, when her nose caught a whiff of something unsuspecting. Her mouth watered as the scent assaulted her taste buds. Her heart fluttered wildly in her chest as her body warmed instantly, humming in anticipation. She couldn't help but lean into the heavenly smell, lifting her head up a bit, catching the breeze as it was blown right in her face.

Cinnamon, cloves, and apples.

Damon tensed at her side. His body responding to hers. She could feel him glancing down at her, taking in her face. Her brow was scrunched and furrowed. The way she was inhaling the air deeply was like she was incapable of taking in a solid breath.

What's wrong? he asked her.

I smell something.

Now he was worried. *Rogues?*

No, no. It smells, she sniffed the air again as the incoming pack adjusted their ranks, accommodating someone in their midst. *It smells amazing. Like coming home.*

Now he was the one with the confused look, but he quickly became distracted as the Twilight Moon Pack's Alpha stepped forward. Flanked by his higher-ranking pack members, the Alpha approached their father.

The new Alpha was quite impressive. He looked only a few years older than herself. Rather tall, even by werewolf standards, and lean, his skin stretched thin over muscles.

Amelia watched as the stranger approached her father. She noticed the way he walked, confident and strong, completely void of care. His face was hard and set as though he had never been taught to smile. His hair was blacker than a moonless sky, and a bit had grown out, hanging in his face. But it was his eyes that grabbed her attention. Silver grey. They were so light and mesmerizing, she couldn't help but stare.

The bats that had once been in her stomach were now more like dinosaurs. Large flapping pterodactyls beating around inside of her. Her palms were sweating. She was unable to help but chew on her bottom lip in nervousness.

What the hell was wrong with her?

"Alpha Thomas, it's nice to finally meet you," the new Alpha said, offering his hand in respect.

Her father instantly took it, shaking his hand firmly. She could tell by the slight dilation of his hazel eyes; he was sizing up the new Alpha. Judging who he was strictly based on what he looked like. Her own father and Alpha was in pristine physical condition, even given his age. Lucky for them, wolves age much slower than their human counterparts. So, even though her dad was over fifty years old, he barely looked a day over thirty with his sandy brown, cropped hair and thin, lean build.

"Thank you for making the trip. You honor our alliance with your presence. Welcome to the Wandering Moon Pack. This is my son, Damon. He'll be named Alpha in tonight's ceremony," he introduced them, gesturing towards her brother.

Damon shook the new Alpha's hand, his grip firm and hard. "It's nice to meet you, Alpha."

"Please, call me Gabriel," he said, flashing him a brilliant white smile.

"And this is my daughter, Amelia."

Amelia could feel his silver eyes take her in. Running over every inch of her body. She wasn't sure if she had ever felt more exposed before. Even having been naked in front of hundreds of wolves had never left her feeling so bare. It wasn't until he looked into her ocean green eyes that she felt something like a jolt of lightning pierce her chest.

She felt frozen. Mesmerized by the way his silver eyes seemed to captivate her. Every solitary cell within her body was attuned to the stranger standing before her. The hairs along her arms and down the back of her neck stood straight up, electrically charged, just waiting for the slightest bit of friction to set off a chain reaction.

His eyes widened as if recognizing her in some way when she was positive they had never met before. The wind had suddenly changed direction, blowing directly in his face, kicking up her hair around her. His nostrils flared wide, catching her scent. His silver iris grew black as his wolf surged forward violently before suddenly settling back down to its calm, cool shade.

She didn't realize how long they'd been staring at one another until the sound of someone clearing their throat caught both of their attention.

Amelia finally felt free of his gaze. The sound of her brother coughing broke her free of his spell. She observed him as he composed himself, rearranging his features to something along the lines of emotionless.

"It's a pleasure to meet you," Gabriel said formally, his monotone voice taking her by surprise. He extended his hand out to her, the same as he did with the Alpha.

"You as well."

Showing no hesitation, she reached out and took his hand, regretting it the instant their skin made contact. Gooseflesh spread across her entire body at his touch. Her heart beat wildly in her chest. Her head was swimming with his intoxicating scent as a tingling sensation of his skin touching hers told her what her soul already knew.

Rey howled in her head, excited and eager. Her other half, her twin soul, recognized him instantly. Amelia could feel her wolf's spirit prancing around, begging to be closer to him. Whispering to her, encouraging her to move in.

He was her mate.

Fuck.

Damon startled at her side, his gaze flicking down to her hand in Gabriel's.

She quickly pulled her hand out of his grasp and hid it behind her back. Rubbing it against the back of her leg, she tried to rub away the lingering feeling. She watched as he moved on from her.

Her father continued the introductions to the top members of their pack. She wanted to run. To get as far away as possible and never look back before this new Alpha had a chance to claim her. To steal her freedom, her rank, and her wildness. He would try to tame her, domesticate her, something she believed to be worse than death.

Men, particularly male wolves, were more prone to dominance and control. Even though her parents were happily mated, fated mates at that, there was no guarantee she'd get lucky in the mate department.

From what little she could remember of her parents together, they were perfect for one another. She could remember her mother's laugh. It was whimsical and soft. Something her father sought out to hear every day. He made it his mission to make her laugh as often as possible. He was quite good at it, but then she died and it was like the light had left his eyes.

She didn't want a mate. She never did, but it looked like fate had other plans for her.

CHAPTER 2

STUPID MATE

Once the introductions had neared the end, Amelia snuck out of the crowd, slipping between her fellow pack members back into the house. She headed directly for the kitchen, pushing through the swinging double doors. The two cooks and half a dozen assistants were flurrying about the room, preparing tonight's feast. She worked her way through the bustle, avoiding those working and made her way to the fridge.

She pulled out a bottle of water, quickly guzzling down the cool liquid. She felt flushed. The type of heat that had nothing to do with the temperature outside. Her heart was racing and her stomach was performing acrobatics, enough to bring back her nausea.

"Is everything okay, dear?"

Amelia snapped out of her daze to discover a short, stout woman with flaming curly hair pulled up into a knot on top of her head, standing in front of her.

"Yes, Ms. McKready. It's just hot out there."

"Make sure to drink plenty of fluids. We have a long night ahead of us," Ms. McKready smirked with a wink, getting back to prepping the chicken.

"You have no idea."

Amelia tossed her waste into the recycling bin before leaving the kitchen. The Packhouse was busier than ever. Between her own pack and the four visiting ones, the house was chaotic.

She recognized her group of friends huddled in the living room. The girls were gawking at the new male beef, and the males were drooling over the unmated females that had arrived. She weaved in and out of varying sized groups, making her way to her friends. Daniel was there, her ex-boyfriend, smiling at her as if she hadn't doused the inside of his car with vomit. She couldn't help but smile back. Even though she had broken up with him, they had still been friends for as long as she could remember. That wouldn't change.

Four of her closest girlfriends were whispering harshly amongst themselves, and each of them couldn't be more distinct from one another. There was Cordelia, the gorgeous, reserved nerd, her closest friend that she couldn't imagine life without. Jasmine, the punk rocker who always had chipped, black nail polish and headphones wrapped around her neck. Melinda, the quiet, mousy red-head with acrylic paint permanently stuck beneath her nails. Finally, there was her cousin Gabby, the pack slut. Known for sleazing from guy to guy and not giving two shits who knew about it.

Amelia managed to jump in at the tail end of the conversation. She caught whispers of dirty comments. Ranging from the various positions they'd love to be put in, to the different flavors they might taste like. Their well-endowed assets were being code named a variety of random objects. Apple pie practically had her choking on her spit.

As she made her way to stand amongst them the conversation quieted. Each of them looked to her to see if there was a male amongst the crowd she would claim first. As the Alpha's daughter, she was amongst the highest ranked, allowing her first pick. But, that was the last thing on her mind. Her heart was still racing from the far from simple handshake she had exchanged with the new Alpha of the Twilight Moon pack.

"Please tell me someone has a drink for me," Amelia whispered amongst her friends.

The girl on her right, Cordelia, promptly handed her a mug she had been holding. Most would think she was consuming coffee, but from the ripe fermented smell of molasses, it was well-aged bourbon.

"Bless you, Cordie," Amelia praised, consuming a deep drink of the burning liquid. She immediately felt more buoyant as the liquor hit her empty stomach. "Goddess, I needed that."

"What's got you so wound up?" Cordelia asked, her detail-oriented hazel eyes were still gazing over the continuously gathering crowd.

"You don't wanna know," she mumbled into the mug before taking another long drink.

"Man, and I thought *we* had some fine-looking men in our pack, but these new beefcakes are making me blush."

Amelia leaned forward to consider the girl on the end, only to find Gabby, her cousin. Her cropped brunette hair filled her slim face. She was constantly looking for her next conquest, causing her to be a bit of a hoe, but who was she to judge? Her cousin knew how to have fun.

The other girls nodded in agreement as they continued their ogling.

"Has anyone seen the new Alpha that just arrived?" Cordelia purred.

"You mean Alpha Gabriel?" Amelia asked. Her heart began to race just by the mere mention of him. She enjoyed the way his name rolled off her tongue.

"What I wouldn't give to mount that fine stallion."

Amelia nearly shot bourbon through her nose as she coughed wildly into the mug. Her head was burning. Her nose itched something fierce; enough to cause her to consider cutting it off. Everyone seemed to have noticed her coughing fit as it appeared all eyes were on her. Her cheeks were flaming red.

Thank God her father wasn't in the room.

"Amelia."

Shit.

Amelia handed the mug back to Cordelia, who looked down at the back washed bourbon with disgust. She glanced over at her father, who stood in a circle of all the visiting Alphas and their heirs, to include Alpha Gabriel. She tried to ignore the burning of his silver eyes as they stared at her. No matter how he was looking at her, he had nothing on her father.

My office. Now.

Amelia lowered her head as his orders rang in her ears. She stepped out of her circle of friends when she felt a hand wrap around her arm, tugging her back. She looked up to find Daniel. His gentle baby blue eyes looked at her as he handed her a handkerchief from his pocket.

"Thank you, Danny," she whispered to him, taking the handkerchief before leaving the main room of the house. She walked down the gray-washed halls decorated with pictures from her childhood, and into her father's office.

Amelia had met some Alpha's who preferred having their office on the top floor near their rooms, but her father always wanted to be accessible to his pack. Since it's normally forbidden for pack members to go up onto the Alpha floor, it never made sense to him.

She pushed the door open to his office. Her nose instantly filled with Old Spice and peppermint. Her dad consistently had peppermint gum lying around everywhere. Thankful for his weird quirk, she swiftly pulled out a piece from his top drawer and hastily chewed it, hoping to remove the smell of alcohol on her breath.

Amelia wiped at her runny nose with the handkerchief. The burning sensation was practically gone. She tucked the piece of cloth into a hidden pocket in her dress when she heard the office door open. She spun around to discover her father standing in the doorway, glaring at her.

She hung her head in shame. She hated disappointing him, yet she couldn't help herself most of the time. Damon was the good twin.

"Amelia, what is going on with you?" he asked.

He stepped farther into the room when she noticed Damon was behind him. Her brother closed the office door.

She turned to follow her father as he moved behind his weathered, hand-carved walnut desk and sat in his oversized leather chair. "Nothing's wrong, dad."

"Are you drinking already?" Thomas asked, his nostrils flaring.

Shit.

You're in trouble.

She glared at her brother before responding to her father. "It was nothing, dad."

"Promise me you will not embarrass this family tonight. We have too many eyes on us today, and I require all of us to be on our best behavior. Do you understand me?" he asked. His voice turned a tad deeper, coming more from his chest and projecting out as his Alpha aura glowed green around him.

She bowed her head in respect. It would be foolish of her not to acknowledge his use of power. It didn't have the same effect on her as it did the rest of the pack but that didn't mean he didn't deserve her obedience.

"Yes, father."

With a shake of his head, he took her in standing before him. She caught a faint twinkle in his eye as he observed her. Amelia recognized what he saw. She had only heard it a million times growing up.

She looked exactly like her mother.

He sighed deeply before getting up from his desk and circling around to stand in front of her. She felt his large, calloused fingers cup her chin, pulling her face up to look at him. "You look lovely my little rose."

She smiled up at him. "Thanks, daddy."

She heard him take in a deep, steadying breath as he moved his hand away. "Just try not to get drunk until after the ceremony," he warned her, his eyes twinkling playfully.

Amelia grinned. He knew her well. "Promise."

"And no picking fights. I don't want to embarrass any of these high and mighty Alphas when my little girl could kick their asses," he laughed over his shoulder as he went to leave the office.

"You just have to suck the fun right out of me!" she called after him, the door shutting behind him.

She couldn't help but smile. Her father had an easy way of making her smile. Making her happy. Her father was her closest friend and confident, well aside from her twin whom she noticed was still in the office, standing just beside her. She could tell he was itching to ask her something.

"Spit it out, Damon. Dad will expect us back out there."

"What's going on with you?" he asked her, cutting her off before she could give him some non-answer, "and don't tell me it's nothing. Don't forget, I know you better than anyone."

She massaged her forehead. A small headache began to form as the effects of the alcohol were already dissipating. "I met my mate."

Damon's jaw nearly broke hitting the floor. "Wait, what?! Like an actual mate? Like a real mate?"

"I think so," she said softly, her heart sinking further into her stomach.

"But who?"

"Alpha Gabriel."

"Christ, Amelia."

She groaned, throwing herself down on the small loveseat, cradling her head in her hands.

"I know. It's bad. What am I gonna do?" she felt like crying but swallowed it down, burying it deep. She refused to spill a single tear on a man she didn't even know.

"There's nothing to do right now. You have to put this mate thing aside. Right now, our priority is the Alpha ceremony. Afterward, we can confront your problem," Damon said, trying to prioritize.

"What if he claims me? I don't want to be a Luna! I want to travel, see the world. I have plans," she could feel her eyes betraying her, tears pricking the corner of her eyes.

Damon seized her by the arms, hauling her up to stand. He shook her softly so that her head rolled back to look up at him. "We will figure this out. I promise you. I won't let you go anywhere if it isn't what you desire."

"But the law clearly states that the male in a mate bond has absolute control of his mate, willing or not," she cried, sniffing her nose.

"Fuck the law. This is not the dark ages. No one will force you to do anything. I always have your back," he promised her, pulling her in, winding his arms tightly around her.

Amelia instantly relaxed against her brother's sturdy form, wrapping her arms around his waist. She quickly pulled out the handkerchief from her pocket, wiping away her tears, and cleaning up her nose.

"We only have a few more hours until the ceremony, and then we can let our wolves out for the pack run," Damon reminded her.

Amelia shuddered in delight. Her wolf bobbed her head, agreeing with her excitedly. It had been a while since she let Rey out. She loved her wolf form and knew her beast within was just itching to run. She never felt freer than as a wolf.

"Alright, let's get back out there," she said, tucking the hankie away.

She watched as her brother left the office. Taking in a deep breath, she made certain her face was dry before leaving the room. She walked down the hall. The sound of voices grew louder by the second as she got closer to the communal room, when suddenly she felt herself being dragged. Her arm was jerked harshly, pulling her into a room. The door clicked shut behind her.

The lights weren't on. The sun was already setting outside, providing little light, but she didn't need to see to guess who it was. Her skin was tingling, gooseflesh spreading up her arm and down her back.

Amelia wrenched her arm free of his grasp. She was fortunate if it didn't leave a bruise. She shoved hard against his chest, catching him by surprise, making him stumble back.

"What the hell do you think you're doing?" she hissed, wanting desperately to scream at him but knew it was better if she didn't. The last thing she wanted was to bring any attention to herself.

Gabriel stiffened, surprised at her strength as she caught him off guard. He swiftly diminished the distance between them, pushing her up against the wall.

Amelia froze. The closeness of his body made her nerves go haywire. Her body felt as if it was on fire. She didn't dare breathe. She didn't need his scent overpowering her too. She had enough going on as it was.

Mate! Mate! Rey shouted in her head.

I know! Shut up already! Like she hadn't already figured that out.

Gabriel reached up, stroking her face with the backs of his knuckles, causing a series of sparks to fly under her skin. She could feel her knees begin to tremble, but she locked them tight. She was taught to never show weakness.

"What do you want?" she asked him again, adding a taste of venom to her words.

Gabriel smirked as he continued to caress her face, as though he was trying to memorize every detail. "I want you, mate."

The way he said mate made her insides shiver. She desperately needed to get a grip. "That's good for you, but I already have plans, and they do not involve you," she said, pushing against his chest, but he wouldn't budge. Instead, he pressed himself harder against her. She could feel something poking her thigh, causing her stomach to burn.

This mate bond was going tp get annoying real fast.

"You think you have a choice?" Gabriel growled.

He reached behind her, gripping her ass tightly, shifting her leg untill it hugged his waist. He pressed his lower half against her even more, angling himself so that she could feel his member pressing against her core.

Amelia tried to stifle a moan. She clamped down hard, biting her lip to keep from getting any louder.

"I'll take you right here and now, and you can't say anything about it. You are mine and mine alone."

Amelia shook her head. Not only to refuse him but to clear the mind-numbing effect he was having on her. Her body craved his touch, wanted to beg him to satisfy her in any way he sought fit, but her mind reminded her that she was a woman, a lady, and deserved to be treated with respect.

"You even think of touching me without my consent. I will carve your dick into tiny pieces and feed it to the crows," she growled back at him.

He has much to learn.

Rey's comment surprised her. She thought she would be all about the mate bond, begging her to let him mate with them but instead, she had her back. She knew she loved her wolf.

"My mate has fire," Gabriel chuckled. "Tomorrow, you will leave with me to my pack and be my Luna. Until you do, I will do with you as I please." He could feel her hesitation. "If you do not comply, I will declare war on your pack and personally kill your brother and father. Trust me, I'll follow through."

Amelia's heart froze in her chest. She's visited the Twilight Moon Pack in the past on diplomatic missions with her father. She's witnessed the size of his pack. The Twilight Moon Pack was equal in size to her own, and their fighters were almost similar in strength. She remembered sparring with a few of their warriors, breaking her arm in the process, but not before she broke at least a dozen of theirs.

"You touch my family and I will end you," she said.

"Is that a threat?" he asked. A touch of amusement could be heard in his voice.

"No. It's a promise," she whispered harshly, leaning up into his face, making complete and total eye contact. She wanted to be sure that he understood how serious she was.

Her deep, ocean green eyes were glaring harshly at him. Something twitched against the top of her thigh. Her defiance aroused him. Her stomach turned sour, flipping what little contents was left. She couldn't decide between kneeing him until he was choking on his own balls or head butting him to hear the satisfying crack of cartilage.

Before she could decide, he leaned into her, crashing down on her lips. She froze beneath him, shocked at the contact as it sent shivers down her spine, igniting a fire so deep inside her she didn't think she'd ever been able to satisfy it without his touch. She couldn't help herself as her arms snaked up around his neck, her fingers running through his silk hair, gripping at the roots.

She could feel the hunger he had for her. Though their bond was but a shadow of what it would be if they ever did mate, it was enough. His blood was coursing through his veins, stronger than a current through raging rapids. It was singing a song. His heart beating, pumping life through his body, calling to her, beckoning her forward. Enticing her to drown in his scent, his touch, his desire. The primal need was over riding whatever sense was left between them and in that moment, Amelia didn't care.

Meeting her own needs and desires, their lips fought, tasting one another feverishly. Her mouth opened under pressure, allowing him entrance, tasting every inch of her. She responded in kind. He really did taste like apples. His hands were roaming down her body, gripping her ass and thighs. His fingertips gripped at the back of her dress, pressing firmly into her lower back like he was fighting with himself on whether or not to rip it off.

His lips moved away from hers, tracing her jaw, down her neck and across her shoulder and back up to the crook of her neck where a mate's mark would reside. He licked the skin between her neck and shoulder, nipping at it, sucking it.

Amelia couldn't help the moan that escaped her lips. Her head rolled farther back in ecstasy, granting him more access to her sensitive skin. If he marked her right then and there, she didn't think she'd care.

Luckily, he didn't.

Amelia! Where are you? Ceremonies about to start!

CHAPTER 3

ALPHA CEREMONY

Damon's voice ringing in her head was like being dunked in a frozen lake in the middle of winter at the North Pole. It shocked her system, yanking her back to reality. Panic quickly settled in her bones. She wasn't ready for this. She swore she'd never let a man take over her mind let alone her common sense.

Amelia could feel his eyes on her as her body went stiff beneath him. She pulled back, resting her head against the smooth plaster of the wall to find him studying her curiously, taking in her every movement. She untangled herself from his clutches, straightening out her dress and adjusting her hair. She just hoped her lips weren't too swollen and there weren't any visible hickeys.

"The ceremony is about to start. I have to go," she ran her hands over the front of her dress, flattening out any creases or wrinkles and took in a deep breath before leaving the room.

Amelia couldn't sense him following her, which was probably for the best. She had no idea how she actually looked. The last thing she needed was for both of them to enter the ceremony looking like they had seven minutes in heaven.

Even though she had no idea how long she'd been in that room with him, kissing him was like nothing she'd ever experienced before. She may still be a virgin, but she'd had her fair share of fooling around. Kissing him, the way he touched her, was addicting to say the least.

She noticed most of those present were already outside for the ceremony. The house contained the last few stragglers making their way out the back door. She blended in with the crowd making her way outside.

Their backyard was large enough to accommodate a thousand plus people. The full moon was rising above the tree line that surrounded their property, illuminating the earth. Tiki torches were flaming around the perimeter and scattered throughout to provide enough light for everyone. A grand stage was constructed along the back of the house where her father, brother, and other high-ranking pack members were waiting.

Since there was no longer a Luna in their pack, Amelia had volunteered to officiate the ceremony. It should have been her mother that presided over the Alpha ceremony, but she believed she was there in spirit.

Amelia forced her way through the crowd and up onto the stage. Her father's eyebrow was elevated as she stepped in between her father and brother.

"You're late," Thomas growled lowly.

"Psh. I'm right on time," Amelia smirked, ignoring her father's looks, glancing out over their pack and visitors.

What could you have possibly been doing for so long?

Amelia glared at her brother. By the deep crease in his forehead to the skin stretched tight over his knuckles, he knew exactly what had distracted her. Clearly, he did not approve, and she honestly couldn't blame him. She had done exactly what she said she didn't want to do.

I know. It's not easy, Damon.

Damon rolled his eyes, huffing in annoyance, but kept silent as their father stepped forward on the stage. The crowd instantly hushed as their Alpha prepared to speak.

"Thank you all for coming here tonight. It means so much to us that you are all able to be present and witness my son take his place as the Alpha of the Wandering Moon Pack. Today is my son and daughter's eighteenth birthday, and tonight we will celebrate." This earned him quite a few cheers in celebration. He smirked before gaining control once again. "But first, my son will become Alpha. As descendants of Ezekial and Rhea, he will take his place in our great pack."

The crowd cheered even louder, howls and hoots ringing through the air.

"Since we are without our Luna, my daughter will preside over the ceremony."

Her father stepped back from the front of the stage back over to his children. Collectively, they formed a triangle around a narrow circular table, which held a golden chalice designed with intricate scrollwork. The chalice was said to be Ezekial's and Rhea's wedding cup and was the pack's prized possession. Beside it was the ceremonial knife.

Amelia looked out over the crowd, smiling brilliantly. She looked up at the stars. Hard to see with all the torchlight, but she could still make out the one she had named after her mother. She knew the words to the ceremony by heart. She memorized them weeks ago, but she knew she had more to say.

"Tonight is a milestone in our pack. The day my brother takes over as Alpha, allowing my old man here to finally retire." The crowd began to laugh. "Our Luna, my mother, should have been the one to perform this ceremony. I know we all feel her loss every day, and even though she may no longer be here with us physically, I know she is always here with us in spirit, watching over us with our ancestors."

She noted her brother and father had unshed tears, glistening in the flickering torchlight. She smiled faintly, clearing her throat before she made herself a blubbering mess.

"Now, let's get this shit started, so we can party." This warranted a serious eye roll from her father, a smirk from her brother, and a few hollers from her friends in the crowd. "Tonight, we are here to witness the passing of one Alpha to another, reforging their bloodline to the succession and continuance of the Wandering Moon Pack."

Amelia picked up the ceremonial knife off the table, holding it across both her palms. Turning to her father, she recited her lines. "Alpha Thomas, are you here of your own volition to step down as Alpha, naming your son and heir as Alpha of the Wandering Moon Pack?"

"I am," Thomas proudly announced, holding out his hand over the chalice.

Amelia took hold of the knife, pressing the blade into the pale flesh of her father's palm. She swiftly sliced into his skin. Blood instantly welled from the wound. Her father held his hand over the chalice, allowing his blood to pool in the bottom of the cup.

"Do you, Damon Smoke, son of Thomas, promise to uphold pack tradition, abide by the laws decreed to all werewolves by the Council of Elders, and perform your duties to the best of your ability?"

"I do," Damon vowed, his words ringing over the chilling silence.

"Do you swear to always put your pack first, conduct yourself with honor and integrity befitting a wolf, and lead your pack with strength and valor?"

"I do."

Damon held his hand out as well, giving his sister a slight smile before she cut into his flesh. He turned his sliced palm over, allowing his blood to mix with his fathers and pulled his hand back, his wolf already healing the cut. Amelia picked up the chalice, holding it delicately with both hands. She held it in front of her as the moon reflected off the crimson red surface.

"With the blessing of the Moon Goddess and the rights being read, Alpha Thomas and Alpha Damon will now drink from the chalice, completing the bond."

Amelia handed the cup first to her father. He took a long drink from the golden cup, blood staining his lips. He passed the cup to his son, his demeanor unphased. Damon took the chalice, raising it to his lips, and completed the ritual by consuming the remaining blood.

She tried hard not to gag as she watched her brother visibly struggle to swallow the thick, clotting blood. A concentrated metallic taste assaulted her senses as she breathed in. The smell was salty and pungent. She was even more relieved it wasn't her performing the ritual.

Amelia bowed down on her knee, the same as every other member of their pack, as she experienced a shift in their bond. It was like an audible pop, confirming his place at the top of their pack. Rey beamed proudly in her mind as their twin took his rightful place.

Damon stepped forward on the stage, signaling them all to rise. "Thank you, everyone. I promise to be the best Alpha I can be. I will bring honor and integrity to our pack in all matters. I will defend us until my dying breath."

The pack all stood up as one before they broke out in cheers. Through their bond, Amelia could hear the congratulations from the mind link, while the rest hooped and hollered, pumping their fists in the air.

"Now, we complete the ritual with a pack run!" Amelia hollered, stepping up beside her brother, clasping his hand.

The Wandering Moon Pack members began to prepare for the run. Some women stepped behind the tree line to shed their clothes, while the rest of them stripped where they stood. Nudity was no new thing in a community of werewolves. Damon and Amelia stepped off the stage, making their way to the center of the gathered pack members. Most already shifted into their wolf awaiting their Alpha's command.

Amelia could feel eyes boring a hole in her back, waiting to see what she'd do, but she could have given two craps for his opinion. Damon and Amelia quickly stripped out of their outer layer of clothes, depositing them on the floor, left only in their undergarments. She could hear a deep growl from behind her, but she disregarded it. They both simultaneously shifted into their wolves before their pack.

Amelia shook out her fur, swiveling her head around, relieved to be in her wolf form. Rey was bouncing on her feet, ready to follow her brother on their run.

She looked over to Damon. He was an annoyingly large wolf, even for an Alpha, with dark silver-grey fur. But lucky for her, she was the same size as him.

Ordinarily this wasn't typical for females. She-wolves were normally smaller than their counterparts but Rey grew as large and as tall as her twin. Large enough to rival most Alpha's. Amelia and her brother stood shoulder to shoulder, equal in size and strength. The sole difference between them was their fur coloring. Her brother was a deeper shade of grey, while she bore a silver-white coat, the moon reflecting off her smooth fur.

"Look at her coat."

"Blessed by the Moon Goddess."

"Why is it so light?"

The murmurings behind her were faint but just enough for her werewolf hearing to pick up. Only her own pack members had seen her wolf. Rey's coloring was rare. It wasn't typical for wolf colorings to be so light, but for some reason, hers was.

Amelia followed behind her brother as he took the pack's head position, directing them into the forest. The soft dirt beneath her feet was still moist from the rainfall the night before. Her claws dug into the turned earth for better grip, kicking up bits of leaves and twigs in her wake. The air smelled fresh and exhilarating, breathing new life into her lungs and invigorating her soul. She could hear the rodents scurrying to their dens as the ground vibrated with their approach. Birds flapped overhead, flying far away from the boisterous, charging pack of wolves.

Damon made sure not to run too fast to ensure the pack maintained ranks and kept together. Whether they were running fast or slow, Amelia just enjoyed the feeling of the wind pushing through her fur, the brilliant smells of the forest, and observing life through her wolf's eyes.

The run didn't last long. They were all itching to get back and start the celebration. They jogged back into the large clearing behind the Packhouse, some already shifting back and pulling back on their clothes. She had torn her undergarments when she shifted, so she knew she'd be naked when she shifted back. It didn't bother her.

Her mate suddenly appeared in front of her, holding out a large, white robe. She inclined her head at him with a glint in her eye. Her pack surrounding her were watching with interest, wondering what this new Alpha had to do with her. Her brother stood beside her, his side pressed against hers, showing he had her back. She quickly nipped his ear playfully before allowing her wolf to shift back into her human form.

Amelia stood in front of Gabriel. Her brother turned his head as he covered her back half. Gabriel stood frozen, staring at her bare-naked body.

"My eyes are up here."

CHAPTER 4

WOLF'S OUT OF THE BAG

G abriel growled deeply, stepping forward with the robe, enclosing it tightly around her body.

"What the hell do you think you're doing?" he asked her. His voice deep. His aura grew red around him.

Her mate's chest was puffed, biceps flexing as they crossed in front of him. She could see the black pupils of his eyes widen, his wolf clawing at the surface, desperate to come out. Apparently, man and beast agreed on one thing. They did not like their mate naked in front of others.

"We're wolves, Gabriel. Nudity is nothing new," Amelia stated, tying the robe around her.

"You are my mate. You will conduct yourself accordingly," Gabriel growled once again.

"Or what?" she asked, challenging him.

Gabriel and Amelia continued staring at one another until they heard the sound of someone clearing their throat. Amelia noticed her father standing before them.

His green eyes were flitting back and forth between the two of them.

"What is going on here? Alpha Gabriel?" her father asked looking between them for an answer.

She knew her father. Knew him extremely well and right now, he was wearing his scary calm face. On the outside he looked concerned given the fact that a stranger was in fact gawking at his daughter, but she could feel his energy shifting between anger and suspicion. She knew he would be having words with the new Alpha of the Twilight Moon Pack, and soon.

Amelia stepped forward in front of Gabriel. "It's nothing, daddy."

"She's my mate."

Amelia swiveled her head. Her mouth hung open. Did he seriously just announce to everyone present that he was her mate? He came up to stand beside her, his stance dominating and ready for a fight.

"Mate?" Thomas gasped. "Amelia, is this true?"

Amelia rolled her eyes, now thoroughly annoyed. "Yes. We have the mate bond."

"And you chose not to inform me? Why?"

"It's kind of new, dad. Not exactly something I wanted to blurt out," she hissed, gritting her teeth.

Gabriel ignored her outburst, his gaze strictly on her father. "She will be leaving with me tomorrow. Back to my pack."

"The hell she will," Damon growled, going to stand beside his father.

"Now, just wait a minute there. We haven't discussed anything," Thomas said.

"This is ridiculous," she mumbled to herself, huffing aloud, pinching the bridge of her nose. "You men are ruining a perfectly good party. In case any of you forgot, it's Damon and I's birthday, so you can shut up, or leave," she shot her mate a glare. "Now, if you don't mind, I'm going to go get changed."

Amelia left the Alpha males to their posturing. Almost the entire pack gathered around, listening and talking amongst themselves. Great. That's just what she needed.

Her fellow pack members parted, allowing her a direct path to the Packhouse.

"Amelia!"

She turned to find Cordelia chasing after her. "Hey."

Cordelia fell into sync, walking alongside her up the flights of stairs. "So, a mate, huh? How come you haven't told me?"

"I've barely had a chance to process, let alone speak about it."

"Hmm. Still, you could have ended up with a worse mate. That Alpha is a fine-looking specimen."

Rey growled defensively. Amelia hadn't realized she'd done so aloud until she noticed Cordelia's eyebrow raised. "I don't want a mate," she said gruffly.

"You should consider yourself lucky. Mates are rare."

"The Moon Goddess did me no favors. She should have chosen someone else."

"Maybe she has a plan for you."

"Yeah? What about my plans? Am I just supposed to throw those away now because some mate wants to claim me?" she hissed, trying to keep her voice low.

Amelia opened her bedroom door, leaving it open for Cordelia to follow. She threw off the bathrobe, letting it fall to the floor, before walking into her closet. Cordelia sat down on the bench at the end of the bed and leaned back on the soft mattress, propped up on her elbows.

Amelia pulled on a fresh pair of underwear and clasped on a matching black lace bra. She looked over her clothing options and decided instantly against a dress. She wanted to be comfortable in case someone challenged her. Getting into fights was always the highlight of her day. She pulled on a pair of ripped black skinny jeans and a form-fitting teal blue top with a built-in corset. It accentuated her full breasts, pushing them up even further and hung off her shoulders, but it was snug enough not to allow anything to pop out if things did get physical. She had fought more times than she cared to admit in that top.

She stepped out of the closet and back into her bedroom, finding Cordelia waiting for her. She walked in front of her, motioning for her to help with the laces. Cordelia stood up, pulling and tightening as she went. Once she was finished, she tied the ribbons into a simple bow.

"Good to go," Cordelia said, patting her on the butt.

Amelia walked into her bathroom, staring at her reflection. Her silver-blonde hair was, wild and tangled. She ran her brush through it until it was tangle-free and twisted her hair up into a high ponytail, leaving her neck bare. Her make-up was still decent. Mascara wasn't running down her face and her eyeliner managed to hold, perfectly smudged in her water-line. For the finishing touch, she added on her mother's necklace. A simple rose gold crescent moon.

Cordelia followed her in, leaning against the quartz counters. "So, what are you gonna do?"

Amelia sat down beside her, sighing. "I don't know."

Cordelia seemed to chew on this. "What's the mate bond like? We've all heard the stories, but actually knowing someone who's mated by fate doesn't happen every day."

"The only people I knew of were my parents," Amelia said, recalling the way her parents used to be. The way her father seemed to always know the second her mother entered a room. The way his eyes would inevitably follow after her, just waiting to catch the small smile she would always save for him. How her mother seemed to know when he needed her. All she had to do was rest her hands on his shoulders for the tension to instantly melt from him.

Oh how in love they were.

She took a moment to reflect. Recalling the brief moment alone she had with her mate. Her cheeks flushed as she replayed it in her mind. It didn't matter how many boys she had kissed before today. Nothing compared to Gabriel and whether she wanted to admit it or not, it wasn't just his kissing or the way his touch seemed to set her on fire, it was the man himself. She couldn't help the gravitational pull she seemed to experience when she was near him. The way her body encouraged her to be near him, to fill a visceral need that was begging to be fulfilled.

"It's all true and so much more, but the worst part about it is I feel like I have zero control. The Moon Goddess threw this man I don't even know in my path, forcing us, telling us this is who I have to be with. No matter what kind of man your mate is, you still have no choice."

"You could reject him," Cordelia suggested.

Amelia scoffed. She had heard tales of mates rejecting one another. It never ended well. "And risk killing myself? I don't think I could do that," she pulled on knee-high leather boots before resting on the counter beside her.

"Just throwing it out there."

"I don't want a mate. I just wanna be free."

"But what if he's a really great guy? You might actually have a chance at love."

"And what if he's not?" Amelia countered, asking the more critical question. "What if he's cruel and violent and tries to force himself on me?"

Cordelia thought for a moment before responding, a sly smirk pulling at her lips. "Then I pity the hell out of the man, cause you won't need to reject him. He'll be dead."

Amelia wanted to smile and laugh it off, but Cordelia didn't know that just an hour earlier, Gabriel had forced her against a wall and kissed her like it was his last wish. Worst of all, she allowed him. She liked it even.

She grasped her friend's hand, towing her from the bathroom. "Come on. I need a drink."

Downstairs, the party was already in full swing. She could barely make out her brother's silver-blonde hair in the crowd, working his way through their guests. Her heart nearly burst with pride. She couldn't believe he was the new Alpha. He was going to be a brilliant leader. She knew the majority of her friends would be outside, so she kept hold of Cordelia's hand, weaving their way through the groups of chattering people.

She took in a deep breath of humid, summer air. The smell of food made her drag her feet over to the huge buffet table. It was stacked high with grilled chicken, burgers, hotdogs, ribs, steak, and every side dish imaginable. Being a werewolf left her starving all the time.

The lawn was littered with picnic tables and chairs scattered across the field. She looked out, spotting her usual group of friends, motioning for Cordelia to follow.

She stuffed a roll in her mouth before picking up her heaping plate and walked towards the table. She slid onto one of the benches beside Daniel, Cordelia taking up residence beside her.

"The gossip of tonight is that you have a mate," Daniel whispered in her ear.

Amelia looked out over the table at her friends. They were all staring at her like she'd produced a second head. "If that's the rumor, then it must be true."

"Are you saying it's not?" Nickolas asked, sitting across from her.

"I didn't say that," she mumbled through bites of her food.

"Makes sense why you broke up with Daniel," Gabby said flippantly, taking a swig from her solo cup.

"Right, cause I totally knew I would meet my mate today."

"Just saying. It is funny timing."

"How about the fact that I was supposed to be leaving tomorrow and didn't know when I'd be back. It's not funny timing. I didn't want to leave him waiting."

"Good thing you did. Now with your mate around, there's no longer any competition."

Amelia narrowed her eyes at her cousin. Did she really need to bring that up now? "I'm going to get a beer," she announced before standing up, walking away from the awkward conversation and hurt expression from Daniel.

She walked over to the stacks of kegs situated near the buffet table and snatched a red cup, filling it from the tap. She leaned back on the heavy keg, drinking deeply. There wasn't enough alcohol in the world to erase her troubles.

"Drinking already?"

Amelia looked over the rim of her cup to find her brother and Dominik approaching. Dominik was the oldest of her cousins, son of her father's Beta. He had the typical golden hair, a hereditary trait of their family, except his was more ash with sun-kissed highlights.

Dominik had always been her favorite cousin. He was laid back, the best sparring partner, apart from her brother, and he knew how to party. His twinkling green eyes winked at her as she handed him her half-drunk cup, filling up another for her herself.

Dominik accepted the drink gratefully, finishing its contents in two large gulps. She moved aside to let him refill it, standing beside her brother. Looking out over the party, she couldn't resist the smile that crept along her face. It was a great turn out. Most of the pack was celebrating.

"I didn't expect him to announce it in front of everyone," Damon whispered out of the corner of his mouth.

Amelia snorted, her cup resting just in front of her lips. "You and me both. But did you see Dad's face? He was pissed," she giggled.

"Of course he was. The man was staring at you naked," Damon growled, his anger rising.

Amelia produced another unladylike sound. "Wouldn't be the first time," she took a swig of her beer, leaving her brother speechless before heading back to her table.

There were a few more empty seats than before. Daniel had disappeared along with a few of the other guys. Leaving just Cordelia, Gabby, and their friend Jasmine. She stepped over the bench, taking back her seat beside Cordelia, once again digging into her plate. She noticed a few items were missing. Those damn boys. They knew how much she hated when someone took her food.

She growled into her chicken as she stabbed at it violently with her fork before tossing it into her mouth.

"You know sometimes I forget you're a girl," Gabby said.

Amelia grinned, her mouth full of chicken, earning her a snicker. She loved tormenting her cousin. Gabby was one of those girls who preferred maintaining her manicure over training. Amelia could appreciate a good manicure, but she had never been afraid to get her hands dirty. She loved her cousin dearly, but sometimes she annoyed the piss out of her.

Damon occupied the vacant seat beside her, Dominik choosing to sit across from them next to his sister, Gabby. Damon leaned over, snatching a chicken wing from her plate before his sister could catch him. Amelia smacked his shoulder in protest, laughing as he consumed her food.

"Hey Cordelia," Damon said around his sister's body.

Cordelia lifted her head up, looking back over at him. Her cheeks flushed. Her hazel eyes were all wide and doe-eyed. She had the biggest crush on her brother for as long as she remembered, and as they got older, it only got worse.

Amelia tried not to laugh at her friend's embarrassment. Instead, she pretended to ignore them as she finished off her food before her brother could snatch any more.

"Alpha. Congratulations on the ceremony," Cordelia said shyly. She was never timid with anyone, except Damon.

Damon rolled his eyes. "Please don't get formal with me. It'll always be Damon for you."

This earned him an even deeper shade of red across her smooth skin.

"Goodness will you two just get a room already," Amelia said aloud, only to be received by two sets of glares. "I bet you two will end up married one day, and I'll get lots of little nieces and nephews."

"Oh, yeah? You may beat me to the punch on kids with that mate of yours," Cordelia snapped.

Amelia turned her head at her best friend, her eyes narrowed. "Like hell. It'll be a decade before I even consider having kids."

"Like you get a say. If he wants to mate with you, he will," Gabby stated.

Amelia looked at her cousin, thoroughly considering the repercussions if she smashed her pretty little face into the table. "Don't you have some new beau to screw?"

Gabby looked out over the visiting packs, smirking. "So many to choose from."

Dominik rolled his eyes, looking as if he might be sick. "Gabby, you're disgusting."

Gabby waved her brother off with her well-manicured hand before leaving the table in pursuit of her most recent conquest.

Amelia was now picking at what remained of her plate, half a role, some coleslaw, and a few ribs. She took another long drink from her cup, savoring the bitter taste as it burned down her throat.

"I can't believe that girl found her mate."

Amelia's ears perked at the sound of a conversation some tables away. She could tell by her brother's tense posture and her friends' sudden silence, they could hear too.

Stupid werewolf hearing.

"And to Alpha Gabriel. That man shouldn't have to be tied down to one bitch his whole life. Have you seen him?"

"I've heard he's a bit of a player. Chasing new tail every night. Who knows, one of us might get lucky enough."

"I just feel bad that he's mated to her. She's got no sense of propriety, loose morals. You know I've heard she's slept with half the males in her pack."

She wanted to act surprised. The fact that someone she'd never met before had the audacity to judge her. She wanted to ignore the petty bitches running their mouths, but she wasn't known for her self-control. Her anger was burning into rage. It wasn't just the fact that they were gossiping behind her back, but the fact that they were speaking of Gabriel was like someone had shoved bamboo needles beneath her nail beds. She couldn't explain it or understand why, but it brought her to a new level of bitch mode.

Amelia pushed herself up from the table, ignoring her brother, who tried to hold her back. Cordelia immediately got up to follow her.

Amelia didn't recognize her. From behind, she could see the woman had dyed blonde hair straightened down her back. Her frame was slim, clearly not a warrior's build. She must be from a visiting pack, sitting at a table surrounded by at least ten other wolves. The few facing her direction saw her coming and instantly stood up, looking wary.

The bimbo was completely oblivious until Amelia tapped her on the shoulder. The girl turned around on the bench. Noticing it was her, she stood up. She was a few inches shorter. She was attractive enough, but that would soon change.

"If you have something to say, I suggest you say it to my face," Amelia said bluntly.

Those gathered around the woman's table all began to stand, taking notice of her stance. She managed to rein in her aura, not wanting to give herself away, but the wolves weren't blind. She was pissed. It was visible by the gritting of her teeth, flushed complexion, and skin stretched taut over her knuckles as she flexed her hands into fists at her sides. Others nearby could detect the tone in her voice that told them she was itching for a fight.

"Amelia's about to fight the bitch," someone nearby whispered.

"She's gonna need some serious plastic surgery when she's done."

Amelia wanted to smirk at her pack's support but didn't want the girl to think she was anything but serious.

"I'm sorry, but I have no idea what you're talking about," the blonde said.

"What's your name?" Amelia asked.

"Brittany."

"Brittany. You know being dumb is one thing, but playing the dumb blonde is just pathetic and a complete cliché," Amelia said, taking a small step forward.

"Who do you think you are?" the blonde shrieked, clearly offended.

"I'm Amelia Smoke. I don't mind a good shit-talking, but the minute you wanna run your mouth and lie about me, then we have a problem."

Brittany scoffed, faking innocence. "I was just saying what I've heard. Your mate is better off with someone of higher class."

"I'm an Alpha bitch. It doesn't get any higher than me."

Before she grasped what was happening, Amelia snapped her fist out, her knuckles connecting with soft tissue. The blonde's nose was spurting blood. Her friends were ready to leap at her defense. Amelia welcomed the challenge. She didn't mind staining the grass red.

"You keep your mouth shut about my mate and I, or else I'll leave you off worse than with a nose job," Amelia growled, her Alpha aura growing, flexing around her, leaving the wolves in front of her backing away.

Thought you didn't want a mate. Damon remarked.

An even deeper growl rippled through the air, making those in front of her instantly direct their gaze down to the floor. The blonde bitch was shaking as she was trying to stem the bleeding from her nose.

Gabriel stepped forward, the surrounding people parting ways for him. He glowered at the idiots in front of her. Only moments ago, they were prepared to challenge her and now looked like they were about to piss themselves, which only meant one thing. They were some of his own pack members.

Gabriel looked over Brittany, blood pooling down her face, her hand holding her broken nose. He overheard enough of the conversation to know what was going on.

"I'll deal with you later," he growled, causing her to flinch back. "Leave."

The blonde quickly fled, her friends following. Gabriel spun around, staring down at Amelia. He gripped her arm tightly before dragging her away from the crowd.

Amelia did not appreciate the way he was manhandling her, but she waved off her brother and pack, assuring them she was fine. She allowed him to haul her away from prying eyes, past the tree line. Once they were a suitable distance away, the sound of laughing and music was distant and barely audible, she dug her heels in the earth and wrenched her arm from his iron grip.

"That's enough," she said.

Gabriel turned on her, letting her go just as quick. "What do you think that was back there?"

"She was running her mouth. She deserved worse than a broken nose," Amelia told him. Was he actually mad at her?

No one speaks about our mate that way. Rey spoke up.

Not now. She said, ignoring her wolf.

"As Luna, you can't just go around punching everyone who says something inappropriate," Gabriel said, trying his best to stay calm.

"I'm *not* a Luna and either way, I will never stand by when someone makes baseless accusations and is trying to spread nasty gossip," she defended herself.

"You need to learn to control your temper. You won't like it when I'm angry," he said, warning her.

Is he threatening us? Rey asked, genuinely intrigued.

Sounds like it.

She stepped closer to him, eliminating the distance between them, tilting her head back to maintain eye contact. "What will you do if I don't? I don't know what kind of woman you're used to entertaining, but I'm not one to generally follow the rules."

"You're going to learn real fast," Gabriel said, his voice deep and husky.

Before she had a chance to reply, she was forced back, pushed up against a tree.

So much for talking.

CHAPTER 5

THE CAKE

Gabriel had her body pinned against a wide Oak. The rough bark pierced into her bare skin, scratching down her arms. His body was pressing hard against hers. Her breasts squished between them, nearly popping out of her corset. She kept her eyes focused on his and extended her hands up, setting them flat against his chest. She couldn't resist the urge to touch him. To feel the weirdly familiar sparks that danced across her skin whenever they made physical contact.

She breathed him in deeply. His scent produced an oddly calming effect that made her brain go fuzzy and warm. She pushed her eyes closed for a moment, gathering herself, recalling what she was saying.

"You can't just force yourself on me every time we have a disagreement," Amelia spoke softly. For some reason, her breath was coming in short and winded. "Otherwise, we'll never get anywhere."

Gabriel growled deep in his throat, tilting his head down, resting his forehead against hers. His eyes fell closed as she noticed his nostrils expand, taking in her scent.

"You're gonna be a problem for me, aren't you?" Gabriel asked.

Amelia chuckled. "Probably."

"I barely know you, and already you're driving me and my wolf mad."

"I've been known to have that effect on people."

Gabriel pulled back, looking deep into her eyes. She looked up meeting his gaze, making out a few flecks of gold near the iris as his eyes warmed before her. His demeanor had changed. Moments ago she could have sworn he wanted to throttle her, but the way he was looking at her now made her knees weak, her stomach quivering with nerves, and her skin flushed.

She swallowed with difficulty under the scrutiny of his gaze. The movement wasn't unnoticed. His eyes flicked down to her neck, right to her marking spot. Unknowingly, she cocked her head to the side, waiting to see what he'd do. Rey was purring like a kitten in the back of her mind, waiting and watching, urging his wolf to claim her. Amelia wanted to silence her other half. Remind her they were nowhere near ready for such a commitment, but she couldn't bring herself to form the words.

She stood there waiting for him to make a move. Do something. Her patience grew thin. The idea of seizing him by his collar and pulling him down entered her mind. That is until he suddenly stepped back.

Amelia was instantly confused. A violent chill crept along her skin from the loss of contact. She could have sworn he wanted to mark her, or at least kiss her, but instead, he backed away. She was impressed. She wanted to step forward. To steal a kiss in this isolated part of the woods,"'",ii89 when she heard a familiar voice in her head.

Amelia! Where the hell did you disappear to now?

What?! she growled, not realizing she'd also spoken aloud. Gabriel looked at her curiously.

Get the hell out of the woods, off of your mate, and over here. It's time for cake.

Amelia blocked her brother, refusing to respond before focusing her attention back to her mate.

"Cake," she said with a shrug of her shoulders.

Gabriel nodded his head, gesturing for her to go ahead of him. Amelia set off, back in the direction of the Packhouse, the voices and music getting louder as they got closer.

"I didn't know today was your birthday. All we knew was there was going to be an Alpha ceremony," Gabriel said, walking alongside her.

"Yeah, Dad didn't want to wait to pass the Alpha rank along. Damon is very mature for his age, and Dad deserves a break. He's been playing Alpha and Luna for over a decade. He could use the time off," Amelia told him.

"What happened to your mother? If you don't mind me asking."

Amelia took in a deep breath, softly shrugging her shoulders. "We're not really sure. She was outside in the garden. She loved working out there. That was when we heard her screams. Dad, Damon, and I ran outside and found her. She had been torn apart, shredded to pieces. There wasn't even enough of her to bury." That day still haunted her nightmares. Still left her shaking, sweating in fear. "We never found who did it. We couldn't track him. There was no scent, no trace, nothing."

"How old were you?"

"Damon and I were six," she told him. "She was pregnant, too. I was gonna have a sister."

He reached down, lacing his fingers in hers, giving her a gentle squeeze. She looked up at him, surprised by the gesture, and found herself smiling.

Together they left the shelter of the lush, green forest and walked out onto the neatly cut lawn. It was still littered with guests and pack members. Children were running around, chasing each other, and dodging their parents. Off to the side, two wolves were wrestling, snapping at one another's necks. Goddess only knew what they were arguing about, but no one seemed to be paying them any attention.

As they walked deeper into the crowd, Amelia felt eyes turning on them. She felt herself inch closer to him, gripping his hand tighter than before while still holding her head high, squaring her shoulders. She was not going to let anyone intimidate her, especially not her own pack.

Amelia spotted her brother near the stage. A large five-tier cake adorned a small table beside him. She could smell the overly sweet buttercream icing and vanilla extract used in the cake making her mouth water. She couldn't wait to devour it. Ms. McKready never disappointed.

She moved in his direction, Gabriel following closely behind her, their hands still entwined. Nearly reaching her brother, she looked back at her mate. He offered her a faint smile in support.

Amelia caught her father's eye as they traveled down to her hand entwined with Gabriel's. She could tell by the tick in his clenched jaw he had words to say about it, but would keep silent with all of their guests present. For now.

She left his side to join her brother.

Thomas stepped forward, "I know a lot of you have already celebrated Amelia and Damon's birthday last night," Thomas glared at them.

Amelia instantly looked elsewhere. Anywhere but her father. Damon beside her lowered his head. They were lucky enough to not be sporting their hangover, but many of the teens present were not so fortunate. She could smell the booze still leaking from their pores, much the same as Damon was experiencing earlier that day. She couldn't help but feel embarrassed at having been called out but they had a blast last night. Even if it did end up with her covered in vomit.

"But tonight is for all of the pack. Today my children become adults. Damon is going on to become one of the greatest Alpha's our pack has ever known, and Amelia ... well, we all know she'll do whatever her heart tells her," her father said.

This earned him quite a few chuckles and an annoyed glare from his daughter. "Raise your glass and let's wish them a very Happy Birthday. The start of the rest of their lives."

Everyone in attendance raised their glasses in the air, wishing them a happy birthday. Amelia smiled brightly, bouncing on her toes beside her brother. Damon stood proudly, his cheeks gaining color by the second.

Amelia cut into the cake, portioning out a slice and placing it down on a plate. She turned to her brother smiling, offering him the first slice. Damon looked at her curiously. Normally, she insisted on the first piece.

He went to take it from her, smiling in thanks.

Silly man. She mind-linked him just before smashing the slice of cake straight into his face. His eyes widened, eyebrows raised in shock as the icing stuck chunks of cake to his skin. Amelia laughed as most of their friends joined in. The adults and elders that knew them couldn't help but smirk, rolling their eyes—typical Amelia.

"Here we go again," Thomas mumbled.

Damon licked the cake that was adhered to his skin around his mouth, before wiping the icing from his eyes. He blinked them open, trying to prevent them from sticking. Amelia laughed hysterically as he pursed his lips. Nodding his head, he reached around her and pulled back a solid hand full of cake in his palm.

"You wouldn't." Amelia narrowed her eyes at him.

"Oh, I would," Damon pushed the cake straight into her face, smearing it in as he went. Amelia gasped, shrieking as he went further, smudging the food into her hair.

Thomas stepped in before it went any farther. They were known for their epic food fights and she could only assume he did not want to make a spectacle with all the neighboring packs visiting.

"So much for being adults," he said to the two of them, his eyebrow raised.

Amelia wiped the food from her eyes before inserting a finger in her mouth, sucking off the delicious buttercream frosting. "We can be adults tomorrow."

Thomas laughed, shaking his head at her. "No food fight tonight. Let's not further ruin this stunning cake Mrs. McKready made."

Amelia pulled a small piece of cake from her brother's face before popping it into her mouth. "It's delicious."

Her father merely laughed at her and pulled out two towels from underneath the table, handing one to each of his children. This had become a tradition of theirs since they were pups.

Amelia took the towel from her father, wiping off the cake from her face while one of the omegas from the kitchen began to cut and hand it out. She felt his eyes on her as gooseflesh prickled down her neck. Like a moth to a flame. Still wiping off the icing, she walked over to him. His eyes narrowed at her.

"I'm gonna have my hands full with you," Gabriel stated once she was close enough. She still had icing streaked through her platinum hair, lining her eyelashes.

"Probably," Amelia reached up, wiping icing down his cheek. His eyes widened. She stood up on her tippy toes, reaching behind his neck, pulling him down closer. She slowly licked the icing off his skin, pulling back to find his eyes shifting from silver to black and back as he fought his wolf for control.

Her heart raced in her chest, oddly satisfied by the effect she was having on him. Rey pushed forward. Her own eyes turned a vivid shade of green as her own wolf pushed through the thin veil that separated man from beast. Her better half wanted nothing more than to meet his wolf, frolic and chase each other through the forest like new pups. But, Amelia pulled her back. She wanted to see how far she could push him.

"I'm also a tease," she whispered in his ear.

CHAPTER 6

LACK OF PERSONAL SPACE

Amelia stepped inside her steaming hot shower. The white subway tiles were already dripping with moisture. She rinsed out the icing from her hair which left a slick, oily feel to it. Washing her hair, she began to run through the night's events.

After teasing Gabriel, she abandoned him to dance with her friends once the music started. The adults retreated inside the Packhouse for coffee, while the younger generation screamed loudly to the music blaring from the speakers. The rest of the night was much of a blur as she continued consuming an unwise amount of alcohol.

Amelia knew he was observing her, hovering in the shadows, letting out low growls to any male that dared approach. She smirked, thinking back on it, secretly enjoying the attention he gave her.

She always thought she didn't want a mate. Always believing that having a mate would hinder her, restricting her from being free. Maybe in some ways, it would. She wouldn't be able to travel as she had wanted, not right away at least, but maybe having a mate wouldn't be so bad.

Gabriel certainly wasn't bad to look at. Her fingertips were itching to reach under the hem of his shirt, trace the contours of his body, outline every plane of muscle. She was dying to get a real look at the tattoo on his bicep that was barely peeking out beneath his sleeve. She wondered what his skin would taste like. Salty or sweat? She imagined it would remind her of the woods, of churned earth, the wind billowing through the trees, and fresh sunshine.

Though he clearly didn't enjoy his authority being challenged, which would most definitely cause them future issues. This was an adjustment for the both of them. Neither of them expected to meet their mates today. This was unfamiliar territory, and maybe, just maybe, they could navigate the troubled waters together.

Amelia stepped out of her shower, all squeaky clean, wrapping a towel around her body. Her hair dripped down her back, pooling onto the tile floor. She grabbed a hand towel off her counter, squeezing out the excess water in her hair before pitching it into her hamper.

She opened her bathroom door. Steam escaped into the brisk air of her bedroom. She reached around her towel, ready to drop it on the floor before going inside her closet when she froze, her hands gripping the white, plush fabric.

Gabriel stood in her bedroom, observing the titles and various colored book jackets adorning her wall to wall bookcase. He turned around at the sound of the door opening and froze. Her skin was still shimmering wet, streams of water glistening down her arms. Her silver-blonde hair was hanging, sticking to her damp skin.

Amelia watched him as he stared at her, taking in every inch of her exposed skin. She immediately retightened the thin towel against her naked body. If he really wanted to, there was nothing she could do to prevent him from removing it. She wasn't even sure she would stop him if she could. His silver eyes roaming every inch of her skin left her body aching with a burning desire.

Amelia cleared her throat, a lovely trait she picked up from her father, gaining his attention. "What are you doing in my room?"

Gabriel fixated his silver gaze on her eyes, forcing himself to regain a semblance of composure. "There are some things we need to discuss."

She nodded her head in agreement. He wasn't wrong. There were about a thousand things they needed to talk about. One of the more pressing matters, what next?

"I agree, but you couldn't have waited for me, I don't know, downstairs? How did you even get in here anyway?" she clearly remembered locking her door.

Gabriel smirked mischievously. "It's one of my talents."

"Picking locks or invading someone's privacy?"

"What's yours is mine."

Amelia narrowed her eyes at him. "Not yet. We may be fated mates, but I know nothing about you. What's mine is mine until you learn some respect for my personal space."

Gabriel advanced on her quicker than she could follow. Even with her werewolf vision, he moved blindingly fast.

"How's this for personal space?" he asked, standing close enough to breathe in the peppermint smell of her shampoo. To see his reflection in the dew glistening along her collarbone.

His breath warmed her cheek. The thin fabric of his shirt outlined his muscles perfectly. She could see the faint stubble already showing along his tanned jawline. His nose had clearly been broken, probably multiple times, given the bump on the bridge of it. His brows hung over his eyes, shadowing the silver iris.

"You're impossible," she wanted to sound braver. To say it with more vigor, but instead, her voice was faint. Her breathing was shallow, trying desperately not to take in a deep enough breath. She was already having issues containing her wolf, adding his scent would only make matters worse.

"You're beautiful," he whispered, reaching up to run his fingers across her collarbone with a feathered touch. He grinned as her body responded with gooseflesh running along her skin. He moved up her neck. Moisture collected along the tips of his fingers as he traced circles in her skin.

Amelia couldn't control herself as her eyes fluttered closed. Her head tilted back submissively. A small moan escaped her lips. He progressed up her face, running along her hairline to tuck a wet strand behind her ear. She swallowed hard, wanting so desperately to tell him to go away. To inform him that she wasn't his, not yet, but her body, her mind, and voice all betrayed her.

Rey was grinning from ear to ear. If she was a feline, Amelia was certain she'd be purring right about now.

Opening her eyes, she found his pupils widened, nearly expelling the silver altogether. She reached up with both hands, relaxing them against his chest just as she had done earlier. Shifting, she ran the tips of her fingers over his muscles. The skin was smooth and blemish-free, stretched taut over his hardened biceps. She could barely make out the beginning of a tattoo beneath the sleeve of his shirt.

Extending her fingers up over his shoulders, she could feel the bulging traps beneath his shirt, transitioning into the tender flesh around his neck. His Adam's apple was hard against his throat, visible and bobbing up and down, almost as if he was struggling to breathe. This made her smirk. She left one of her hands along the nape of his neck. Beneath the thin skin, she could feel his heart beating rapidly, matching the tempo of her own.

Reaching up with her other hand, she spread her fingers through his onyx hair. It was long enough to just hang in his eyes, producing a stark contrast against the silver. She'd wanted to stroke his hair since the moment she saw him. Wondered what it was like to touch it, if it was as soft as it looked. It wasn't, it was better.

Running her fingers through his hair caused a groan to rumble in his chest, making her smirk grow wider. Amelia and her wolf were both grinning that they could please their mate in this way. It wasn't sexual gratification. No, this was more intimate.

Gabriel wrapped his brawny hand around the base of her neck, bringing her closer to him. The only thing holding up her towel was their bodies pressed together. Amelia bit her lower lip, anxious about what he might do. Would he kiss her, or would they continue to touch, to linger breathlessly against one another?

Amelia.

Amelia jerked at the voice in her head, causing Gabriel to drop his hand from her skin. By reflex, she grabbed for her towel, securing it around her body.

What? she growled.

"What's wrong?" Gabriel asked, his eyebrows furrowed.

"My dad."

My office, 5 minutes. Thomas demanded. *Bring your mate with you.*

Amelia looked up at Gabriel guiltily. Her father knew he was in her room.

Dad, it's two in the morning. Can't this wait?

Now.

He left no room for argument, sealing the connection. Amelia huffed loudly, rolling her eyes.

"What is it?" Gabriel asked again.

"He wants us in his office," she told him, stepping into her closet to put on actual clothes. "Now."

She dropped the towel with her back facing him, rapidly slipping on underwear, sweatpants, and a tank top. She turned back to him to find his eyes black once again.

"Close your mouth. I don't want drool on my carpet," she said, brushing against him.

Wrapping her hand around the handle, she pulled her door open. She could feel Gabriel following closely behind her as she made her way down the five flights of stairs, down the hall, and in front of her father's office door. Not bothering to waste her time knocking, she pushed the door wide, stepping inside.

Her father was already seated behind his desk in his large leather seat. He was leafing through a pile of papers on his desk with a fountain pen in hand. Thomas owned several small businesses in Boston and keeping up with them took a lot out of him.

Thomas looked up over the rim of his metal-framed glasses, perched on the end of his pointed nose. He pulled them off, setting them down neatly on the desk before leaning back into the cool leather seat.

"Please, sit," he said, gesturing to the sturdy chairs in front of the desk.

Amelia and Gabriel both moved their way through the room, each taking their seats. Amelia arched a brow at her father. What was he up to?

CHAPTER 7
SLEEP WITH ME

"Now I'm sure you're both wondering why I've brought you here at this ungodly hour," Thomas started, "but since Gabriel has already stated he was taking my daughter away the following morning, I figured there was little time to waste."

Amelia didn't like the sound of this. "Dad-"

Thomas held up his hand, effectively silencing her. "No, Amelia. You two may be fated mates, but that does *not* mean he can take you against your will."

"She is *mine*," he growled.

A shock jolted her system at his words, causing her to turn towards him. Overlooking the fact that she barely knew him, she felt oddly proud, elated even over the fact that he was willing to fight for her. While another part of her was irritated and not just with him but herself as well. She wasn't an object for them to fight over.

Amelia noticed her father sitting up straighter in his chair, his hands clasped in front of him against the worn desk. His shoulders twitched, his tell-tale sign of holding back. She could tell he wanted nothing more than to throttle the Alpha beside her.

"Alpha Gabriel, I understand the pull of the mate bond. Amelia's mother and I were also a fated pair. So, believe me, when I say, I understand the attraction. The fear of not being near her," Thomas said grimly. "But that doesn't give you the right to force her from her home."

"Actually, according to the laws put forth by the Council of Elders, I have every right. She is mine by law," Gabriel stated.

"I don't give a damn what the law states. You are not taking my daughter anywhere," Thomas jumped to his feet. The chair slammed into the wall behind him.

Gabriel stood as well. A deep growl emanated from his chest. His claws extended, ready to complete the shift.

"That's enough!" Amelia shouted, moving to stand between the two fuming Alphas. She allowed Rey to blend with her consciousness as she released a sliver of her aura. She felt her body warming as she displayed a taste of her power, showering the room in a purple tint that tasted of fresh ozone after a lightning strike.

Both men halted their aggressions as they refocused their attentions on her. Thomas cocked his head, staring at her curiously. Gabriel took a step back, wary of her.

"Neither of you gets to tell me what I am doing," Amelia glared at them. "Not one of you asked me what I wanted," she shot a look at her father. "You don't get to defy the Council of Elders, especially not for me. None of our pack members will be put at risk. I will not allow it," she whipped her head, staring daggers at her new *mate*. "And you. This whole 'she's mine' crap ends now. I am not an object or a thing for you to possess. Do you understand me?"

Not giving him a chance to respond, she continued, looking back at her father, her posture calmer and more reasonable. "Dad. I know you're worried about me, but Gabriel is my mate. The fates have spoken, and this is their will. I am going with Gabriel to his pack tomorrow."

"You are?" both men stuttered, each giving her a questioning look.

Her father looked at her as if she had lost her head. The corner of Gabriel's lip was twitching, resisting pitifully to smile.

"It's as you said. The mate bond is strong," she spoke to her father, all the while gazing into his silver-gray eyes. The bond between the two of them tugged on both ends, gravity forcing them towards one another. "And as I said, I won't have a war started because of me. I was already planning on leaving tomorrow anyway, just now for different reasons," she said with a shrug of her shoulders.

Her father stepped wide around his desk approaching her. She could sense Gabriel beside her, hovering, keeping her father in his sight. She tried to ignore the over protective side and focus on the man before her. The man who raised her to be strong and independent. He rested his hands on her shoulder, giving her a light squeeze that instantly quieted her mind and soul, putting her at ease after a long day of frenzied events.

"You are so much like your mother," he told her. "She was selfless, annoyingly brave, fiercely protective, and incredibly strong, even for a Luna. You are exactly like her."

Amelia let out a small smile, tears glistening in her eyes. "I don't think anyone's ever called me selfless before," she chuckled.

"Oh, my girl," Thomas pulled her in, winding his arms around her. "You are more selfless than anyone I know."

"Thank you, daddy," she breathed him in deeply, imprinting his scent of spicy aftershave, big bear hugs, and his constant scolding's, forever in her mind. The Wandering Moon Pack and Twilight Moon Pack had been allies for decades. She knew she would be back at some point in time, but for some nagging reason, she felt uneasy leaving her father.

She knew both packs couldn't afford to go to war. Too many lives would be lost and for what? Because she didn't want to be mated? This was her moment to put her pack first. Both of her packs. The Moon Goddess set this path for her for a reason and she would be damned if she wasn't going to see it through.

Amelia pulled back from him. Gabriel's arm wrapped around her waist in support. She wanted nothing more than to lean into his body and take comfort in his presence, but she needed to be strong. Her father needed to know she could overcome anything, even leaving her home for good.

"You two should get some rest. It's a long drive to the Twilight Moon territory. Amelia, take what you can pack. I will have the rest of your things boxed and sent over," Thomas told her.

Amelia smiled. "Goodnight, daddy."

Gabriel followed her out of the office, shutting the door quietly behind them. His room was on the main floor. A few doors down from where they stood. He reached out, lacing his fingers in hers, pulling her into him.

Amelia was caught by surprise. She had expected to retreat to her room, disappear under her comforter and lay awake until the sun colored the sky. Knowing full well, she wouldn't be able to catch a wink of sleep that night, not with the fact that she was leaving her home in the morning. Tilting her head back, she looked up into his eyes. The exact ones that looked down on her, puzzled and confused.

"Why did you agree to come with me?" Gabriel finally asked her.

"What do you mean?"

"I expected more of a fight out of you."

"I clearly remember you threatening my pack and family if I didn't agree to leave with you," she told him, making him flinch. "Am I wrong?"

He seemed to ponder that question, longer than he probably should have. "I'm not gonna lie. I want you with me."

"Because of the mate bond," Amelia finished for him.

Gabriel reached up, cupping her chin, keeping her focus on him and only him. "Not just because of the mate bond."

"You can't know that. As of this morning I was dead set on never having a mate. Never settling down and living life on my own terms. Yet, here I am, abandoning all of my plans to follow you back to your pack. You can't tell me that isn't the mate bond digging its claws in me. Altering my feelings towards you. Forcing us together."

"I won't deny I want you, because I do. Yes, it most likely is the mate bond nudging us, influencing us to do things we hadn't yet considered. But, I can tell you right now. I want to get to know you, cause whether we like it or not, the Moon Goddess has paired us for a reason."

"I know," she sighed, his words reflecting her own inner turmoil.

His lips pulled into a small, genuine small. A smile that wasn't laced with sarcasm, or teasing. Just a modest, sincere smile.

"I just have to ask for one thing."

Gabriel's smile instantly turned into a frown. "What?"

"I will go to your pack. We can be mates, and I will learn to be a Luna for you, but I want to arrive at your pack on my own," she watched as his frown grew further displeased. "Don't get mad. I'm still going to your pack. All I'm asking is that you don't force me to ride with you. Let me say goodbye to my friends, my family, and pack. I will come to your pack, but I need to do this part on my own."

Amelia watched as he struggled internally, instantly regretting having to ask.

"Gabriel," Amelia said, regaining his attention. "Look at me." His silver eyes finally focused on her. "I promise you. I will be there. I do not plan on running off and disappearing. You can trust me."

Gabriel's eyes flitted back and forth between both her eyes, looking for any tells of lying. Finally, against his better judgment, he nodded. "Fine. But if you are not at my Packhouse by four o'clock, I will personally hunt you down and eliminate anyone who might be helping you."

Amelia resisted the urge to roll her eyes, especially considering how serious he was. His Alpha aura flexed around them. His reminded her of a sunset, painted in oranges, reds, and yellows. It brushed against her. Winding around her, enveloping her in its warmth. She felt protected and snug, as though cocooned in a soft, plush blanket. She could feel his aura blending with hers. Strands of orange and purple bleed together until she could no longer distinguish between the two, marking her as his. She wrapped her arms around his waist, needing to find a way to pacify him, to reassure him.

"Come to bed with me," she whispered.

Gabriel's eyes widened. "What?"

"Come to bed with me," she repeated. "Not to have sex, not yet, but come sleep with me. Please."

She couldn't explain why or how she knew, but having him close was the only thing she could think of to keep him calm. Prevent his mind from wandering.

Gabriel nodded hesitantly.

Together, they walked back up the flights of stairs and into her bedroom. Flicking off the light turned the room to total darkness. She pulled off her sweats, leaving them in a pile on the floor, before climbing onto her bed and pulling the covers over her body. She could hear him wrestling with his own clothes. The bed beside her dipped as he moved under the covers, laying back against the pillows. He reached out, snaking an arm around her torso and pulled her back into his chest.

Amelia adjusted herself, molding her body to his, fitting against him perfectly. His skin was warm against the thin cotton of her shirt. She could feel his face pressed into her hair, breathing her in deeply, his body relaxing against hers.

Before she knew it, her eyes closed heavily, her mind wandering off into a dreamless sleep.

CHAPTER 8

SECURITY BLANKET

Amelia woke to the sound of jean fabric being stretched and shimmied on. The sun was already up, painting the earth in stunning yellows, oranges, and reds. The birds outside began their morning song, annoyingly loud just outside her window. Her back was cold and abandoned. She distinctly remembered sleeping against a solid, warm chest.

She sat up, rubbing the sleep from her eyes. Her right arm was numb from laying on it all night. Trying to shake it out to restore blood flow, she looked up to find Gabriel standing in her room, buttoning his jeans.

She tried not to stare, but it was like her eyes were caught in a snare. The snare being his deep v-line. His tanned skin was stretched taut over hard muscle, eight delicious abs begging to be touched. He had a significant black tribal tattoo covering half his right bicep, running up his shoulder and down across his chest. Her fingers were itching to trace the design.

"Good morning," she said smirking.

Gabriel smiled back. "Morning. How did you sleep?"

"Like a baby." Having the most peaceful sleep, she could remember. "You?"

"Same," he forced his hands in his pockets, adjusting the fit of his jeans before pulling his shirt over his head. "I have to head downstairs. Make sure those I brought with me are ready to go. We're leaving in an hour."

Amelia pushed off the comforter, standing up and stretching out her limbs. She caught his eyes instantly lowering, staring at her midriff that was exposed, revealing the small rose tattoo she had above her left hip. The cold air stung her exposed legs. Looking down at herself, she had forgotten she was only wearing a tank top and underwear. Noticing his still lingering gaze, his eyes lusting her body, she knew she needed to redirect him.

"I have a couple of suitcases I'll need you to take with you to tide me over until my father can get everything packed and shipped," she told him.

"What about your car?"

"I don't have a car."

"Then how are you getting to the territory?"

"Oh, you'll see," she smirked. "Here, I'll walk you down."

"No, that's okay. You have packing to do," he told her. "Now, I'm allowing you to stay here and say your goodbyes but-"

"I know. If I don't arrive at your pack by six o'clock-"

"Four. I said four, not six."

Amelia's lips pulled into a teasing smile. "I know. I'm just teasing you." By the expression on his face, she instantly realized that was a poor decision on her part. The man already believed she was going to run away. She had to prove him wrong. Prove to him that she could be trusted. Otherwise, they really didn't stand a chance. "I'm sorry, I shouldn't have teased. I promise I will be on your territory no later than four."

Gabriel nodded his head solemnly. She was hesitant to believe if he was relieved or not given is stoic nature.

"Relax," she reached out, rubbing her hands against his arms, bringing warmth to his skin. "I won't let you down," she promised. "Now get out of my room so I can pack. You're distracting me."

Gabriel bent down, brushing his lips against hers, tasting her flesh. Amelia was momentarily surprised. She didn't like that. Only she was the one allowed to do that, but right now she didn't care. He tasted so good. The kiss wasn't rushed or desperate. It was slow and painful, soft and pleasant. She pulled back, her head swimming.

Amelia opened her eyes to find him smiling down at her. She couldn't help but feel giddy. The way he looked at her made her feel singled out and somehow important.

She blushed, shaking her head, squirming to get out from under those piercing silver eyes. "Get out of here. I'll see you in a bit."

Gabriel chuckled, leaving her room, closing the door behind him. Amelia continued staring at the door. His scent still lingered in the air. She turned around to face her room. The very room she spent her entire life in, from newborn to adulthood. It had seen all of her firsts, all of her joy, her heartache, her anger and regret.

Even though she was leaving, no longer to live in this house again, she knew this wasn't the end. She had so much more to do and experience and was finally being given a chance to make a whole different set of memories elsewhere, with her mate.

She entered her walk-in closet, pulling out three glossy black, plastic suitcases. She zipped open each of them, laying them out on the floor. She walked back into her closet, freeing clothes from their hangers and tossed them into the suitcases. She grabbed everything clothes-wise she felt she would need to last her at least two weeks. Hopefully, her father wouldn't wait any longer than that to send her stuff. Most of the clothes fit all in one suitcase.

Amelia threw in a few pairs of shoes she wore regularly, her toiletries, and the few weapons she had stashed under her bed into her second suitcase. She flipped the knives expertly in her hand. The silver metal glinted in the fluorescent lighting. Werewolves, as a breed, were deathly allergic to silver. Their skin would blister on initial contact, but not hers.

For some reason, silver was like any other metal, cold and shiny. She packed them carefully away in the suitcase, keeping them sheathed so as not to slice a hole in the plastic. The thin scars on her hands were proof of how sharp they were.

The third suitcase she saved for a specific purpose, housing something of great importance. She ran her fingers along the books decorating her shelves. Finding the ones she needed, she began packing some of them away. One dust jacket in particular caught her eye, her fingers lingering over the worn cover.

Cradling it in her arms, she traced the lettering of the title, Narnia. It was the only memory she had of her mother. Her soothing gentle voice, reading aloud the colorful language. Telling her of fantastic creatures and children lost in another world. The memory was faint, sometimes she believed it was only a figment of her imagination, but it was all that was left of her mother.

Amelia placed the book atop the others. The suitcase was stuffed with enough reading material to last her a month. She flipped each of the cases closed, zipping them shut.

"Damon!" *Damon!* she screamed aloud and through the mind link.

Damon tore open her bedroom door, nearly ripping it off its hinges. His sea-green eyes were wide with a determined look by the set of his brows. He searched around her room. Shoulders pushed back, fists clenched at his sides, ready for a fight.

Amelia couldn't help but laugh. He looked absurd.

Her brother relaxed his posture as he took in the fact that she clearly wasn't in danger, before setting into a scowl.

"What are you screaming like that for?!" Damon shouted, clearly annoyed.

"Help me bring these down. Gabriel's taking my stuff with him and I can't get it all down by myself," Amelia stood up, pulling along the suitcase filled with books. The thing easily weighed a hundred pounds. She was surprised the suitcase didn't explode, unable to contain the pages within.

Damon picked up the remaining two suitcases, holding one in each hand. "I thought you were leaving with him. You're not going like that, are you?" he asked, gesturing towards her clothes and lack of pants.

Amelia looked down at her clothes, completely forgetting she was still only wearing a tank top and underwear.

"Shit," she hissed, jogging into her closet. She threw on the first thing she could reach, a pair of jeans, a clean bra, and a new tank. "Okay, now I'm good."

Together they both carried the luggage. Normally this would be a struggle, given the weight of each suitcase. Thank the Goddess for werewolf strength. They made it down the five flights of stairs, barely breaking a sweat. Amelia beelined for the front door, following the smell of cloves and apples.

Outside, three black SUV's were parked in the driveway. A dozen men and women were buzzing around, loading bags into the car, checking that each member was accounted for. Gabriel stood to the back of the procession, his head bent close to another large male, talking low enough that not even *her* hearing could make out what they were saying.

She noticed his head snap up, scenting the air before turning towards her. Amelia smiled at him, approaching with her brother and bags in tow.

"Do you have room for these?" Amelia asked.

Gabriel sized the three large black bags, eyebrows raised. "I'm sure we can make it work," he said.

"Oh good," Amelia sighed, feeling instant relief.

"I'll see you back inside," Damon said behind her, leaving her alone with Gabriel and her future pack.

She was apprehensive. Nervous to leave her home and join the Twilight Moon Pack. She had visited them a handful of times in the past, but arriving as their Alpha's mate left her feeling uncertain of her place. There was no way of telling how she would be received or if the pack would accept her.

"Amelia, this is Kaleb, my Beta. Kaleb, meet Amelia, my mate and Luna," Gabriel said, introducing the two.

Amelia stuck out her hand, smiling at the attractive man. His hair was a sun-kissed, ashy brown that hung down into his cat-shaped, brown eyes. He was thinner than Gabriel and shorter by just a few inches, but he looked fast, definitely a runner. Kaleb shook her hand firmly, wincing as he pulled away, flexing his stiff fingers.

"That's quite a grip you've got there," Kaleb laughed.

"I'm sorry. I am so sorry," Amelia said, completely mortified. "Are you okay?"

"I've endured worse," Kaleb said with a smile. "Glad to know we have such a strong Luna."

Gabriel smirked, reaching out, taking the suitcase she was still carrying.

"What the hell is in here?" he asked. The weight of the case was more than he expected as the case sagged beneath its burden.

"Books," Amelia said shyly, her eyes focused on the tinted windows of the car. They were so dark she couldn't make out a single detail inside.

"Did you bring a whole library with you?" Gabriel asked, stowing the bag inside the back of the SUV.

Amelia dragged over the other two bags, setting them down beside him. "No. Just the ones I need," she could tell from his expression, he clearly thought she was eccentric. "They're like my security blanket, okay. Books are my thing."

Gabriel chuckled. Making quick work of her remaining bags. The SUV was packed and ready. He approached the middle car. Kaleb left them alone, making his way to the opposite side of the vehicles.

He stopped short of the rear passenger door. Amelia looked at him, squinting at the early morning sun that glinted over his shoulder. She could feel his emotions through their bond. Like her stomach was doing flips. Nerves wracked through her system, but the sensation wasn't her own. Instinctively, she reached out, resting her hand on his back. Her thumb rubbed back and forth through his thin shirt.

"Four o'clock," she told him.

He looked down at her, cupping her face in his large hands. "Four o'clock, or I'll come back here and drag you there myself."

Amelia bit her lower lip, trying to keep from smiling. "Don't tease me."

He leaned in, kissing her. It was simple and short, too short, but it was effective. She stepped back a bit, watching as he climbed into the back seat of the car. With a small wave, she stayed frozen in her driveway until the black cars had disappeared from view.

It would only take them four hours to reach his pack. She pulled her phone out of her back pocket, checking the time, barely nine, and she could make it there in three. Giving her enough time to have a last meal with her family and give them proper goodbyes.

Amelia huffed aloud sadly. Today may be the best and worst day of her life.

CHAPTER 9

GOODBYE'S

Back inside the house, a mouthwatering smell attacked her senses. Buttermilk pancakes, cinnamon sugar topped French toast, and fresh strawberry jam caused her stomach to growl loudly. She followed the demands of her stomach, stumbling into the dining room where a feast was laid out. Every breakfast food imaginable was stacked high, along with her favorite, fresh strawberry pancakes and homemade strawberry syrup. She was shocked, surprised, but mostly overwhelmed, and it wasn't just the food having such an effect on her.

Her father, Damon, Cordelia, every one of her cousins, aunts, uncles, and friends were all gathered around the table, looking at her. Amelia clutched at her chest. Her heart was fit to burst with love and appreciation for each of them. Her Aunt Linda, her mother's youngest sister, sat near her father, her eyes brimming with unshed tears.

Aunt Linda never had kids of her own and had made sure to be there for Amelia and Damon since their mother died. She had become like a second mother to them during a time when they needed one desperately.

Amelia laughed awkwardly, trying to ignore the pressure growing behind her eyes. "If any of you make me cry, I swear I will make sure your beds get stuffed with pig shit."

This earned her a room full of broken laughter, sniffling cries, and rolled eyes.

"That's my girl," her father said proudly.

Amelia walked around the table, greeting each of her friends and family, thanking them for coming. She moved towards the head of the table, finally sitting between Cordelia and her brother. Reaching out, she took ahold of Cordelia's hand and gave her a light squeeze.

Amelia couldn't help but shake her head as her father stood up, preparing himself to make a speech. He was very fond of speeches, especially if it involved embarrassing his children.

"Thank you all for coming on such short notice. I'm sure most of you know, but for those who don't, the fates have decided to bless our Amelia with a fated mate. Alpha Gabriel of the Twilight Moon Pack has claimed Amelia, and she has graciously accepted. So, in just a few short hours, she will be leaving us to join him. I ask you all to raise your glass, wishing our girl well on the journeys that lie ahead. May you handle them with all the grace and modesty you can muster," Thomas winked at his child, taking a large sip from his glass of mimosa.

Amelia felt her cheeks go hot at her father's words. This next chapter in her life was going to test her in ways she couldn't fathom. Maybe it was time to grow up and no longer behave so childishly. She wanted to make him proud.

Everyone around her clinked their glasses, cheering and toasting her name. She had never felt so loved and cared for in her entire life. She clinked her glass with both Damon and Cordelia beside her before guzzling down her glass. The champagne bubbled in the back of her throat.

This was her chance to say what she needed to say.

Amelia stood up, her chair scraping against the hardwood. Everyone at the table immediately went silent, giving her their full attention.

"Thanks, Dad, for that riveting speech," Amelia laughed nervously. "I just wanted to thank you all for coming. It means the world to me. You *all* mean the world to me. This pack, my family, you all have raised me to be the woman I am today, and there's nothing I could ever do to repay you all. Even though I am leaving for another pack, fate has called me to something I never imagined for myself. My heart will always be here with all of you. The Wandering Moon Pack is the best, the oldest, the most distinguished pack in the world, and I am so proud to call you all mine. I love you all."

She picked up her refilled glass, toasting them all, taking a small sip this time from the crystal. Most of the women at the table were misty-eyed, dabbing their cheeks with their napkins. The men were beaming proudly. Most of them had trained with her at one point or another, making her the effective warrior she is today. She owed them everything.

Amelia sat back down, swallowing down the rush of emotion that was swelling within. Cordelia beside her was a blubbering mess, her eyes swollen and red. Damon, on the other hand, was cool and composed. They had already said their goodbyes days before. Nothing had changed.

"Alright, enough crying," Amelia laughed, trying her best to lighten the mood. "Let's all eat before the rest of the pack finds us."

Her family and friends laughed with her, allowing her shoulders to relax.

Amelia piled her plate high with strawberry pancakes, sausage, bacon, biscuits, and hash browns. Most around the table were doing the same.

Amelia observed her family around the table. Dominik was sandwiched between his girlfriend and Gabby. She had a feeling that Dominik and his girlfriend, Anya, would announce that they were mates soon. They'd been together for as long as she could remember, and they were a great couple. On the other hand, Gabby was too busy sleeping through mateless wolves to be bothered by something as frivolous as a mate. Gabby had her own ideas on how a she-wolf should behave, and nothing was going to change her mind.

Her Aunts and Uncles, countless cousins and all her friends were all eating, stuffing themselves full while talking loudly over one another. The younger pups were chasing each other around the dining table, avoiding the reach of their parents. It was absolute chaos, and she would miss it all. She noted the time on her phone. It was almost noon. Gosh, how time flies.

Pushing her chair back once again, she stood up from the table, sneaking out of the dining hall unnoticed. Her family was happy. She didn't want to sour the mood. Instead, she headed back upstairs to her room for the final time, taking the stairs two at a time.

Once inside, she went directly to her closet. Her clothes were appropriate enough, but she knew she would need her leather jacket for the ride. She pulled it out, adding on a layer of socks and pulling on her black leather boots. She zipped up the sides, making them snug against her calves.

Inside her bathroom, she took out her spare toothbrush and toothpaste from a drawer, brushing her teeth. She quickly tidied her hair, pleating it down the middle of her back. She grabbed a small backpack out from under her bed, stuffing her remaining toiletries inside. Along with a spare set of clothes, just in case.

Standing up, she looked around her room once more. Slowly circling, she took in every inch. She froze when she came face to face with her father, standing in the middle of her doorway.

Amelia smiled sadly. "I'm gonna miss you."

"Me too, my sweet Rose," her father stepped forward, taking her in for a big bear hug.

Amelia held onto her father tight, for once allowing a single tear to pass, soaking into his shirt. "I love you, daddy."

"And I love you."

She pulled back, wiping quickly at her eyes, giving him the bravest smile she could muster. "I'm ready."

"You don't have to go, Rose. We'll find a way."

She shook her head. "We can't. Besides, I have to do this. You know, I do. The mate bond is so much more than what you told us. I have to see this through."

Thomas sighed in defeat. "I had to try."

Amelia chuckled, snaking her arm around her father's waist as they left her room together for the last time. "I know you did," she said. "Don't forget to ship the rest of my stuff. You've got two weeks, mister."

He smiled. "Yes, ma'am."

Downstairs, a few remaining family members lingered. Ms. McKready stood at the foot of the steps, a small bag in hand. The petite woman was a blubbering mess, handing her the small bag of food before skittering away. She tucked the bag of snacks into her backpack on her back before tightening the straps around her arms.

Amelia walked out the front door. Her brother and Cordelia waited for her at the bottom of the porch steps. She skipped down the old steps her and Damon spent last summer repainting and ran into her best friend's arms. Wrapping herself tightly around her, she breathed in her familiar scent, vanilla and caramel. Cordelia was crying into her shoulder loudly, hiccupping between sobs. Amelia smoothed her hair down, rubbing circles into her back, biting down on her lip until the taste of salt and copper filled her mouth. She couldn't cry in front of all these people.

Amelia pulled back, cupping her friend's face between her hands. Cordelia was a hot mess, but she knew she was leaving her best friend in capable hands.

"We will talk every week, and I promise we will see each other soon," she kissed both of her cheeks, tasting salt on her lips. "I love you, Cordie."

Cordelia sniffled. "I love you more."

Amelia turned to her twin, giving him a slight shrug of her shoulders. "Take care of the pack, Alpha. Don't make me come back here and do your job for you," she taunted him.

Damon snorted, laughing. "I'll do my best," he said, holding out his arms to her.

Amelia folded herself in his embrace, taking comfort in their bond once more. The boy that had been by her side all her life, the man he was now, would rule the world one day.

I'm always with you. Damon said.

Amelia untangled herself from his grasp, looking into the eyes that mirrored her own exactly.

And I you. She said, making him a silent promise that no matter what, she would always be there for him.

Her heart felt as though it was tearing in two. The call of her home tugged at her. This was where she had been born. Where her ancestors had lived for hundreds of years, long before white men settled on these shores. Her blood and the blood of her kin had soaked these lands, defending what was theirs for generations and now that she was leaving, she felt as though she was somehow betraying them.

It wasn't unheard of. Joining a new pack was usually due to the mate's rank. The pair would join whichever pack that held the highest position. She just never imagined this would be her path, her future, her destiny. Twilight Moon would be her new home and the uncertainty of that left her feeling unstable.

With a final breath, she turned toward her bike in the driveway. A matte black speed bike, her helmet placed neatly on her seat. She ran her fingers across her baby before picking up her helmet, preparing the straps. With one final look at her family and the pack gathered outside of the house, she smiled at them all, taking a mental photograph. One she would never forget.

Pulling the helmet on over her head, she fastened the clips. She swung her leg over the bike, kicking up the kickstand and started the motor with her key. Pulling on the exhaust, it stuttered to life, kicking up a cloud of dirt behind her. Without looking back, she took off down the driveway and away from her childhood.

On to new beginnings.

CHAPTER 10

THE TWILIGHT MOON PACK

The farther Amelia drove from her pack, the fainter her connection became. When she was just an hour outside of their territory, she felt the connection snap, like a rubber band breaking when pulled. She quickly pulled over on the side of the road, nearly losing control of the bike.

Clutching at her chest, she struggled, trying to force oxygen into her lungs. The pain of severing her connection to her pack was painful, but it gradually turned into a dull, smarting pain.

Are you okay?

Amelia straightened at the sound of her brother in her mind. Unable to contain it, she released a deep sigh of relief. She wasn't certain if they would keep their connection after the pack bond broke, but now that she knew for sure, she felt elated. Even if she was no longer connected to her pack, she still had her brother and that was something she would hold onto like a life line.

Yeah, I'm good.

Did you feel that?

Of course, I did. Hurt like a bitch, too.

Just be careful. Until you enter the Twilight Moon Pack's territory, you're technically considered a lone wolf. Most packs don't look kindly on them.

I know, I know. I'm going.

Amelia closed off the connection, restarted her bike, and tore off down the road. The rest of the drive went by without a hitch. The roads were clear and open, barely coming across any cars. By the change in smell, she knew she was coming up on the pack territory. Even through her visor and helmet, she could make out the distinct scent of the Twilight Moon Pack. Pine trees and maple sap.

She crossed the boundary line. The scent was even more pungent, burning her nose hairs—definitely something she'd have to get used to. In the dense brush, she could spot a wolf running alongside her on each side. Their brown fur blended in beautifully with the forest. They were probably already alerting Gabriel of her arrival, which made sense since they hadn't stopped to question her.

Driving on her bike, the motor purred beneath her as she weaved through twists and turns, taking her deeper and deeper into the unfamiliar territory. Even though she had been there a few times, she still felt uneasy in a new place, surrounded by unfamiliar forests and smells. Some roads branched out from the main one. Probably leading into other parts of the territory where pack members lived, but she knew to get to the Packhouse, to Gabriel, she had to continue straight.

Finally, the Packhouse came into view. It was large, much like the one she grew up in, but this one was a little more country farmhouse themed, whereas Wandering Moon was more brick, European style. The house was beautiful and charming, painted brilliant white with sets of blue shutters adorning each window. The house's entire length contained a wraparound porch. The scene set with over a dozen rocking chairs spread across the deck.

Amelia pulled her bike to the front of the house, stopping in front of the porch steps leading up to the front door. She was surprised Gabriel wasn't out front waiting for her, unable to help but feel slightly disappointed. Now that she thought about it, not a single person was outside. No one wondering who the newcomer was. No warriors to threaten or interrogate her. No pups nipping at her heels, nothing—just silence.

She swung her leg over her bike, pulling her helmet off with ease. Setting her helmet down on her seat, she smoothed out her hair and looked around anxiously. Her upbringing taught her better than to just walk into a house without being invited, so that was out of the question. Instead, she left her bike in the driveway, not like she knew where to park it anyways and headed around the back.

As she got closer to the backyard, her werewolf hearing could make out sounds that she knew all too well. Someone was fighting. Picking up her pace with a pep in her step, she rounded the corner of the house. The backyard was large, much like her old pack was. Perfect for pack parties and get-togethers, but she didn't see any signs of fighting. Suddenly, she remembered from her last visit. The training grounds were just beyond the tree line that led to another, even larger clearing at the edge of a lake.

Amelia walked across the empty yard, pushing through the few dozen feet of trees until she came upon the packs training grounds. About fifty members were in the clearing, broken off into five groups. The one on her immediate left was paired off, sparing with one another in their human form. Next to them was another group practicing knife throwing. This surprised her immensely. Not many wolves bothered with weapons. Out in the lake, a group of ten were doing laps across the length of the water. To her right, the remaining members were in their wolf shape, learning to fight in their natural state. Half working on defense, the other half offense.

Amelia instantly felt excited, observing all of them practice and train. The smell of blood and sweat permeated the air. The sound of wolves growling, knives splitting wood and flesh connecting with flesh made her want to dance with excitement. She froze when a man caught sight of her, approaching her with caution.

"Who are you?" he called out, his voice carrying out over the clearing, halting all present.

Fifty pairs of eyes trained on her. Amelia took a hesitant step back before her stubbornness won, and she stood her ground. Rey bristled at the wolves vocally growling, challenging her.

The man approached her slowly, getting closer and closer before finally stopping a few feet from her.

Amelia recognized him with his buzz cut, chocolate brown eyes, and goofy face. "Christian?"

Christian straightened, no longer stalking towards her, his name catching him off guard. He looked at her closer, his eyes widening. "Ella?"

Amelia laughed, thankful he recognized her. She didn't think she could fight fifty of them off, no matter how good she was. "Man, you've grown since I last saw you. You've filled out nicely," she said, smirking.

Christian blushed fiercely, his cheeks turning a flaming red. "Ella, that was two years ago, besides you don't look so bad yourself," he said, gesturing to her now fully mature body.

Amelia waved him off playfully. "How're your ribs doing? Still healing from that ass beating I gave you last time?"

Christian snorted. "I distinctly remember breaking your arm during that fight."

"That might be true, but I made you regret it immediately after. Don't say I didn't," she said, holding her finger up at him, daring him to say otherwise.

"I don't want to talk about it anymore," Christian grumbled, earning him a whimsical laugh. "What are you doing here, anyway?" Christian asked, looking behind her as if he was expecting someone else to appear. "Our Alpha just got back, is something wrong?"

Amelia's eyebrow arched high. Guess Gabriel didn't tell any of them she was coming. Interesting. Play it cool. "Nope, nothing's wrong. Just thought I'd come by, say hi."

Lame Amelia, just lame.

He clearly didn't believe her, now standing with his arms crossed against his chest, leaning back on the balls of his feet.

"And why don't I believe that?"

You really suck at this. Rey said, coming out of the recesses of her mind.

You are not helping.

Before she could have a chance to think of a response, she heard feet pounding into the earth, coming up behind her fast. She spun around to find Gabriel running up to her. He was in a clean pair of jeans and a grey shirt. His hair combed back from his face.

"Amelia," Gabriel said, sounding winded. "I didn't know you were here already."

Amelia eyed him up and down. "Yes, I could tell from your lack of being there when I pulled up."

"You were early," Gabriel told her, looking down at the watch on his wrist. The time was only half-past three.

"Didn't your guards at the border tell you I was coming through? Cause I know they saw me." Now she was getting annoyed, crossing her arms over her chest and sticking out her stubborn chin. "If your security is that lax, then you have a much bigger problem than just little ole me."

Gabriel did not look too pleased with her accusing him of not setting up proper border patrols and procedures in place for intruders. Anger was rolling off of him in waves. His aura glowed red around him. The pack may not be able to see his aura like she could, but they could sense their Alpha's displeasure as they all backed away; keeping their heads down.

Amelia didn't care if he was pissed or not. She pulled her shoulders back, crossing her arms over her chest, ignoring his macho posturing that he was trying to use to intimidate her. She wasn't a timid she-wolf and he had a lot to learn if he thought she was.

"I told those at the border that if they saw a woman coming through, they were to let her in, no questions asked," Gabriel growled through his teeth.

Amelia took a step closer to him, challenging him. "So, because I'm a woman, I'm not a threat? Is that what you're insinuating? And you'll just let any woman through your borders? How very promiscuous of you."

She couldn't explain why she was saying the things she was saying except that her anger was boiling over, her words coming out faster than she could think. But she would be damned if he believed her to be less than him just because of her sex. Teaching him that lesson would be her absolute pleasure.

"Hey, boss," Christian chimed in, sensing the crackling tension between the two. "How do you know Ella?"

Gabriel shook his head, not sure he heard him right. "Who's Ella?"

Amelia raised her hand as if to say, *duh*. "That would be me."

"Your name's Amelia," Gabriel said slowly.

Amelia couldn't help but roll her eyes. Men are so obtuse. "I go by lots of nicknames. Christian's always called me Ella."

"And how did you two meet?" Gabriel asked her accusingly.

Now she wanted to punch him. Was he seriously getting jealous? "You are unbelievable. You didn't even bother to be there when I arrived because your border patrol failed to tell you I was here. Now you have the nerve to be jealous?"

"I am not jealous," he growled.

Will you stop messing with him?

No! He deserves it. He's being an ass.

She could feel her wolf roll her eyes at her. *It takes one to know one.*

Amelia bit her tongue from yelling aloud at her wolf. She closed her eyes, able to feel the shift just beneath her skin, taking in deep breaths before she really started to lose her cool. She could feel her aura around her sparking, flexing erratically, tied tightly to her emotions. Unable to help but feel insecure in a new pack and slightly abandoned by Gabriel, she was overreacting big time, and she knew it.

She opened her eyes to find Gabriel staring at her inquisitively. His head cocked to the side. Could he see her aura?

Christian coughed loudly, causing her to remember they had an audience. She broke eye contact with Gabriel, once again disregarding him.

"I'll ask again," Gabriel said. "How do you two know each other?"

"Boss, Ella is the girl I told you about. The one that came here two years ago," Christian explained. "She took on ten of us at once and only walked away with a broken arm."

Gabriel's face scrunched in confusion. Amelia wanted to scoff at his reaction. As though he found it hard to believe she was capable of holding her own. Let alone challenge ten men and walk away with barely a scratch.

"You never told me she was the Alpha's daughter," Gabriel said.

"We didn't know," Christian shrugged his shoulders.

"I came with my father's Beta during one of the treaty negotiation meetings. I wanted to see how other packs worked," Amelia told him, even though she didn't feel she owed him an explanation. "Now if you don't mind, I'd like to be taken to my room. It was a long ride, and I'd like to get cleaned up."

"You're staying here?" Christian asked.

Gabriel shot him a warning look, making him snap his mouth shut. Amelia noticed the silent exchange, reawakening her insecurities.

"He didn't tell any of you?" Amelia asked, speaking loud enough for most in the clearing to hear. "He's my fated mate. Lucky me, right?"

Paybacks a bitch.

CHAPTER 11

THE UNEXPECTED
BOOKCASE

Amelia stood in front of her bike, staring up the front porch steps at the French doors. More than anything, she wanted to get back on her bike and flee this territory forever, but her honor held her bound to this pack, to him. She made a promise, and she wasn't going to go back on it just because things hadn't gone the way she expected. She was bigger than that.

Walking up the few steps onto a sturdy, wooden porch, she approached the massive front door, knocking on it three times. She stood there waiting. Her wolf hearing picked up the sound of feet shuffling towards the door. It opened to reveal a short, middle-aged woman with chestnut hair, reminding her much of Mrs. McKready.

"Yes?" The woman asked, looking at her suspiciously.

Amelia tried to smile at her, nerves making her heart hammer in her chest. "I'm Amelia," she said, hoping Gabriel had told at least one person in the house about her arrival.

The woman's eyes widened, taking a step back and appraising her with a big, gap-toothed smile. "Luna, blessed by the Moon Goddess, you are beautiful!"

Amelia couldn't help the blush that was making her face feel like a million degrees. The woman grabbed her hand, pulling her inside the house and slamming the door shut behind her.

"My name is Lena Anderson. I run the kitchens and am in charge of the Omegas. I pretty much oversee that all the household chores are completed. Although now that you're here, I'm sure that'll change," Lena said, looking up at her expectedly.

Amelia held her hands up in surrender. "I'm not here to take over, and honestly, I don't want to be a Luna confined to the house. If you're okay with it, I think it's best if things stay as they are for now." Or forever.

Lena smirked, bobbing her head. "That is fine with me, Luna. Whatever you desire," she looked behind her at the door, frowning. "You don't have any bags with you?"

"No, Gabriel brought some of my things with him this morning. I just have my bike," Amelia told her.

"Samuel!" Lena shouted over her shoulder into the house.

Amelia jumped, the boom of her voice shocking her to the bone. Note to self. This woman was not to be trifled with.

A youthful, scrawny teenager came running towards them. His shaggy, ginger hair hung in his eyes. His brown eyes flitted between Lena and herself, staring at her a longer than she was comfortable with.

Lena flicked her wrist, smacking the boy upside the head. "Show some respect. This is your Luna boy."

Samuel's eyes widened, fear distorting his face as he bowed, tilting his head in submission. Amelia tried to keep herself from rolling her eyes but unable to hide the smirk that was pulling at her lips. She was kind of falling in love with Lena.

"It's okay, Samuel, you can call me Amelia. It's nice to meet you," she said, trying to offer him a smile.

"Samuel, our Luna's bike is parked out front. Be a dear and bring it to the garage," Lena said, making it more of an order than a request.

At the sound of the word bike, Samuel's ear perked, his interest instantly peeked. "You ride a bike? What kind of bike is it?"

"Suzuki GSXR 600," she told him, smiling at the awe written on his face.

"Wow. That's so awesome," he said, practically jumping, racing for the door.

Amelia stuck her hand out, grabbing him by the arm, looking him straight in the eye. "Scratch it, and you'll wish you were never born. Got me?"

Samuel swallowed hard, nodding his head slowly before she let him go. He walked out of the house with slow, controlled steps, shutting the door behind him.

Amelia turned back to Lena to find the woman smiling at her.

"I think you and I will get along just fine," Lena laughed. "Come on, follow me. I'll show you to your room. The Boss already had your luggage brought up."

Amelia followed her into the house, past an empty dining hall and through a common room with a few people mingling about. She followed her up four flights of stairs, down a dimly lit hallway, until they reached the last door on the right.

Lena pulled out a key, unlocked the door and pushed it open, entering without a word. Amelia followed hesitantly, nervous about what she might see. Taking in a deep breath, she pushed down her nerves and stepped into the room where Lena was waiting.

Inside the room, it wasn't exactly what she was expecting. She honestly wasn't even sure what she was expecting, but it wasn't this.

"This is the Alpha's room?" Amelia asked.

"Yes, Luna."

"And I'm supposed to sleep here?"

"The Luna typically lives with the Alpha, in his room. So, yes."

Amelia could hear the teasing in her voice, but she was too distracted to care. The room was painted in a light gray color, similar to the color of his eyes. There was a king-size bed in the middle of the room, set between two large bay windows that overlooked the back yard.

On the right side of the room were two separate doors. She assumed they led to a bathroom and closet. Along the wall by the door was a dresser and armoire in dark mahogany wood. The thing that puzzled her the most was the whole side of the wall on the left was empty, but she could tell from the carpet's impressions that there was furniture there and recently too.

"Why is this wall empty? Where did the furniture go?"

"The Boss asked us to remove it. He's ordered a wall to wall bookcase to be installed there later this week."

Amelia snapped her head towards the woman, her mouth hanging open. "A bookcase?"

"Yes, Luna," Lena smiled. "I'll leave you to get settled. Dinner is in two hours."

She turned back to the blank canvas, faintly hearing the door shut behind her. He was installing a bookcase. A wall to wall bookcase. Why? Was it for her? Did he like to read too? She instantly felt bewildered. What was he playing at?

Amelia approached the bed. Her three suitcases were placed along the right side, waiting for her. She picked up the one closest to her. Judging by its weight, it was her books. Hauling it across the room, she left the suitcase along the blank, empty wall. Lifting the second, she heard metal clinking against metal. Sounds like her curling iron and straightener battling for dominance. She set that one aside for later, leaving the last suitcase to be the only thing left, her clothes. Laying the suitcase down on top of the bed, she zipped it open to reveal her hastily thrown in clothes, instantly regretting not taking the time to fold them.

Amelia turned back to the two doors along the wall beside her. She approached the door closest to her, turning the handle and pushing it open. Inside was a black and white bathroom. The tile on the floor was a black and white checker with black cabinets running along the wall, containing plenty of storage. On top sat a delicate white quartz counter holding two porcelain sinks. The wall was decorated in white subway tiles in a herringbone pattern. In the back corner was a giant walk-in shower with a clawfoot tub tucked to the side.

Backing out, she shut the door and approached the next one. It must be the closet. Twisting the knob, she opened the door finding herself in total darkness. She groped along the wall, her fingers fumbling to find a light switch until she felt something plastic against her skin. Flicking it up, the lights went on, illuminating the space in front of her. The closet was huge. It was at least double the size of the one she had back home.

In the middle of the closet was a light gray ottoman, probably for someone to sit on when getting dressed. Every inch of wall space was covered in storage, shoe racks, and hanging rods. The closet's entire left side was full, brimming with neutral-colored clothing, shoes for every occasion, even a small area for watches, cufflinks, and the like. The right side was bare, waiting to be filled.

Amelia couldn't help but smile. She approached the empty side of the closet, running her hand along the bare shelves where her shoes would fill. Pulling her hand away, she discovered dust covering the pads of her fingers. Rubbing the dust between her fingers, her smile grew. No one had ever occupied this space. She felt oddly comforted by that.

Mate's been waiting for us. Rey chimed in.

Amelia snorted. *Maybe.*

Please give this a chance Amelia. I have a good feeling about this.

Yeah? Then why do I have a bad one?

Maybe because you're pessimistic?

Right, and you're the eternal optimist.

See. We balance each other out.

Amelia rolled her eyes at her wolf. She left the closet, flicking off the light and shutting the door. Back to her suitcase, she dug through her mess until she found a clean pair of jeans, a navy floral shirt that was flowy and loose against her body, and clean undergarments. Pulling the backpack off her back, she tossed it on the bed. She went back into the bathroom for a second time with her clothes under her arm. Setting them down on the counter, she opened each of the cabinets until she found a clean towel.

Knowing she didn't have enough time for a full shower, she could at least wash her body before she met her new pack. She released her hair from its plait, tying it up on top of her head. Stepping inside the insanely large shower, she turned the knobs, releasing raindrops of water from three various heads coming at her in different directions.

She stepped outside of the bathroom. His smell smacking her square in the face. Looking up, she found his back to her, sitting on the edge of the bed on the opposite side. Ignoring him, she grabbed her backpack off the bed, ripping open the zipper, and pulled out her brush. She yanked out the band from her hair, her long blonde locks falling around her, sticking to her damp skin.

"I see you've made yourself comfortable," Gabriel said, not bothering to turn around.

Amelia froze at his words, her brush halfway down the length of her hair. Was he annoyed with her? "I can stay somewhere else if you like. I don't want to inconvenience you," she said with more bite than intended, but the man did something to her, getting on her nerves more than anyone else she'd ever met. If this is what the mate bond was like all the time, she wondered what she did to piss off the Moon Goddess so royally.

Gabriel turned around, facing her, still sitting on the bed. "That's not what I meant."

"Then what did you mean?" Amelia asked him, continuing to brush through the tangles in her hair.

Gabriel sighed, unsure of what to say. "I don't know."

Amelia frowned, her brows scrunched together. She couldn't figure him out, and he was beginning to give her whiplash. She put her brush down on the nightstand and walked around the bed to stand in front of him.

"Gabriel."

He looked up at her. His silver eyes were unsure.

"I'm here like you wanted. I showed up earlier than you expected. I'm *here*. If you don't want me to be, then you need to tell me that," she said to him slowly, holding her breath.

What if he really didn't want her?

Gabriel stood up, his height towering over her. Her head came up just under his chin. He wrapped his arms around her waist, lifting her up and into his chest. He buried his face in the crook of her neck, breathing her in deeply.

This took Amelia by surprise. She was expecting him to tell her to get out. Not hold her, breathing her in as mates do. She found herself hugging him back, running her fingers through the baby hairs at the nape of his neck.

"I'm glad that you're here," Gabriel breathed into her shoulder. "I'm sorry I wasn't there to greet you. I should have, and I'm sorry."

Amelia was further shocked. She never expected to get an apology out of the man, *ever*. Maybe he really did care.

Told you so.

She internally rolled her eyes at her wolf, ignoring her altogether. She felt him lower her back down to the ground, feeling the soft carpet once again beneath her feet. Leaving her arms around his neck, she kept her fingers in his hair, enjoying the soft silky feel of it.

"It's fine," she said, then thinking back, "I mean it's not fine, you should have been there. You should have been the one to show me around the Packhouse and to our room, but it's over with now."

Gabriel nodded his head. "Come on. Dinner should be done. The pack is dying to meet their Luna," he said with a smirk.

Amelia snorted lightly. "So, you actually told them about me?"

"Of course, I did," Gabriel said with a reassuring smile.

CHAPTER 12

CHALLENGE ACCEPTED

Downstairs, approximately fifty people were gathered, talking amongst themselves in the communal room. Once they walked in, the room became silent; all eyes turned on her. Amelia forced herself from taking a step back in hesitation. The notion of fleeing the room to never return crossed her mind. She hated being the center of attention and especially hated being put under a microscope. Someone for everyone to gawk at.

Gabriel reached down, clutching her hand in his, giving her a slight squeeze, silently telling her he was there for her. "For those of you who don't already know, this is Amelia, my fated mate, and your Luna. I want you all to show her the respect you show me, so let's welcome her to our pack in true werewolf fashion."

Amelia looked at him, curiously. What did that mean? Suddenly, every single man and woman in the room raised their nose to the ceiling and all at once howled to the sky. The sound sent chills down her spine. Her heart raced in her chest as her throat went dry. Rey was scrambling in her head, itching to join. The wolves sang in perfect unison, howling in greeting. When their song ended, they all smiled at her, waiting for her response.

Amelia bowed her head in respect to each and everyone one of them, grateful for such a genuine welcome. She could tell she shocked most of them, bowing to them. Bows were reserved for Alpha's and Elders, not ordinary pack members. Even though this was only a small fraction of the Twilight Moon Pack's numbers, she still felt that much easier about her decision.

"Thank you all for accepting me into your pack. I hope I deserve it," she said, making eye contact with as many of them as she could.

"Dinner's ready," announced Lena standing in the archway to the dining room.

"Let's eat," Gabriel said.

That was all they required from him as each of them filled into the dining room. Gabriel and Amelia were the last ones to follow. Gabriel held her back before following the others.

"You're incredible. Did you know that? You continue to surprise me," he whispered into her ear.

Amelia smirked, cuffing him lightly across the chest. "Back at ya."

Gabriel, still holding her hand, walked them inside the dining room. The room was rather large, housing four long tables, each seating easily twelve people. It was more of a dining hall than a room. Gabriel motioned for her to sit opposite him at one of the tables. This momentarily surprised her, not to find him sitting at the head of one of the tables, but instead sitting with his pack, mingling in the midst of them.

Amelia smiled, following his lead and sitting down at an empty place between a male and a female wolf. Gabriel took the seat opposite her.

Lena came into the dining hall carrying a plate of chicken. Behind her followed seven Omega's carrying similar looking plates. Two plates of chicken were set on each table. Amelia waited, afraid to disturb anything. Instead, she waited for cues from the Alpha. Here, she would follow his lead.

Lena came back in a few more times bringing in the additional sides, gravies, and rolls, covering the table with an abundance of food.

The smell caused her stomach to rumble. Making her quickly realize her last meal was that morning with her family. She quickly realized this was her new family. She would *make* them her family.

Gabriel reached for the chicken, stabbing one with his fork before putting it down on his plate. The second the poultry touched the white pottery, there was a clatter of forks. Arms reached across each other, wolves' hissing and bickering at each other while they all filled their plates.

Amelia smiled at the familiar atmosphere. No matter which pack it was, wolves were all the same, controlled by their hunger and impulses. She began to pile food onto her own plate, those around her respectful of her rank. Gabriel had already started digging in, so the rest were doing the same.

She worked on her food, cutting up her chicken before putting each piece in her mouth. She observed Gabriel, who seemed to be watching her in return. Both of their eyes taking in each minute detail about the other.

Rey, at the back of her mind, was becoming antsy, almost jittery with anticipation.

Down girl. Can we eat first?

Rey snapped at her, making her chuckle in response. Gabriel's eyebrow rose in response, curious as to what made her laugh. She just shook her head in response, taking another bite of food.

"Hi, I'm Kelsey," the girl beside her said, her hand out in front of her.

Amelia smiled, shaking her hand lightly. "Hi, I'm Amelia."

"Oh, I know who you are, Luna. I saw you earlier at the training field," Kelsey chatted away, her voice high and excited.

Amelia at least had the decency to flinch at the mention of the training fields. She caught a flash in Gabriel's eyes at the sound of it too. "Yeah, sorry about that."

"Oh please," Kelsey said, waving it off. "Is it true you beat ten of our warriors? At once?"

Amelia looked off to the side, catching a glimpse of Christian smiling behind his beer. She gave him a good hard glare across the room. "I'm sure whatever you heard has been greatly exaggerated. Besides, it was two years ago, hard to remember," she was lying, big time, but she wasn't going to flaunt it in front of her new pack that she had kicked their warrior's asses single-handedly.

"Luna, my name is Jamison, I assist Christian with training," the man on her left said.

"Please, it's just Amelia," she told him, ignoring Gabriel's squinty eyes.

Jamison ignored the correction and continued, "We would be honored if you would join our training tomorrow. Our warriors would be glad to give you a demonstration."

For the first time since she arrived, she was excited. "That would be great."

"Perfect. Training starts at eight," Jamison informed her.

"You got it. I'll be there," she smiled brightly, taking a swig from her glass of water.

"Don't you think you might have more important things you should be doing tomorrow?" Gabriel asked her from across the table.

Amelia raised an eyebrow at him. "Really? Like what?" she asked, assessing him.

Please don't be a douche.

"Learning your Luna duties. Learning to run this house," Gabriel said, stating the obvious.

Amelia leaned back in her chair, setting her fork down on the table gently. Most of the conversations around them died. No one dared to make eye contact, but she would bet money all ears were trained on them, curious as to how the unfamiliar Luna would respond. This would demonstrate to them who she was and how she would lead them beside their Alpha.

She never failed to rise to a challenge, and Gabriel was going to prove to be the biggest challenge of her life.

"Gabriel, while I appreciate your views of a Luna are a bit outdated, I want to make one thing clear. I am not a housewife. I will not live in this house, polishing the floors and waiting around to prepare your food. I am a warrior first. I have worked my ass off to be better than most men.

"You need a party planner? I'm sure I can do it. You need help in a business meeting? I'm organized and efficient with numbers. Running the Wandering Moon Pack's finances for the last few years taught me a thing or two. But never assume that just because I'm a female, I am obedient."

The she-wolves around her openly stared at her in astonishment. Some of the men shook their heads, whether in disappointment or for disrespecting their Alpha, she wasn't sure. She knew there was going to be a growing period for all of them. Most of them didn't know her, but soon they would.

Gabriel stared at her hard, looking as if he was fighting internally with how to respond.

Was I too harsh? Amelia asked her wolf.

No. They will learn, or we will make them.

Amelia internally smiled, making sure to keep her external posture serious and composed, ready to take whatever backlash Gabriel might give.

The wolves around them were silent, awaiting their Alpha. This could go two ways. One, he lashes out at her or two, he lashes out at her and then sends her to her room, which might be funny. Either way, she didn't think it was going to end well.

"You're right."

Now her jaw was the one to hit the floor. "Excuse me?" she was pretty sure she had brimstone wedged in her ear.

"I said you're right," Gabriel said, slowly repeating himself, ignoring the blatant stares of his pack. "I've underestimated you at every turn. Tomorrow we'll see what you're made of."

Did he just challenge us? Amelia asked Rey, looking for confirmation, maybe even clarification if she was still speaking with his wolf.

Pretty sure that was a challenge. Rey confirmed.

Amelia nodded her head, holding his stare, refusing to blink or look away. "Yes, you will."

Gabriel's lips turned up into a smirk, getting back to the task of eating. The tension in the room immediately fizzled as the others quickly realized there would be no outburst from the Alpha. Now the pack had something new to chatter about, their Luna at training in the morning.

Amelia watched Gabriel intently, taking in every detail about him. The way he held his fork in his hand like a pen. How he chewed each piece methodically before taking another bite. The way his presence consumed the room, each member of his pack hanging on his every word. They worshipped him, and what's not to like?

Gabriel looked up, startling her. She quickly looked down at her plate. She could feel the blood rushing to her face, her body temperature rising fast. Embarrassed at being caught, she shoveled food in her mouth to distract herself.

The meal lasted an hour. Everyone moved about the room after their plates were finished, mingling with one another. Amelia was seriously impressed with the relaxed atmosphere. The lack of formality. She hated when simple things such as a meal would be hung up on ceremony. Unfortunately, she had met one too many Alpha's that paraded themselves around like a King. It was pathetic.

She had moved over to where Christian was sitting. His face was one of the only ones she recognized. Sitting down beside him, she leaned against the table, elbow propping her head up.

"What am I to expect from tomorrow?" she asked him seriously.

Christian refused to meet her eyes, which only meant one of two things. The least likely, Christian didn't know. Most likely, Gabriel already put a gag order in place to prove who the Alpha was. Not that she minded. He was Alpha, and he had every right to defend his title. She didn't know if she should be flattered or insulted that he felt the need to defend it from her. She'd relieve him of his misogyny once and for all, even if she had to beat it out of him.

"That's fine. Don't answer. I appreciate your loyalty to your pack and your Alpha," Amelia said. The look on his face meant that he took it exactly as she meant for him too. That he was loyal to the Alpha but not the Luna.

Christian went to respond, but she silenced him with a wave of her hand. "Don't. I like a challenge, and I don't fight fair. You of all people should know that," she winked at him before leaving him alone at his table, speechless.

Amelia stood up from the table, instantly spotting Gabriel from across the room. He was leaning against the wall near the communal room, watching her. She could smell his jealousy from where she stood. Goddess, he was easy to rile up, but she didn't like it. She didn't like that he was jealous. Either he didn't trust her, or he didn't trust his pack. Both scenarios didn't sit well with her.

She strolled over towards him, stopping just short of his reach. She cocked her head to the side, observing his posture.

"What are you staring at?" Gabriel asked her.

"I'm just watching you. Wondering why you're jealous," she said bluntly.

"I am not jealous," he spat out, faster than he should have.

Amelia chuckled. She saw right through him. "You were. I can smell it on you," she stepped closer to him, now just a foot apart. "Question. Are you jealous because you're afraid I'll be unfaithful or because other males might find me attractive?"

A snarl slipped through his lips unwillingly.

"So, the latter," Amelia said, stating the facts. They may be human, but the animal side never lied. She took the final step that would close the distance between them. "First of all, to ease your mind, I am the most loyal person you'll ever meet. I will never be unfaithful to you. It's not how I'm built," she reached out, laying her hands over his arms across his chest. "And second, men can look all they want. There is nothing in this world you can do to stop that, whether you like it or not. If one gets too brave, I'll be the first to put them in their place. But I am only yours to touch."

Gabriel unfurled his arms, relaxing them at his sides. She pushed in closer to him, winding her arms around his waist. Tilting her head back to look at him, she smiled.

"Let's get out of here," she said, a small smirk playing on her lips.

Gabriel's eyebrow rose. He found himself nodding his head, following her out of the dining hall.

CHAPTER 13

MUCH, MUCH MORE

Amelia's hand was laced in his, towing him behind her to the base of the stairs. Taking two of the steps, she turned around, now on an even level with him. His eyes were consuming her as she stared into his silver melting pools, rich with warmth and hunger. She reached up, stroking the hair back from his eyes, leaving her hand to rest on the base of his neck.

"Do you want me as much as I need you?" Amelia whispered, realizing too late she had spoken aloud.

Gabriel looked taken aback. The sheer honesty in her voice startled him. He slipped his arms around her waist, pulling her in against him. "No," he finally said, "I need you much, much more."

He crashed down on her lips. Hungry. Ravenous. Tasting her like a man parched of thirst. She could feel her body burning where they touched. The small sparks that danced across her skin were growing, consuming her body, propelling her towards something more. She gripped his hair at the roots, pulling and tugging, bringing him in closer.

Her heart hammered in her chest. Kissing him could never compare to any other boy. With the mate bond pulling on both ends, forcing them to meet, she couldn't help but fall into it. The depths of their fate were swallowing her whole and she prayed she wouldn't drown.

Their tongues danced against one another. She had never tasted anything so sweet, so refreshing, like she was finally being kissed for the first time. Even though she had more practice than she'd ever admit. His hands dug into her lower back, tugging and teasing at the hem of her shirt. She felt him skim down over her butt to her thighs, gripping and elevating her until her legs were wrapped securely around his waist.

Amelia's' head spun. Somehow at that moment, she knew those hands, his brawny arms, would always be there to catch her. She didn't recall him carrying her up the stairs. Only his hands moving along her body, his lips sucking on her marking spot, causing elicit moans to escape her lips.

She felt her top being pulled off, thrown over her head. Reaching down, her fingertips curled under the hem of his shirt. She pulled it off between kisses.

Whenever she imagined losing her virginity, she always thought she'd be nervous, scared, and yet, it was the exact opposite. She barely knew Gabriel. Barely knew a damn thing about him, and yet she had never felt more comfortable.

Amelia had virtually forgotten how to breathe. The taste of him consumed her. His every breath, every touch, molded with hers until they became one. A small blissful existence that she basked in with fervency.

Amelia felt herself being lifted back down on the plush carpet. They were in his bedroom, their bedroom. Gabriel stepped back. Filtered moon-light cascaded through the windows. Her heightened vision picked up the firm lines of his muscular form. She didn't like that he was so far away. Her hands demanded to be on him. She needed to be touching him. From the fever in his eyes, she knew he felt the same.

She reached out to him, tugging him by his belt buckle and reduced the distance. Her shaky fingers somehow managed to unfasten his belt. Pulling it free, she dropped it on the floor before she unbuttoned his pants, letting them to his ankles. He wore nothing beneath his jeans.

Her eyes bulged at the sight of him. A fire burned in the deepest part of her stomach with such intensity her mouth felt parched. She tried to swallow, lick her lips to rid herself of the dry sensation when she heard a growl from above. He hauled her up quickly, bringing his lips back to hers.

Gabriel's hands were swifter. Her pants already in a pile at her feet. Her core was burning. Desire tore through her entire being. She was wet, and by the way his nostrils were flaring, he was more than well aware. He lifted her back up on his waist, their mouths finding each other again. The only barrier between their union was her thin cotton panties.

Amelia reached behind her, unclasping her bra, pitching it to the floor. Gabriel laid her down in the middle of the bed before pulling back to admire her. She should have blushed, maybe even been embarrassed. It was the first time she had ever been in this situation, naked with a man staring at her in such a way that stripped her soul bare. But she wasn't. There was no shame, no insecurity or doubt.

It didn't matter that they had only known each other for less than forty-eight hours. It didn't matter how different they were or the challenges that surely awaited them. He was her mate, her fated mate. They were made for each other, and that was all she needed to know.

"Condom," Gabriel breathed, his voice husky and questioning, telling her he didn't want the thin barrier between them.

"I'm on birth control. I had the shot," Amelia shook her head. She didn't want anything between them either. She'd been enduring the injections every three months for the last four years—a standard procedure with wolves and their temperamental hormones. Babies were not something she wanted to deal with.

Gabriel came back to her, leaning over her body. His hands rested on the bed on both sides of her head. He kissed her, this time softer and more tender. She cupped his face with one hand, gripping his waist with the other.

He pulled back again, hovering just above her, his breath mixing with hers. "Are you sure about this?"

Amelia swallowed with difficulty, licking her lips. Nerves took residence in her stomach in the form of bats. Her insides were quaking. The bond that was forcing them closer and closer together was demanding to be completed. Fate screamed at them not to fight, not to push against destiny, for she would surely push back.

She nodded her head. "Saving myself for you was the best choice I ever made."

Gabriel's lips pulled up into a genuine smile. "I'll go slow," his voice husky and thick with need. "At first."

Amelia bit her lip before pulling him down on top of her. Their mouths devoured one another with a new type of need. His hard member was pushing against her thigh, inching its way up to her tender core.

He trailed his fingers down over her chest, her nipples hardening in the brisk air, across her stomach, and down to her soaked panties. With one pull, he tore them off, leaving her completely exposed. From the smell of her, she was more than wet and ready. He trailed his hand back up to rest beside her head, the other hand slipping between her and the bed, resting along the small of her back.

With one swift movement, he pushed himself inside her core. Amelia gasped, covering her mouth with the back of her hand. Gabriel hovered over her, allowing her a moment to get used to the feeling. He peppered her with kisses, distracting her with his lips, trailing down her neck and back up again. He began to move slowly inside of her.

Amelia initially clenched. The feeling of his hard member inside of her was shocking and a bit painful, not used to being stretched so intimately. But he was patient with her. He kissed her, distracting her, and soon she found herself kissing him back, the fire within back to a blazing inferno.

Soon, he began to move inside her, and the intensity grew, morphing into something that had her crying out in ecstasy. Before she realized, she found herself bearing all of him, her body claiming every inch, and he was all hers. His hand was pressed into her back, guiding her, moving her body to his rhythm.

Amelia could feel a strange warmth burning through her chest. It wasn't like the ache between her legs that signaled pleasure. No, this was something else. There was something passing between them, opening a door into one another's souls. She could taste him, though his lips weren't against hers. His scent washed over her in a wave of spiced heaven. The mate bond was forming, tethering them together for the rest of their lives.

Her fingers dug into his back, her body responding in such a way that she never imagined. He picked up his pace, pushing into her harder and faster. A pressure began to build above where he was pounding, hitting a heavenly spot repeatedly. Her moans were becoming more erratic, her breathing heavier and faster. Gabriel looked down at her, enjoying the view.

"Look at me, baby," Gabriel called out to her without failing to miss a beat.

Amelia opened her eyes, looking up to find him staring down at her, watching her.

"Stay with me. Don't look away," he said, his voice deep and heavy. He lifted her off the bed, still buried deep inside of her, overturning them so he was sitting, and she was straddling him. "That's it, now move with me."

Amelia licked her lips, following his directions. She began to move her hips against his, grinding down onto his manhood, eliciting a new kind of pleasure deep within her walls. Gabriel moaned, a rumble coming from deep in his chest. She smirked, glad she was able to satisfy him the way he had been doing to her.

She rode him faster, her body picking up speed, their bodies moving simultaneously against one another. Gabriel gripped the back of her neck, keeping their eyes locked on one another. Amelia could feel her orgasm grow, expanding until she was sure to explode.

"Wait for me, baby. We'll cum together," he told her, pulling at the root of her hair.

Amelia hissed, her eyes boring into his. "I can't," she begged.

"Just another second," he breathed, his voice hitched with each thrust.

Amelia felt possessed, her body acting on its own, guided by sheer instinct. She thrust down on him harder, the tip of him slamming into the entrance of her womb. Shots of pain and pleasure combined into one. She didn't know which way was up. Which way was down. She was reaching her peak, unable to contain it any longer.

Gabriel groaned beneath her just as she screamed out loud. Her orgasm finally released but not before she felt white-hot pokers slicing into the soft spot on her neck. She felt a jolt of pain, racing down her neck, along her spine and down to her toes. As soon as the pain appeared, it was just as quickly replaced. A second orgasm tore through her body, making her spasm against him, the way his manhood was twitching inside her, releasing his seed.

Riding out the end, she felt herself go limp in his arms. He removed his canines from her neck, licking the spot, sealing the small holes. A fresh shiver rippled down each vertebra. Her mind was mind-fuckingly numb as they collapsed together, back on the bed. He twisted her hair to the side, off her face and shoulder, before kissing her forehead as soft as a whisper.

Amelia didn't move. She didn't think her legs would work properly even if she tried. He was still buried inside her, but she didn't care. For the first time in her life, she felt whole.

CHAPTER 14

UNCERTAIN

Amelia reached out, her hand connecting clumsily with her phone, knocking it off the end table. Groaning, she rolled over, stretching down to the floor, frantically searching for the device that was honking at her like a car alarm. Her fingers finally connected with the stupid thing. Raising it up to her face, she squinted at the screen until she found the stop button—finally, silence.

A warm, firm arm snaked around her waist, pulling her in closer. Amelia smiled, turning to face him, snuggling against his solid chest. She nuzzled her nose into the crook of his neck, the place where his scent was strongest. Sweet honey apples and cinnamon flooded her mouth. Gradually, she trailed her fingers along his tender flesh, her touch as soft as a whisper. She couldn't help but smirk as he shivered at her touch, gooseflesh prickling along his arms.

Gabriel squirmed against her, pulling her in tighter along his body, making sure she knew the effect it was having on him from the evidence of the wood poking her stomach. Amelia's mind instantly flashed back to last night.

Her core ached with the memory of him buried deep inside her. How gentle he was. The noises and sounds she released, never having experienced such bliss and pleasure. She extended her hand up, brushing against the mark he left on her.

He marked her. She should be happy about that, but the idea that now she belonged to him didn't sit well with her. Did he do it because they were both caught up in the carnal pleasure, the gratification, and satisfaction of having sex? Was that really a reason to mark someone?

Amelia found herself frowning, unable to lessen the feeling of self-doubt that was now clouding her mind. Why did she have to sleep with him last night? She barely knew the man, and she just gave it up to him in one night? The mate bond took away her freedom, her choices, forcing her into circumstances that compromised her beliefs and resolve.

She squirmed in his arms until he loosened just enough for her to escape his grasp altogether.

Gabriel tilted his head off the pillow, his eyes squinting, sleep still at the forefront of his mind. "Where are you going?" he asked, his voice rough like sandpaper.

Amelia stood up from the bed, completely forgetting she was naked. She had plenty of time before training started, so she dashed into the bathroom, feeling sticky in places best left unmentioned. Shutting the door behind her, she went right for the shower.

The frigid water shocked her system, waking her up fully. She shivered, completely submerging herself under the raining shower head. The water warmed rapidly, but it didn't keep her in the shower any longer than she needed to. Hastily cleansing her body, she felt peculiar. She couldn't explain the change, but having sex with Gabriel altered her in some fundamental way. Maybe it was the mark. Now she was forever connected to him physically, psychically. Even if the bond hadn't been completed fully, since she had yet to mark him.

Stepping out of the shower, she wrapped her towel around her body, shaking out her long hair. She looked around, stupidly realizing she now had to go back in the room with only a towel keeping her covered since she had none of her clothes with her.

Mate wants us. Rey said, her voice making her jump.

I know Rey, but it's more complicated than that.

Why?

Amelia sighed. Sometimes she wished she could see things as simple as a wolf, but the reality was much harsher and even more complicated. *Rey, we don't know him. He marked us, and we literally know nothing about him. It's too fast.*

Hmm. Rey grunted, contemplating her words. *But we like mating with him.*

Amelia rolled her eyes so hard they almost stuck in the back of her head. *Rey, there is more to mates than just sex. There has to be. I need to know he wants us for us, not just because we're destined. Not just because our pheromones happen to align with one another. There has to be more. Otherwise, how can we spend the rest of our lives with someone only for physical attraction? That's not real.*

Like, mom and dad. Rey sighed sadly.

Amelia couldn't speak, her throat instantly closing, the pressure behind her eyes building. She didn't remember much about her mother, but the one memory that always stayed with her was the love she always had in her sea-green eyes whenever she looked at her mate. When they were in a room together, it was hard to miss the warmth and adoration they exhibited towards one another.

Her father always said that she and Damon were a product of their love. A blessing from the Goddess. They had so much love for one another; one baby wasn't able to contain it all. Her father was a complete cheese ball, but she believed him. It was hard not. It was clear how much he loved her. He wasn't one of those widowers that refused to speak of his deceased wife. He rejoiced in her life, constantly telling them stories about when they were younger. It always made them feel closer to her, better able to retain the few memories they did have.

Amelia always told herself she didn't want a mate because it would force her into connecting with someone she may otherwise not choose. She wanted the freedom to select a mate for herself—someone she could love just as hard as her father loved her mother. Now, here she was in a new pack, with a fated mate that left her confused about her own feelings. Adding sex to the mix made her feel even more uncertain.

She took in a deep breath. She couldn't very well hide in the bathroom forever.

We can do this. Amelia told herself.

Fighting will help us. Rey chimed in.

This made Amelia truly smile, remembering training was soon. Soon, she would lose herself to sweat and blood. Burn off some of the sexual energy she now had brooding inside of her.

Stupid mate bond.

Reaching out for the handle, she opened the door, instantly noticing the empty bed. Glancing around the room, he was nowhere to be seen. Lifting her nose to the air, she breathed in his scent stale. She couldn't help but feel confused. He just left?

Going to her suitcase, she pulled out workout clothes; a pair of shorts, a sports bra, a tank top, and sneakers. Quickly changing and throwing the towel in the hamper, she went back into the bathroom. Plaiting her wet hair down her back, she wrapped the braid in a bun on top of her head, pinning it in place. Harder for someone to grab during a fight.

Amelia left the room and headed down the stairs. The smell of bacon drove her forward into the dining hall. A table had been set up along the back wall, containing plates stacked with every breakfast food known to man. There were already some wolves eating, some alone, others in small groups—still no Gabriel.

She made her way to the table, grabbing herself an empty plate and filling it with plenty of bacon, sausage, and biscuits. She poured herself a tall glass of orange juice before sitting down at the nearest table. Only one other person was sitting at the opposite end of her. She wasn't up for conversation, so she kept her eyes on her food, eating quickly.

Last night's activities left her particularly famished. After round one, she was pretty sure there were at least two more similar occurrences.

A shadow lay over her, dousing her plate in darkness. Amelia looked up to find Christian sitting down across from her, a plate similar to her own in his hands. Now that her attention was no longer focused on her food, she realized there were a dozen pair of eyes, all trained on her.

Amelia growled in response. The other wolves instantly lowered their gaze, unable to deny her aura.

"Don't be upset with them," Christian said, a playful smirk tugging at his lips.

"What's got you so happy this morning?" Amelia asked him, annoyed by the chipper look on his face.

"I'm just wondering why you aren't happier," he joked, playfully wiggling his eyebrows at her, causing a blush to color her face. "Nice mark."

"Is it that noticeable?"

"I'm not sure where his scent ends, and yours begins," Christian smiled, giving her his dumbass goofy grin. "Besides, you've got that after-sex glow."

Amelia stuffed a biscuit in her mouth. The soft buttery dough tasted like ash in her mouth. She felt herself growing more and more agitated, and now it was screwing with her food.

Christian could sense her mood growing darker. "Ella, what is it? What's wrong?"

"I don't want to talk about it," she grumbled, her mouth still full of food. She took a big swig of orange juice before pushing back her plate away and storming out of the room, out to the back yard.

Outside, she breathed in the fresh air. The smell of pine and sap permeated the air. Another reminder that it wasn't the Wandering Moon Pack. She suddenly felt increasingly homesick and alone. Already feeling confused and conflicted with Gabriel, combined with the fact that he was nowhere to be seen, wasn't helping. She hated herself for wanting him to be there, to hold her and comfort her.

Quickly, she shoved that notion aside. She didn't need some guy to hold her together. She could take care of herself, and now it was time to make that clear to her new pack. Whether Gabriel liked it or not, she was his equal, and she will not be pushed around.

"Ella!" Christian panted, running outside beside her.

"What now?" she growled.

"What's gotten into you? You're not normally like this."

"You barely know me."

"That's not true, and you know it. The last time you were here, we spent nearly every day together."

"Yea, every day of me kicking your ass."

"Amelia," Christian moved to stand in front of her, blocking her way.

Amelia stopped, almost stomping her foot in protest. "What?"

"You can talk to me."

The sincerity in his voice had a weird calming effect on her. She tipped her head back, eyes closed, hands resting on her hips, completely unhinged. She looked back at him, simply standing there waiting patiently.

"I don't know what I'm doing here," she admitted. "I don't know why I willingly agreed to come."

Christian's brown eyes grew light as his expression softened. "It's all new. It's okay to feel a bit lost."

She shook her head. "I don't do lost. I know what I want, and I go for it, but here I have no place, no purpose."

"You're our Luna. You're Gabriel's mate."

"But I don't wanna be someone's something," she countered. "I just wanna be me, not whatever it is he wants me to be. Which I wouldn't know because we haven't had an actual conversation."

"I think I know what'll help," he said, smirking at something behind her.

Amelia turned around to find a large group of over fifty wolves, making their way towards them. She immediately felt her spirit lighten. Finally, a chance to fight. It's been a couple of days since she doled out a good beating, and her patience was wearing thin because of it.

Christian laughed, noticing the distinct change in her aura. "Come on. You can help me get them warmed up."

Amelia checked the time on her phone. "I thought you said training was at eight. It's seven-thirty."

"Yep. I lied. Wanted to see if you'd show up early."

Amelia gave him a hard shove, causing him to nearly loose his balance. She practically skipped out to the middle of the clearing. Christian running to catch up with her. Soon the field was full of bodies, shifting their weight, waiting for the start of the day—still no sight of Gabriel.

"Good morning. For those of you who don't already know, this is Amelia. Some of you may recognize her from her last visit, but now she is here in a different capacity. Amelia is Alpha Gabriel's fated mate, our Luna. She will be leading today's training with us," Christian announced.

Amelia looked at him, surprised, not expecting to do anything but participate and observe.

"She's just a woman, and you expect her to lead us in training?"

Amelia's head snapped to the crowd, no one giving up who spoke. Her aura automatically grew, Rey growing more and more furious at the blatant disrespect. She could feel her aura expanding around her, licking the air. She was able to taste the fear of the wolves in front of her that were now cowering, their heads tilted to the side in submission. She could kill them all at that very moment and not even bat an eye. It would be as easy as breathing.

Amelia stepped back, her aura snapping back around her, her anger dissipating as quickly as it appeared.

What the hell was that? Amelia nearly shouted in her own head.

Never before had she felt so much power.

I'm not sure. Rey said faintly, clearly just as stunned.

Christian looked at her, his eyes wide.

She shook her head, shaking off the unnerving feeling she had. "Ten laps around the territory!"

Not a single one of the warriors made a peep. Not even a sigh. Amelia didn't wait for them to fall in line. She took off at a run, leaving those behind to catch up. She quickly realized she didn't know the territory at all, but she knew to follow her nose. Even still, she slowed down a bit, allowing Christian to catch up and take the lead. This time.

Amelia enjoyed the run a lot more than she probably should have. Her muscles were tense, coiled tightly with unuse. She'd been lazy the last few days, between her birthday and planning the Alpha ceremony. A long run was exactly what she needed to burn off some of her pent-up energy.

The day grew hotter as her muscles began to burn from lactic acid. The long-run gave her a perfect excuse to see the layout of the territory for herself. It was expansive, even bigger than the Wandering Moon's territory, and that was saying something. The land was beautiful. It wasn't overly packed with brush, which was a relief, and the canopy of the trees allowed a cool breeze to sweep the floor, keeping the majority of the sun off them.

Her shirt's thin, cotton material was beginning to act like a second skin, making her itch as she sweat, rubbing uncomfortably. She pulled it off, leaving it to hang on the branch of a tree, not really caring if she retrieved it or not. More comfortable in just her sports bra and shorts, she breathed in deeply, finishing their last lap.

Nearing the end, Amelia jogged into the clearing, her body feeling instantly lighter. The warriors behind her were breathing heavily, leaning over their knees, lying on the cool grass. One was even heaving in the bushes. She smirked at their misery. Serves them right. They looked like death while she was barely out of breath. Even Christian looked a bit winded.

Amelia's ears perked, whispers traveling across the breeze straight to her. Someone, a male someone, was gripping and whining about her presence. Only two other females in the training group were present, and their eyes were permanently glued to the floor.

"Everyone, break off into your groups. We're rotating from yesterday's exercises! Wherever you were yesterday, move to the left!" Christian announced to the group, his voice carrying across the clearing.

"Chris," Amelia hissed under her breath, low enough to not be heard by the masses, but just loud enough for his werewolf hearing to catch.

Christian jogged over, bouncing to a stop just in front of her. "What's up?"

"Where are all the women? Why aren't there more of them here?" she murmured, keeping her voice low.

Christian turned his back to the group, keeping his head bent. "Women haven't really been encouraged to learn to fight here. It's always been strictly male. Over the last few years, a couple have shown interest, but not many stick around."

Amelia looked back at the group. A good majority of the men were giving her sidelong glances and hostile looks. She bit the inside of her cheek, drawing fresh blood. Knowing full well from Christians wary face, her eyes were drastically changing from her normal sea-green to black, Rey bristling at the sexism.

"I want you to go inside and gather every single female in there. I don't have the pack link yet, but you do. Use it. I want as many women as I can get. You have fifteen minutes," she instructed.

Christian shifted uncomfortably. "Gabriel won't like this. Most of the women inside are working."

"Cleaning? Cooking?" The nod of his head was enough to tip her over the edge. "If Gabriel has a problem with it, he can take it up with me. You have fourteen minutes."

CHAPTER 15

THE LESSON

Not needing to be told a third time, Christian bolted for the house. Amelia turned back to those training, ignoring the misogyny. She immediately approached the group the two women were participating in.

They were clearly excluded from the men present, left to figure out the knives themselves. One of the women, a petite blonde no more than a year older than her, was handling a knife that would guarantee her a missing digit.

"May I?" Amelia stepped in, acknowledging the two girls huddled close together.

The blonde handed her the knife in her open palm, hilt first. At least she had some knowledge on how to handle a blade.

"What are your names?" she asked them.

"Marissa, Luna," the blonde said meekly, afraid to meet her eyes.

"Nicole," the girl beside Marissa said. She was tall, taller than even her. Her raven hair was pulled up into a ponytail. Amelia instantly liked her based on how easily she made it look to meet her eye. She had a fighting spirit.

"Has anyone shown you how to throw a knife?" Amelia asked, not even surprised by the shaking of their heads. Of course not. "Well then, I'm going to show you."

"You can throw knives?" Nicole asked in awe.

"I can do more than throw knives," giving them a wink, she smiled gently.

Spending the next ten minutes with them, she demonstrated how to position their bodies and place their feet to balance their weight properly. How to hold the blade correctly to avoid slicing off your own skin and when to release.

Nicole was a natural. Her blade was bouncing off the target, but at least her aim was correct. It took time to get used to holding a knife and learning when and how to flick your wrist just right. Marissa struggled, but she was persistent, continuously throwing the knife and retrieving it each time.

The clearing suddenly became alarmingly quiet. All training came to a halt. She turned around and found Christian approaching them, over twenty women at his back. They all looked extremely nervous, like they were being shepherded out to the butchers. Lambs to the slaughter.

She definitely had her work cut out for her.

Amelia collected them in the front of the clearing, leaving the men to glare at her back. She made sure to make eye contact with every solitary woman in attendance, giving them all encouraging smiles. They ranged in age from young teens to mature adults with pups.

"Thank you ladies, for coming. I really appreciate you dropping everything for me," she clasped her hands together in front of her, her body jittery with anticipation. "The reason I called you all out here is because I've noticed a few troubling things in this pack in the short time I've been here. Now I may not have been raised here, but I am a werewolf, the same as any of you, and I've noticed women are severely underrepresented in our group of warriors."

Amelia smirked. A few of the women in front of her perked up. The men behind her grumbled. "That may be because some of you chose not to. Preferring other jobs, and that's okay. We all have things that we're good at, jobs we might be more comfortable with. *Or* you may have been made to feel uncomfortable. Told you weren't competent enough because of your sex." She struck a chord with the last one. Most of the group in front of her were visibly flinching, just as she suspected.

Amelia began to walk, her pace slow and deliberate. "If you believe that men and women were made equal, you're mistaken. We're not. Men and women are extremely different from one another. Men are generally bigger, faster, and stronger than us. That's why they call us the weaker sex. They think we're vulnerable, more fragile than them because we don't possess brute strength."

The women's eyes were all trained on her, unblinking and unwavering. "They're right. We're not as strong as them, but we have something far superior. We have our brains. Men tend to think with other body parts."

A scream rang out in the clearing. One of the biggest group members, a middle-aged warrior, fell to his knees, clutching his hand. There was no blood, no visible wound, but the man was crying, fat tears streaming down his face, with Amelia standing directly behind him. A devilish smirk played on her lips. The men around her instantly grew wary, gradually coming to the realization she'd been orbiting them, herding them closer together. The women were wide-eyed.

"Men think with their fists, on most occasions they're dicks." The women chuckled, most nodding in agreement. "They're prone to blinding fits of rage. Women are more vindictive. We like to take our time. We don't have to be stronger to beat them; we simply have to be smarter."

Another warrior screamed, an audible cracking sound rippled across the field. Amelia stood behind yet another man, his calf twisted at an odd angle. She remained completely unfazed, leaving the warrior to cry on the floor.

"You think just because you've managed to pick off two men from behind that makes you strong?"

Amelia snapped her piercing glare on a man towards the middle of the group. He was a big, burly man. Taller than her by at least six inches. Thick with bulging muscles and wide enough to barrel through three of her. She observed some of the women immediately direct their eyes down at the sound of his booming voice, clearly terrified. The real question remained, was his bark worse than his bite?

"I wager that none of the men present can lay a hit on me. If you win, I'll never return to another training session again. If I win, women will be permitted to choose whether they train or not, and you will be gracious about it. If not, I'll make certain your lives are a living hell, suffering in the kitchen with Ms. Lena for a week," she noticed most of the men grimace at that prospect. "Deal?"

"Amelia," Christian said softly in warning, fearing for her safety.

"Shush, Chris. I'm trying to teach a lesson," Amelia waved him off.

"This isn't the same as last time."

"No, this is better."

"This is three times that number."

"Exactly," she laughed, rubbing her hands together eagerly.

Christian just shook his head.

The big, burly man yelled, charging straight for her. Amelia frowned at his approach. Did the idiot really have to make it so obvious? Just as he was about to barrel into her, she sidestepped him, sticking her foot out in the process. The man kissed the hard, packed dirt with his face.

"Like I said, not smart at all," she sighed, tisking at him as he struggled to get up. The remaining men around her seemed outraged, angry at their fallen comrade, and angry with her for making a fool of him.

The thirty-odd men began to approach her cautiously, circling in around her. Amelia shifted on her feet, keeping her eyes and ears open and trained, looking for any visible sign of advance. This is what she lived for.

The men began to move in on her, one after another, each one attacking back to back. Amelia dodged their punches, deflected their kicks, sidestepping their attempts to tackle her. Like cat and mouse, except for she was the lion.

Is it time yet? Rey asked, stepping in, sounding annoyed.

But I'm having fun!

We're here to make a point. Not to play with the insecure boys.

Ugh, fine.

Amelia growled deeply, her voice echoing through the trees, freezing the men. She used their momentary pause and struck, placing them on the defense. She lunged for the man closest to her, seizing him by his shirt and hurling him over her body, knocking down another two in the process. Spinning around, she back kicked a man across the face, elbowing another in the jaw, and suckering punching one in the gut, making him stumble back, gasping for breath.

She ran through the men, punching and kicking faster than her mind could keep track of, but it didn't matter. Instinct was taking over, and that was all she needed. Their feet were churning the earth, turning it to mud. Their feet slipped, unable to gain traction. Amelia smiled. She liked the mud.

The men's numbers were already cut in half, but they still hadn't learned their lesson as they continued to come after her. She slid between the open legs of one, punching out his knee. Sweeping out the feet of another beside her, she got back up on her feet. Kicking out in front of her, her foot connected with a man's chest, ribs audibly cracking. She rolled across his back as he leaned over, clutching his side, knocking out another with a swift boot to the side of his head.

"They can't hit you if they can't catch you," Amelia yelled out, dodging punches to her face, attempts to grab her hair, and kicks aimed for her stomach. "Make yourself small." She turned side face, narrowly preventing a hit to the head. "Small targets are harder to hit." Snapping out with her elbow to his temple, knocking him out cold.

Five left. The last stragglers were now wary of her, but still stubborn enough not to admit defeat. She admired that. Three of them shifted, charging at her together. One of the women called them cheaters, another coward. Amelia waited for them patiently, allowing them to get closer and closer until she suddenly flipped her body, soaring above them to land just behind them. She reached out, securing a firm hold of the russet wolf in the middle by his tail. Utilizing his own body against him, she flung the wolf, using his body like a bat, effectively knocking down the two remaining wolves.

Amelia turned back to the remaining men, she cocked her head. A blonde and a redhead, appearing to be around the same age as her. "And when in doubt." The dumb blonde ran for her. "Go for the jewels." She flicked her leg out. The boy sank to the floor, gasping in pain, clutching himself.

The remaining redhead immediately went down on one knee, head bent and turned to the side in submission.

"Good boy," Amelia toyed with him, turning her back on the field of bodies. Most clutching some part of themselves in pain, the others knocked out cold, dragged away by those less damaged.

"Infirmary's gonna be full today," she shrugged, earning her a few laughs and cheers from the women. She extended her hand, effectively silencing them. "I didn't do this to show off. I did this to show you; we are more than we seem."

"Now, I understand some of you have pups and may not want to be dragged into a war that may never come. But as wolves, we must always be prepared for a fight. Even if you don't want to become a warrior, every woman will learn self-defense. You should be able to protect yourself and your families. There may not always be a male around to save you. We're no damsels."

"No, you're certainly not."

The familiar voice caused a shiver to run down her spine. How long had he been watching?

Gabriel stepped out from behind the tree line, out of the shadows and into the light. Nearly everyone in attendance lowered their head in respect, all except for her, of course.

He approached her slowly, his composure calm and steady to those around them, but thanks to the mark on her skin, she could feel his displeasure. He stopped just beside her, setting his hand against her lower back, sending wisps of fire licking across her skin.

"Your Luna is right. It's high time everyone learns self-defense at the least. From now on, all women will report to training by nine a.m. If you wish to only participate in self-defense, training is an hour. For those that wish to extend their training beyond defense and join our warriors, training is an additional two hours," Gabriel smiled at the women, most of them swooning over his charm and good looks. "You're all dismissed."

Amelia crossed her arms over her chest, her foot tapping against the floor. The women immediately turned away, leaving them and headed back to the Packhouse. Most of the men were already gone for the infirmary or retreating into the house for an ice pack and a nap.

Christian came up beside her, offering her a pat on the back. "Excellent job, Ella. You're even better than I remembered."

Gabriel growled a warning, glaring at the hand resting on her shoulder. Christian hastily withdrew, head bowed, leaving them to be the two remaining on the field.

Amelia flicked her hand out, striking him across the chest. "Why did you have to do that?"

"No one touches you," he snarled, "and who the hell do you think you are coming into *my* pack like you own the place? Who gave you the authority to call on the females? To humiliate my warriors?"

Amelia could feel his anger coming off him, like the wind blowing in during a squall, fierce and fast. She honestly hadn't even thought that what she did might be considered a betrayal. It had never been her intention to overstep their Alpha, but that didn't mean that she regretted what she did. Cause she didn't.

"I'm sorry if you felt that I made you look weak-"

"I am not weak," Gabriel growled, his Alpha aura flexing around him. "But you conducting training like that, should have been something we discussed together. My pack is not at your beck and call to be used as amusement."

"How can we discuss anything when you're not around?! You ran out this morning before I could even get a word out!"

"I thought you might need space," Gabriel sighed, rubbing his hand down his face, appearing drained.

"I never suspected your pack was here for my amusement, but you don't know what it's like. There were *two* females at training today, and neither of them had any help. None of the wolves had their backs. How can you let this happen? What kind of Alpha are you when you only allow half of your pack train?"

"I don't have to explain myself to you! You pull something like this again without my approval; I will have you locked in the dungeons for a month," he said, diminishing the distance between them, his eyes glaring daggers into her soul.

"Oh, I'm so scared," Amelia mocked him. Childish, but the effect was the same. He was pissed. "Go ahead and lock me up, you brute. While you're at it, send me down a slice of beef. I'll need something to keep me entertained."

Wrong tactic.

Gabriel gripped her by the arm, his fingers digging into the soft tissue. Amelia gasped despite herself, his reaction startling her.

"You'd like that, wouldn't you? I'll eviscerate any man that dares to touch what's mine," he promised her, his eyes large and black, his claws elongating, cutting into her skin.

Amelia jerked her arm from his grasp, flinging her hands up in the air, fed up with his crap. "You are such a damn caveman! Am I supposed to go growling and marking my territory, pissing on every woman that bats an eye at you? Should I go and hunt down every woman you've slept with, you've ever fucked? I'm sure the list is long."

"Should I for you? How many guys have you let crawl in your bed, slipping between those thick thighs?"

A resounding slap vibrated through her, jarring her hand, the flesh on her palm stinging. Gabriel's head was snapped to the side. A handprint was visible on his skin, angry and red looking.

"Fuck you," she hissed through gritted teeth, storming away.

CHAPTER 16

ROGUE

Amelia stormed off into the tree line. Away from the Packhouse, away from super hearing, away from him. She could feel the stinging in her eyes, the anger and frustration overwhelming her nerves. Unable to control herself, she shifted, her clothes shredding around her in a cloud of cotton confetti.

Rey shook out her fur, stretching her limbs before taking off at a run. She now knew the borders from earlier. She wouldn't risk crossing them, but she couldn't stay there with him a moment longer. Pushing herself more vigorously than before, she ran deeper into the forest, jumping over fallen logs, leaping across wide dips in the earth.

With Rey in control, Amelia slunk to the remotest corner of her mind, sulking. She was furious with him for insinuating she was a whore. She knew she gave it up to him too quickly. She looked desperate, too eager, too loose. Thinking back to last night, she could have sworn she told him he was her first. Did he not believe her?

For most girls her age, it wasn't typical for a wolf to wait as long as she did. Werewolves are physical creatures, constantly craving touch, smell. They're creatures of comfort. That's why a mate's scent is one of the most powerful tools a mate has. Having the ability to calm them down just through the sensory glands. Once a wolf hits puberty, it's hard to resist the urge for sexual gratification.

It had been hard for her to resist. She had to refuse a lot of unwelcome attention over the years, but there was always one main reason she rejected so many, even Daniel. No matter who she was with, it never felt right. They would fool around, make out, but she never felt comfortable enough to go further. That is until last night. It's standard for wolves to be sexually active and often. Not giving into those urges can make the wolf side unstable, imbalanced even.

Some wolves have gone rogue due to the lack of physical touch. A rogue is one of the most dangerous, lethal members of the werewolf society. They're wolves who have completely lost their humanity, feral and unreasonable. Becoming a rogue can happen for many reasons; losing a mate is one of the most common, but some wolves have been rejected in the past, losing contact with family and their pack, turning rogue as a result.

Rogues are one of the main reason's packs train so often. Even one single rogue is lethal to most. End up with a couple on your territory, and you could have a critical issue on your hands.

Rey froze, her paw lifted mid-step. She turned her head each way, assessing her whereabouts. They were past the boundary line. She could smell it a hundred yards back. Amelia scolded herself and Rey for getting so lost in thought they ran right past the boundary. Rey went to turn around when a deep growl got their attention. The silver-white hairs along her spine lifted in response; her tail erect in warning.

Rey.

I know.

A Rogue. The smell was unmistakable.

Once a wolf turns rogue, their lack of humanity, the ability to think rationally and maintain any source of self-preservation, is gone. It stunk of dung and mildew, making her nose burn something fierce.

Now her nose was burning to the point of itching unbearably. Rey backed away slowly, lifting her paws quietly, inching her way back the way she came. She could only smell one, thank the Goddess, but one was enough. Amelia and Rey were good, but they had never gone against a rogue.

She recollected the one time a rogue had drifted onto the Wandering Moon's territory. It took twelve wolves to take him down, killing three warriors in the process. She was twelve at the time, hiding in the panic rooms with the rest of the pups, and she hated every second of it.

Now, Amelia regretted not marking Gabriel as well. She may not be linked to the pack, but she could have at least been linked to him, warn him. Rogues didn't travel in packs like other Were's, but it has happened, though normally on a much smaller scale.

The rogue stepped into view, pushing through a dense column of brush. He was large for a wolf, nearly as tall as her, but skinny. His bones protruded through his emaciated skin. Chunks of hair were missing from his coat, matted down with bits of dirt and leaves woven in.

Rey pulled her lips back, baring her teeth, snarling at the rogue. He snapped the air, his jaws crunching the space between them, stalking slowly towards her. They had two options. One, try and run away, possibly make it back to the pack, and put those there at risk. Amelia immediately scolded herself. Injuring a good majority of the warriors at training was just dumb. The pack was near defenseless.

She could stand and fight, try to kill him. Probably her stupidest option. She'd definitely end up injured, but it was either her or the pack she was supposed to protect. Whether she liked it or not, she *was* their Luna.

Rey stopped backing away and stomped the ground with her paw. Holding her ground, she let a terrifying growl rip free from her chest, shaking the earth beneath them. Birds fled their nests in trees overhead, their wings beating against the air, hard and fast. Animals scurried from their nests, running far away from the stench of death heavy in the air. One of them was dying today, and she would be damned if it was gonna be her.

The rogue barely flinched at her growl. It only seemed to make him angrier. The wolf charged for her, straight and true. Rey stood her ground, waiting for him to get closer before she launched herself over his head, landing on his back. She dug her claws deep into his shoulder and sides, clamping her jaw down on his neck, shaking him like a ragdoll.

The rogue tried to reach behind, his breath hot on her neck, but she clung on. The metallic taste of blood filled her mouth enough to make her gag. He continued to jump around, bucking and kicking, biting behind him in an attempt to get some kind of grip on her. She felt a searing pain in her back leg, teeth grazing against bone.

He wrenched her off, hurling her against the trunk of a tree.

The air was knocked clear out of her lungs. Struggling to get her paws underneath her, she tried to stand. Her back leg was burning, unable to bear her weight. Something was broken. She barely had a chance to get a first real breath before he charged at her again. The blood dripping from his numerous wounds didn't even leave him winded.

Rey pushed past the pain and ran at him as well. She struck him with her paw, claws extended, racking down the side of his face. The rogue barely paused. They both reared back, striking at one another in a flurry of fur and sharp claws, teeth and snarls. She felt herself being hit, thrown back on the earth. Her head was spinning, her vision doubling, tripling. She tried to shake it off, but the pain was ringing in her ears.

His smell was getting stronger, she knew he was coming back to finish the job, and there was nothing she could do. As a Were, their healing was incredibly fast but not two seconds fast. She struggled to get her front paws beneath her. She'd be damned if she was going to die lying down. If she was going to die, she'd die on her feet like a true warrior.

The sound of paws striking the earth was getting closer. This was it. She waited for the impact, but it didn't come. A growl ripped through her consciousness, igniting her soul, setting her blood on fire. It was Gabriel.

An obsidian wolf came storming through the forest. His massive paws shook the ground beneath her, ramming his head into the side of the wolf, knocking him askew. The rogue whirled around on him, snapping at her mate.

Amelia began to panic, watching the scene unfold before her. Gabriel was assaulting the rogue in a flurry of claws and teeth, but the rogue was just as deadly as the large Alpha, if not more. Wounds and near-fatal injuries didn't seem to hinder him.

Rey, get up! Amelia yelled.

Rey struggled again, pushing herself harder to gather her feet beneath her.

Rey, you have to get up. We have to help him.

The rogue managed to bite into his shoulder. Gabriel howled in pain. Rey stumbled beneath her own weight. Agonizing pain raced down her arm. The same spot as Gabriel's wound. Stupid mate bond, she didn't have time for their weird, psychic link.

Rey shook her head, clearing the cobwebs once and for all. The rogue was forcing Gabriel back, pinning him against a tree. Rey launched herself through the air, landing on his back once again. Extending her claws fully, deep into his flesh until she could feel his bones grazing against her nails. She wrapped her jaws around his throat, composed of mostly skin and bone, and clamped down as hard as she could. Her teeth slid through his artery like butter, filling her mouth with blood. Making quick work, she snapped his neck with a swift jerk of her head, his body dropping on the ground with a final exhale.

Rey rolled off the dead wolf, pulling her claws free, and extracted her teeth from his flesh. Nearing complete and utter exhaustion, Amelia forced the change, bones cracking and reshaping back into her human form. Her leg was nearly healed, but it was still incapable of carrying her weight, needing only a few more minutes, but she didn't have a few minutes.

Amelia dragged her naked body across the earth, sticks scratching against her, sand chafing her skin. Gabriel was quickly shifting back as well, his black fur shedding into human skin. His silver eyes found her green ones, and what she found there shocked her to her soul. He was terrified. Terrified, he had lost her, terrified she was hurt.

"Gabe," she heard herself call out, her voice pleading.

Gabriel got up, stumbling, rushing to her, falling at her side. Amelia pulled herself up on her knees, her ankle nearly healed but her head was still swimming. They both reached out for one another, running their hands along each other's body, checking for serious damage.

Gabriel's shoulder was still bleeding. The bite mark was deep and wide, but she could tell it was already healing. The holes were significantly smaller than just moments ago. His hands grazed across her ribs, causing her to wince, hissing aloud. He looked down to find long, deep gashes down her flank. His face instantly frowned. His lips pressed in a thin line.

"I'm okay. I'm fine," she said breathlessly. Between the fight and his hands on her skin, her head was swimming. She reached up, threading her fingers through his hair, pulling him down closer to her, resting her forehead against his.

"What were you thinking? You could have been killed."

The tone of his voice wasn't angry or disappointed, but instead sad and distraught, as though the thought of losing her would be the end of the world. His world.

"I couldn't bring him to the pack and put everyone at risk. I had to try and handle him here, away from them," Amelia tried to explain.

"You're too stubborn and headstrong," Gabriel sighed, shaking his head.

"Says the man who just ran headfirst into a rogue." Pot meets kettle.

"Fine, we'll be the death of each other," he pulled her in closer.

"Definitely."

She crashed her lips against his. Gabriel pulled her against his body, holding her tighter and more firm along the length of him. Their lips devoured one another, their tongues slipping past teeth, tasting each other as if they'd been starved to death. She didn't care how dirty they were, or that they reeked of blood and rogue. All she knew was she needed him, needed him like a fish needs water, like a flower needs the sun. She had to feel him, all of him.

Gabriel lifted her off the ground, her legs wrapped around his waist, her arms encircled his neck. She pulled at the roots of his hair, making him hiss in her mouth. Licking him, she nibbled on the sensitive skin of his bottom lip, teasing him. She hissed back as rough bark scraped down the length of her back, biting into her skin.

She felt his hard member at the entrance of her weeping core, swollen and begging. He pushed himself in forcefully, causing her to yelp, moaning as he slid in and out. His need for her was rough and unrestrained, rutting like a mindless beast. Their blood was up, fresh after a fight. No matter what was between them, they both needed the release.

Gabriel sank inside of her over and over, pounding flesh against flesh. Amelia reached up, holding onto a sturdy branch just over her head, holding herself steady as he plowed into her. She was close to release, and by the sound of his own moans, so was he. She cried out, the tip of his manhood buried deep.

Gabriel called out her name just as he unleashed his seed, when she cupped the back of his neck, sinking her fangs into his marking spot. He continued to push his way inside her, riding out the second orgasm her marking inevitably caused. When he slowed down, his movements becoming less fluid, she removed her teeth from his flesh, licking the mark closed. The taste of dirt and blood was heavy on her tongue.

Amelia felt her legs slip from his hips, hitting the ground roughly, leaving her feel unsteady. Gabriel staggered back a few steps, his eyes fogged over, her mark taking effect. She reduced the distance between them, her legs quivering beneath her, her core still humming and wet. She thrust her finger in his chest, looking up at him in all seriousness.

"I am yours, and *you* are *mine*," she growled at him, her warning clear, issuing her final statement via the mind link they now shared. *Mate.*

CHAPTER 17

WHISPERS

Amelia and Gabriel had no choice but to shift
back into their wolves. Amelia could feel their
mind link snap into place the moment her fangs
entered the tender flesh of his neck. Their mate bond
tethered them together, keeping her anchored forever.
Running back to the Packhouse, she could feel the
warmth in her chest. She could feel his uncertainty, his
confusion, and his doubts. Mixing with her own, she felt
more disoriented than ever.

Gabriel pressed against her side, steering them home,
forcing her back to the present. She tried to clear her mind.
If she could feel his uncertainty, then he could definitely
feel hers. Things were complicated and unspoken enough.
She didn't need it to get any more difficult.

The run took them about thirty minutes. Amelia was
slightly stunned over this, not realizing she made it so
far past the territories border. Now she really felt like
an idiot. She deserved that rogue ambushing her. Serves
her right.

Gabriel delayed her, nipping at her back legs. The Packhouse in sight, she turned on him, her large wolf head cocked to the side.

Stop blaming yourself. It wasn't your fault.

Amelia nearly jerked back at the sound of his voice in her head. It was bad enough she had to share her mind with her wolf and her brother, seeing as she's been doing that her whole life, but adding in a third voice felt uncomfortably restricting.

It wasn't easy for wolves to be able to mind-link. Unless connected by blood or the mate bond, mind-linking took practice and concentration. The higher placed wolves had an easier time with it but to do it without permission would be considered a serious violation of privacy.

I'm fine. She said, her voice a little snappier than she intended.

Gabriel scoffed, a deep rumbling coming from his wolf's chest. He clearly didn't believe her.

He pushed past her, flicking his bushy, black tail in her face, causing her to snap her jaws at him, missing by a breath. She followed after him to the house. Up the back porch, the doors were already open and waiting. Pack members moved aside for their Alpha, heads bowed, offering her the same courtesy as she followed behind him.

Amelia could hear some of the wolves whispering to one another. Her earlier training demonstration was clearly headline-worthy. Most were impressed with the new Luna. One of them called her a show-off, putting the pack at risk by injuring so many warriors.

She couldn't do more than hang her head in shame. If only they knew what happened just past the border, the fact that a rogue had been so close to the border. They didn't know how right they were.

She could feel Gabriel's presence in her mind, rubbing against her conscience, seeking admittance, but she kept him out. She didn't deserve to be consoled.

Gabriel didn't head for the stairs like she assumed he would. Instead, he headed down the hall to where she guessed his office was. Amelia tried ignoring the disappointment blooming in her chest and pushed herself up the stairs, all the way to the top floor. She nudged the door open with her snout, kicking it shut with her back leg.

Once inside the room, Amelia shook out her soiled, blood-stained fur and shifted. Back in her own skin, she stretched out her sore, beaten limbs. Between the training, fighting a rogue and the rough sex, she was disgustingly dirty and exhausted.

She half walked, half dragged her way across the room, onto the cool black and white tiles of the bathroom. Her ankle was still tender from the rogue bite. She reached inside the shower, flipping the water on to steaming hot. Glancing at herself in the mirror, she looked worse than she thought possible.

Dried blood coated her shoulder, where Gabriel had pressed her body against the length of the tree. Long, claw marks down her side were just barely visible as the skin was nearly finished knitting back together. Her hair was a mess of tangles, leaves, even a broken stick.

Spinning around, she found chunks of bark still clinging to her back. Narrow slivers embedded in her skin. Hopefully the water could work those out. Her eyes finally drifted over her mark, placed in the tender spot where her neck meets her shoulder. Delicately, she brushed her fingers along the two holes in her flesh that covered her scent with his. To other wolves, it was a warning, marking his territory, asserting his dominance. To her, it was something else. Something that had her nibbling on her bottom lip, craning her neck to the side as she remembered the feel of him, full and swollen.

Amelia instantly snapped out of it. Gabriel's consciousness brushing against hers. He knew what she was thinking about—stupid mate bond.

She got in the shower, allowing the hot water to run down her body, eradicating every trace of filth. Tensing her back, she pushed out the remaining bits of wood from her skin, finally allowing the remnants of her escapade to heal closed. She took her time, allowing the heat to soothe her aching body. Even though technically she was recovered, she hurt everywhere.

Forcing herself to wash and properly care for her hair, she unwillingly got out of the shower. Lugging her butt to the bed, she flung herself down. Not giving two craps whether she was naked or not.

Her stomach rumbled loudly, reminding her of yet another thing that pained her. She groaned, turning her head against the firm pillow. Food would have to wait.

Sleep dragged her under faster than she could grasp, darkness swallowing her whole.

* * *

The forest was impenetrable. The shadows moved along the ground, sinister and inviting, beckoning her forward to join in their depths. The woods smelled of pine and sap. She was in the Twilight Moon Pack's territory. Sniffing again, she lifted her nose to the air. A black snout blocked her vision. Distracted, she looked down. Her feet weren't feet at all but paws, covered in a thick silver, white fur. She was in her wolf form, but where was Rey?

Finally, she caught the smell. The air tickled her cold nose. Her blood ran cold. Her body tensed. Blood. The smell of blood and mildew was pungent in the air, causing her nose to itch. Her eyes burned to the point of tears. She shook her head. Her fur captured the pregnant moon's light hanging in the sky above.

Perking her ears, she could hear distant snarls, wolves growling in warning, jaws snapping as teeth sought after something to latch on. A familiar sound pulled at her heart, his whimper crying out in pain.

Amelia forced her paws harder against the pact earth, racing forward. The sounds of wolf fighting wolf grew louder. Her right paw slipped in something, causing her to slow down, her paws now unable to support her body. Looking down, she found herself standing in blood-soaked dirt. Red colored mud that she was now unable to get a purchase in.

Finally, taking in her surroundings, her heart dropped to the floor, her stomach flipped inside out. Bodies. Dead wolves, everywhere. Wolves with their throats ripped out, necks broken, eviscerated, butchered like animals. The dead were a mix of pack and rogues. The sole difference between them was the state of their fur, their muscle tone. Whether or not emaciation was visible. There were so many, she refused to count, more than enough to cover the forest floor in every direction she turned.

Amelia stepped gingerly through the bodies. The glazed eyes of countless dead stared at her, beckoning her to join them. The shadows reached out to her, calling to her, muttering something not even her werewolf hearing could pick up. Her heart picked up on something her eyes refused to see; a lifeless body with beautiful obsidian fur.

Rey came through her consciousness, tilted up, and howled to the moon.

(((

Amelia bolted up out of bed, her breath labored and panting, her skin covered in dew.

"What the fuck?"

CHAPTER 18

PAWS OFF

Amelia placed her hand over her chest. Her heart hammered against her breast bone. The overpowering smell of blood still burned in her nose. The metallic taste lingered at the back of her throat. Checking her phone on the nightstand it read nine am. Shit.

She ran her hand through her hair, pulling at the roots in frustration. She literally sleept all afternoon and night, not to mention missing the first half of training. To top it all off, she felt like her stomach was devouring her insides, being starved of nutrition for almost twenty-four hours.

Looking over at the side of the bed, she noticed his side was untouched. Glancing down at herself, she found herself wrapped under the comforter, still naked. The last thing she remembered was face planting on her pillow.

Mate tucked us in.

Amelia startled at the voice of her wolf. *He was here?*

Yes.

But he didn't stay with us?

No.

"What the fuck?" she exclaimed for the second time that morning. "What is his problem?"

I don't know. His wolf wouldn't talk to me. Rey whimpered.

Don't worry, Rey. We'll figure this out.

Amelia flung the comforter off her body. The sheets were adhering to her skin. She practically had to peel them off. Standing up, the frosty temperature of the room sent gooseflesh down her body. Looking down, she realized she was still naked. Knowing she was already late, she didn't want to miss the rest of training. Maybe she could still grab something to eat.

Her hair would never dry in time, and it didn't look too unreasonable, so she left it in a bun on top of her head. Making quick work out of it, she jumped in the shower, scrubbing fiercely at her skin. Getting out, she towel-dried her body and went to her suitcase. She really needed to remember to unpack her bags.

Pulling out a pair of black workout leggings, a teal blue sports bra, and a light gray tank, she quickly changed into her clothes. Running back into the bathroom, she decided her hair didn't look too bad up in the bun, so she left it. Hastily, she applied deodorant. The least she could do was not stink.

Snatching her phone off the nightstand, she left the room, slamming the door behind her, running down the stairs like a vampire out of church. The dining hall was empty of both people and food. Frowning, Amelia went straight for the kitchens, praying to the Goddess she could find something to eat.

Inside the kitchen, wolves were bustling about, preparing lunch that was yet to take place for a few hours. Amelia spotted Lena's perfect brown sock bun across the room, fishing items from the large fridge. She narrowly avoided a small Omega, her arms stacked with an unreasonable amount of porcelain plates. Amelia instinctively reached out, catching the plates just as they started to slip from the uneven stack.

"Thank you, Luna. Thank you," the girl bowed in respect, her eyes wide, sweat beading on her forehead. "I didn't even realize they were slipping."

Amelia smiled at the girl who couldn't be more than sixteen. "It's okay. No need to thank me. It's Amelia, please. Is this okay?" she asked, gesturing towards the counter just behind them.

"Yes, of course," the girl said, continuously thanking her and bowing her head as she skittered from the room.

"Luna!"

Amelia placed the plates on the counter just as Lena spotted her. She sighed in relief, her lack of food making her head spin.

"Lena, thank the Goddess."

"You look peaked," Lena said, studying her face.

"I'm not peaked," Amelia whined, gripping at her growling stomach. "I'm fucking starving."

Lena snorted in the most unladylike manner that made Amelia laugh. The woman flicked her kitchen towel at her, beckoning her to follow with a tilt of her head.

"Come with me."

Amelia obeyed, following her to the other side of the kitchen towards a basket filled with plastic Tupperware. She arched a brow at the woman, curious as to why this was all set aside. Raising the containers to her face, she could see all her favorites, perfectly stored and waiting for her.

"You are a saint," Amelia breathed, ecstatic to see so much food.

Lena chuckled, shaking her head. "It wasn't me. You can thank the Boss."

Amelia immediately straightened. "Gabriel?"

The woman merely nodded her head, swept back up in the bustle of the kitchen, leaving Amelia alone to her conflicting thoughts.

He made sure we had breakfast. Amelia said, half to herself, half to Rey.

Why are men so dumb?

Amelia couldn't help but smirk. Rey wasn't wrong.

Breakfast would have been much nicer in bed. Rey huffed in annoyance.

Amelia couldn't help but laugh aloud at that, earning her some curious glances. She pressed her lips together, grabbing the basket of food and left the kitchen.

You be sure to tell his wolf that the next time you two talk. Wouldn't kill him to wake up in bed with us, either. Though, on second thought, she wasn't sure if that was wise either.

Shaking her head of such stupid notions, she walked out the back doors, through the yard, and past the tree line. The training yard was active. Christian was standing to the side; his arms crossed as he supervised a group of wolves practicing the proper way to jump on another wolf's back.

Amelia headed directly for him, his eye catching hers as she got closer. Looking out over the clearing, she instantly noticed a large number of females in attendance, to the point where they almost trumped the men. She couldn't help but smile at that, glad her demonstration had some effect on the she-wolves.

"Finally decided to grace us with your presence?" Christian teased her, his grin taking over most of his face.

"Well, no one woke me, so here I am," Amelia shrugged, placing the basket down on the ground between them.

Christian leaned over to reach for the bag of biscuits on top when Amelia smacked his hand, making him flinch back in response.

"Paws off. I haven't eaten since breakfast yesterday and I'm starving," she glared at him coldly, a touch of her Alpha aura slipping out.

"What were you up to all day yesterday?" he asked, wiggling his eyebrows at her.

Amelia couldn't help but feel flushed, remembering their brief but steamy moment in the woods, followed by her marking him. He started to chuckle at her response, causing her to push him away for teasing her. She hated how hot she felt now that he brought it up, her core aching in a way she wished it wouldn't.

"Shut up. No, it wasn't that," she said breathlessly, trying to control the blush on her face. "I took a run after training, and I ended up outside the border. A rogue attacked me."

"What?!" Christian yelled, suddenly lowering his voice as the trainees began to stare.

"Damn Chris, yell louder. I don't think the whole state of New York heard you." Amelia rolled her eyes, pulling out the container of sausage links from the basket.

"What do you mean a rogue attacked you? Are you okay? How did you get away?" Chris rambled, firing question after question.

"I attacked it."

"What?!" Christ yelled again, this time earning them every pair of eyes in the clearing.

"If you don't keep your voice down, I will give you something to yell about," Amelia growled under her breath, her eyes flicking down to his more sensitive bits.

Christian immediately cringed in on himself in automatic response.

"I attacked it since I was the dumbass that took out nearly fifty warriors. I couldn't exactly lead it straight to the Packhouse."

"Yeah, but rogues are different compared to training warriors."

"Yeah, no shit," she responded, frowning down at her now empty container.

"Did it hurt you? Are you okay?" Christian asked, his eyes scanning her body for any visible damage.

"No. I mean, yes, it did get me, but Gabriel showed up at the right time. If it weren't for him, I'd be dead," she said matter-of-factly. Whether she liked it or not, it was the truth.

"Gabriel killed a rogue?"

"Not exactly."

"You killed a rogue?"

"It was a team effort."

Christian whistled softly, knowing full well she was being modest.

"Do you guys get rogues here often?" Amelia asked him, now digging into the bag of pancakes.

"No. They're a rare occurrence," Christian said, shaking his head. "The last one on our lands that I know of was back when I was a pup. I barely remember. They normally don't bother us."

She nodded her head absently, her eyes distant. "That's good."

Amelia thought back to her dream. The countless rogues raging through the territory. The infinite sea of blood and bodies. Gabriel's wolf lying still.

"Amelia."

Her eyes refocused, catching Christian staring at her oddly, concern etched in his face.

"I'm good. Just spaced," she tried smiling to assure him, but it didn't quite reach her lips. Placing her food back in the basket, she looked back over those still training.

Most of the men she had the pleasure of taking down yesterday were in attendance, giving her weary, cautious looks. In the crowd of trainees, she recognized a familiar face from the night before.

Amelia waved over her shoulder to Christian before beelining straight for Kelsey; at least she hoped that was her name. The girl noticed her approach, bouncing on her toes, smiling.

"Luna!"

"It's Kelsey, right?" Amelia asked, fingers crossed behind her back.

"Yes! Yes, it's Kelsey," the girl smiled brightly.

"Thank the Goddess. Sometimes I really suck at names. And it's Amelia, please."

"Amelia," Kelsey said, trying it out. "Such a pretty name."

Amelia chuckled. She spent the next hour working with Kelsey going over different defensive moves. The girl was quick, able to pick up the moves with ease. She even managed to flip her over her body, landing on the compact earth with a force that knocked the air from her lungs.

Kelsey immediately started to freak, apologizing profusely, but all Amelia could do was laugh. She was proud of her for doing it so well in such a small amount of time.

Pulling herself up from the ground with the help of Kelsey's offered hand, Amelia stood up, bouncing up and down on her feet. Her back spasmed from the impact.

"Are you sure you're okay? That looked like it really hurt," Kelsey asked again for the ninth time.

"Really, hun, I'm okay." Amelia stretched out her back as she spoke. Her body was still sore from yesterday's fiasco. She tried not to wince as a sharp pain shot down her spine. "Let's go inside and get some lunch."

The other trainees were beginning to break off and head inside for the day. The sun beat down above them in the June heat. Her clothes were sticking to places they shouldn't, and all she wanted to do at that moment was try out the soaker tub in her bathroom. But, given the discomfort in her stomach, she knew that would have to wait.

Kelsey and Amelia both headed for the backdoors of the house, passing Christian on the way. Amelia observed him as he kept a wary eye on her, his eyes glazed over, the tell-tale sign of being mind linked. She wondered who he was talking to.

As soon as they crossed the threshold, the smell of pasta wafted up her nose. Amelia's stomach growled loudly at the notion of food. Internally, she was grinning like a Cheshire cat.

"Mmm, Lena has done it again," Kelsey said, her nose tilted to the ceiling, taking in all the delicious aromas coming from the dining hall. "We're lucky we're werewolves, otherwise with her cooking, we'd all be huge."

Amelia nearly snorted, knowing full well it was true. With how much food she could pack away, it was a wonder her metabolism even kept up.

The girls both walked into the dining hall, wolves already clambering over one another to reach the line now forming. A buffet had been set up along the wall, complete with stations of various pastas, sauces, vegetables, even a fruit display.

Amelia went to the back of the line with the other wolves just entering, Kelsey following beside her. The wolves in front of her bowed, gesturing for her to go forward.

"No, no, thank you. I can wait," she said, flashing them a smile.

The wolves around her regarded her cautiously, almost as if they expected it to be a trap. She ignored the weird stares and instead tried to focus on Kelsey, who was endlessly chattering beside her. Kelsey was the type of girl who didn't need her to interject too much, happy to fill the time talking about one thing or another without really caring if she was heard. Amelia liked that. It reminded her of her easy friendship with Cordelia.

Getting up to the buffet table, Amelia immediately dove in, scooping up copious amounts of pasta into her bowl. She grabbed a plate as well. She couldn't have her fruit touching her pasta. That's just gross.

Nearly jumping up and down in excitement, she spotted her favorite, vodka sauce. Filling up her bowl with the sauce and her plate with varying fruits, she spotted a few vacant seats at a table near the windows.

Knowing Kelsey was right behind her, she made her way over, sitting down with the sun to her back. Sitting across from one another, silence ensued as they dug into their food. Amelia didn't bother looking up until the sound of a chair scraping against wood forced her attention away.

Christian sat down, carrying two bowls brimming with pasta alfredo, plus a heaping plate of fruits and vegetables. How he managed to carry all that himself and not drop it was a mystery to her.

"Hey Ella," Christian said, glancing at her nearly empty bowl. "How are you feeling?"

Amelia raised an eyebrow at him. "I'm fine, thanks."

"Yeah? That was a pretty nasty hit you took. You know, after everything that happened yesterday."

"What happened yesterday?" Kelsey jumped in.

Amelia turned in her chair, facing Christian head-on. The man's eyes were glued to his food, refusing to make eye contact with her. Now the puzzle fit.

"You can tell Gabriel if he wants to know something, he can ask me himself," Amelia growled under her breath, her words sending shivers along Christian's skin.

Not wanting to deal with the curious looks, Christians guilty face that made her instantly regret not reigning in her anger, or Kelsey's open-mouthed expression, she pushed away from the table and left the room.

(((

Amelia settled herself down into the bubble-filled, hot water. Her muscles instantly relaxed on contact. Her body was still tense from yesterday and her takedown today, not to mention her nether region was sore from a certain someone. She submerged herself nearly completely underwater, her head tilted back against the cool ceramic, sighing in relief.

Her eyes closed heavily, her mind beginning to drift off when she heard heavy footsteps on the floor. Someone was in her room.

Amelia didn't move, his scent already filling her nose, making her head swim in a way that she wished it wouldn't. Keeping her eyes closed, almost afraid to make eye contact, his scent doing plenty enough to her body already, she could hear him moving closer.

"It's a little weird, you just standing there and staring."

"How are you feeling?"

Gabriel's voice was deep and full of concern. So much so, she risked cracking open her eyes. He stood towering over her. His ebony hair hung in those silver eyes of his that were heavy, but not with lust as she expected. No, this was considerably deeper than just him needing her body. This was him genuinely worried for her safety, her health.

"I'm fine, Gabe. Really," she said, sitting up a little straighter in the water, trying to make sure their eye contact didn't waver.

"You need to be more careful," Gabriel said, his voice clear with a warning. "You can't keep putting yourself at risk. One of these days, I won't be there to save you."

Amelia furrowed her brow at him, her eyes shifting to a deeper forest green in warning. She could feel her color was no longer flushed from the hot water she'd been sitting in, but the anger that was now boiling inside of her. She pulled herself completely out of the tub, standing in front of him, suds running down the length of her body.

"I saved you from getting killed by that rogue, so let's not get shit twisted here. Training is a part of our life;

what makes us wolves is being able to fight, to defend our pack. I will not stop doing that. I am not some fragile doll for you to tuck away for safekeeping."

"If I hadn't shown up when I did, you would be dead, so let's not get *that* shit twisted. I know you're not fragile, but I also don't enjoy being worried every time you scrape your elbow."

Amelia scoffed, her temper now running the show. "We don't know what would have happened with that rogue, but one thing I do know is you can take your stupid mate bond and shove it up your ass. Don't worry your pretty head about me. Next time just let the rogue eat me."

Her last words brought forth a different beast in the man standing before her. The exact opposite of what she meant, but the wolf within him didn't seem to care. Gabriel's eyes grazed over her body, leaving a trail of fire in its wake. His eyes shifted back and forth between man and beast.

Amelia stood her ground, challenging the man to do something. Her stubborn chin stuck out farther than usual as she witnessed him struggle. Through their bond she could feel the conflicting emotions he was experiencing. A part of him wanted nothing more than to throttle her. Pin her to the ground and force her to submit, teaching her her place. She narrowed her eyes at him, slightly wishing he would try.

While the other half of him wanted to take advantage of her naked state. Ravage her body and slip between her legs until she begged for him to give her what she really wanted. Use that hot mouth of his to make her moan in ways she'd never heard before. Taste her until stars flashed in her eyes and her head felt like she was floating endlessly in the Milky Way.

Amelia clenched her legs together in response.

Gabriel turned around, storming out of the bathroom, slamming the door in his wake. Amelia felt like she could finally breath even though the air felt thick and warm. Her heart was beating against her breasts, her core burning with unquenched desire. Not even a bath could soothe her now.

CHAPTER 19

UNPACKING

The next week was less than uneventful.

Amelia had barely seen Gabriel. It was almost as if he was going out of his way to avoid her. He hadn't bothered showing up for meals. His side of the bed remained untouched, and thanks to them marking one another, their lack of skin touch was driving her mad. Her temper was becoming shorter and more irritable. The strangest part of it all was she knew he was lingering. She could sense his presence, constantly watching her, observing her. Even though she couldn't see him. He was constantly around, during training, meals, and most especially at night when she was asleep.

She knew he was having wolves keep tabs on her. Their vacant expressions gave them away. Christian had to restrain her several times from unleashing her fury on them. It wasn't their fault; they were following their Alpha's orders, which was another thing that was digging at her like a knife between the ribs. They chose to mark and mate with one another, providing her a direct link to him, but he had yet to induct her into the pack.

While she may be his mate, he had yet to make her an official member. Leaving her with no official standing in their ranks, no mind link to connect with the other wolves. According to their customs, she was as good as a lone wolf, visiting another pack's territory. It left her feeling isolated and disconnected, on top of Gabriel freezing her out.

She had enough.

Her nightmares were another story. They were persistent and unwavering. Every night, for the last week, she had gone to bed and every night, the same nightmare plagued her. No matter what she did, it was the same each time—the same feeling of hopelessness, the familiar smell of blood, and churned earth. Rogues coming at her from all sides and no matter what she did, it ended the same. Hundreds of wolves, dead.

Could it be her own insecurities, masking themselves as rogues? Was it some sort of post-traumatic stress disorder from being attacked? She'd definitely seen and endured worse, so that didn't seem likely. But nothing else seemed to make sense.

Inside their room, Amelia had yet to unpack her suitcases. They still laid out on the floor, open and in shambles, her stuff shoved in with no rhyme or reason.

The wall to wall bookcase had been installed yesterday. It was beautiful. Whitewood, solid, perfect for all of her books back in her old room. That was the one thing she couldn't let sit any longer. Her suitcase full of books was presently taking residence on one of the bookshelves. They deserved better than being thrown in some plastic sweatbox.

Today her stuff would arrive. Damon had managed to mind link her when she first woke up, informing her that her stuff was loaded on the truck and would be delivered in just a few hours. She was glad to have all of her familiar things within reach again, but another part, the oblique part, was weary. What if it didn't work out? She'd have to pack it all up again.

Amelia turned her head away from the bookcase, her fingers still lingering on the worn leather cover of Narnia, when she heard a knock coming from the door. Gabriel wouldn't knock.

"Come in," Amelia called out.

Lena poked her head inside, catching her standing beside the new build. "Amelia, there's a moving van out front for you."

Amelia's heart managed to skip a beat and fall to the floor in the same instant. "Thank you, Lena. I'll be right down."

Turning back, not waiting for her to leave, she gazed at the used book for a moment longer. Recalling the soothing voice of its previous owner, reading the sacred words printed on its paper. Taking in a deep breath, Amelia straightened her blouse before vacating the room.

Outside, a white moving van parked in the driveway. Its back doors were already swung open, waiting for its contents to be emptied. Amelia saw the dozens of boxes stacked to the roof. Crap, did she really have so much stuff?

Yes, you do.

Shush, I didn't ask you. She snickered at her wolf.

Ignoring Rey, Amelia jumped into the back of the van, picking up the first box she touched. Hopping down onto the gravel drive, she spotted thirty-odd pack members, walking through the double doors, stopping in front of her.

Christian came forward, flashing her his goofy grin. "We're here to help. Just tell us what to do."

Amelia couldn't resist the smile that spread across her face or the warmth that grew in her chest. At least someone cared. "Grab a box. They're all going up to my room. Whatever doesn't fit can be left in the hallway for me to go through."

Christian looked back over his shoulder to the wolves behind him, flashing them a grin. "You heard your Luna."

Amelia left them to handle themselves. She didn't think it was necessary to direct traffic, seeing how there were enough of them present to only warrant one round trip. Moving the boxes in would take them ten minutes, whereas it would have taken her hours by herself.

Back at the top of the stairs, Amelia dropped her box on the floor near the bookcase, knowing full well from its weight, it was more books. As each pack member came up, delivering her things, she made sure to thank each one of them. Even if a certain unnamed mate was responsible for them helping her, she still appreciated it.

The room was already brimming with boxes, to the point where she could no longer find the bed. She didn't even want to see what was left in the hallway. Christian came inside with a box labeled photos in his arms.

"Last box, Ella. Where do you want it?" Christian asked her.

"Find a spot. Anywhere."

Amelia spun around, overwhelmed by the number of boxes that needed to find a home. She felt a hand rest on her shoulder, warm and solid. Turning around, Christian stood behind her; concern etched in the creases of his forehead.

"What's wrong?"

"Am I making the right decision? Is it even worth unpacking any of this when Gabriel could care less that I'm here? I left my damn pack for him. I trusted in this stupid mate bond, and all it's given me is a damn headache," she said, pinching the bridge of her nose, her anxieties finally rising to the surface.

Christian now laid both hands on her shoulders, leaning down to her eye level. "Listen, Ella. I don't know what's going on in that thick Alpha's head, but I do know that this pack is thrilled to have you here. Since you arrived, you have completely won over the hearts of every single Twilight wolf. Gabriel, well, he's a complicated man. He may not show it right now, but he wants you here too."

Amelia scoffed, shaking her head. "He has a hell of a way of showing it."

"I want you here," Christian smirked, holding his arms out to her.

Christian reminded her of a giant cuddly bear. That is if bears were six-six giants made of hard muscle and a face that made you laugh just by looking at it. Amelia couldn't help but step into his arms, wrapping her own around his waist as he nearly squeezed the life from her, but she didn't mind. This was the closest skin contact she had since that brief encounter in the woods, and it was nice to be held.

Christian chuckled, pulling back. "So, where do we start?"

Amelia and Christian devoted the next several hours unpacking nearly all of her boxes. Together they moved around each other as though in a synchronized dance. They passed the time swapping jokes, reminiscing over childhood memories, and who had the most embarrassing moment ever. Amelia still thinks she's won. Running up behind Danny at the mall to pinch his butt, only to find out it wasn't Danny. She had never been so embarrassed.

Amelia was busy arranging the books on the wall, grouping them by author, to then line them up on the shelves from top to bottom in order of importance. The less spectacular books ditched to the bottom. Surprisingly, she managed to fill nearly all of the shelves, leaving just enough room for some pictures and baubles.

Since they were already busy unpacking, Amelia went ahead and ditched the suitcases, jamming them, now empty, to the back of the closet. The walk-in looked extra full now that her clothes were finally hung. Her shoes lined the shelves along with her other knick-knacks. Oddly enough, she felt at ease with it. Like she was finally home, with her stuff all around her, making the space feel like her own. If he didn't like it, he could just shove it where the sun don't shine.

"Where do you want these last few boxes?" Christian asked, standing in the hallway, a box of winter clothes in his arms.

"Is there an attic or somewhere for storage?"

"Yeah, we have an attic. The door for it is just at the end of this hallway."

"Then that's fine. The rest are just winter clothes anyway. Won't be needing them anytime with this hell fueled heatwave."

Christian nodded, readjusting the box's weight before disappearing out of sight down the hall. Amelia turned back, continuing her mundane folding, the last bit of clothes left that would take up her side of the dresser.

Hey, Mia.

Amelia straightened, smiling at the sound of her brother's voice. *Hey, creeper. You know the phone works just as well.*

Where's the fun in that? When I could just pop in whenever I feel like it.

Eww. You know, one of these days, karma's gonna come back and bite you in the ass.

Hmm, I like it kinky.

Amelia couldn't help but gag, suddenly plagued with images she never wanted in her head. *Did you need something, or do you just live to torment me?*

I just wanted to check in, make sure you got your stuff. See how you're settling in.

Tell Dad; I said thank you. You guys did an excellent job packing it all up. I'm amazed by how organized it all is.

I'll be sure to pass on the message.

Amelia smiled. Her brother's silence left her wondering if he had closed the link, when he managed to sneak back in.

You didn't answer me, though. How are you doing there?

Amelia gritted her teeth, resuming her folding. *It's fine.*

She could almost hear him chuckle. *Liar.* He knew her better than that. *What's wrong, Mia?*

It's nothing.

It's not nothing. I'm always here for you; that's the joy of having a twin. You're stuck with me for the rest of your life. Now spill, what's going on?

Amelia sat down on the edge of the bed, throwing the shirt in her hand on top of the semi-neatly folded pile. *He's just such a dick.*

Has he hurt you?

Pfft. Like he could. Amelia rolled her eyes. *No, he just ignores me instead. I don't know what to do. He doesn't even try.*

Do you want me to come and beat his ass? I feel like it's my duty to fight for your honor.

Amelia couldn't help but laugh out loud. She could almost picture him in his office, right that very minute. His face in a scowl, ready to fight the world for her. *No doofus. I can fight my own battles, but thank you.*

Meh, that's okay. I didn't want to have to explain to the Council why they're short an Alpha anyway.

Amelia rolled her eyes for a second time. She honestly wasn't certain who would win that fight. *What's going on there? How's the pack?*

Not much is happening here. Same old, same old. Other than the nuisance with the rogues -

What do you mean rogues? Amelia asked, bolting upright. *What rogues?!*

There have been more sightings of rogues around the territory. We've seen at least ten, in and around the border.

Has anyone been attacked?

A couple of ours got too close. No one died, but a few were injured, including Dominik. Most of the rogues are keeping their distance, like their watching for something.

Amelia could feel the start of a headache just behind her eyes. Her mind flashed to the dozens of dead wolves littered on the forest floor. *Why would rogues be watching for something? Rogues are wild; without humanity, they don't think, let alone have respect over boundaries.*

Gabriel mentioned having the same problem. We're not really sure wh-

We don't have the same problem. We had one rogue, one. It wasn't even that close to the border. Once I killed it -

Amelia Rhea Smoke!

Amelia winced as his booming Alpha voice bounced off the delicate walls of her brain. *Bro! Keep it down! This is still my brain. Fuck. Yes, I killed a rogue, but as I said, it was only one.*

I'm not even going to comment on how reckless and stupid you were to take on a rogue by yourself. But Gabriel has told us that there have been multiple rogues spotted along your border. None of them have crossed, but they're there.

Amelia stood up off the bed, her hands flexing at her side. *Damon, I'm gonna have to get back to you.*

CHAPTER 20

MAD WOMAN

Amelia charged out of the room, down the stairs to the main floor, and down the hall, kicking in the door to his office. The wooden door splintered on impact, exploding inward with significant chunks of wooden shrapnel. She stepped over the wreckage to find Gabriel, Kaleb, and an elderly gentleman staring at her wide-eyed and surprised.

"Amelia!" Gabriel yelled, standing up from his desk so fast his chair flipped to the floor. "What the hell do you think you're doing?"

Amelia directed her attention to the elder, clearly a member of the Council, and inclined her head in respect. "I am so sorry to disturb you, councilman …"

"Edward," the man offered his name meekly.

"Edward," Amelia said his name sweetly, her smile pleasant while her eyes were that of her wolf. "But I'm going to have to ask you to leave. Now."

Her aura was slipping out of her control as her anger raged within. Kaleb and Councilman Edward flinched beneath the force of her command. Her voice was nothing but polite and calm, but the intent behind it was murderous. She ignored the glaring stare of her mate while the two men fled the room, stepping around the remains of the door.

"You have five seconds to explain your actions before I-"

"Before you what?! Huh? What are you going to do to me? *Mate*," Amelia challenged him, fed up with his attitude, over his superiority complex. It was wearing her thin. She was no longer in control of herself or her wolf.

"What is the meaning of this? You can't just come charging through here like some madwoman," Gabriel yelled, throwing his hands in the air for dramatic effect.

Amelia froze at his words, her heart stiff in her chest. Rey moved closer and closer to the surface. Her sea-green eyes flashing between human and wolf.

We can always show him a madwoman.

Amelia let her lips twitch into a small smirk at her wolf's remark. She stepped closer to her mate. The energy in the room crackled and raged. Her aura flexed around her. Noticing the slight adjustment in his stance, the set of his shoulders, the wary look in his eyes, he was nervous.

Good. He should be.

"You haven't even scratched the surface," Amelia said, her voice cold and harsh. "You have ignored me for a week, avoided every room I'm in, and hidden in the shadows, watching me like some fucking psycho. Your bullshit ends now. I don't know what your problem is with me, but there is one thing I will not tolerate. You not bothering to keep me informed when it comes to what's going on with the pack."

Gabriel's eyes widened slightly before rearranging back into his typical stoic self. "I don't know what you're talking about."

"Cut the bullshit, Gabe. Why haven't you said anything about the rogues? Or maybe that my brother is dealing with the same thing? My cousin was injured, and you didn't bother to say a word to me," she said, her voice sounding more desperate and upset than she would have liked.

"*I* am Alpha here, Amelia, not you. Don't forget your place in this pack. You've spent the last week walking around here like you own the place, but this is unacceptable. I do not owe you anything," Gabriel snarled.

Amelia unconsciously stepped back. Her facade of strength and poise faded instantly. "How can I forget my place here when I don't even have one? You've abandoned me to fend for myself. You haven't bothered to induct me into the pack. I haven't seen or heard from you since the rogue last week. What am I supposed to do? Mope around, waiting for you to show interest?"

Gabriel sighed, massaging his forehead. "No, it's not that-"

"Then what? Because I'm doing my best here. I never asked for your love or your heart, but I do expect your loyalty and respect. I never expected us to live happily ever after like those stupid fairytales humans seem so fond of. But I guess some naive part of me was hoping that you'd show a tiny bit of interest."

Amelia could hear her own voice cracking. Rey whimpered in the back of her mind. She shook off the rush of emotions that were threatening to engulf her. Her stomach cramped, twisting into knots. She felt as though something was wrapping tightly around her neck, cutting off her air and circulation. But, she refused to look weak in front of him. She would not let him see how much he was hurting her.

Gabriel took a step toward her, making her step back as a result. He froze, his hand half stretched as if he wanted to hold her, console her. Or maybe that was simply wishful thinking.

"No," she said, holding her hand up for him to stop. "You're right. You don't owe me anything. I apologize for expecting you to treat me like a person. God forbid your Luna. Who is *supposed* to be your equal. This pack is like family. I will defend them till my dying breath, but the Wandering Moon Pack *is* my family. You should have told me."

"Who told you?"

Amelia scrunched her brow at him. Was that really all he had to say?

"It was Christian, wasn't it?" he asked accusingly.

Amelia rolled her eyes. The jealousy in his voice was uncalled for. He was fortunate she was in control of herself when all she wanted to do was smack the shit out of him.

"No. Christian didn't say a word. It was Damon. He informed me."

"How? You two haven't spoken since you left. He hasn't called you once."

"What are you screening my calls now?!" Amelia yelled.

"How did he tell you, Amelia?" Gabriel asked her again through gritted teeth, ignoring her.

"Through the mind link," she huffed loudly.

"What are you talking about? That should have broken the moment you left," Gabriel noted. "Unless you didn't actually sever the bond."

"The bond snapped an hour outside of the territory. Trust me, that's not something I'll ever forget," she said, rubbing her hand into her chest as if she could still feel the break. The cold ache it had left.

"Then how can he still mind link you?" Gabriel asked her.

"We're twins. It's a twin thing. I've always had a different bond with my brother than anyone else. No matter how far apart we are, I can always reach him," she said flippantly.

What the hell did it matter? What was he getting at?

"And you didn't think that was something you should have told me?"

"What does it matter?! He's my twin, my family. Who cares if I can still link with him?"

"You don't think that's a conflict of interest. Still being connected to your old pack? How do I know you won't put their priorities over ours?" Gabriel asked, his voice thick with unspoken accusations. "This is your pack now."

"If you want to get technical, I'm a lone wolf. I don't belong to any pack. Thanks to you, I severed my bond with the Wandering Moon, and also, thanks to you, I'm still not a part of the Twilight Pack. So right now, I belong to myself."

Even though that wasn't at all how she felt, she didn't really care. She was a member of the Twilight Moon Pack, whether she was linked with them or not. These wolves were her family, and this was her home. But the way he was behaving, practically accusing her of being a traitor, was wearing her thin.

Gabriel eliminated the distance between them before she could even react. His fingertips dug into the tender flesh of her arm as he gripped her tightly against his rigid form. "You are mine," he growled.

Amelia struggled to release herself from his grip, but the more she pulled, the tighter he squeezed. "What the hell is your problem?! Let go!"

Gabriel lifted her, the tips of her toes barely touching the floor, as he forced his mouth on hers. Amelia stiffened beneath him, shocked by the force of his lips against hers. The feel of his skin against hers melted her resolve. Their bond opened, flooding the two of them with one another's emotions and what she could feel from him left her unable to hold out.

At that moment, she could feel his need, his desire for her as she opened her mouth to him. The desperation and hunger had her tongue slipping past his teeth, tasting him. A fresh wave of passion and remorse led her to reach up, weaving her fingers through his silk hair, pulling him down farther.

But then something else started to flow through. She could feel his shame, his concern, his fear, even his superiority. Amelia could feel each of them worming its way inside, crawling under her skin. She shoved hard against him, his grip on her breaking, nearly causing her to fall back on the floor.

"What the fuck?!" she breathed, her voice shallow and heavy. Her body desired him more than ever, but her mind was repulsed. He wanted her. More than she could have ever fathomed, yet he feared her? She could feel his desire for her, but he was troubled by it? "Is this all I am to you? You avoid me all week and then think it's acceptable to just assault me like that?"

Gabriel just stared at her, his breathing labored and harsh, almost as if oxygen was lacking in the room. His silver eyes wild and unfocused. "Amelia, I-"

"I wish the Moon Goddess had never given me such an ass of a mate."

Without bothering to wait for his response, Amelia stormed out of his office.

CHAPTER 21

THE STRANGER

Amelia ran away from the house, away from him, away from it all. She rushed for the garage. Luckily it wasn't locked. She flung the door open, easily spotting her bike parked along the back wall, nestled beside a muscle car.

She noticed a key holder hanging on the wall, easily finding her keys. She sprinted for her bike. Her helmet was neatly balanced on the seat. She was grateful she had the sense to keep her ID and money tucked in her pocket at all times. Being raised to be constantly prepared for anything was certainly paying off at the moment.

Amelia hit the garage door opener beside her, pulling on her helmet over her plaited hair. She straddled the crotch rocket, twisting the key in the ignition, and kick-started the bike to life. The noise of the bike was sure to garner some unwanted attention.

Without bothering to push herself out of the garage, unwilling to waste any more time, she leaned down low, pulling on the gas. The bike jerked forward, tires skidding against smooth cement. Burnt rubber filled the air as her bike propelled her forward.

Gravel kicked up beneath the bike as she raced ahead. Pack members were running out to discern what the noise was. Christian came from along the side of the house. His face was a mixture of pride and worry. Amelia ignored them all and raced away from the garage, down the driveway, and away from the house.

Wolves were racing beside her but kept their distance. She could feel Gabriel brushing against her mind, demanding entrance, his temper boiling. But she didn't care. She pushed him away and forced him out, completely blocking all contact with him.

Passing through the pack's borders, she felt as if she could finally breathe. No longer suffering under the constant glares and judgments. No longer questioning herself and her decisions.

It was nice to finally feel the wind pulling at her skin again, whipping her shirt around her. She wasn't exactly wearing the proper riding gear, but none of that seemed to matter. She simply enjoyed the freedom after a week of being cooped up. She couldn't resist the smile that spread across her face.

Amelia tried to push their fight away. Tried to disregard the guilt that was taking root in her chest for running off. The anger towards him that boiled her blood, and the unexpected pain their fight had caused. He didn't trust her, and that cut deeper than any knife.

She knew she had to go back. It's not like she was actually running away, being that she just unpacked twenty boxes, but for now, she would enjoy her time alone. Hell would be waiting for her no matter what time she returned.

Up ahead, a sign pointed her in the direction of a town not five miles from the territory. Maybe she could find a bookstore, grab a drink.

Turning off the road, she followed the signs, and within a few minutes, she entered a quaint town with small stores lining the main road. She couldn't spot a bookstore, but she did see a small cafe. Pulling to a stop, she parked her bike in front of the glass windows.

Dee's Cafe reminded her of something out of a Hallmark movie. The brick face was worn and covered in ivy. The entrance door dinged above her head as she pushed it open, signaling her arrival. The interior was small and intimate, with large comfy lounge chairs around two-seater tables. The walls were adorned with a variety of plants, producing necessary contrast against the dark brick. It was charming and comfortable and instantly put her at ease.

Cradling her helmet beneath her arm, she took it all in. The smell of ground coffee, vanilla syrup, and cinnamon rolls wafted in the air. It was like heaven.

Looking around, she secured a vacant table near the corner by the window. Sitting down, setting her helmet on the floor beside her, she flipped open the small menu on the table. The options were limited but delicious-looking none the less.

An attractive, middle-aged woman with raven colored hair pulled up into a messy bun, approached her table. A pen and notebook in hand.

"Welcome, Darlin. What can I get you?" the woman asked, her accent thick and southern, which was odd being they were so far up north.

Amelia noticed the name Dee embroidered in her apron. Must be the owner.

"Can I get a cappuccino and a cinnamon roll, please?" Amelia smiled, laying the menu back down on the table.

Dee swiftly noted the order down before turning away without another word. Amelia didn't mind. She wasn't fond of chit chat and preferred the quiet silence of her own thoughts.

That is until a certain someone was acting persistently annoying, banging on the walls of her mind. She winced at the intrusion, hissing in response, drawing unwanted attention to herself from the other patrons. She smiled politely before turning away, directing her gaze out the front window, trying to act as normal as possible.

If having your subconscious assaulted was normal.

He's furious. Rey said.

I know, but I'm pissed too. How much longer can we continue to be silent? He doesn't trust us!

I know. She said grimly. *But just answer him. They're worried about us. You know he's afraid of you leaving him. He has abandonment issues.*

How do you even know that?! Amelia snarled, feeling extra defensive.

Amelia, I'm always on your side, but we have a mate now, and we need to be considerate of his feelings too.

I can't be considerate of his feelings if he won't even talk to me!

He's trying to talk now. Rey said, just as a more persistent force was used against their blocked link.

Amelia took in a deep breath to steady her anger before she cracked open the door. Gabriel seized full advantage, kicking it wide open. She winced in response, biting her lower lip to keep from yelling out. He was forcefully entering her mind, stomping through without a care. Even when her head did feel like it was splitting open from the inside.

Where the fuck are you, Amelia? Get your ass back here right now!

Amelia closed her eyes, steadying herself. She could feel her body twitching, her bones humming with the desire to shed her human skin and transition into fur. She couldn't very well phase in front of a cafe full of humans, but her anger was beginning to get the best of her.

Gabriel quit yelling in my head. You're giving me a headache. Even she surprised herself with how calm and level headed, she sounded.

She could almost feel him, forcing himself to relax.

Where are you?

I'm out. I needed a breather from you, from everything.

You can't just run away whenever you feel like it. I won't allow it.

Amelia snickered. *You don't have a choice. I'm already gone, and in case you didn't hear me the first time, you have no control over me. I am not a member of your pack.*

Whether you're a member of this pack or not, I am your Alpha, your mate. So, when I say come home, you come home!

She could feel his Alpha aura through their link, exerting the force of it behind each of his words in hopes of bending her to his will. Typically, this would work on any other wolf. But not on her. Alpha commands had zero effect on her.

Amelia laughed through their link. Laughed at his attempt to command her. Why couldn't he just get that she needed some space? No, instead, he has to try and go all Alpha.

Well, that shits about to backfire.

I'll come back if and when I'm ready. So, fuck off, Gabriel. She smiled, just envisioning the look of shock on his face as he realized his command didn't work. *Ta ta for now.*

With that said, she sealed the link once again, forcing him out for good.

Amelia had been so preoccupied with her little mind chat that she hadn't realized Dee had already come by. A steaming cup and a cinnamon roll were waiting in front of her. The cinnamon roll was smothered with icing that dripped off the sides, pooling onto the plate. The cinnamon sugar had her stomach growling with delight.

Not wasting another minute, she made quick work of the cinnamon roll, savoring each bite. It was glorious. The roll was soft and packed with tons of flavor. She would have ordered ten more if she didn't already anticipate the look of judgment she would receive. It was one thing to eat like a whale in front of the pack, none of them were any better with their appetites, but humans were much more delicate and judgmental.

Instead, she pushed her empty plate away, leaning back in her comfy seat, sipping on her cappuccino. She closed her eyes, enjoying the warming rays that streamed through the windows. She hadn't even thought to grab her phone before she stormed out of her room, and she was oddly glad. Being technology-free was liberating.

Taking a sip from the hot beverage she cradled in her hands, the light from the window was suddenly blocked. A large shadow fell over her.

Amelia looked up to discover a man standing in front of her, his back to the window, shrouding her in darkness.

"Do you mind if I sit here? It seems the rest of the cafe is full," the man asked her.

Amelia looked around at the cafe, and sure enough, almost every other seat had been taken, apart from the one across from her.

"No, of course not. Please sit," she gestured to the seat in front of her.

The man smiled in thanks, sitting down before ordering himself a cup of coffee. Amelia took in the stranger before her. He was definitely older than her, given the wrinkles around his mouth and along his forehead, but unsure by how much. His mousy hair was trimmed short against his head, revealing three long scars over the left side.

Amelia puzzled over that, curious what kind of scrap he got himself into to earn himself such a nasty wound. She could feel the stranger's dark brown eyes on her, taking her in as much as she was doing to him. Flicking her gaze down, she examined the nearly empty contents of her cup.

"You're not from around here, are you?"

His voice stole her attention, causing her to look back up. She scrunched her brows at him in confusion.

"I'm sorry, I don't mean to be nosy. It's just I come here almost every day, and I don't think I've never seen you before. Most of us here are regulars," the man said, offering a smile.

Amelia smiled back, finding him charming. His accent was almost Bostonian. "I just moved here about a week ago," she informed him.

"Well, welcome to the neighborhood. It's a peaceful town; we don't get much excitement this far from the city. Unless you count the wolves, which most here don't," the man sipped on his black coffee.

Amelia straightened in her seat. "Wolves? That can't be that surprising up here in the wilderness. Worse things are lurking in the woods besides wolves."

The man chuckled, setting his coffee cup down in front of him. "Maybe so, but these wolves aren't your typical beasts."

Amelia felt a chill crawl down her back, her senses on overdrive. Rey crept forward in the back of her mind, scenting the air between them. She recoiled instantly, which left Amelia puzzled, not smelling anything obvious. He smelled of petrol and antiseptic. An unusual combination.

It's to hide his scent. Rey informed her, clearly able to tell more than she could by the smell of the man.

"You're a beautiful young lady. I bet you have all the men chasing tail," the stranger smirked, leaning back in his chair.

Amelia would have found the man attractive if not for the creepy, unsettling tone in his voice. "I get by," she added, keeping her answer short. She suddenly had the strong desire to go home, surprising even herself to call the Twilight Moon pack home.

"I'm sure you do," the man grinned. His lips were pulled up into a smile, but his eyes were flat and unexpressive. "You're quite stunning."

Amelia squirmed in her seat. The way his eyes lingered on her body felt like someone had poured a bucket of worms on her. She felt dirty and unclean.

Time to leave. Rey ordered.

She didn't need to be told twice. Amelia stood up, pulling out a twenty from her back pocket and flung it down on the table. Grabbing her helmet off the floor, she went to leave when the man stepped in her way.

"I really need to be going," Amelia insisted, glaring daggers at the man. The last thing she wanted to do was cause a scene.

"It was nice to meet you ..."

Amelia glanced down at his outstretched hand. She really didn't want to take it, to let him touch even a single inch of her, but politeness won out.

"Amelia," she said, shaking his hand.

A shock of cold engulfed her body the instant they made contact, causing her to jerk her hand back in response as though she was struck by a snake, venom freezing her blood.

The stranger didn't seem fazed in the slightest, continuing to smile down at her. "The name's Michael."

Amelia tried to smile, side-stepping past him. Refusing to offer him even a goodbye. She had to keep herself from running out of the cafe and to her bike, forcing herself to move at a seemingly reasonable pace. Once she reached her bike, she started the engine, allowing it to warm up while pulling her helmet on.

As she backed the bike out, away from the cafe, she could still feel the man's deadly gaze watching her as she drove down the road and out of sight.

CHAPTER 22

ONE DAY AT A TIME

The drive back to the territory was a quick one. Not nearly as long as she would have liked. The border was directly ahead, the smell of pine and sap already washing over her. The scent instantly reminded her of her mate.

Home. She was home.

For a moment, the scent warmed her to her very soul, providing comfort in ways she never knew possible. That is until she recalled what waited for her at the Packhouse. One pissed off man-child.

Wolves followed her through the territory, escorting her up the drive. She wasn't certain if this was to support her or ensure she actually made it to the Packhouse. Probably the latter.

The massive house came into view, growing larger and larger by the second. She couldn't see him, but she could feel him. The closer she got, the stronger their bond became. Her head was already pounding in preparation for round two.

Driving past the house, she headed directly for the garage. The door was already ajar and waiting. She pulled up, backing the bike into its original spot beside the muscle car. Twisting the key, she shut off the bike and removed her helmet. Her hair was sticking to her neck and face thanks to the sticky humidity. All she desired was a bath.

Christian and Kelsey came running into view. Christian looked worried, concerned even, while Kelsey looked fascinated, her eyes glued to the crotch rocket beneath her body. Amelia smiled at her. Maybe she could teach Kelsey how to ride one day.

"Alpha's pissed, Ella," Christian said in warning.

Amelia couldn't help but snort. "No, shit. He's been screaming in my head since I left."

"You drive this?" Kelsey asked, her eyes still glued to the sleek bike.

Amelia smirked, hoping that maybe they had another thing in common. "You like it?"

"It's sexy as hell!" Kelsey exclaimed, her face bright and alive.

"Yeah, it can be. I can show you how to ride sometime," she smiled, "that is if I'm not thrown in the dungeons."

Kelsey gasped, suddenly remembering the real issue that lay ahead of her. "He wouldn't do that to you. You're his mate, his Luna."

"I'm honestly not convinced that any of it matters to him," Amelia sighed, suddenly feeling extremely tired. She was *not* prepared to deal with him.

"It's going to be alright, Ella. We've got your back," just then Christian's eyes looked distant. Someone was linking him. Coming back to, he seized Kelsey by the arm, producing an apologetic look. "Sorry, Amelia."

Together, they scampered away quicker than a fox chasing a hare.

Amelia got off the bike, setting her helmet back where it belonged. She returned the keys back to where she found them before closing the garage door and exiting.

We can do this. Amelia tried reassuring herself.

I have your back. Rey said, rubbing against her conscience in comfort.

What are we going to do, Rey? I can't keep fighting with him like this. It's exhausting, and honestly, I just don't want to argue.

I know. Maybe we can make him understand.

Amelia snorted. Some people had more faith in her mate than she did.

All we can do is try. But we have to try. Rey insisted, appealing to her more stubborn side. The side that refused to back down from a challenge.

Amelia huffed in annoyance, knowing full well her wolf was right. The damn canine was always right. *You know, sometimes you're too clever for your own good.*

She headed directly for the house. By the smell inside, she could tell the pack was anxious, nervous like a bomb might detonate at any moment. They probably weren't wrong.

Judging by his lingering scent, he had passed through the commons at some point. At the moment, he was likely in his study, restraining himself. She hoped he hadn't taken it out on any unsuspecting pack members. They didn't deserve his wrath. Not when she was the cause of it.

Lena rushed towards her just as she shut the front door. The poor woman looked terrified.

"Luna, thank the Goddess! There you are! Alpha, sir, has been in a right fit since you left. He came out here, terrorizing half the pack, frightening the pups!" Lena exclaimed.

Amelia reached out, laying her hand on the woman's shoulder, patting her back. "It's okay. I'm back. Don't worry about Gabriel. I'll speak with him," she said, offering her an encouraging smile. "Please, tell the rest of the pack it'll be alright."

Lena bobbed her head, suddenly looking very calm and relaxed under her touch. The housekeeper turned away, heading back the way she came, disappearing into the dining hall.

The few pack members she did see milling about were huddled together, whispering amongst one another. Amelia gave them all warm, heartfelt smiles, trying to calm the thick tension in the house. They seemed to respond, smiling in kind.

Amelia went straight for the stairs, knowing full well Gabriel would be behind in her moments. Once his thick head realized she wouldn't confront him in his office. Up in their room, she flung the door closed, not caring how loud of a bang it made.

That should get his attention.

Inside, she looked around at all of her freshly unpacked stuff. All of her books lining the shelves and the pile of clothes that she left half folded on the bed. She began to finish the clothes. No point in getting ready for a bath when he could walk in at any moment. She would not allow him to catch her off guard again.

Just as she was placing the last few articles of clothing away in the dresser, the bedroom door opened. Amelia disregarded him, closing the dresser drawer quietly. After no longer having an excuse, she turned to meet him head-on.

Gabriel looked like a mess. His usually sleek, combed hair was rumpled and out of place, like he ran his hands through it too many times, pulling on his hair. His knuckles were healed but coated in dried blood. Clearly, he put his fist through something. She was suddenly relieved she didn't go to his office, afraid of what it might look like.

Unable to help herself, she stepped towards him, reaching out, grasping his large hands in hers. She ran her fingers over his rough knuckles, identifying scar tissue built around the bones. There were no visible signs of an open wound.

Looking up, she caught him watching her, his silver eyes like warm pools. Amelia folded herself against him, surprising him even further by winding her arms around his waist. She didn't care anymore what they were fighting about. She was tired. Tired of the anger that was eating away at her. Tired of the millions of emotions that plagued her thoughts and dreams.

Amelia wasn't sure if he was going to remain stiff or hug her back. She rubbed her nose into a patch of skin, just above the opening of his shirt, tickling the hair on his chest. Breathing him in deeply, she savored his smell, expanding her lungs with the warm aroma.

Gabriel encased her with his long, rigid arms, hugging her firmly against himself. For the first time in over a week, they both relaxed against one another. His nose was in her hair, breathing her in just as she was doing to him.

They stood there like that for some time, the minutes bleeding together. Time was no longer a concept. At that moment, however brief or long, they just held each other. Basking in the bond that bound them. However hard she fought against their connection; it was moments like this where she couldn't deny how she felt. Instead of allowing it to confuse her, she simply closed her eyes, feeling safe and secure in his arms.

"Amelia?"

"Hmm?"

"Where did you go?"

Moment over. The sharpness in his tone made that very clear.

Amelia untangled herself, placing a few feet between them to clear her head. No longer in his arms, she felt detached, unhinged from the one thing that was supposed to tether her to this world.

"I went into town. The one right outside the pack's borders."

"What were you doing there?"

Amelia turned back to him. His face was impenetrable, like it had been carved of stone, unyielding and unapologetic. She sighed at his demeanor.

"I stopped at a cafe," she told him, sitting back on the edge of the bed. "Is that a crime?"

"I specifically ordered you to return home," he growled softly in an attempt to keep himself and his wolf under control. He was failing.

Amelia knew where this was heading. She didn't think she had it in her to fight with him. "Gabriel, you can't just order me around. I'm not one of your pack. I'm your mate."

"Were you with another man?"

The tone in his voice caused her to stiffen. He was suggesting something. Something absurd and immature and completely insane.

"What are you talking about?" she breathed deeply, trying to calm herself down.

"I can smell another male on you. Don't deny it." His eyes were shifting between man and wolf.

And you said to try and talk to him! Amelia hissed. *Men are stupid!*

She wasn't wrong.

"If you're trying to suggest something, Gabriel, then please, go ahead. I'm really tired of you constantly accusing me of things I'm not capable of doing."

"Really? I hardly believe you're not capable of -"

"Choose your next words carefully." That was it. She was rising to the occasion. "No matter what you believe, no matter what your past drama may be, I am not a cheat, or a traitor, or whatever other bullshit you want to accuse me of being!

"I don't know what else I have to do to prove it to you! I left my home, my pack, my family, for you! I severed my connection to the only pack I've ever known, for you! I gave you my body, something I never shared with anyone else, and you have the nerve to accuse me of something I would *never* be capable of!"

Amelia knew her voice was starting to crack. She hated the way this man could shatter her resolve. Her mind and body were torn between ripping out his jugular and screwing him where they stood.

"I had a conversation with a man at the cafe. I shook his hand to be polite. But at least someone wanted to talk to me. The man found me beautiful, and my own mate can't bother to be in the same room with me, much less look at me. Am I that repulsive?"

Amelia turned away from him, afraid to meet his eyes, afraid to see the disgust in them. Maybe she was right. She angrily wiped at the wetness in her eyes; her own body was even betraying her.

"I'm sorry, Amelia."

Amelia looked back over her shoulder, her ears straining. She must have heard wrong.

His boots pushed against the carpet as she heard him walking towards her. Amelia held her position, afraid to move, afraid to breathe. She felt his warm, large hands grip her shoulders, sliding down her arms. It felt like she'd been freezing in the dark, and his touch brought the sun out, chasing away the shadows, warming her all the way through.

"Look at me."

The sound of his voice was stern yet gentle, coaxing her to turn and face him. She did as he asked, looking up to find his eyes sad.

"I'm sorry. I'm sorry for accusing you and doubting you," he said, his words completely honest and sincere. "I never thought of having a mate, much less a fated one. I don't trust easily. It's not in my nature, but I never meant to hurt you."

"The truth is Gabriel; we know nothing about each other. You wouldn't know that I never wanted a mate. Never wanted to be tied down to a pack, much less a man. I wanted to travel the world. Live out of a backpack. Sleep in dirty alleys and live off ramen noodles," she smiled as his face began to lighten, taking in everything she had to say. "You wouldn't know any of this because you never bothered to ask or take the time to get to know me."

Gabriel nodded solemnly. She could see there was something else, something he wasn't saying. Unconsciously, she reached up, cupping his face in her hand. Her fingertips brushed against the hairs on the nape of his neck, her thumb brushing along his jaw bone. He leaned into her touch, closing his eyes, breathing her in.

"I'm afraid of the effect you have on me," Gabriel whispered into her skin, brushing his lips against the tender flesh of her palm.

Amelia's breath hitched in her throat. Never expecting to hear anything so sensitive, so honest, to pass through his lips. Her heart was skipping in her chest, her stomach twisting itself into knots, her core humming in response to their intimate contact.

"You're not the only one who feels like they're losing control," Amelia admitted aloud, for the first time. She was falling for the man, and it was beyond her control.

"I've been trying to stay away from you ever since the first night we made love. I've been falling for you, and I can't seem to stop myself," he leaned down into her, resting his head against hers, taking in gulps of air. "You infuriate me to no end."

Amelia chuckled softly. "The feeling is completely mutual."

She let her words hang between them, giving each other time to process. No matter what, she never expected this.

"What do we do?" Gabriel asked her.

"We take it one day at a time. We try, but we'll figure it out together."

CHAPTER 23

BETTER TO BE PREPARED

The days had started to bleed together. It had been more than a week since their heart to heart. Since they admitted to one another that feelings were deeper than either of them knew.

Amelia was kept busy learning about the pack, Luna duties she was willing to entertain, and training with the warriors. She'd been appointed as an official trainer, joining Christian in leading the sessions. The warriors were beginning to trust and recognize her authority and skill. Every day, more women were continuously joining.

Gabriel had started training again, joining them during their morning sessions. She was seriously impressed with his form and technique. He excelled in fighting, even more so in wolf form. She couldn't help but watch him as he worked with other members of the pack. Taking in his stance, the way he carried himself, how easily he talked with other wolves. He was a natural-born Alpha.

Gabriel had even included her in some meetings, keeping her briefed with the territory's security and pack treaties under review. He was trying and she appreciated every minute of it.

Even though he was kept busy most of the day, he made sure to show up for dinner every night. They didn't always sit near each other, making sure to interact with various wolves, but she could constantly feel his eyes on her, watching her.

They hadn't had intimate contact since their forced kiss in his office, and she was beginning to go a bit crazy. Luckily, he started sleeping in their bed again, each time holding her tightly as they both slept comfortably in one another's arms. The bit of nightly skin contact was enough to prevent her from going insane, but she still craved a deeper, more intimate encounter with the man.

It was early in the morning. An hour before training was supposed to start and already she was in Gabriel's office discussing the continuous rogue sightings. They were still staying on the other side of the border, a hundred yards out, but still there. The Wandering Moon Pack, as well as other neighboring packs, were all reporting the same things. Rogues were gathering on the borders or passing through other pack's territories.

Given her nightly nightmares, it left her completely unsettled, frightened even. Each night was the same; the bodies, the vicious rogues. It was the same dream on repeat, and with the absurd number of rogue sightings in the last few weeks, she didn't know what to believe.

"If they attack, we'll lose more wolves than them," Amelia said, reading over the reports in front of her. According to the other pack's numbers, over a hundred rogues were massing across two states. "My brother got lucky no one was killed."

Gabriel walked around his desk, resting his hand against her shoulder, kneading the tension from her neck. Amelia couldn't help the moan that escaped her. Between the gentle prodding of his fingers in her skin and the automatic arousal she experienced every time he was near, she couldn't control herself.

"Amelia."

"Hmm?"

"You smell sweet," he whispered, his lips brushing against the sensitive skin where her shoulder joined her neck, hovering right over her mark. She knew he knew that was a sure-fire way to unravel her completely.

"Your point?" Amelia tilted her head to the side even more, allowing him better access.

He brushed his lips over her skin, kissing and sucking at the mark he placed, permanently marking her as his. She felt her knees tremble, her spine melting until she was sure there were no longer any bones left in her body to support her. She leaned back into him further. Something hard poked into her backside.

Unable to hold out any longer, she turned in his arms, capturing his face and luring him down. Their lips devoured one another whole. His hands gripped her by her waist, lifting her and setting her down on the edge of the desk. His fingertips dug into her back, tearing at the thin cotton shirt she had on.

Amelia tore his shirt in two, no longer able to withstand the material beneath her touch. She needed to feel him, needed to feel the warmth of his skin. She had been starved of his touch, dying of thirst, her body parched, and now she would be damned if he didn't quench it.

She bit his lower lip, earning her a throaty growl in her mouth. Her core was throbbing, begging for attention. Her arousal was heavy in the air, enticing him, telling him she was wet and waiting.

Gabriel didn't require any further encouragement. His hand grazed up her thigh, past the thin, breathable material of her shorts to her soaked panties. She was more than ready for him.

Amelia devoured him thoroughly with her tongue, slipping past teeth, tasting the coffee and danish he ate earlier. She gasped in his mouth as she felt his fingers slip past her wet slit, traveling up into her core. She grabbed on tightly to his shoulders, her nails digging into his back as she leaned back on one arm against the desk, arching her back.

Gabriel observed her as he flexed his fingers inside. Her aromatic smell overpowered every one of his senses. He'd been dying to touch her, dying to take her every time he laid eyes on her, but he'd been patient. Afraid to push her before she was ready. Judging by her reaction, she was more than willing.

Amelia held onto him and the lip of the desk tightly, sure to break the sturdy oak beneath her. His touch was firm. Responsive to each elicit moan, every gasp, every spasm. He moved within her like a man desperate to please, desperate to make her scream his name. At this point, she just might.

She was near the tipping point, the tips of his fingers grazing, flicking, prodding her sweet spot. Amelia leaned into him further, grinding her body and his hand along with it against his rock-hard member. Gabriel snarled at the contact, his own groan lost in her panting.

The office door flung open.

"Hey, Amelia, you're gonna be la... Oh, my God!" Christian's eyes were bug-eyed, wide, and terrified at what he was witnessing.

"Get the fuck out!" Amelia screamed, her orgasm already fading, diminishing before she had reached her peak.

Gabriel growled. His Alpha voice shook the walls. Christians inner wolf immediately tucked tail, exposing his soft underbelly.

"Sorry!" Christian yelled, slamming the door shut behind him.

Gabriel withdrew his fingers, her arousal already dissipating from the room. The mood was dead.

Amelia propped her head against his hard chest. The hairs tickled her nose. She sighed deeply, struggling to calm herself and Rey. Her wolf was pissed, ready to rip Christian's head off for interrupting a moment with their mate.

Gabriel rubbed calming circles into her lower back until she was able to relax once again.

"Training," Gabriel said, his breath skimming across the top of her head.

"I'm going to slaughter him," Amelia gritted her teeth.

Gabriel chuckled, making her head bounce against his chest. She pulled back, looking up at him. She expected him to be mad, angry, something. But instead, he was just looking down at her with laughter in his eyes; his lips pulled up into a smile. It was a smile she wanted to see every day for the rest of her life.

"Why are you not mad?" Amelia couldn't help but ask.

"Oh, I am. I could throttle him right now. But, I'm just happy to have gotten such a reaction out of you," he said, smirking.

Amelia couldn't help but smile in return. "Why would you think I wouldn't?"

"It's just nice to see. To know that I have the same effect on, as you do to me," Gabriel spoke, his voice low and husky. His eyes shifted once again as he ran the tips of his fingers, still slick with her need, down the length of her spine.

Amelia shivered in response, leaning back into his touch. Her arousal once again filled the air.

"Training!"

Amelia glared daggers through the door, wishing she could shoot laser beams from her eyes, smiting her friend down. She looked back to Gabriel, who was now full-on laughing at her. Not even two seconds ago, he practically had her dripping for him once again.

Amelia snarled, knocking him back, causing him to stumble into the wall behind them. But it didn't seem to faze him. Gabriel continued to laugh.

"Stupid mate bond," Amelia growled, straightening her clothes out as best she could before turning for the door. "You'll pay for that," she informed him over her shoulder before leaving him in the office.

Standing in the hall was Christian. His face beat red with embarrassment, his eyes glued to the hardwood floors, refusing to meet her gaze.

Amelia wasn't ready to forgive him, either of them. "I'm going to go shower. I will meet you outside in ten."

(((

Running outside, she caught sight of the warriors already gathered in the clearing; Christian was beginning to pair them off.

"Wait!" Amelia called out, causing them all to stop mid-step.

Christian caught sight of her, the tips of his ears reddening by the second. Amelia ignored his embarrassment and addressed the group.

"Today, we're going to start doing things a bit different," she said to the seventy-odd warriors present. It wasn't even a third of their warriors, but it was impossible to train them all at once. Instead, they were rotated out every day.

"What do you have in mind, Luna?" Asked one of the more considerable warriors, Rick. He was the man who challenged her the first day of training, the one whose forearm she snapped during her demonstration. Now he was one of her biggest supporters.

"I'm sure most of you already know about the rogue sightings around the territory. It's not just us that's having an increase in rogues. Many of the territories surrounding us are experiencing the same thing." Amelia paused, honey apples and cinnamon engulfed her, letting her know he was approaching.

Gabriel came up to stand beside her, tucking his arm around her waist, pulling her in against him. His touch alone was enough to set her skin on fire, igniting the embers, ready to be stoked into a raging inferno.

No! Stop it! Amelia told herself, convincing her body to focus.

"Amelia is right. Many territories from here to the Wandering Moon, up towards the Crescent Wolves, are all reporting the same things. Rogues are gathering," Gabriel announced.

The wolves in attendance began to whisper amongst themselves, voices rising in fear and anxiety.

Amelia regarded the wolves in front of her. The smell of fear choked the air. She couldn't allow them to lose their heads. Now was not the time to let fear cloud their judgment. Rey came forward, her aura stretching out over the wolves' present.

Before her eyes, the wolves instantly calmed, giving her their undivided attention.

"What was that?" Gabriel leaned down, whispering in her ear.

Amelia's mouth hung slightly open, her eyebrow raised. "I don't know," she whispered back to him before turning back to the now relaxed group of wolves. "Since the threat of a rogue attack is very real, we will be shifting our training tactics. Typically when we train, we work on learning to take down a wolf, learning how to get them to quickly and efficiently submit. That won't work with rogues."

Amelia left Gabriel's side, pacing in front of the wolves. Their eyes followed her every movement, their breathing timed with her own. Her nightmares were at the forefront of her mind.

"Rogues are void of humanity. They no longer feel pain. The only thing that will stop a rogue is death."

"Luna!" One of the younger warriors, a redhead she distinctly remembered rearranging his family jewels, extended his hand. "Have you fought a rogue before?"

Amelia glanced back to Gabriel, who nodded his head, offering her his support. She turned back to the group. "Your Alpha and I eliminated one a couple of weeks ago."

"Did it hurt you?" A female voice lost in the crowd asked.

"Obviously not. She's here breathing, isn't she?" Another female snickered.

"Yes, the rogue did injure me. I would be dead if not for Gabriel. He managed to distract the wolf long enough for me to deliver a kill shot," she admitted to them all. "This brings me to my point. When fighting other packs, were taught to engage them head-on. Rogues, we can't do that with. We have to fight together as one body. One rogue could easily kill five warriors if those warriors attack separately, but together, working as a team, we could hold our own."

Stepping forward by her side once again, Gabriel addressed his pack. "From now on, until the threat of the rogues has passed or they attack, we will be changing our training to learn to work together. How to fight with one another, using each other's strengths and weaknesses to our advantage," Gabriel said. "Rogue's are mindless beasts, but we're not, and that is how we win."

"From now on, each of you will start to carry silver knives with you wherever you go. It's better to be prepared than caught unaware," Amelia said, reaching down into her own shoe and pulling out a thin, silver switchblade, flicking it back and forth in her hand. "They may be without their humanity, but they're still werewolves. Silver is just as deadly to them as it is to us. A silver blade might just save your life. So, get comfortable carrying them."

Amelia tucked the blade back into her shoe before straightening herself out. "I want you all to break up into groups of four. One of you will be the rogue, and the other three will work together to eliminate the target. Go."

The warriors didn't waste any time, dividing amongst themselves into groups of four. She stepped forward to join them, to demonstrate various techniques, when a hand grabbed her arm, pulling her back around.

Amelia looked up to find Gabriel, his arm already snaking around her waist and held her tightly. She looked around nervously, some of the wolves eyeing her, smirking at the intimate position she was in.

"Gabe," she hissed softly, trying her best to keep her voice under control.

"Do you know what you're doing to me in that top of yours? In front of all these males?" Gabriel huffed, his voice deep and thick, his silver eyes pooling with lust.

Amelia smirked, folding her arms, pushing her breasts up higher. "Karma's a bitch, isn't it?"

Gabriel smirked as well, his canines elongating past his lower lip. His wolf was just beneath the surface, ready to come forth and claim what is his. Rey responded in kind, her eyes shifting to that of her wolf. Large emerald iris. Her aura grew around them, encasing them in a warning to everyone present. They belonged to each other and no one else.

"You're just full of surprises, aren't you?" Gabriel asked, his canines already retracting, his wolf responding to his mate's dominance.

"Sometimes even I surprise myself," Amelia admitted truthfully, not quite sure what any of it meant.

Gabriel leaned in, brushing the tip of his nose against hers, breathing her in.

"Go out with me tonight."

Amelia pulled back, her brow furrowed. "What did you just say?"

"Go out with me tonight, Amelia."

"Like a date?"

Gabriel chuckled. "Yes, a date."

Amelia couldn't help the smile that pulled at her lips, a rosy flush heating her face. "Okay."

"Good," he brushed his lips on the tip of her nose before pulling back.

Amelia cleared her throat, trying to refocus, trying to ignore the jittering, giddiness she was experiencing. "We should train now," she said, pointing over her shoulder.

"Not like that you're not," Gabriel advised her, adding a deep growl to enhance his warning.

"Silly Alpha, don't you know I'm already yours?"

CHAPTER 24

SAFETY RULES

"Did he tell you where you're going?"

Amelia stuck her head out of her closet to find Kelsey running her fingers along her bookshelves, perusing through the titles. She noticed her reach for the worn leather binding.

"Don't touch that one."

Kelsey jumped at the sound of her voice, jerking her hand back as if she'd been bitten.

"It was my mom's; it's extremely fragile. You can touch anything else, just not that one," Amelia smiled before ducking back inside the closet. "And no, he didn't tell me where we're going. He just said, 'dress casual.'"

"What does that even mean? Casual could imply a million things," Kelsey complained, her voice exceptionally high.

Amelia chuckled. The girl wasn't wrong.

Kelsey had already curled her hair into long, loose beach waves that gave her hair some great body. She hadn't gotten dressed up in weeks and felt like a new woman.

Kelsey clapped her hands excitedly as Amelia exited the bathroom, complete and ready to go.

"Damn, girl, you clean up well," Kelsey smiled, pointing at her up and down.

Kelsey wasn't wrong. After training, she looked like she had taken a mud bath, caked in dirt, with leaves and twigs sticking to her body. Training was intense, but extremely productive as each of the warriors took the new training seriously.

"Thanks," Amelia said, bouncing back on her heels. "You think he'll like it?"

"I don't think he'll be able to keep his hands off you."

Rey licked her lips in anticipation. Amelia bit down to keep from smiling; her face already beet red. That was the plan. Being edged earlier had made the heat between her legs nearly unbearable. She tried to lessen the sting in the shower but was incapable. Her body demanded him and only him.

"Hopefully it's not too casual," Amelia said. She took notice of Kelsey's blank stare. "What is it?"

"Alpha is waiting for you downstairs!" Kelsey squealed, nearly jumping up and down.

Amelia pursed her lips, tugging on the bottom of her top, fidgeting with the fabric of her tight-fitting corset. She suddenly felt extremely nervous. Every part of her wanted this date to go well. It wasn't just about the sex. A part of her wanted more of him than just his body. She wanted to understand the man.

Kelsey took notice of her friend's composure, instantly forcing herself to settle down. "Are you okay? You seem nervous."

"What if we have nothing in common?"

"The Moon Goddess would not have given you Gabriel as a fated mate if you two had nothing in common. There's a reason you two are bonded together, trust in that," Kelsey smiled, playing with the ends of one of Amelia's curls that lay over the black fabric.

"Thanks, Kels."

"Anytime, now get out of here."

Amelia took in a deep breath before leaving the safety of her bedroom. She rushed down the first few flights of stairs, but forced herself to slow down the last treads, taking each step with as much control and concentration she could muster.

Finally reaching the main floor, she spotted Gabriel waiting near the front door with his back to her. He must have caught her scent because the next instant, he spun around to face her.

If she ever thought he was good-looking before, she was dead wrong. His tall, hard frame was tailored to perfection in a tight-fitting silver button-up shirt. The sleeves were rolled up against his biceps. His tattoo peeked out just beneath the fabric. His shirt was tucked into a pair of fitted blue jeans, a simple black belt tying it all together, with hard leather boots.

Gabriel's ebony hair was arranged back from his face, allowing her to clearly see his silver irises that were currently taking her all in. If he kept looking at her like he was, undressing her with his eyes, they'd never make it out of the house.

She reduced the distance between them; his eyes never wavering from hers. They weren't fixated on her breasts or her curves; no, they were simply possessing her eyes. As if he could really see her. See straight down in the depths of her heart—the place where his name was beginning to engrave its way into her every beat.

"You look beautiful," Gabriel stated, his voice deep, dripping down her spine.

Amelia smiled, her stomach twisting wildly. She took one last lingering look. Now that she was closer, she could see the small scar just above his left eyebrow. The bump in the ridge of his nose where he broke it in the past. The outlines of his tattoo shadowing against the light color of his shirt.

"You look stunning," she breathed.

"Let's get of out here. Unless you want our night to end before it even begins," Gabriel flirted, arching a suggestive brow.

Amelia scoffed, rolling her eyes. "The night better consist of food, or you'll endure the longest dry spell of your life."

Gabriel chortled, offering his arm out for her to take. "I hope you like buffalo wings."

Amelia felt her insides humming for the man beside her. Her heart fell just a little bit harder as she looped her arm in his. "Does a bear shit in the woods?"

Gabriel continued to chuckle under his breath, causing Amelia's heart to race in her chest. Her hands were feeling clammy. Being so close to him and touching him in such a casual way had butterflies fluttering in her stomach.

Could it really be this easy between the two of them?

Outside, a black full cab, 4x4 F-150, was parked in the driveway, the engine already running.

Gabriel opened the passenger door for her. Amelia refused his hand, pulling herself up into the cab. He mumbled under his breath, something that sounded like, "stubborn woman," before shutting the door behind her.

Amelia ignored his comment with a smirk and took in the interior of the truck. It looked brand new. The dash was shiny and sleek, the seats unblemished. It even had that new car smell. She buckled herself in nervously. Never had she been in a vehicle so high off the ground.

Gabriel climbed in the truck behind the wheel. He glanced across the truck at her, noticing her knee jigging up and down. He reached out, placing his hand over hers, instantly quieting her jitters.

"Nervous?"

"No," Amelia scoffed, her reaction too quick, revealing her lie.

"You said you wanted to get to know me, right?"

"Yeah," Amelia dragged the word out, suddenly more nervous.

"Well, now's your chance," Gabriel pulled on the gear shift, transitioning the truck from park to drive and slowly pulled away from the house.

For as big as the truck was, the ride was surprisingly smooth, the shocks absorbing every minor bump in the road. The drive was quiet. Gabriel's hand rested comfortably over hers on the center console.

An hour later, the truck pulled into an empty gravel parking lot. A large red and black bullseye painted on the side of the white cinderblock building.

Amelia looked to Gabriel, eyes wide. Was this a joke?

He brought us here to kill us.

Rey scoffed. *He wouldn't hurt us. You need to learn to trust him. Follow his lead.*

I don't like following. She grumbled internally.

Who cares? Do it anyway. It might be nice to surrender to someone else finally.

Amelia had a feeling Rey was no longer talking about their date.

Gabriel was already out of the truck, walking around the vehicle, opening her door. Amelia unbuckled herself before sliding out of her seat, landing neatly on the pebbled ground. He opened the back door, pulling out two black hard cases, one considerably larger than the other.

"Follow me," Gabriel beckoned her with a tilt of his head, a case in each of his hands.

Amelia gathered the courage she lacked and followed after him inside the desolate building. The interior was much like the outside, bare and lacking in decor. Inside was a row of lockers, sizes assorted, lining both walls of the entrance hall. At the end of the hallway, she saw a counter and a metal door on the right.

Behind the counter sat an older gentleman, his hair buzzed short, his skin brown, and tough as leather. The man noticed Gabriel and smiled, his face instantly twisting from a bored bystander to a friendly face.

"Gabriel, good to see you again, son."

Gabriel nodded in acknowledgment to the gentleman. "Howard, how are you?"

"It's been a slow night," Howard grumbled.

Amelia stepped out from behind Gabriel, meeting Howard's steely gaze. The man instantly smirked at her appearance. "You've never brought a lady friend here before. She must be something special."

"She is," Gabriel said plainly, without a drop of sarcasm.

"Lane 1 and 2 are available. You know where everything is," Howard gestured to the door on their right. His hand slipped beneath the counter, releasing a buzzing sound.

Gabriel pushed the unlocked door open with his backside, holding it open for her.

"Thanks Howard."

Amelia slipped past Gabriel, through the door, and into a well-lit room. It was the size of a bowling alley, with stalls sectioning off each row. She walked up to the stall with the number one painted into the wall, coming face to face with a chest-high counter. It looked down a narrow alley, straight to a target hanging on the wall.

Behind her, she found Gabriel propping his black cases on a table, unlocking them to reveal guns and ammo lying safely on a bed of black foam.

"You've got to be kidding me," Amelia faltered, her mind racing.

"Have you never shot before?" Gabriel asked over his shoulder, busy assembling the gun parts into one cohesive weapon.

"No! Why would I need to shoot when I have claws? Guns and wolves do not mix."

Amelia crossed her arms over her chest and watched as he expertly assembled the various parts. Pushing the magazine in with a quick flick of his wrist, he cocked the weapon, ready to fire.

"Please don't tell me my mate is anti-guns," Gabriel pleaded with the universe, going as far as to look up to the ceiling and beyond.

"I'm as American as they come. I believe everyone has the right to bear arms and defend themselves. I've just never felt the need to handle them, much less fire one."

"Well, today we're going to change that," Gabriel held out the Glock in his hand.

Amelia stared at the gun warily, as if the metal deathtrap would fire at will. Gabriel noticed her apprehension, his lips twitching, trying not to smile. He rotated her body, facing the target head-on, sliding a pair of what looked like headphones over her ears. The sound was muffled, but thanks to her uncanny werewolf hearing, she could still hear him clearly just behind her.

Carefully, he placed the gun in her right hand, guiding her pointer finger to rest along the smooth barrel.

"Rule number one, always treat the weapon as though it's loaded. In fact, this one is loaded. Which leads me to rule number two. Keep the muzzle pointed in a safe direction. Don't point at anything you're not willing to kill," Gabriel brought her left hand around, wrapping her hand around the bottom of the pistol grip.

"Rule number three?" Amelia breathed, trying to focus on the loaded weapon between her palms, but her body couldn't ignore his surrounding hers.

"Keep your finger off the trigger until you're ready to shoot. Triggers are sensitive creatures. The slightest pressure can set it off, so keep your finger off until you're sure of what you're shooting at," he instructed.

Gabriel straightened her right arm, locking the joint, elevating it so that her sight looked down along the slide of the gun. "The final rule, always be aware of your surroundings. Anything can happen when you're shooting, so constantly be aware of what's going on around you."

Amelia felt him step back, releasing her arms to wield the gun on her own. She felt oddly empowered. A gun in the wrong hands, could be either a force of mass destruction or a tool used to protect and defend.

"Now, use your dominant eye and close the other. Line up your weapon with your target. Exhale, pause, and shoot."

Amelia steadied her breathing, Gabriel's voice was calm and steady behind her, offering her additional support. Closing her left eye, she focused her right down the gun's slide, lining up the middle point with the target ten meters out. Aiming for the bullseye, she took in an even, steady breath and exhaled. Holding her breath, she brought her pointer finger down and squeezed the trigger.

The gun recoiled in her hands, jarring her to the bone. The weapon packed a bit of a punch, stinging muscles she didn't even know she had. She looked over the weapon and examined the hole her bullet left in the target. Slightly askew, off by a few inches to the left.

Amelia narrowed her eyes at the target. She would not allow a piece of paper, only ten meters away, best her. Raising the gun back up to her line of sight, adjusting her stance, she carefully gripped the butt of the weapon. Exhaling fully, she paused, holding her breath, and squeezed the trigger again. This time she continuously squeezed the trigger, refusing to inhale, keeping her right eye levelled down the sight, aiming for the bullseye.

Lowering the empty weapon, keeping it secure at her side, her trigger finger resting along the side of the barrel, she narrowed her eyes down the lane. Six out of ten bullets tore a hole through the middle of the target. She couldn't resist the smile that tugged at her lips, pride swelling inside of her.

Guns had always made her nervous. Hunters were prone to use silver bullets on their kind, hunting them down like animals. But now, after having shot one, she didn't feel so intimidated as when she first walked in to the shooting range.

That is until she turned around.

Gabriel stood behind her, a smile plastered on his face, grinning from ear to ear. Clearly, he was proud of her for shooting so well, but that wasn't what caught her off guard. The large, heavy-duty, tricked out sniper rifle he held between his hands had her heart hammering in her chest. It was angled with the barrel pointed down, away from any visible targets.

The way he supported the rifle with an air of confidence and familiarity unnerved her. It was one thing to shoot a small handgun, but the weapon in his hands was for an expert marksman. Someone trained to kill.

"That was impressive, Amelia. You're a natural," Gabriel praised her.

The sound of his voice snapped her out of her own thoughts. She carefully placed the handgun back down in its case, resting it on the black foam lining.

"Thanks," she smiled timidly, unable to tear her eyes from the rifle.

Gabriel followed her line of sight, the smile fading from his face. "Are you scared?" he asked her for the second time that night.

"No," she said with confidence, this time meaning it. "Just curious how you know all of this. Guns aren't exactly a weapon of choice in our world."

"They're not, are they?" Gabriel pondered aloud, glancing down at the high-powered rifle in his hands. "Come on."

Gabriel began walking down the hall, past the endless stalls.

"What about our stuff?" Amelia called to him, her voice echoing off the cement walls.

"Don't worry. Howard doesn't allow anyone in when I'm visiting," Gabriel responded over his shoulder, his stride not slowing.

Red flag? Maybe.

Amelia jogged to catch up to him, just as he pushed through another steel door. The sun blinded her for a moment. She quickly blinked the white spots from her vision and her eyes focused on their surroundings.

They were outside, behind the shooting range. The sun was hanging low in the sky, making its steady descent. The rays of light painted a beautiful canvas of oranges, reds, and yellows. Gabriel continued walking out into the abandoned field. It was stripped of all signs of life, targets placed hundreds of meters out, stretching farther and farther back along the property until they were no longer visible to the naked eye.

Amelia followed him until they came upon a mat in the dirt, marking their place to stop. Gabriel immediately settled down on his knees, lifting the weapon as he moved. He extended what looked to be a metal kickstand along the rifle, propping it open. Positioning the rifle on the ground, he laid flat down on his belly, the butt of the rifle pushed into the crook of his shoulder.

Without waiting to be told, Amelia laid down beside him, making sure they didn't touch. The last thing she wanted was to be a distraction. But she observed him. How precise he was with his body, as though his movements were pure muscle memory. The brain no longer needed to process the motions. The body already knew what to do.

Gabriel fiddled with the scope on the rifle, adjusting it as he looked down its glass. The bulk of his weight was held in his shoulders. His forearms were parallel with the ground, supporting the rifle's weight evenly. She watched as he made slight adjustments to his posture, rounding his shoulders back, the tilt of his head as he pressed his check along the barrel, his knees shoulder-width apart, one slightly bent more than the other.

She listened to his breathing, his heart beating at a steady rhythm. He exhaled slowly, and at the end of his breath, he squeezed the trigger. A sharp popping that reminded her of a firework rang across the vast space. Thanks to her enhanced sight, she could see the six-hundred-meter target. A wooden board in the shape of a man with a hole straight between the eyes.

Gabriel readjusted himself, modifying the scope for the next target, eight hundred meters out. He continued firing for the next hour. Each time aiming for something farther away and each time hitting his mark straight between the eyes.

Amelia couldn't help but stare and watch with fascination. Even though a part of her was a bit freaked out by her mate's ease and expertise with the high-powered rifle, most of her was just downright turned on. His control and fluid movements with which he handled the weapon had her wondering what else he might be fluid in with those hands.

Gabriel finally pulled away from the rifle. Deep, red lines cut into his cheek where he'd been resting against the barrel and caught her eye. His eyes were black. Amelia looked elsewhere hastily, her cheeks reddening.

"I think that's enough for one night," Gabriel said, his voice deep and filled with unquenched desire.

He pulled himself up off the ground, his body stiff and rigid as he tried to sit up. Lifting the rifle, he closed the kickstand, rocked back on his heels, and stood up straight, shaking his body out. Audible cracks and pops could be heard as he loosened his stiff muscles.

Amelia straightened herself out as well, patting the dust off her shirt and jeans, pulling the corset down into its original position since it had crept up from laying down for so long. A deep growl caught her attention, causing her to look up from herself, only to be met with his eyes fixated on her body.

Amelia swallowed hard. His gaze unraveled something inside of her, causing her breath to hitch in her throat, her heart to flutter erratically against her breast. She cleared her throat, looking up at the sky behind him. The sun was officially set. The sky now painted in oranges, purples, and blues.

"We should get going. You must be starving," Gabriel cleared his own throat, fighting for control over his body and wolf.

"I am."

She just wasn't sure for what.

CHAPTER 25

SOLDIER BOY

Gabriel made quick work of disassembling the weapons, arranging them back in their cases, and locking them up once again. Amelia sat back and watched, admiring how his hands carefully worked over the seemingly harmless metal, springs, and pins.

"You ready to get out of here?" Gabriel asked, catching her staring.

"Uh, huh," Amelia smirked, unashamed. She was his mate after all; what did it matter if he caught her watching him.

He carried the two hard cases. Amelia hurried ahead of him, pulling open the door to their exit. Howard still sat behind the counter, now flipping through some gun magazine.

"Good night, Howard," Gabriel smiled at the gentleman.

"Enjoy yourself, kids," Howard called out to them as they made their way to the exit.

"Bye, Howard. Thank you!" Amelia turned back to the older man, waving, before turning back, exiting the building entirely.

Outside, Gabriel was already loading the cases in the truck's back row and opened her door, waiting. Climbing up into the truck, she felt his hand graze along her ass, before snapping back, sharply smacking her. Gasping, she sat in the cab, her but stinging from the contact. Looking down at him, her mouth gaped open.

"What the hell was that for?"

"Quit being such a tease," he growled under his breath.

"Me? Being a tease? All I did was say goodbye to the man!" Amelia chortled, unable to believe his jealousy.

"Yes, and I'm sure he's now in the back, flipping through a playboy magazine with you in mind," Gabriel suggested, his left eyebrow arched high.

"You're disgusting," Amelia scrunched her face, the visual permanently ingrained in her mind.

Gabriel chuckled, slamming her door shut. Amelia buckled herself in, still unable to erase the sick image in her head. Even Rey wanted to hurl.

"So, where to now?" Amelia asked, watching him get in the truck and start the engine.

"I promised you buffalo wings, didn't I?"

"You did."

"There's a bar not far from here. They've got some of the best wings I've ever had."

"You're taking me to a bar?" Amelia raised a brow, her lips pulling up into a teasing smirk.

"Not okay?" Gabriel asked, doubt obscuring his face.

"No, no. I'm just surprised. Bar sounds great," and she meant it. She wasn't typically into the flower petals and candlelight, finding both extremely cheesy and stereotypical. A bar meant comfort food, alcohol, and easy conversation.

Gabriel still didn't look so sure when he pulled away from the gun range and back onto the main road. They drove for another ten minutes when Amelia spotted signs for Fort Drum. They really were far north.

A sign indicated the post was five miles ahead when they pulled into a dingy bar named *The Pony*. Surprisingly, the parking lot was packed. Car bumpers loaded with military plates and back seats filled with camouflage uniforms occupied the lot.

Gabriel pulled the truck all the way to the back, away from any street lamps or cars that could dink the giant. Amelia slid out of the truck, walking around the beast to meet him by the tailgate.

The bar looked like any other bar built on the side of a busy road. There was nothing particular that stuck out to her. She could hear country music from inside. The smell of fryer grease, cigarette smoke, and stale beer wafted from the kitchen's back door.

Amelia's stomach growled at the smell, alerting both of them to the fact that she was, in fact, starving. Gabriel chuckled beside her, resting his hand along her lower back, guiding her to the front entrance.

Inside the bar, the smells were more intense. If not for Gabriel's firm, steady presence beside her, she was sure she'd tip over. Cigarette smoke was heavy in the air, obscuring her vision. Her lungs felt heavy as the nicotine coated them, making her cough. They both spotted an empty bar height table tucked away in the corner of the room. It was farthest they could get, away from the couple smoking at the bar, and beelined straight for it.

Once settled on the wooden stool, Amelia was able to observe the patrons frequenting *The Pony*. Many men and women were in uniform, their camouflage pants and green cotton tee's made it obvious they were from the post just down the road. This was clearly a regular spot for the soldiers.

Amelia glanced over at Gabriel, watching him as he observed the crowd. He seemed relaxed in this atmosphere. A kinship reflected in his eyes as he watched the men in green shoot pool across the hall.

"Were you stationed at Fort Drum?"

Amelia caught him off guard. She could tell in the way he held his breath, his face blank and expressionless, as though he was figuring out a way to respond. But before he could answer, a cute brunette approached their table.

The waitress was tall, with long legs and silky straight hair. Her skin was perfectly tanned, blemish-free, and smelled like cotton candy, causing her nose to wrinkle. The girl's golden hazel eyes were focused on Gabriel. Her smile revealed everything she needed to know. They knew each other.

"Gabe! It's so good to see you again! How have you been?!"

Even her voice sounded beautiful. Amelia couldn't help but flinch at the use of his shortened name. Like someone had slipped a knife between her ribs.

Gabriel seemed unphased, smiling politely at the woman. "Gina, hey. How are you?"

"Oh, you know. Busy working," Gina said flippantly, waving her pen in the air. "I haven't seen you in six months.

Where did you disappear too? The girls and I missed you." Gina gestured to the two equally beautiful women behind the bar.

Amelia leaned back in her stool, crossing and uncrossing her legs. Rey was snapping in her mind, her fur bristling, ready to break the girl's neck like a twig.

Easy girl. Amelia cooed to her wolf. If Rey lost her shit, she wasn't sure how long she could keep her at bay.

Let me bite her.

No. We're not a rabid dog.

Oh, I'll show a bitch rabid.

Rey. Amelia growled at her own wolf.

If he thinks this impresses us, he's got another thing coming! Date my damn ass!

Amelia stared up at the ceiling, no longer wanting to watch the obvious flirting going on before her. She heard him laugh at something the waitress said.

Did he bring her here as some joke?

"Actually, Gina. My girlfriend and I are here together," Gabriel reached across the table, taking her hand in his.

Amelia jolted at the contact. The familiar tingles raced up her arm. Gina, for the first time, noticed Amelia sitting across from him. Her smile never wavered.

"Gabe has a girlfriend? Now I really have seen everything. We never thought you were the settling down type," Gina smirked suggestively.

"Guess it just took the right kind of woman," Amelia finally spoke, stunning the girl.

Gina's fake smile finally faltered, understanding her hidden meaning. She plastered on a feigned smile and pulled out a small pad from her back pocket. "What can I get you?"

"Buffalo wings, cheese fries, mozzarella sticks, and a draft beer, whatever you have on tap," Amelia recited, reading off the single page menu that lay on their table.

Gina's eyes widened at the order but kept her mouth shut. Wise choice. Gabriel was trying to conceal his amusement but was failing miserably. He ordered himself wings and a beer as well, sending Gina scampering away.

Amelia twisted her hand out from underneath his, rubbing the back of it against the rough denim on her thighs, trying to extinguish the feeling he left on her skin.

Gabriel frowned, visibly hurt. "What's wrong?"

Amelia scoffed, shaking her head. *Men are so fucking clueless.* "Did you just bring me here to rub it in my face?"

"Rub what in your face?" Gabriel asked, his frown cutting deeper lines in his forehead.

"Did you sleep with her?"

Gabriel's eyes widened in understanding. His gaze flicking between his mate and the waitress walking over with their beers. Gina was at least smarter than she looked, setting the beers down quickly and leaving them at once.

His silence was all the answer she needed. Amelia picked up her tall draft. The glass was chilled and filled with frothy alcohol. She chugged it down. Every last ounce. She didn't care who was watching or what they thought. All she knew was that she needed to feel the effects as quickly as possible, allowing the alcohol to numb her mind.

Gabriel watched her in stunned silence as she set her now empty glass down on the table. Amelia didn't appear to be fazed, let alone buzzed.

The tension between them grew to an unbearable degree.

"I'm getting another beer," Amelia left the table, collecting her empty glass with her, and approached the bar. One of the female bartenders, probably another one of his other hookups, accepted her empty glass from her and proceeded to fill her up with a new one. "A shot of tequila too, please."

Waiting for the beer and her shot, she felt a coldness bloom between her shoulder blades, dripping down her spine in an almost painful way. The hairs on her arms were raised. Rey bristled in her mind. Someone was watching her.

"Make that two. My tab Macy."

A masculine voice made the coldness recede instantly. Amelia looked up from the wooden counter to discover a man standing beside her, leaning against the sticky bar. The man's head had been recently barbered. It was shaved on the sides, leaving the top a few inches long. His baby blue eyes were sparkling in the dim lighting, looking glassy as ever, clearly drunk. He wore the typical green uniform of an Army grunt, his pants neatly tucked in his tan boots.

A shot glass was placed in front of them. Amelia tipped it to him in thanks before knocking the liquor back, enjoying the feel of it burning its way down her throat, hitting her empty stomach.

"You have the most radiant eyes I've ever seen," the man slurred, swaying where he stood.

Amelia couldn't help but giggle; his breath reeked of whiskey. "Thank you, yours aren't so bad yourself."

"Thank you," he said proudly, puffing out his chest. "Names, Riley." Setting his hand forward.

"Amelia," she replied, shaking his hand.

A deep growl erupted behind her, startling most in the room. Amelia turned around lazily to find Gabriel at her back. His eyes pitch black, and his upper lip pulled back. The beast within was ready to lunge.

Well, that escalated quickly. Rey chimed in, giddy over their mate's reaction.

Amelia confronted her mate, laying her hand on his chest. His heart thrummed beneath her fingertips. Not even her touch was enough to soothe him at this point. The human was too far gone, Ren, forcing his way to the surface.

"The fuck is your problem, man?"

She heard Riley behind her, but no one in the bar mattered. They couldn't risk exposure, and she wouldn't have a stranger's death on her hands because Gabriel was jealous.

Gabriel growled again, louder this time. Amelia noticed his claws coming through, his canines elongating. She didn't have long before he was fully shifted. By then, it would be too late.

Doing the only thing she could think of, she reached up on her tiptoes, entangling her fingers in his hair and pulled him down, pressing her lips against his. She kissed him hard, enticing him to move with her, licking his bottom lip for entrance.

Their soul bond opened between the two of them. She could feel his wolf, Ren, clawing at the surface of his mind. Rey slipped through the cracks, rubbing her conscience against his, instantly settling him down, encouraging him to enable Gabriel to come back. This was the mate bond she grew up hearing about.

She knew she got through to him when his arms winded tightly around her waist, pulling her up against his flat, hard body. His lips parted beneath hers, responding to her touch, her taste.

Amelia broke their kiss, breathing hard. Between the alcohol burning through her system and the fire of his touch, her head was swimming, pleasantly numb. She didn't need to look around to know that all eyes were on them. Between his beastly behavior and their public display of affection, it was obvious they attracted more than enough attention. But neither of them seemed to care.

All that mattered was the two of them together. Their bond still open, flowing freely between them.

Amelia grabbed her fresh beer from the bar top without a glance back, following him back to their table in the corner of the room. The bar instantly lightened, resuming its normal loud chatter.

Gabriel scooted his stool closer to hers, draping his arm around the back of her seat, pulling her into the crook of his body. Amelia rested her head on his chest, breathing him in deeply.

"I'm sorry," Amelia sighed, afraid to meet his eyes.

"No, it's me who should be sorry. I didn't think before bringing you here. I guess I forgot about the way single soldiers can act with alcohol in their system," Gabriel snarled, his eyes fixated on Riley across the room.

"It's not just the soldiers, trust me." By the way his breath froze in his chest; it wasn't the best choice of words. Amelia chanced it, pulling away and looking up at him. "What I mean is, I shouldn't be surprised you had a life before me. You *are* four years older. You've clearly seen more of the world, and have way more experience. It's only natural that you had relationships with other women."

"And that bothers you?" Gabriel asked her honestly.

Amelia shrugged her shoulders lightly. "Yeah, I guess it does."

"Why?" he asked.

"If I told you I wished I had more experience with men before meeting you, would you be upset? Goddess knows I had plenty of chances, lots of drunken nights to lose -"

Gabriel growled, his eyes already shifting.

Amelia pointed at his face, her face breaking into a smirk. "Ha, there! That's what I'm talking about. You can't stand the thought of another man touching me, but I'm supposed to not be jealous over the fact that you've slept with other women?"

Gabriel's eyes settled in their human form; his cool silver iris's softening. "Yes, I've been with a few women, but I can tell you one thing. None of them meant a thing to me. You're the only one who's managed to make me truly lose myself, to enjoy the moment."

Amelia nibbled on her lower lip, her cheeks blushing fiercely.

"Can I ask you something?" Gabriel asked.

"Sure."

"How come you never did it before? Before me, that is. What made you wait? Usually, that's impossible for wolves."

He wasn't wrong. When a wolf hit late puberty, it was nearly impossible to keep wolves from craving sexual gratification. Their wolves pushed them for any kind of stimulation.

"It just never felt right. I was with Daniel, a guy in my old pack for years. I'd known him my whole life. There were a few times we tried, but I would always stop. I just could never go all the way. Rey would always talk me out of it," she confessed.

"Your wolf?" he asked, taking the soft nod of her head as an answer. "She sounds like a smart wolf."

Mate was out there. We had to wait.

Rey's revelation surprised her. Her wolf knew all along that they had a mate out there, waiting for them. Now she understood better why Rey was never comfortable around other males. Constantly insisting they wait.

Gabriel tucked her hair behind her ear, rubbing his thumb along the tip of her ear. "I'm glad you saved yourself for me."

Amelia swallowed with difficulty, the moment interrupted by food being placed in front of them. The spicy buffalo wings just once again reminded her of how hungry she was. Wasting no time, she dug into the food. Gabriel ate his own silently beside her.

Appreciating the silence, they both sat and ate, enjoying one another's company. She could feel his occasional glances, watching her, taking in whatever details he could find. She wasn't sure what he was seeing. She just hoped she didn't have chicken stuck in her teeth.

Once her wings were picked clean, she sipped on her beer, picking at her cheese fries and mozzarella sticks.

"So, you served in the Army?" Amelia asked him once again, disrupting the silence.

"Four years."

"You joined when you were eighteen?"

"Yes."

"Why?"

It wasn't the most ridiculous question. Werewolves didn't typically outsource jobs. They usually stuck close to their packs, working in the pack owned businesses. She'd never heard of a wolf joining the human military, let alone a future Alpha.

"I was an out of control teenager. My wolf was wild. I was wild. I got into a lot of trouble as a kid. My father refused to make me Alpha until I could control my temper. Kaleb suggested joining the military. Maybe they could give me the structure and discipline I'd been lacking," Gabriel said. His body was in the present, but his mind was in the past. "So, I joined right after graduation. I'm pretty sure the school only passed me just to get rid of me."

Amelia smiled, but something was nagging at her. "What happened to your dad? I haven't seen him since moving to the pack."

Gabriel grunted, leaning back into his chair. "The old man split as soon as he made me Alpha. I haven't seen him since. Last I heard he was living in some cabin up in Canada somewhere."

"I never liked that old man," Amelia admitted candidly. "He was too quick-tempered and always looked so miserable."

She remembered visiting his pack a few times over the last few years with her father's Beta. Each time she disliked the Twilight Packs Alpha more and more. Judging from the few moments she spent with him and Gabriel's demeanor when talking about him, his father was abusive.

"And your mother?"

Gabriel's eyes softened, his face fell. "She died when I was twelve. She was human and developed breast cancer. By the time the doctors caught it, it was too late. It had already spread."

Amelia reached out, laying her hand over his against the table, giving it a light squeeze. "I'm so sorry," she knew what it was like to lose a mother. The grief was a terrible burden to bear. "What was her name?"

Gabriel smiled in remembrance. "Grace."

Amelia smiled as well. "That's a lovely name."

Knowing they were treading on dark and depressing waters, Amelia pressed on. "So, you joined the Army. Then what? You were a pretty great shot back there. Did that have anything to do with your job?"

"I enlisted in the Special Forces Unit and got recruited into the Delta Force. From day one, shooting was just easy. Gave me something to focus on. Calm myself. Every time I had a weapon in my hands; I was the one in control. My expert marksmanship caught the attention of a specialized group, and they enlisted me to be a sniper."

"Did you deploy?"

"A few times," Gabriel said flatly, unwilling to go any deeper. "After three stints overseas and four years under my belt, it was time to move on. My dad was getting worse, and the pack was struggling under his command. It was my time to be Alpha."

Amelia bobbed her head, dozens of more questions churning in her mind, but she held them back. They had plenty of time for all that. She was pleasantly surprised he opened up as much as he did.

"And you?"

She frowned, biting down into a mozzarella stick. "What about me?"

"Alpha commands clearly don't work on you."

Amelia choked on the fried cheese. The marinara sauce burned up her nose. She took a deep swig from her beer, chasing the rest of the food down.

"Goddess, can you at least warn me next time?"

Gabriel chuckled, but he was still quite serious. "You're not like other wolves, Amelia. The Moon Goddess paired us together for a reason," he said, hinting around something. "What else don't I know about you?"

"Well, my favorite color is lavender. Favorite movie is Terminator. I hate mushrooms. Slimy bastards. And I prefer cake over ice cream, every time."

He arched a brow at her, his lips pressed in a thin line. "While I appreciate the insight, I was suggesting something a bit deeper. Why does it seem that Alpha commands have no affect you? Why do you have an Alpha aura greater than any other Alpha I've met? And why is it that you can calm anyone with the slightest touch?"

Amelia reeled back in her seat, the temperature in the room suddenly dropping. Should she really tell him what she knew? Granted, it wasn't much, but her father had always instilled in her to keep everything about her and her brother a secret.

We can trust him. Rey interjected.

How can we know that?

Trust me, Amelia. I trust him. He would never do anything to hurt us.

Amelia inhaled deeply before biting the bullet and throwing her fate to the wind. "Fine, fine. Look, I don't know much. My mother died before I could ever think to ask her, and my father has always refused to talk about it. All I know is that I am a direct descendant of Rhea and Ezekial, and this gives me a certain connection to the Moon Goddess."

"Ezekial and Rhea? As in the first mated pair?"

"The very one."

"What do you mean, connection to the Moon Goddess? What can you do?"

"Well, I have the freaky connection with Damon. No matter how far apart we are, we can always mind link one another. He and I can also heal others. I can use it on my own, but he can only do it if he's connected to me. As far as the Alpha thing goes, I really don't know. Alpha commands have never worked on me, though I never let on until recently. And the aura, well, that's been a new development. Ever since we mated, actually."

"You think this has something to do with me? With us?"

"I don't know," Amelia shrugged her shoulders. "The story goes that Rhea inherited her abilities after they completed the mate bond. The Moon Goddess instilled in each of them gifts to complete the other. Ezekial was stronger, faster, bigger, his senses more honed than any other wolf. Whereas Rhea could heal from far distances, sense the future and receive visions from the Moon Goddess herself."

"Ya, but those are just stories," Gabriel insisted.

"So was the fated mate bond. Yet, every woman in my family has had one. Most of them were brutally murdered in some way. My father made me swear up and down to never tell a living soul about what I can do. There has to be a reason for that."

Gabriel cupped the back of her neck with the arm he had draping over her chair, forcing her to meet his gaze. "I would never let anyone hurt you."

The intensity of his glare spread ripples over her skin, trickling down every vertebra. "I know," she breathed, her voice soft and deep with need.

All this talk about fate and destiny, and their pasts, was all a wash. She was tired of waiting. Her unfulfilled desire from earlier that day was clouding her mind, bringing her arousal back in full force.

Gabriel's silver eyes darkened to orbs of onyx, his eyes wandering leisurely over her body.

"I think it's time to leave," Amelia said faintly, not sure when she started leaning into him.

"I think you're right."

CHAPTER 26

EVERYTHING I NEED

The drive back was torture. Amelia made sure to restrain her hands, folding them in her lap. The last thing they needed was for her to distract him and crash the truck. That wouldn't benefit either of them.

She could tell he was struggling almost as much as she was. The vein in the side of his neck was bulging against the thin skin. His knuckles were white, gripping the steering wheel with such force she was convinced it would break.

The hour was long, but soon enough, the Packhouse came into view. Amelia let out a breath of relief she hadn't realized she'd been holding.

Gabriel hastily pulled into the driveway, skidding to a halt in front of the porch steps. Amelia slid out of the truck, landing nimbly on the gravel drive. Gabriel was already standing beside her, shutting the truck door. He rested his hand on her lower back, the tips of his fingers pressing firmly into her skin.

Amelia couldn't help but lean back into his touch. Only for him to spin her around facing him. His hands gripped her waist, digging into her flesh, lifting her into his body as his lips crashed down on hers. She wound her hands up into his hair, gripping him harder. Her nails cut into the tender flesh of his neck.

"Inside, now," Gabriel gasped in her mouth, his voice deep and thick.

Amelia forced herself to turn away, his hands never once leaving her waist. He followed behind her, keeping her close and tight against him, his hard wood poking into her back. Her core was tight with an insistent throbbing, her arousal widespread and heavy in the air.

Gabriel slung the front door closed behind them, directing her straight for the staircase. It was too far away. She needed him now like she needed air to live.

"Boss."

Gabriel and Amelia stopped where they walked, their attention pulled away from their lust, from their desperate need, to find Kaleb, standing in the hall. The Beta held a manila file in his hand, looking expectantly at his Alpha.

Kaleb took in the scene he interrupted, his ears turning red as he caught a sweet aroma filling the air. He directed his eyes away from the mated pair, realizing he interrupted something intimate.

Amelia could recognize the displeasure coming from Gabriel, his chest rumbling beneath her back. She couldn't help but feel annoyed. Being interrupted twice in one day was leaving her murderous. At this rate, she was going to have to satisfy herself.

"Go ahead upstairs. I'll be right up," Gabriel whispered in her ear, his breath tickling her skin.

Amelia left him without a glance back. She headed straight for the stairs, seriously considering stomping her feet all the way up to her room, but decided against it. With her arousal permeating the air, she didn't want to attract any unwanted attention.

Inside her room, she shut the door behind her. The soft click was oddly comforting. Maybe a shower would help cool her off. It wouldn't be the first time she had to attend to herself.

Unzipping her boots, she placed her knives on the dresser and kicked the leather off in the direction of the closet. Ripping her socks off, she flexed her toes in the soft carpet. She hated shoes. If it were socially acceptable, she'd go barefoot everywhere.

Walking towards the bathroom, she undid her jeans, shimmying out of them as she shuffled across the floor when she heard the door shut behind her, a lock clicking in place. Amelia spun around with her pants halfway down her thighs. Her mouth hung slightly open at the sight of a tall, dark figure standing in her doorway.

She hadn't even bothered flipping on the lights. The moon's radiance streamed through the open windows coating him in a sterling hue, allowing his silver eyes to twinkle in the darkness.

"Where do you think you're going?"

Amelia tried not to react to the huskiness of his voice that caused her body to shiver deliciously. "Shower," she whispered, managing to regain her voice.

He stepped towards her, his face now outlined by the subtle lighting. His eyes were wicked with desire, hooded, and fixated on her jeans still pulled down her thighs.

"You weren't thinking of doing anything to yourself, were you?" he asked, clearly smelling her still present arousal.

Amelia stood up straighter, allowing the denim to fall loosely, pooling around her ankles. She stepped free, reducing the distance between them.

"What if I was? It may be the only way I'll ever get to finish," she challenged him, suggesting he was unable to complete the job.

Gabriel growled in response, just like she knew he would. He reached around, gripping her ass in his vast hands, lifting her until her legs wrapped around his waist. The bulge of him, concealed beneath a layer of denim, pressed against her weeping core. She moaned on contact as he escorted her to their bed.

Amelia kissed up and down his neck, nibbling and sucking on his mark. She could feel him shudder at the contact. The mark of a mate is one of the most sensitive parts of their bodies. He gently set her down on the bed, hovering over her as she laid back against the soft mattress.

He kissed her with unkempt yearning, his tongue doing wondrous things to her mouth. Leaving trails of kisses down the side of her neck, he brushed his canines against her mark, causing her to spasm beneath him, already near the tipping point.

Gabriel ran the tip of his tongue down her collarbone to her breasts, bulging out the top of her corset. He sucked on the exposed cleavage, pulling at the strings, loosening the stays until the corset was unraveled around her. In the blink of an eye, her chest was completely exposed. Ripping the shirt from underneath her, he hurled it to the floor.

Her nipples sprung up, fully exposed to the brisk air. Gabriel took his time with each of them, rubbing the firm buds between his teeth, pulling and sucking on them with fervor. Amelia gripped the comforter beneath her, her nipples sensitive against his touch.

Gabriel looked up at his stunning mate, her body already so close to release.

"Tell me what you want," Gabriel spoke softly, causing her to look down at him.

Amelia was breathing heavily; her skin felt like it was on fire as though all the blood in her body was sent directly to her core. "I want you to taste me."

Gabriel's full lips pulled into a smirk. He flicked his tongue down her stomach, tormenting her, peppering her with kisses along the top of her panties. Amelia pulled her legs up on the bed, her body urging him to initiate more immediate action.

She heard the sound of fabric tearing. Looking down, she found the remnants of her black silk thong.

"Really?" Amelia couldn't help herself. Did he have to destroy her clothes?

Gabriel shrugged, "They were in my way."

Before she could utter another word, his mouth was tasting her. His tongue licked her folds, flicking against her sensitive nub, burying itself in her sweetness. Amelia arched her back, covering her mouth with the back of her hand, burying her screams.

Gabriel stopped, causing her to sit up on her elbows, looking down at the dark form between her legs.

"Why'd you stop?!" her labored breath almost squealed with sexual frustration.

"Don't cover your mouth. I want to hear you," his voice reached her ears, unable to see his expression in the shadows.

"Fine, but if you stop again-" Amelia gasped, moaning loudly as his mouth closed over her most sensitive bit, licking, sucking, and blowing on it.

Amelia could feel herself ready to burst, knowing he was nearing the end game. She had been getting herself worked up all day long, and now, with his tongue eating every inch of her, she could finally let go.

Her orgasm tore through her body, her legs spasming as she rode the overwhelming waves. But Gabriel didn't stop there. He plunged a finger, then two past her folds, massaging her walls as his tongue continued to work its magic. She clenched hard around him, her legs shaking uncontrollably, clamping around his head, holding him in place. She was torn between begging him to stop and crying out to keep him going.

It wasn't long before she was cuming again, this one more powerful and longer than the last. Her hands were shaking, her throat hoarse as she struggled for breath.

None of that mattered; she still wasn't done. She needed to feel him, needed to feel his fullness.

Gabriel sat up, licking his lips like the ravenous wolf he was. Amelia ignored the weakness in her limbs and pushed past the exhaustion. This wasn't the end. It was only the beginning.

She stood off the bed to confront him as he stood. The man was still completely clothed. That wouldn't do.

Amelia smirked at his button-down shirt. Clutching his collar, she tore the shirt open, smiling at the satisfying sound of buttons tearing from cloth. Gabriel frowned at his now shredded shirt on the floor.

"Fairs, fair," she said plainly before getting on her knees.

Her fingers more confident than her mind as she undid his buckle, tossing it to the floor. She unbuttoned his pants, pulled on the zipper, and slid his jeans down to his ankles, where he gracefully stepped out. Standing at attention in front of her was his loose member. She bit her lip, forgetting he wasn't one to wear boxers.

Amelia stroked it gently, the skin softer than she imagined, like fine silk. The head was large and swollen, a single tear weeping, begging her to taste. She took as much of him as she was capable in her mouth, allowing her hand to tend to the rest of him. He tasted sweet and salty.

Gabriel moaned loudly above her, his fingers running through her hair, gripping her head by the roots. Amelia reached around with one hand, gripping his butt, causing him to jolt beneath her. She laughed, nearly choking on him in the process.

Suddenly, hands gripped her arms, hauling her to her feet. Amelia whimpered. She wasn't done.

Gabriel kissed her insistently, their tongues tasting each other.

"I need to feel you," Gabriel whispered against her lips, his hands tangled in her hair.

Amelia could feel Rey purring in her mind, her wolf eager to bond with his. "I'm all yours, Gabe. Always."

She rested her hand above his heart, their mate bond opening beneath her as he set her back on the bed once again. She could feel his need, desire, and longing for her heart, body, and soul. It was overwhelming, her head swimming with his thoughts, his emotions, his scent.

His fingers laced with hers over their heads pressed deep into the bed. Amelia squeezed his hands, wrapping her legs around him as he lined up with her core, her body more than willing to grant him entrance.

Gabriel pushed inside. Her walls instantly contracted around his member. Her body full, taking every inch as he buried himself deeper and deeper. Amelia moved with him, grinding her pelvis against his as he thrust into her depths.

His hands, still pinning hers above her, forced her to look up. Gabriel's eyes were fastened on hers, noting her every expression, every moan. He finally released their hands, his movements becoming more erratic, plundering into her soul.

Amelia winded one arm around his waist, digging her nails into his lower back. The other arm cupped the back of his neck, lacing her fingers in his now unruly hair that hung over his eyes.

She could feel his manhood throbbing inside her; both of them approaching their climax. She tugged him down, stealing his moans with a kiss. Their soul bond was completely open between them as their wolves joined as well.

Amelia flipped them over with inhuman strength and speed, straddling his body, barely missing a beat. Gabriel's eyes widened, a smirk playing on his lips but was quickly replaced by a moan as she began to move her hips in a circular motion. She gripped him by the back of his neck, elevating him until their chests, slick with sweat, were rubbing against one another.

She bounced in his lap, the tip of his manhood hitting a spot so deep she screamed in ecstasy.

Gabriel held her gaze. Amelia locked eyes with him, lost in the silver twin moons staring at her with such emotion. She could get lost in them forever.

As if reading her mind, Gabriel whispered, "You're everything I'll ever need."

Amelia felt her heart cracking wide up, picking up her pace. The pressure in her stomach was fit to burst, her walls quivering with stimulation.

Gabriel's breath hitched in his chest. He was ready. She could feel it.

Just as their climax's reached their apex, hers causing fireworks behind her eyes, his filling her to the brim with his warm seed, Rey slipped out, latching on to her mate's neck. Her canines buried in his flesh, ripping another orgasm from him.

Satisfied, she meant to retract her teeth when she felt a white, hot searing pain lance down her neck, reigniting her core. Once again, she spasmed in his arms. His grip on her tightened to prevent her from slipping.

She wasn't sure how long they stayed like that. His manhood, still buried inside her, their teeth puncturing each other's flesh.

When her heartbeat and breathing finally calmed, she extracted her canines, licking the fresh mark clean, sealing it with a kiss.

Gabriel did the same. The feel of his tongue on her skin made her insides hum, her body pleasantly numb.

They collapsed back on the bed, Amelia removed herself from him, laying down on her side. A small part of her wanted to go in the bathroom, clean up the mess between her legs, but the dominant part of her said fuck it. Lying blissfully in his arms.

Gabriel was right. This was everything she'd ever need, as long as she had him.

CHAPTER 27

SCRAMBLED EGGS

The forest was dark. Sinister shadows taunted her, beckoning her forward. The crescent moon hung low in the sky—a faint sliver of silver, contributing to the darkness that threatened to consume her whole.

Pine and sap. Twilight Moon scent.

The earth churned beneath her paws as she raced through the wood. The closer she got to the sounds, the more she could smell them. Blood and mildew. Rogues, her pack, the distinct tang of metal and salt penetrated the air. Blood.

Perking her ears, she could hear distant snarls. Wolves growled in warning. Jaws snapping as teeth sought after something to latch on. A familiar sound pulled at her heart, his whimper, crying out in pain.

The ground was blood red, her paws slipping as she got closer to the massacre. Bodies were scattered everywhere, as far as she could see. Rogues and pack members, each torn apart, broken necks. Fur colors were no longer visible, only red.

She looked around the sea of dead wolves, looking for the familiar obsidian fur. She couldn't find him.

A whimper came from behind, human and faint.

Spinning around, she encountered a small child. A young boy stood amongst the dead wolves, his bare feet drenched in blood. Tear tracks ran down his soot-stained face. His ebony hair was sticking out every which way. Sea-green eyes welled with tears.

A mud-brown wolf appeared from behind, creeping up out of the darkness.

"Mommy."

☾ ☾ ☾

Amelia's eyes bolted open, her body slick with sweat, her breathing labored. She looked around the room, taking in her surroundings. She focused on the sleeping form beside her, grounding her to the waking world. She was in their room, Gabriel sleeping blissfully beside her.

I'm home. I'm safe. It was just a nightmare. Amelia tried to tell herself.

They're getting worse. Rey said meekly, her voice fainter than normal.

I know, Rey.

It had been over a month since their arrival to the Twilight Moon Pack, and dreams still plagued her every night.

Amelia glanced down at Gabriel. His face was soft and smooth, free of stress and worry. He looked so peaceful asleep. Jet black hair hung across his forehead with his arm raised above his head. Her eyes traveled over his exposed upper half, their blanket only covering him from the waist down. His muscles were etched into his tan skin. Fine hair dusted across his chest.

"You're staring."

Amelia smirked. Gabriel's eyes were still perfectly closed, looking blissfully unaware, except for the slight tug on his lips.

"Can you blame me?"

Gabriel smiled. Before she had a chance to protest, he struck out, gripping her by her waist, pulling her body on top of his, straddling him. Amelia looked down at herself. The only thing protecting her body from him was a thin lavender bralette and matching panties.

Ever since their first date, they had been taking full advantage of one another, daily, usually multiple times a day. But last night, she had been so exhausted, she was lucky she was able to get out of her jeans before crashing on the bed. The nightmares didn't allow her a solid night's rest, and it was taking a toll on her.

Gabriel tightened his grip on her waist, flexing his hands against her skin, holding her firmly on top. Amelia twisted her hair over her right shoulder, knots, and tangles matted to the side of her head. Bedhead was definitely a problem.

"You were restless last night. Again," Gabriel said.

Amelia wasn't paying much attention. His morning wood was firm beneath her as she slowly rotated her hips, grinding against him. The feeling sent fire straight between her legs.

"Amelia."

"Hmmm?"

"Can you stop that for two seconds, please?"

Amelia pouted, sticking out her lower lip. "What?" she whined.

Gabriel chuckled, rubbing his thumb along her bottom lip. Amelia couldn't help but smirk. The man seemed to know exactly what to do, whether it was her begging him for release or smiling like a love-sick school girl. Either way, she reveled in it.

"I said, you were tossing and turning all night, mumbling in your sleep."

Amelia sat up a bit straighter, sucking her lip back in. "Was I?"

"It's been going on for weeks."

"It's just nightmares," she said, blowing it off.

"Every night?" he asked.

"It's nothing," Amelia said in frustration, wanting to move on from the subject. It was bad enough she had to experience them at night. She did *not* want to have to talk about them during the day. "Now, are you going to lay there and ask me about my dreams, or are you going to take advantage of the woman on top of you?"

Gabriel gazed at her hard, pitching her over onto her back, causing her to squeal in response before he made love to the woman of *his* dreams.

☾ ☾ ☾

Amelia skipped down the stairs, her racerback tank flowing around her. Unable to restrain the giddy feeling in her chest, her heart was full and content. If every morning began like this one, she would die one satisfied woman.

Strolling through the commons, fellow pack members bowed their heads in respect as she passed, offering each of them a smile in thanks. The smells from the dining hall reminded her of yet another need that had to be satisfied.

Her stomach churned in anticipation. Her hunger was so overwhelming it was bordering on nausea.

Amelia discovered the line to the self-serving buffet to be nonexistent.

Thank the Goddess. She prayed.

She beelined straight for the buffet, bypassing the dozens of tables filled with ravenous wolves. Grabbing herself a plate, she piled a heaping amount of scrambled eggs and toast onto the stoneware. The salty aroma filled her nose, making her nearly groan in delight.

The room was half full, with wolves eating and chatting quietly. Amelia spotted Kelsey's usual high ponytail and headed in her direction. Her friend was already midway through her own food, chowing down before training began. Today was Kelsey's rotation. She was a quick study and getting better every day.

Kelsey barely looked up from her plate as she sat down beside her. Not bothering to waste any time, she began shoveling the eggs in her mouth, nearly moaning aloud. They were whipped to perfection.

"That's a lot of eggs on that plate," Christian commented, taking the seat across from her.

Amelia glanced up at his own plate, her brow arched. "It's the same amount as you, doofus."

"Yes, but I eat eggs for breakfast every day; you don't."

Glancing down at what remained of her scrambled eggs, she frowned. She'd always hated eggs. The taste of them made her gag, growing up. It unnerved her that he noted something so subtle about her habits, and yet it left her feeling uneasy because he wasn't wrong.

Amelia shrugged her shoulders dismissively. "What's your point? I like eggs now. So what?"

Christian merely shook his head, his attention back to his own food. Amelia tried to ignore him, but his words left her feeling unsettled. It was just eggs. Why'd he have to go and make it weird?

She pushed her half-eaten plate away, nibbling on a slice of toast. Now she just really wanted to hit someone. If someone happened to be Christian, she wouldn't mind.

Glancing at the watch around her wrist, she noticed the time. Training. Finally.

Standing up from the table, along with most of the other wolves' present, she made her way outside.

The sky was cloudless. A perfect blue stretched across the sky. While the day was stifling. A typical New York summer. Her shirt immediately clung to her skin. She couldn't wait to shift and let her wolf out. The opportunity hadn't presented itself very often days, and she was itching with the need to run.

Today's group consisted of seventy wolves. Since her arrival and her female empowerment demonstration, more and more wolves had been joining the ranks, coming out of retirement. Especially given the rogue threat, no one was taking any chances.

Amelia started them off with their usual ten-mile run. Oddly enough, she had to push herself to complete the last few laps around the pack's borders. Her sides cramped, and her head felt fuzzy. She was already feeling fatigued, her muscles sore.

Stupid dreams. They were stealing her sleep, and now they were affecting her training. Her favorite part of the day. Now she definitely wanted to fight. To push through her body's fatigue and lose herself in a fury of teeth and fur.

Back in the clearing, the wolves congregated in the center for their morning brief. Most of them were barely winded as though they hadn't just sprinted ten miles. She used to feel like that. Right now, she wanted a nap, but she pushed that thought back to the remotest recesses of her mind.

"Today, we're going to focus on fighting in wolf form. I know we've all had our wolves for our entire lives, but trusting them completely can sometimes be hard to do," Amelia spoke clearly. Her voice rang out over the clearing, ensuring every wolf present could hear her.

"Surrendering ourselves, giving up complete control, is not easy for most. The human side thrives on control. But, if we want to be effective, cohesive fighters, we must learn to surrender completely. Wolves are brilliant creatures; pack members used to working as a whole. Their senses are unparalleled, their intuition flawless. Most of the time, they know what's going on before we do."

She could see she was getting through to them as most were beginning to bob their heads in agreement. "So today, we're going to focus on fighting as wolves. Allowing our wolf to take control of the situation. If you can't surrender to your other half, that can hurt you and your pack in battle. When you're in the middle of a fight, you don't have time to debate tactics. Wolves have better instincts than we ever will."

"You have ten minutes to shift before we break off into groups. At the end of the lesson, we'll break off into teams. Rogues against Pack. The two showing the most improvement will be team leaders. Rogues will go as savage as they can. The pack will work together to bring them down," Christian said, enticing them with a game.

The warriors were bristling with excitement. Most of them dropped their clothes where they stood, transitioning from mortal flesh to thick, coarse fur. The sound of bones cracking and popping as over seventy wolves shifted was audible. Some of the women, new to training, stepped behind the tree line, shifting in private.

Amelia followed suit, heading for the trees. Normally, before Gabriel, she would have joined the men, stripping her clothes and shifting in front of everyone present. But now, she had a mate who didn't appreciate her opinion on nudity, and honestly, she didn't blame him. She certainly didn't like the idea of him being naked in front of other women either. This was a healthy compromise.

Standing behind a clump of pine trees, she began to pull off her clothes until she was completely nude. She anticipated the usual pull of her bones as they morphed into a new shape. The pinching of her skin as it shed from smooth skin to fur. The elongating of her spine as it took on the shape of another mammal. But nothing happened.

Amelia frowned, her brows furrowed. She called on Rey, forcing her wolf forward, but nothing. No claws, no canines, no fur, nothing. She felt like one of those stupid anime characters that failed to perform a magic trick.

What the fuck?! Amelia screamed internally.

No.

What do you mean, no?

We're not shifting. Rey's tone was completely calm and firm.

What do you mean we're not shifting?! We're a freaking werewolf, and training is starting without us! We have to shift!

No.

Amelia's blood was boiling. Never before had Rey flat out refused her anything.

Are you serious right now?

Yes.

Amelia stomped her feet, pulling her clothes back on her body. Now, not only was she tired and moody, she was being denied the one thing that could put her in a better mood. Fighting was what she lived for, why she breathed. It was one of the only things that allowed perfect clarity. Her body's way of releasing stress and focusing all that energy into the one thing she was good at, kicking ass.

Storming out of the tree line, she could see every pack member in wolf form, ready to train. She spotted Christian's russet brown wolf and walked over to him. She still wasn't linked to the pack, which was becoming more inconvenient, but *he* at least understood her. He just couldn't respond.

"You're on your own today," Amelia gruffed, her arms crossed over her chest. If steam could come out of her ears, she's pretty sure it would.

Christian's wolf cocked his head to the side at her, his bushy eyebrows furrowed.

"I don't want to talk about it. You're just going to have to handle training without me today. I'll send Kaleb out to help."

Amelia noticed the wolf's sly grin. His lips pulled back into a wolfy smile as if he was in on some joke. She shoved him hard, nearly pitching him over before stomping her way back into the house.

What the fuck did he know?

Whatever was going on with Rey, Amelia could think of only one thing to help her calm down. She just hoped he was in his office.

CHAPTER 28

REY WON'T SHIFT

Amelia walked in through the back door. The house was silent; most wolves were outside training or working at the pack company's construction site.

She headed directly for his office, walking through the commons, when she spotted Gabriel heading straight for her. Stopping in her tracks, she froze, her brow furrowed in confusion. His eyes were dilated, his posture tense, and he was directing all of his nervous energy towards her.

Did something happen?

"Gabe, what are you doing here? I was just coming to see you," Amelia said, gesturing in the direction of his office.

Gabriel made his way to her. His hand instantly reached out, stroking her hair, cupping the back of her neck. "My wolf was freaking out. He was worried about you."

"Me? What about me?" Amelia asked, her heart pounded in her chest.

Rey?

It wasn't me. Rey said, still sounding faint.

"I don't know, he just said to check on you," Gabriel pulled her in against him, hugging her.

Amelia stroked his back; his body tense. He really was worried. What was going on with their wolves today? "Hey, I'm okay. Rey is just being fickle today."

"What do you mean?" he asked, pulling back, looking down at her, trying to read her face.

"I'll tell you in a minute. First, where's Kaleb?"

"He's in my office. We just finished our conference call."

"Great," Amelia took his hand, leading him back the way he came.

Inside the office, she found Kaleb sitting in one of the armchairs across from the desk, shuffling through papers on his lap. His chestnut hair hung in his eyes as his lanky frame hunched over his lap. He looked up at the sound of their approach, instantly standing up at the sight of her.

"Luna," Kaleb bowed his head.

"I'm not the Luna," Amelia reminded him. The topic was beginning to feel like a wound that was festering. "If you don't start calling me Amelia, we're going to have a problem."

Kaleb smirked. "Yes, Amelia."

"Would you mind helping Christian with training today?" she asked the Beta.

Kaleb frowned at her in confusion, obviously curious as to why she couldn't do it, but he was smart enough not to ask. "Of course. I'll head out now."

Kaleb bowed to both of them before vacating the office, shutting the door behind him.

Amelia felt Gabriel's hands gripping her arms, whirling her around to face him. His eyes were narrowed. The wrinkles in his forehead were more defined and his lips were set in a thin line as though he was biting the inside of his cheek. He looked baffled, even angry.

What the hell did he have to be angry about?

"What's going on, Amelia? Why aren't you out there training with Christian? Did he do something to you? Did one of the other males?"

Amelia sighed with annoyance, swatting at his hands that were gripping her too tight. Why did his mind repeatedly have to go there? "Stop it! No! There was nothing of the sort, now calm down."

Gabriel seemed to relax by a fraction, letting her go. But he still frowned with confusion. "Then why are you here and not outside?"

"What's wrong? You don't like spending time with me now?" she asked seductively, advancing toward him slowly.

"Amelia," he growled in warning.

Amelia rolled her eyes. She moved to his desk, leaning back on the firm wood. Remembering the last time she had sat on that very spot. The friction, the excitement, and then the disappointment.

"You are too damn easy to rile up. You know that, right?"

Gabriel ignored her, not giving in to her attempts at deflection.

"Fine," she hissed in annoyance. Such a buzzkill. She looked down at her black converse, admiring the dirt caked ties. For some reason, she didn't feel confident enough to make eye contact with him. "Rey won't shift."

Gabriel cocked his head back, his brow furrowed. Clearly not the answer he was expecting.

"What do you mean she won't shift?"

"We're supposed to be training in wolf form today, and when I tried to shift. I couldn't. She won't let me."

Gabriel shook his head, "I don't get it."

"Yeah, you and me both." Amelia leaned back on the desk, glancing at the papers strewn across the desk. She picked one up, reading over the notes. "More sightings?"

Gabriel ran his hand through his hair. The bags under his eyes were more pronounced than she remembered. The whites around his radiant silver iris were blood-shot. He looked drained, bone-weary. The rogue issue was becoming steadily greater and more alarming. "Yes. They seem to be headed south-east."

Amelia perked up, "But that's Wandering Moon territory." A cold sensation dripped down her back.

"I know. We're keeping ahead of it. Damon's doing everything he can to prepare his pack for an attack, and we're not that far away to respond if he needs help."

She took in a deep, quivering breath. Her mind flashing back to her nightmares. The dead wolves, the rogues. Was there something she was overlooking?

Gabriel reached out, sensing her distress, but she prevented him, laying her hand against his chest. "I'm fine."

Part of her wanted his comfort. To lose herself in him. Drown in his scent, his body. But she was stronger than that. If her brother's pack was going to be attacked, then they all needed to prepare.

She slipped off the edge of his desk, ignoring the pained expression on his face. She couldn't worry about him and his bruised ego right now. Right now, she needed to figure out why her wolf was so defiant. Otherwise, she was no good to anyone if she couldn't fight.

"I'll let you get back to your work," she said, making her way to the door.

"Amelia."

Turning back around, she faced him. A strange smirk was playing on his lips. "What?"

"Is two weeks enough time?"

"Enough time for what?"

"Your Luna ceremony. Is two weeks enough time to prepare?"

Amelia stared at him, her mouth slightly gaping. "What?!"

"I think it's high time this pack receives their Luna formally," Gabriel approached her, her face now a broad smile. His silver eyes held hers steadily. "I want you to be a part of this pack. Officially. There's only one woman in this life that will ever be my Luna, and that's you."

She couldn't believe what she was hearing. Her nerves felt frazzled, shooting off randomly as her stomach did somersaults. Her mind began to race with all that lied ahead of her. Being a Luna was a full-time job with many expectations and menial tasks she knew she wouldn't enjoy. But the other part, the more dominant one, was ecstatic. Her palms began to sweat. Her legs were suddenly filled with a burst of energy that she felt she wouldn't be able to run off no matter how long she ran. To finally be a part of a pack again had her nearly bouncing on her toes.

Amelia flung herself into his arms, startling him, nearly causing them both to end up on the floor. Though somehow, he managed to stay upright. She kissed his neck, pecking at his mark. The man moaned beneath her in response, his chest vibrating through hers as his hands gripped into her back tighter.

"I'll take that as a yes," Gabriel said softly, his voice deep and thick.

The huskiness in his voice warmed her all the way through. She heard him inhale sharply, taking in her scent, her arousal that was soaking through her thin cotton panties. Moments ago, she wanted distance. Now she wanted to remove every atom of oxygen between them and devour him whole.

Amelia found his lips, pushing past his teeth, and tasted him. She was famished, starving for his touch. She needed to feel him buried deep inside her, required the release that came from mating. The wolf within, primal and without shame, needed to take him like a hound took a bitch.

She knocked him down on the ground, taking him by surprise. His eyes widened, his eyebrow arched, wondering what she had in mind. She pulled off his pants in one swift movement, tugging off her own shorts, and straddled the man.

"Amelia, the door," Gabriel warned, looking behind her to the door that was shut but not locked.

"Fuck it, let them watch."

☾ ☽ ☾

Amelia fixed her clothes, tugging on her shirt so it lay just right over her chest, straightening out her shorts. Gabriel was busy buckling his pants. His hair in disarray, hanging in his face. It was her favorite look on him. He looked like he'd been well ridden. Pride swelled inside. Flashes of her riding him, wild and without restraint, replayed in her mind, and she couldn't help but smirk.

Rey was stirring more than earlier but was still quiet. Normally after mating, her wolf was like a kitten who'd just been given cream for its super. Content and satisfied, but not now. Something was definitely going on with her.

Amelia made her way to the door, her hand on the knob when an arm wrapped around her, spinning her into a solid chest.

"Trying to give me whiplash?" Amelia teased, looking up into his silver eyes. Goddess, she could drown in those eyes for all of eternity. They complemented the complexion of his skin perfectly and added amazing contrast to his ebony hair.

Gabriel cupped her face in his large warm hand, his thumb stroking along her jawline. "You have two weeks to arrange your Luna ceremony. All of our ally packs will be here to witness. Check with Lena. She'll know where to start."

Amelia couldn't help but smile, her insides twisting into knots. She was ecstatic and anxious. It had been almost two months since they found out they were fated mates. Well, over a month of living with the Twilight Moon Pack, feeling left out and disconnected, but in two weeks, she'd finally take her place at his side.

She reached up, sweeping the hair from his eyes. Her fingers brushed against his forehead before running through his hair. "You shouldn't put so much product in your hair. I love it like this."

"Do you?" Gabriel asked, amusement in his voice. His hands folded at the small of her back, holding her tighter against him.

Amelia nodded, continuously running her fingers through his hair with a feather-soft touch. She could feel his manhood pressed against her stomach once again. Unable to help the smirk spread across her face, she tried to reign in her hormones before he could smell her arousal once again.

"Long hair on guys is incredibly sexy," she purred, pulling him down into a searing kiss.

Would she ever get tired of his touch? Goddess, she sure hoped not.

Gabriel groaned in her mouth, forcing her back against the door. "What kind of spell do you have on me? No matter what, I can't seem to get you out of my system," he panted between kisses.

Amelia leaned her head back against the wooden door. His eyes were now black, his wolf pushing through to take control. Apparently, his wolf wasn't finished with her either. "I was going to ask you the same thing. Stupid mate bond."

She nipped his bottom lip, teasing him before pushing him off her. Opening the door, she slipped out, but not before sticking her head back in, a smile playing on her lips. "Don't worry. There's more fun tonight."

Amelia grinned, shutting the door behind her, holding the solid piece of wood firmly against her back. She could hear a string of curse words flying from his mouth behind the door. Chuckling to herself, she headed off in the direction of the kitchen. If Lena were anywhere, it would be there.

Passing through the commons, her senses were attacked by something putrid, rotting, dead. Her stomach churned, twisting uncomfortably. Throwing a hand over her mouth, she ran for the nearest bathroom. Fortunately, there was one in the hallway just outside the commons.

As soon as she flung open the door, she barely had time to open the toilet seat before throwing up the entire contents of her stomach. The acid burned her throat. The taste of rotten eggs was thick on her tongue. That's the last time she ever eats those.

The vomiting continued for some minutes. Her stomach cramped with the effort, sweat beading on her forehead and down her back as she tried to hold her braid from falling in the toilet bowl.

Finally over, her stomach now empty, she leaned back against the cold, white subway tiles of the wall. Her body was exhausted. Her hands shook.

What the hell is going on? She wondered to herself. She couldn't remember the last time she'd been ill.

Pup. Rey said timidly.

Amelia froze, her heart beating loudly in her ears. *What did you just say?*

Pup, Amelia.

Amelia's heart officially fell out of her ass.

CHAPTER 29

VISIONS

"You're leaning too far into the punch. That makes your legs an easy target. Balance is everything. Go again!"

Amelia circled a group of three warriors, each in human form. Two females against one male. Not many were comfortable with such a match up, but they needed to prepare for every scenario. Unfortunately, statistics suggested males were more likely to turn rogue, losing their humanity to the beast within. The female warriors needed to become accustomed to fighting men on their own.

All the warriors established a perimeter around the fight, observing from the sidelines. It was crucial for each of them to become aware of each of their strengths and weaknesses. To observe how they all fought. Most of those watching were offering words of encouragement and advice. It was heartwarming to see them all so eager to support one another.

It had been nearly a week since Rey dropped the bomb on her. She hadn't told Gabriel. Rey disagreed with her, but she would never betray her trust. Rey already believed Ren, Gabriel's wolf, suspected something had changed with her, but the man was still completely oblivious. She wasn't sure if she should be grateful or thoroughly annoyed.

It didn't make sense to her how she could be pregnant. She'd been on birth control for years. But clearly, fate had other plans once again.

She'd been keeping busy. Between planning her Luna ceremony with Lena and training the warriors, she'd been able to keep her mind off the pea-sized alien growing inside of her. Her symptoms were manageable as long as she stayed away from eggs and chicken.

Thank the Goddess nothing physical had changed yet. Except for the fact that her breasts were increasingly sensitive, and she had the hormones of a teenager who just discovered carnal pleasure. Gabriel didn't seem to mind tending to her every need, and boy did she have many of them.

Training was becoming difficult. Her senses had become alarmingly heightened, most smells making her nausea skyrocket. In good conscience, she couldn't put the pea in jeopardy. Rey had already forbidden shifting, and she was trying to avoid hand to hand combat entirely. Running was still okay, but even then, sometimes she had to make an excuse to branch off and vomit in the bushes. She wasn't sure how much longer she could keep it to herself.

Given the continuous Rogue sightings, she was nervous if Gabriel knew, he would lock her in the safe rooms until she gave birth. It wasn't uncommon for male wolves to be extra protective if their mate was expecting. Gabriel was an Alpha, so he could only be worse.

The idea of being restricted and him reversing back into the asshole she first met, scared her. They were in an amazing place. Though they didn't refer to each other as a couple or boyfriend/girlfriend, they were mates. In the werewolf community, they were as good as married. She was already bound to him through the Moon Goddess, but she was afraid of losing her last taste of freedom if he found out.

Her vision blurred out of focus, causing her to stop her pacing. *A branch cracked. The wind blowing directly in her face, carrying with it the scent of dirt and blueberries. A young boy cried in pain, bones splintering.*

Amelia's vision refocused on the present. Her attention was no longer on the fight. The smell in the air didn't give anything away. Christian was asking her something, but all she could think about was the boy.

Branches cracked overhead to her right. She forced her way through the warriors still gathered. Most moved out of her way before she had a chance to touch them. The smell of dirt and blueberries reached her nose. She sprinted for the tree, praying to the Goddess it was the right one.

A shrill voice screamed as the sound of tree limbs snapping rang through the clearing. Just as she reached the cover of the pine tree, she jumped forward, arms outstretched, catching the child.

The boy had his eyes fastened firmly, still waiting for the severe impact that was inevitably coming. Amelia chuckled. The boy couldn't be more than six. Precocious kid.

"Aaron!"

Amelia watched as the boy's eyes opened at the sound of his name. One of the warriors, Margo, ran towards her. Her face was a mixture of sheer relief, terror, and fury. Amelia was glad she wasn't the one in trouble. She did *not* want to be on the receiving end of that much turmoil.

The boy, Aaron, finally looked up at her own face, his brown eyes wide. Amelia set him down on his feet, squatting down beside him to where they were on eye level.

"Are you okay, kid?" Amelia asked him.

The boy simply nodded his head, his eyes inspecting the grass beneath his sneakers, too intimidated to meet her gaze. Amelia chuckled, tousling his hair.

"Aaron James Scott! What do you think you were doing climbing in a tree?!" Margo shrieked as she came closer.

Both women inspected the boy for any significant damage. Aaron was lucky. Only a few scrapes and bruises.

"Luna. Thank you so much. I don't know what I would have done if you hadn't caught him," Margo breathed, pulling her son against her chest.

Amelia rubbed circles into the boys back, the child crying against his mother's shoulder. Poor kid must have been terrified. That was quite a height he was at up in the trees.

"I'm just glad he's alright," Amelia smiled, standing up alongside Margo, who cradled Aaron in her arms.

"How did you know he was up there? I didn't hear or smell him," Margo asked, bouncing Aaron against her body.

Amelia tried to ignore the fifty pairs of eyes on them. She couldn't exactly tell them all she'd had a vision warning her. "I heard a branch snap, and with all the rogue sightings, I thought I should check it out. That was when I saw him in the tree."

Not a complete lie, Amelia internally shrugged.

Not the truth either, Rey said.

Her wolf had been quiet, more than usual, since finding out they were pregnant. Apparently, pregnancy takes a lot out of Rey, though she doesn't understand why. Something to do with the inability to shift and transferring that energy to the baby to keep it viable. Who knows.

"Well, thank you again, Luna," Margo smiled before heading for the Packhouse, her boy in her arms.

Amelia watched the woman carry the child away. A brief picture flashed in her mind of one day cradling her own child. Would it have Gabriel's coal black hair or her sea-green eyes? She imagined swaddling the baby in the softest blanket, promising to always keep it safe. Reading Narnia to him before bed. Scolding him for climbing trees and kissing booboos.

Christian behind her was ordering the warriors to resume training.

The visions were becoming more frequent. First, it was small things; a glass tipping over, walking into someone, a woman tripping over a crease in the carpet. Then it grew to bigger events. A phone call Gabriel received from the Crescent Pack, their Alpha died from a heart attack. One of the new moms going into labor an hour before it happened. Now, the boy falling from the tree.

They seemed to start shortly after their mating, but since she discovered she was pregnant, they'd been becoming more and more frequent. Maybe it was time to speak with her father about all this mate nonsense. It was time for him to finally crack open. She always had an inkling that he knew more than he was willing to admit. He was her mother's fated mate for crying out loud. He definitely knew something.

"Amelia!"

Snapping out of her own thoughts, she caught sight of Kelsey bouncing her way. Taking in the state of training, it seemed the day was over for the warriors. Had she been lost in thought that long?

"Hey Kels," Amelia smiled, not quite feeling the cheer beaming her way. Her mind felt too cluttered, too conflicted.

"Are you ready to pick out some cake for your Luna ceremony? Lena has about six different flavors ready to try," Kelsey looped her arm through Amelia's, dragging her towards the house.

The mention of cake had her stomach rolling. She inhaled sharply, holding her breath in an attempt to fight the bile rising. Throwing up in the middle of a cake tasting would definitely raise suspicion.

"What is this, a wedding? I had no idea so much went into this," Amelia complained.

Planning the ceremony was getting to be a pain in the ass. It was a little over a week away, and the list was still insanely long. Thank the Goddess she had both Kelsey and Lena in her corner.

"Oh, just wait till your wedding. Now *that* will be the event of the century!" Kelsey squealed excitedly.

Amelia's heart skipped a beat at the thought of marrying Gabriel. They'd been together a little over two months, she was already pregnant, and the thought of a possible wedding really had her feeling the urge to hurl. It was all moving so fast. They hadn't even had one significant conversation regarding their relationship. Steps were seriously being skipped.

Inside the house, the smell of cinnamon and apples engulfed her, warming her all the way through. Their bond made her chest feel fuzzy and heated like she'd been placed in a microwave and set to pop. He was close.

Gabriel walked around the corner into the commons, straight into her line of sight.

"I'll meet you inside the kitchen," Kelsey whispered in her ear before disappearing.

"Hey," she smiled at him, her nausea instantly abating in his presence.

Amelia could feel Rey stir as he got closer, sensing Ren. The two wolves were a match made in heaven. She couldn't get over how attentive Gabriel's wolf was. He'd been compelling Gabriel to be the same.

"Hey beautiful," Gabriel gathered her in his arms, clinging to her tightly. "You okay? You look pale."

Amelia smiled, trying to ease the frown that was causing his forehead to crease. "I'm fine. Just hot outside." Her shirt was adhered to her skin with perspiration.

"I heard what you did for Margo's boy. You're incredible. You know that?"

"I did what anyone else would have."

"You're wrong there," Gabriel pressed, "was it another vision?"

Amelia nodded her head. Ever since she told him what she knew about her lineage and her connection to the first mated pair, she'd been trying to be more open with him. Though she hadn't told him about her nightmares, she had been telling him about the visions.

She rested her head against his chest. Listening to the steady beat of his heart. His lungs filling with oxygen soothed her own nerves. The future was so uncertain. She felt as if the walls were closing around them all. But in moments like these, she felt content and finally able to breathe.

CHAPTER 30

BLOOD AND GUILT

Amelia, Kelsey, and Christian were busy in the weapons rooms, sharpening knives and cleaning the various pointed objects hoarded away. Amelia couldn't believe their stockpile, and yet, no one seemed to use any of it.

She happened upon the room only a few days before when she was searching for a mop. No one was nearby to ask, and she made a bit of a mess in the bathroom. She couldn't exactly ask Lena to stop cooking chicken, but the smell of raw meat upended her stomach every time. Meanwhile, she found a random storage room that ended up accommodating the pack's entire arsenal.

Amelia could make out a few guns, obviously Gabriel's since she didn't know anyone else comfortable around them. The rest were various-sized knives, some as thin as her pinky finger, others as long as her forearm. There were throwing stars, bows and arrows, crossbows, axes, and of course, plenty of handcuffs.

Cause what pack didn't need handcuffs for the occasional prisoner?

Many of the weapons were titanium metal. Some were steel, while a few were a hundred percent silver. Amelia went straight for those, tucked within a metal cage. It wasn't even secured. She pulled the doors open and immediately grabbed for one.

"Amelia, careful!" Kelsey shouted.

Amelia raised a brow behind her at Kelsey, who stood there gaping. Her mouth hung open as Amelia expertly flipped the knife until the flat of the blade landed purposefully in her hand.

"Silver doesn't burn you?" Christian asked from beside Kelsey. He looked to be in a state of shock and awe as the metal laid in her hand, unscathed. No burning, no blistering, nothing.

"Silver doesn't hurt me," Amelia shrugged her shoulders as she played with the knives in the case. They were exquisite. Too beautiful to be left in an abandoned room collecting dust. "Why in the hell does no one use these?"

Christian shrugged his shoulders in response. "We've been using them more since you got here, but I think most wolves prefer the simplicity of fighting fair. You know, fists and teeth."

"Hey, I'm all for those, but why fight fair when they're trying to kill you? If you can have an advantage, then you should. Especially against rogues!" Amelia said, jabbing the knife in the air at an invisible target.

"Easy killer. No rogues have stepped foot on our land," Christian chuckled.

"I sure hope they don't! Rogues are freaking terrifying!" Kelsey cried, taking a wet stone to one of the blades in her hand.

"Well, you better get used to them, Kels. They seem to be everywhere these days," Amelia put the knife back in the case before closing the cage doors.

Kelsey was an excellent fighter. She quickly picked up new fighting moves and executed them quite flawlessly, but she did not like confrontation. She was always hesitant to hit first, which wasn't what a warrior needed to be in battle. Hesitation meant death, and she worried for the day when Kelsey might be confronted with a problem that required mindless execution.

Something odd wafted through her nose. She tilted her head, breathing the smell deeply. All she could make out were scents that were familiar to her. Christians hair gel, Kelsey's vanilla body spray, the roast beef from dinner, and of course, pine and sap, Twilight scent. But underneath all of that, there was something else. It was barely there, but she could taste it just faintly in the back of her throat.

Mildew.

Howls rose in the air causing the hairs on her arm to stand on end. The border patrols we're under attack. Amelia looked to Christian and Kelsey. Christian was already mind linked. Kelsey looked terrified.

"It's rogues," Amelia turned back to the cage and began inserting knives into her boots and back pockets before grabbing two twin daggers, their blades carved in a fashion that would cause ultimate damage if twisted once it slipped into its victim.

"How do you know that?" Christian asked, grabbing for his own weapons.

"I can smell them. Let's go," Amelia hesitated, catching Kelsey's look of sheer terror. "Kels, why don't you stay here. We've got this."

Kelsey merely bobbed her head, leaning back against the wooden block table.

Amelia ran out of the room before she felt a hand seize her arm, pulling her back. She swung around to find Christian restraining her from going any further.

"What the hell?" she asked him, glancing down to his fingers digging into her arm.

"You should stay here. We can handle this," Christian hissed, keeping his voice low for some odd reason.

"Fuck that. If there's trouble, then I'm going to help," she wrenched her arm from his grip before he could protest any further.

Amelia, we shouldn't go. Rey spoke up.

I won't sit back and do nothing. Not when the pack is in danger. Amelia shook her head, pushing out the back door, joining the other warriors running for the woods.

But the pup-

The pup is the size of a pea. At most. You worry about the pup. I got this. Amelia pushed past Rey's resistance and ran through the pine trees, dodging under low hanging branches.

The moon was a few days shy of full, casting enough light overhead to guide her way. Branches snapped, leaves were being crunched underfoot. The sound of feet being pounded into the earth penetrated the woods as warriors from every direction ran for the border. Most covered other points, ensuring no surprise attacks, but Amelia was running straight for the target. Their smell became more pungent the closer she got.

Amelia, where are you?! Gabriel's voice rang in her ears.

I'm almost there! The sounds of fighting were getting closer, louder—wolves whimpered in pain. Hopefully, no one was seriously injured.

No! Turn back now! Gabriel growled in her mind. His fear and worry vibrated through her, jarring her to the bone.

Amelia ignored him. He couldn't expect to hold her back every time there was an ounce of danger. She was a warrior first and always. Protecting her pack was engraved in her DNA, and nothing could change that. If someone was in danger, she'd do everything in her power to help. She just hoped he would understand.

She was nearly there. By the stench in the air, she could make out ten rogues. Not as bad as it could have been, given all the sightings, but ten more than she would have liked.

The flat of the blades in her hand rubbed along her forearm as she ran with them in her grip. The wooden handle was grooved, the dips and curves fit perfectly in her grasp. Her legs were pumping beneath her body as she pushed through a clump of brush, only to be knocked from the side.

Something large and fur-clad bouldered into her, knocking the breath from her lungs. Amelia landed on her back. The wind knocked out of her as she came face to face with a rogue. She scrambled for the blades that were knocked from her hands-on impact. The rogue stalked towards her; his lip pulled back snarling, teeth snapping in the air.

Amelia pulled out a blade from inside her boot. It was smaller than the ones she was carrying, but it would have to do. She got up on her hands and knees, bracing herself for impact as the wolf inched closer. Unable to shift, she had to wait for the rogue to come to her.

Just as the matted wolf went to lunge, it hurled itself back in pain. Whimpering, it pushed its muzzle against the floor, dragging its face in the sticks and leaves. Amelia didn't hesitate. She hurled her knife straight into the side of the wolf's head, ending him quickly.

Not waiting to see it die, she pulled the knife from the body and ran back in the direction where the sounds of snarling were loudest. Following her nose towards the scent of blood was heaviest.

What she came upon made her proud. Pack members worked together, fighting the rogues in groups, just as they'd been training for these past months. The rogues we're putting up a fight but gradually losing. Their numbers were down by half.

Amelia jumped right in, working with four other warriors to take one down. It was lashing out viciously. Claws slashed through the air, catching the arm of the warrior beside her. She could make out Rick's profile just across the rogue. His huge build and russet brown hair were hard to miss.

A heavy paw, its claws extended, was aimed for her throat when the rogue got pulled back. The wolf's legs gave out, making him land on his chest. Amelia felt a slight sting across her breasts, but she disregarded it, recognizing her moment of opportunity. Her blade in hand, she leaped forward and slit the wolf's throat.

Standing back up, Amelia looked around. Most of the other rogues were already being taken care of. No one seemed to have any serious injuries, seeing as how the pack had ten times their number.

Rick stepped towards her, narrowing the distance between them. "You alright, Princess?" he asked, gesturing towards her chest and arm.

Amelia looked down to where he pointed and found faint scratches across her chest, cutting through her tank top. The scratches were minor but deep enough for blood to bead against her skin. The wounds were already healing, but they still stung like a bitch.

She felt a warmth running down her arm. Raising her hand up, she found a deep gash cut into her forearm. The flesh was cleanly cut through, no jagged edges like the type caused by claws. She wanted to smack herself on the forehead. One of the blades she was holding must have scored her when she was knocked down.

Cut by her own blade. Rookie mistake.

Rey, are you okay? Is the pup? Amelia reached out to her wolf.

We're fine, but this was beyond foolish, Amelia. You can't keep taking these risks. There's more than just your life on the line. Rey growled, upset and fed up.

Amelia couldn't help but hang her head at her wolf's words. She was right. It was stupid. She should have been more careful. The rogue ramming into her could have had a considerably worse outcome.

"Amelia!"

She flinched at the sound of her name. Gabriel's voice boomed through the trees. The leaves on the branches quaked with the force of his aura. His Alpha side, large and in charge.

He's pissed. Rey chimed in.

Amelia internally rolled her eyes. *No, shit.*

You're lucky he doesn't know about the pup yet. You'd be in deeper sh-

Amelia cut her off, blocking her wolf before she could say another word. She already felt guilty and irresponsible for her reckless decision. She didn't need a lecture from her other half as well. Being pregnant may have taken her by surprise, but it wasn't something she should take lightly.

Gabriel stormed towards her, his aura flexed around him, warning all pack members to back away in submission. Rick instantly flinched back under the terrifying Alpha's command, giving her a look of sympathy as he put ten feet between them.

Amelia held her head high. Whatever he had in store for her, she would take. She defied his orders and could have put him in jeopardy because of it. The mate bond was still a new concept to her. Never before had she had to worry about keeping herself safe to protect someone else. If she's injured, that's a distraction for him. But that doesn't mean she has sit on the sidelines either. If he's in danger, she'd rather be by his side and take it on together.

Gabriel stopped just in front of her. His silver eyes were nearly black as they took her in. Between the low lighting and his wolf coming through, she tried not to flinch under the scrutiny. His gaze roamed over her body, pausing at her chest and the blood dripping down her hand. The cuts on her chest were nearly closed, and the blood flowing freely from her arm had already came to a halt.

She flinched when he extended his hand. Not because she thought he meant to harm her, but her overwhelming anxiety and nerves were making her jumpy. His eyes automatically softened, his hand wrapped around the back of her neck, causing her to look up into his face.

He received a handful of scratches on his arms, but all in all, he was unharmed. His hair was a mess, sticking out in every direction. Her hands itched at her side to reach out and run her fingers through, but she kept still, hesitant as to what kind of state he was in.

Gabriel's thumb pressed under her chin, forcing her to meet his gaze. She reluctantly did. The sight stole the breath right from her chest. There was a vacuum in the air, and it seemed to remove the oxygen from the immediate vicinity. He didn't look angry or upset, but rather heartbroken and concerned. She never wanted to see that look on his beautiful face ever again.

"Are you okay?" Gabriel asked, his voice calm and gentle like.

All Amelia could do was nod her head, afraid to talk through the lump forming at the back of her throat. Her blood was up from the fight. Her anxiety was excessive, unsure of his reaction. He was touching her, looking at her in a way that caused her to feel like she was the only woman in the world, because to him, she was it. For the rest of their lives.

"Does it hurt?" he asked, lifting her arm for a closer inspection.

The cut had stopped bleeding. The edges already looked like they were beginning to close. Thank the Goddess for werewolf healing and the blade slicing clean through. Gabriel still looked troubled studying her wound, but his touch was delicate and soothing. Their mate bond calmed them down as their scent and touch worked their magic on one another.

Amelia had to resist the urge to close her eyes, allowing them to roll to the back of her head completely. At that moment, after a fight, her body was begging for more, and she knew he could feel it. But with more than a hundred pack warriors in the immediate area, that wasn't an option.

"Amelia," Gabriel said; his voice was like a whisper against her soul. Promising her eternity, safety, devotion, and something she never thought she'd have.

"Yes?" Amelia looked into his eyes to find the brilliant silver iris back. The shade that so perfectly matched his personality and contrasted his hair. The eyes she'd jump off the edge of the world for; if only he'd continue to look at her this same way for the rest of her life.

"You fought brilliantly tonight."

His words caught her off guard. She nearly teetered over in response. "You're not mad?"

"Oh, I was furious," Gabriel chuckled, his face lightening with each passing second. "But how can I stay mad when my mate can kick ass and defend herself, defend her pack. You're hurt, and it doesn't even phase you. You're a warrior queen."

His arms snaked around her waist, pulling her in against his body. It didn't matter that her arm was wet with her blood or how filthy either of them was. All that mattered was that he accepted her, all of her.

"I know you want to protect me, but I won't stay on the sidelines if I know I can help. I can take care of myself," she jutted out her chin, reinforcing her position on the matter. She wasn't a helpless female.

"I know, and we can talk about it more in the morning, but first," he leaned into her, his lips brushing against her ear. The feel of his hot breath kissing her skin nearly had her moaning in response. "Let's go upstairs."

CHAPTER 31

TOGETHER OR NOT AT ALL

The silence was deafening.

The wind was blowing through the trees, yet she was unable hear the sound of leaves rustling. Dead wolves were scattered around her, blood-soaked the dirt, but the smell of iron and salt refused to reach her. The moon was full in the midnight sky, and yet the light defied all law to illuminate the forest around her. Leaving her unable to distinguish rogue from pack, friend from foe.

Her feet trailed through the woods. Cold mud squished between her toes. Glancing down, she noticed her clothes were in tatters. Dirt and blood mixed, streaked across her skin. There was a warm sensation spreading down her thighs, sticky and wet. Her stomach was cramping, but she couldn't feel the pain.

The point of her toe caught on something. She fell hard, landing on a firm body coated in downy soft fur.

Sitting up, the moon's silver rays finally cast down through the trees. The sight of the wolf before her caused bile to clog her throat. Tears streamed down her face. Her hand covered her mouth to hold back the scream. Withholding the pain that threatened to devour the world.

Her magnificent, obsidian wolf laid dead before her. His silver eyes were glazed over by death. She reached out a hand and stroked his silky fur as her heart shattered. This is what hell must feel like.

She laid her head down on his body. Tears soaked his lifeless fur. Her fingers played with the softness beneath her face as she sobbed into the wolf of the man she loved.

Movement out of the corner of her eye drew her head up. Hopefully a Rogue was coming to finish her off. Then she could be with him in the peaceful afterlife.

The figure of a willowy woman walked silently between the trees, moving closer towards her. Her dress was like smoke, billowing around her, conforming to her body with every step. Her movements were distressingly noiseless. Not a single distinct sound was produced as her bare feet struck the earth. The long, silvery wisps of hair moved around her, defying the laws of gravity.

The woman stopped in front of her before bending down. On eye level, she noticed the woman possessed violet-colored eyes, shocking her straight to her soul. The wolf within recognized the woman immediately, bowing down in submission.

"Do not disregard my warnings," the woman said, her voice soft and whimsical, like beautiful sweet music plucked from the strings of a harp. "Your pack will die. Your mate will die. Your child will die."

(((

Amelia bolted upright in bed. Sweat ran down her back, her chest, and soaked her hairline. She wiped her eyes only to find wetness coating her hand. Her breathing was ragged, her throat sore from choking back screams. She pulled her knees up to her chest and wrapped her arms around them.

The bed beside her moved. Gabriel reached out to find her sitting up in bed. He pulled himself up drowsily, wiping the sleep from his eyes.

"Amelia, what's wrong?"

"It's nothing," Amelia shook her head, her voice quivering despite her best efforts to manage it.

This time Gabriel sat up straighter, sleep erased from his mind. He winded his arms around her, pulling her in against his chest.

"You're shaking. What's this about? Another nightmare?"

Amelia could feel the pressure behind her eyes building. The concern in his voice nearly shattered her resolve. She concealed her face against his neck, breathing in the scent of him deeply. Her frazzled nerves began to soothe. The trembles shaking her body began to quiet. She was nervous to open her mouth. Afraid of what she might say.

"Amelia," he pushed her away only to cup her face, forcing her to meet his eyes. "What is going on? You've been having nightmares for weeks. You're barely sleeping, and you're losing weight," he said, listing things off like it was a checklist. "What are you not telling me?"

We're pregnant. Rey piped up.

Shut up, Amelia growled at her wolf.

She wasn't prepared for that discussion just yet. They never discussed their own relationship, let alone what either of them thought about having children. Given that she had thrown herself in the middle of a rogue fight only hours before, she was not ready for the throw down that would ensue.

Inform him about the nightmares, at least.

Amelia took in a deep breath, remembering the sensory deprivation of her dream. Not being able to hear, smell, or speak was the worst feeling she had ever experienced. The memory of it was torture enough.

"Since we've mated, I've been having dreams," she started, unsure how much she should tell him.

We should tell him everything.

"Dreams, what kind of dreams?"

"They typically start with us in the woods. Sometimes we're here, and sometimes it's at the Wandering Moon. But every time is the same," she licked her lips nervously. The memory of hundreds of dead wolves filled her vision. "Our packs were slaughtered by rogues."

Gabriel rubbed his hand up and down her spine, pressing the tips of his fingers against the tense muscles of her back.

"They're just nightmares," Gabriel said softly, trying to soothe her troubled mind.

Amelia shook her head. "I don't think so. Not anymore. Gabe, I think something bad is going to happen," she heard herself whisper. As if announcing it any louder would make it more true, more real.

"Like your visions?"

"Maybe. I don't know," she sighed exhaustedly. "This one was different, though. I could barely see even though there was light. I couldn't hear or feel anything. It was like I was completely cut off." She looked away from him, afraid to meet his gaze. "Until I f-fell over your body. You were d-dead Gabe, and there was nothing I could do. I couldn't save you."

She could feel the hot tears streaming down her skin. Her body betrayed her. She hated crying, hated looking weak. But the thought, the idea of his death, the feel of his cold corpse beneath her, terrified every cell of her body. He'd only been in her life for a little over two months, and he had already wormed his way in her soul. Imprinting his name on every beat of her heart.

Gabriel pulled her in tighter, setting her on his lap as he cradled her against his chest. His fingers gently stroked her hair. Tender kisses feathered against her forehead.

"I'm not going anywhere. I could never leave you," Gabriel whispered, his breath brushing against her skin, causing shivers to ripple down her spine.

"She said you'd die. That I'd lose everyone," Amelia cried against his chest. Her arm wrapped around her stomach, clutching at the small life that was developing inside of her.

"Who said?" Gabriel asked, confused.

"The Moon Goddess. She came to me and told me that you'd die. Our pack would die," she sniffled, holding back the last line.

Our pup, Rey, whined, remembering the Goddess's exact words.

Amelia nibbled her lip, biting back a fresh wave that threatened to engulf her. She felt Gabriel's arm tighten around her. The thick cords of muscle strained against stretched skin.

"Nothing is going to happen to me. I won't ever lose you. And if the Moon Goddess herself wants to come and take us, then she can take us together or not at all," Gabriel declared.

Amelia could hear his heart hammering in his chest. Their bond was open and exposed, like a nerve shocking her system. He was definitely alarmed when she mentioned the Goddess. But he was also firm with his words. He believed every word she said. Her heart sank deeper, drowning in warmth.

Even though the expression hadn't been said aloud, she knew those three singular words could never amount to the way she felt for the man.

Gabriel pulled her back against the bed with him, keeping her body firmly pressed against his. She snuggled against him, enveloped in his warmth, his comfort, and security. No place made her feel safer than in his arms as she finally drifted into a dreamless sleep.

((((

For the first time in weeks, Amelia finally experienced a peaceful sleep. Wrapped in Gabriel's arms, his smell fueling every inch of her, she was able to awake on her own. She felt lighter, like a weight had been lifted off her shoulders.

Amelia was glad she finally told Gabriel about the dreams. Though she no longer believed they were dreams. Gabriel was right. They were most likely visions. The Moon Goddesses' appearance was a wake-up call. Rogues were coming for them. She just didn't know where or when.

Even though she slept peacefully, she woke up with an eerie, jittery feeling in her chest. She kept jigging, unable to keep still. Something within her was off. Her body was in a battle, at war with itself. Fight or flight mode was coursing through her. She just had no idea what she should be fighting or running from.

Down in Gabriel's office, they discussed border issues, the rogues, and of course, her Luna ceremony next week. It felt like it would never be prepared in time. The list continued to grow from flower arrangements to guest lists and her dress. It was endless.

Munching on a piece of toast, trying to quell the nausea that was always present, she felt a sudden twinge in her chest. She bent forward, gasping for breath as she felt a string, a tether she never realized was there, snap. Dropping the bread from her hand, she gripped at her breasts, her heart pounding against her ribs. An arctic cold dripped in her veins, spreading throughout her entire body.

Amelia could hear Gabriel shouting at her, asking what was wrong. But his voice sounded altered, far away. She couldn't focus on him. All she could feel was the ice spreading down her spine. Damon.

"*Damon!*" Amelia screamed, aloud, and through their bond.

Amelia.

She could hear her brother through their link. Sighing with relief, she took in a deep breath, but it was short-lived. The tone of his voice caused her body to stiffen.

What's happened? Are you okay?! I felt something snap.

Rey was pacing, anxious, and terrified.

"Amelia, what's going on?" Gabriel growled beside her. Patience was never his strong suit.

Amelia threw a finger up at him, asking him to wait a moment. One thing at a time.

We were ambushed, Damon finally said.

Amelia staggered back. A sturdy arm wrapped around her waist, supporting her.

What happened? Are you okay? She asked him again. There was something he wasn't saying. Something she knew she didn't want to hear but needed to. Something that would alter her world forever.

Rogues came. There were so many of them. Twenty, thirty, forty. We couldn't keep track. They overwhelmed him. I couldn't reach him in time. His voice drifted off.

Who? What happened, Damon?! They were attacked the same night? That couldn't be a coincidence.

Dad's dead.

Amelia stopped breathing. Oxygen was lacking in the air. No matter what she did, she couldn't get her lungs to respond and take a breath. Her head felt fuzzy as black fog crept over her vision. Her heart slowed in her chest, Rey howled in her mind, and her eyes rolled back as darkness consumed her.

CHAPTER 32

NEVER GOT TO SAY GOODBYE

The world was moving around her. She felt warm and secure. Brawny arms were wrapped around her body, their firm presence constricted her. There was a slight breeze against her cheek, causing her eyes to flutter. Forcing her eyelids to separate all the way, she found herself looking up to the underside of Gabriel's face. His jaw was hard and squared, focused on the space in front of them.

She realized they were walking somewhere while he carried her bridal style. Squirming in his arms, he finally looked down, noticing she was conscious.

"Amelia," Gabriel let out a breath of air in relief.

How long was she out?

His eyes were wide with fright. Through their bond she could feel his terror, gripping him in its vice to the point where she wasn't certain how he was still standing, nonetheless breathing.

"Where are we going?" Amelia asked, glancing around at their surroundings.

"To the doctor. You fainted," Gabriel said, his eyes still fixed on the direction they were headed.

The doctor? No, she couldn't go to the doctor. They'd know about the baby, and she wasn't prepared for that. She wiggled harder in his arms, pushing against his chest.

"Put me down. I'm fine," she protested.

"No, you're not. You were in pain, and then you fainted. That's not nothing," Gabriel said, her struggles futile in his arms as he clearly didn't believe her when she said she was fine.

Panic began to set in. She shoved him harder, pushing more of her strength into her movements until his grip on her began to loosen, forcing him to stop.

"You're such a stubborn woman," Gabriel muttered to himself before setting her down on her feet.

Amelia swayed as she tried to force her legs to support her weight. For some reason, she felt disconnected from the rest of her body. Like her mind was no longer in control of its functions. Gabriel kept his hands firmly on her hips, holding her against his body. Her head was swimming. Nausea was rising in the back of her throat and threatened to appear. Her vision was beginning to fog over again. Black spots swarmed her as she put her palm to her forehead, trying to steady her breathing.

"You are not okay. Please, let me take you to the doctor," Gabriel pleaded.

"I just need a minute," she said, holding her hand up. She closed her eyes for a few moments, breathing in and out deeply. In through the nose, out through the mouth. Repeating the process until she felt her head begin to clear, and her nausea abate. Finally opening her eyes, she looked up and found silver pools shining with worry.

"What happened?" Amelia asked, finding her voice thick with an emotion she couldn't place.

"I was hoping you could tell me. What do you remember?"

Amelia thought back. She remembered being in his office going over normal pack stuff when she felt a cold sharpness spread throughout her body. Her hand automatically laid over her chest, clutching at the thin fabric of her shirt. Something had snapped. Someone had died.

Dad.

Tears slipped from her eyes. She turned away from him, not wanting him to see her looking so lost. Her knees buckled as grief swept over her like a tsunami crashing on the beach. Gabriel's grip on her tightened, pulling her back flat against him. One arm was snaked around her waist, the other around her chest. Her breathing was erratic, as though there wasn't enough oxygen in the air to sustain her body. She could hear Gabriel speaking in her ear, calm and assertive, trying to convince her to breathe with him.

The rise and fall of his chest against her back forced her own body to respond, mimicking the movement. She could feel their mate bond opening between them. Gabriel tried to siphon some of her despair, her grief so that she could function. She could feel him shaking beneath her, but she felt better. The tide of grief lessened. It was still there but no longer drowning her.

"Amelia."

Amelia finally turned to look at him, only to discover his eyes shining and wet with unbridled emotion. She reached up, brushing her thumb against a tear that was already falling down his cheek. His hand extended to her face as well, brushing away her own tear stains.

"My dad's dead," Amelia whispered, fresh saltwater leaking once again.

Gabriel pulled her harder against him, wrapping his arms even tighter around her like he was trying to fuse her body with his. Amelia gratefully laid her head against his chest and allowed herself to be held. She cried into his shirt. The cold nagged at her heart from the bond that was so forcefully shattered. She never realized its constant presence, but now that it was gone, she couldn't ignore the empty void that resided in its place.

She was officially an orphan now. There were so many things she never got to say. So many things she needed to know and now would never have the chance to ask. She couldn't even remember the last time she spoke with him, told him how much she loved him. How amazing of a father he was.

The tears continued to fall until her body had exhausted itself of all hydration. She felt drained, fairly certain the only thing keeping her upright anymore was Gabriel. The back of her throat was drier than the Sahara. All she desired at that moment was water.

Gabriel lifted her once again, but this time headed in the opposite direction.

"Where are you taking me?" she asked, her voice coming out like a dying frog.

"You need water. You're dehydrated," he said, not bothering to look down.

"But how...?"

"Mate bond, sweetheart. Or did you forget I can read your mind?" his lips pulled into a smirk.

I certainly hope not. Amelia grumbled to herself. Rey nodded her head in agreement.

He carried her into the kitchens. Only a few people were working but quickly skittered out at the sight of their Alpha and Luna. Gabriel carefully set her down on the island's granite countertop, leaving her there while he grabbed a cold bottle of water from the fridge.

Twisting the cap off, he handed her the open bottle, which she quickly took, gulping the water down greedily. The cool liquid soothed her aching throat but only added to the frigid pain in her breasts.

"Better?" Gabriel asked, his eyes not once leaving her. Probably afraid she'd faint again.

"Much," she nodded her head, finishing the bottle. "I need to speak to Damon. I probably freaked him out when I fainted."

Gabriel nodded, taking the empty bottle from her and tossing it into the trash. He laid his hands against her knees, rubbing small circles against her skin.

Amelia took in a deep breath, pushing back her grief. She wasn't the only one who had lost a parent. Damon had likely been with their father when he passed. She couldn't imagine watching her father die.

Damon? she called out through their link.

Amelia! Thank the Goddess! Are you okay? The link just ended, and I was so worried.

Amelia winced from her brother's panic, chafing against her like sandpaper. His voice echoed off the chambers of her mind. Even Rey felt overwhelmed by her brother's barrel of emotions. Gabriel's grip on her knees tightened to stabilize her, sensing her spiking heart rate.

I'm okay. I just fainted. The bond breaking was horrible. It was like I felt him die. She shuddered at the memory, biting the inside of her cheek to keep from crying again.

I know. I felt it too. Damon's voice dropped a few octaves.

At that moment, all she wanted to do was throw her arms around him and hold him close.

What do we do now? Amelia asked the obvious question. Of course, there were his affairs to put in order. A funeral to arrange. But knowing her brother, he was already five steps ahead.

The funeral is in two days. We'll have a remembrance ceremony the following day.

Amelia nodded her head, relaying the information to Gabriel. She could tell he recognized what she was about to say next and appeared hesitant.

"I have to go. I have to be there for my brother, my family. I have to say goodbye," she said, her eyes pleading with him to understand, and by the softening of his brow, he did.

"Fine. But you're not going alone," Gabriel's voice was stern, making it known it wasn't a request. "Given the attack last night, we're not taking any chances."

Amelia nodded, a slight appreciative smile pulled at the corner of her mouth.

Damon, we're coming.

What? Like, now?

We're leaving in an hour.

Are you sure? We could be attacked again. With all this rogue nonsense, it might not be such a good idea.

Amelia's mind flashed back to her dreams. The Moon Goddesses warnings. It was possible her brother was right, but she'd be damned if she didn't attend her father's funeral. No one would take away her right to say goodbye.

I'm coming, Damon. You are not doing this alone. I have to be there. There was no way in hell she was missing this, but she could feel the pressure building in her chest again. The yearning to scream and throw things was staggering. She did her best to reign it in, but the thought was still there.

Gabriel grasped her hands in his, massaging the delicate tendons beneath the skin. Her body instantly relaxed under his touch. The tension evaporated from her muscles. She had the desperate urge to take him where they stood and lose herself in their bond and his body. He would probably let her, but that wouldn't relieve the gnawing sensation of loss. It would only delay the inevitable when she would eventually break.

Of course. I'll be waiting for you when you arrive.

Amelia sighed in relief. She didn't really expect her twin to fight her on it, but she knew he would do anything and everything to protect her.

I love you, bro.

I love you, Mia.

Amelia blocked the connection before she really started to lose it. She pulled Gabriel closer, drawing him in between her legs until she could fold herself against him. Burrowing her face in the crook of his neck, she breathed him in deeply, allowing his scent to wash over her.

How did we ever survive without him?

We need to tell him, Mia. Rey reminded her.

I know. I will soon, I promise. But right now, there's just too much going on.

Rey whimpered in the back of her mind. It wasn't just Amelia that lost a parent. Rey had too.

Amelia pulled back. Gabriel looked down at her, waiting for her to speak.

"I want to leave as soon as possible. My brother needs me."

Gabriel gave her a soft smile; his eyes warm and genuine. "I've already linked Kaleb. He's setting it up now. We'll leave as soon as you're ready."

Amelia couldn't help but grin. She slid off the counter, giving his hand a last squeeze before they both went their separate ways. Gabriel went off to his office to square things away with the pack, seeing as how they'd be away for a few days. Meanwhile, she advanced up the stairs to gather some things. Just as she reached the third floor, she felt hands grip her upper arm, hauling her down the hall and into someone's bedroom.

Before she had the chance to kick and punch her attacker, she caught the familiar sight of someone's goofy-ass face.

She punched him in his shoulder, causing him to yell out.

"You dick! What do you think you're doing?! Trying to give me a heart attack?" Amelia yelled at him as he tried to shush her. "Don't you shush me. What the hell do you want?"

"I heard you fainted," Christian said, his voice full of concern. "I wanted to make sure you were okay. You and the baby."

"I'm fine, I just … wait, did you say, baby?" Amelia hissed, now trying to keep her own voice down. The last thing she needed was for the entire pack to find out before the father. "How do you even know?!"

"You've been eating eggs, which you hate. You haven't shifted in weeks and no longer participate in active training. Plus, you smell like vanilla. Wolf's scents don't just change overnight for no reason. You've already been marked, so that can't be it. You have to be pregnant. It's the only thing that makes sense," Christian shrugged his shoulders.

Amelia crossed her arms over her breasts, frowning.

"Plus, your breasts are huge."

She stuck him across his chest, letting her arms fall to her side. "Jerk," she said, shaking her head.

The fact that Christian was able to put it together left her feeling uneasy. Her best friend could tell she was pregnant, and yet her mate was still completely oblivious. She wasn't sure if she should be grateful or annoyed.

CHAPTER 33

THANKS A LOT ASSHOLES

Amelia stepped out the front door; her black duffel bag slung over her shoulder. She felt the straps slip through her fingers as the weight shifted from off her back. She caught sight of Christian walking past her, her bag in his hands. Great. Now he was going to be weird about it. He was fortunate she couldn't mind link him just yet. Otherwise, he'd be experiencing a major headache.

Parked in the driveway were two fully loaded buses and three black SUV's. Amelia frowned at the vehicles. Not sure what was going on. She felt a warm hand press against her lower back. Familiar tingles raced up her spine.

"What's with the buses? We going on tour of Massachusetts or something?"

Gabriel chuckled beside her. "We're bringing over fifty warriors with us. Given that the rogues did just attack, I'm not taking any chances. I've left plenty of warriors here to defend our borders, but I'm not leaving without some added protection."

Amelia swallowed the lump forming in her throat. Nerves plagued her mind. Last night the Twilight pack was attacked. Albeit a small attack, but an attack nonetheless. Then, at the same time, the Wandering Moon Pack is attacked, and her father is fatally injured. That can't be a coincidence.

Christian jumped off the last step of the bus before the black doors swung closed behind him. "Everyone's on board and ready," he announced to his Alpha.

Amelia heard muffled footsteps cuffing the wooden deck behind her. She spun around to find Kaleb stepping out of the house, wishing them farewell.

Gabriel shook Kaleb's hand formally before patting him on the shoulder. "We'll be back in a few days. Try not to burn the house down."

Kaleb scoffed, rolling his eyes. "That was one time. We were teenagers. And I'm pretty sure you're the one who started the fire."

Gabriel chuckled, letting go of his best friend and Beta. "I never liked those curtains."

Amelia smirked at the playful tone in Gabriel's voice. She didn't get to hear much about his past and wished to know more. His warm hand pressed against her back again, fingertips pressing against her skin, indicating her to get going.

"Thank you for doing this, Kaleb. I really appreciate everything," Amelia said. Surprising herself and him, she pulled him into a quick hug. Kaleb was rigid beneath her, but she held on anyway. That is until a low growl rumbled behind her.

Amelia turned away for the vehicles, abandoning the stunned men on the porch. Quickly wiping away the moisture gathering in her eyes, she scolded herself—stupid hormones.

Christian held one of the SUV doors open for her, offering her a supporting smile. "You got this, Ella."

Just before she could lift a leg to pull herself up into the car, she experienced a startling chill running down her spine. The hairs on the nape of her neck rose in warning as gooseflesh decorated her skin from head to toe. Someone was watching her. Someone that shouldn't be there.

Amelia froze and turned around. Her eyes trained on her surroundings. Scouring the woods for any signs of movement. Anything out of place. She scented the air carefully but could smell nothing but Twilight Moon Pack and the fumes from the cars.

"Everything okay?"

Amelia snapped her head in his direction. Gabriel came up behind her, his brows furrowed.

"Yeah, everything's fine."

☾ ☾ ☾

The drive to the Wandering Moon Pack was almost four hours long. They were over three hours into the trip, and the entire time Amelia stuck to her side of the vehicle. Leaning against the door, her eyes were glued to the scenery passing them by. Her mind was bothered by Christians admittance to knowing her secret, yet her mate had failed to see it. Her heart was conflicted between her dreams and losing her father.

Something was going on behind the scenes. Someone was pulling the strings of these rogues. Never before have so many rogues assaulted a pack before, on purpose. None of it made any sense. But most importantly, why was the Moon Goddess getting involved?

On one hand, she was grateful to be going back home. Back to the pack that raised her, but the circumstances left a heavy weight on her heart. She couldn't believe he was really gone. The coldness of his death was already beginning to fade as if he had never existed at all, and that bothered her even more. Her body was accepting his death before her mind could process.

Christian sat in the front seat, constantly looking over his shoulder, ensuring she was okay. Like the big brother she never wanted and yet loved.

Amelia could feel his silver eyes on her, constantly checking to see if she was all right. She'd barely spoken the whole drive. Luckily, she wasn't one to get car sick, the nausea having the sense to disappear. She didn't think she could deal with it on top of everything else.

She could sense his desire to console her. To embrace and protect her, but she was grateful he didn't. She felt confused and conflicted—her hormones, doing nothing to help with any of it.

She appreciated the distance he was giving her. He didn't know it yet, but between the pregnancy and losing her father, it was all just too much. Then there was their mate bond. Pushing her towards him. Nudging her to lose herself in the man, but that was something she wouldn't do. She would *not* allow herself to succumb to that part of the bond. She could hold herself up just fine on her own.

But none of that compared to the hormones wreaking havoc on her body. Her senses were in overdrive. No matter how hard she tried, she could smell Gabriel everywhere. The smell of spiced apples was permanently ingrained in her body. She could smell him from miles away, of that she was sure.

Though, it wasn't just his smell driving her crazy. She was aroused constantly. She was beginning to experience a love/hate relationship with her sex. Constantly igniting itself whenever she could detect his presence. The moment he touched her skin left her ravenous, ready to consume the fuel he gave that stoked the embers within. She could never get enough, always craving more.

It was exhausting and thrilling all at once—stupid hormones.

The smell of maple and tree bark filled her nose. Home.

Crossing through the pack borders, Amelia spotted familiar wolves racing through the tree line, following their vehicles to the Packhouse. Her fingers twitched with excitement, itching to join them. To enjoy the freedom of shifting and running with her pack.

Until she remembered she wasn't a part of any pack. It was as though her bond had broken all over again, removing her link to the only pack she had ever known. Not to mention the fact that she couldn't shift even if she wanted to. Shifting at all during pregnancy could kill the pup. The fetus was too small to withstand the trauma of the transformation process.

The SUV pulled up to the house. The smell of home assaulted her senses the minute she breathed in the fresh Massachusetts air. She could nearly taste the maple on the back of her tongue. Amelia jumped out of the car before it even came to a stop. Gabriel and Christian yelled at her as she did so.

Damon and Cordelia stood on the front lawn, waiting. Amelia stopped in front of them. Damon looked like a wreck. Bruises covered his body. Deep-set circles rimmed his eyes as if he hadn't slept in days. Superficial cuts could be seen across his skin. The attack was more severe than he let on.

Cordelia beside him didn't look any better. While she was missing the visible signs of battle, her eyes were bloodshot and swollen. Her lips were chapped, and her hair, for the first time in living memory, was in a messy bun on her head.

But the most shocking was their hands intertwined between them. Cordelia leaned into her twin's body. As though, without his support, she might tip over. She almost wanted to laugh. They were finally together—crappy timing of it all.

Amelia rushed towards her two-favorite people on the planet and hugged them both. She felt their arms wrap around her small frame, embracing her tightly. Their scents filled her nose, warm and comforting, breaking down all her barriers and walls. On instinct, she began to hum her comforting tune. Damon joined her on impulse.

The air around them grew thick, charged with a power not often seen in this world. The song ended almost as quickly as it began. Amelia instantly felt lighter and well-rested. She pulled back and found her twin to be completely healed, not a scratch or bruise to be seen. Even the dark circles under his eyes had faded completely. Same with Cordelia. Any evidence of her crying from grief had been erased as if by magic.

Gabriel came up beside her, his hand wrapping around her waist, luring her in against him. She knew he didn't like others touching her. She despised it, but it equally made her smirk.

Silly Alpha.

The men shook hands, their faces solemn.

"I'm so glad you're here, Mia," Damon sighed in relief.

Amelia couldn't help it. She pulled out of Gabriel's grip and wrapped her arms around her brother's neck. For the first time since she left, she felt her body completely relax. No matter who her mate was, there was a bond she had with her twin that could never be matched, and right now, it was exactly what the both of them needed.

Damon pulled back, his nose crinkled as if she stunk. "What's that smell?"

Amelia frowned, her lower lip sticking out in a pout. She lifted her hair to her nose but smelled nothing other than her lavender shampoo. "That's freaking rude."

"No, seriously. You smell sweet. Like vanilla," Damon said, sniffing the air around her.

Amelia swatted at him, causing him to flinch back. When suddenly, her heart froze in her chest. Christian had said something very similar only a few hours earlier. Something about her scent being different.

Shut up, Amelia warned him through their link. Her eyes wide and glaring for added emphasis.

"It must be my perfume," she said aloud.

"What are you talking about? You don't wear any perfume," Gabriel commented beside her.

Amelia wanted nothing more than to roll her eyes and smack herself on the forehead. No better yet, smack him for being so dense. He noticed she doesn't wear perfume but not that her scent had completely changed?!

Cordelia scented the air as well. Her nose scrunched at the unfamiliar smell. "Damon's right. You do smell different."

Just then, her best friend's eyes widened with realization. She could see the small bounce in her friend's stance. She was certain if it weren't for Damon clasping her hand, she'd be jumping up and down screaming.

"You-your, but-your," Cordelia stuttered, her voice growing increasingly louder.

Amelia just shook her head at her friend. Praying to the Goddess above, she might take the hint. She could hear a chuckle from behind her and wanted nothing more than to sucker punch Christian in the gut. Baby or not, she was prepared to kick someone's ass.

"Oh, my Goddess, you're pregnant!" Damon shouted, his own eyes widening with the shocking realization.

Amelia glared daggers at her supposed best friend and brother, who should now fear for their lives.

"Thanks a lot, assholes."

CHAPTER 34

SUN AND MOON

Amelia hung her head. Gabriel was shocked beside her. She could feel her aura slipping. She was furious with the two that were supposed to have her back. Instead, they just outed her in front of her mate. Completely overlooking every single sign she threw at them.

What part about shut up, did you not understand? Amelia growled at her twin. She could see him visibly wince under the pressure of their link.

"What are they talking about, Amelia?" Gabriel asked, his voice in disbelief with an undertone of anger.

Amelia ignored the guilty looks of both Damon and Cordelia and turned to her mate. Gabriel was searching her face, probably in hopes that it was all a lie. That she hadn't been keeping such a secret from him, but he wouldn't find what he was looking for.

"I'm pregnant, Gabe," Amelia breathed, her heart slamming against her chest. The palms of her hands were sweating as her anxiety skyrocketed.

Gabriel took a staggering step back. Glancing from her face to her stomach and back again. Even though he had the pieces, he was still trying to fit them together. He really had no clue.

Should we be pissed at him? Amelia asked Rey. Uncertain how to take his reaction.

Give him a minute! He's processing!

Men. She internally rolled her eyes. *I thought you said his wolf knew.*

He did. He could smell it on us.

Then how is he so blind?!

"How long have you known?!" Gabriel growled. His own aura expanded around him. The glint in his eye nearly made her flinch. He was furious, and it was solely directed at her.

Amelia glanced around. They were beginning to gather a crowd of onlookers. Damon and Cordelia looked like they wished to be anywhere but there.

Good, they should suffer.

"A few weeks," she said softly.

"A few weeks?!" Gabriel's voice boomed across the yard.

Amelia visibly flinched from his thunderous tone. His temper was flaring. His aura grew red around him. She reached out to grip his hand. If she couldn't quiet him down, then every pack member would be out on the lawn within minutes in response to his aura, drawing in all those below him.

Gabriel tried to pull away from her, which stung more than she wished it would, but she held on nonetheless. Rubbing small circles into the bends of his wrists, she applied a steady pressure.

"Can we talk about this somewhere more private?" she urged him, gesturing towards the house.

Gabriel gritted his teeth before nodding his head. Escorting him inside, she made sure to look back, shooting Damon and Cordelia a look that told them they were not off the hook. She towed him inside the house, smiling at the few pack members that offered her greetings but stayed back due to the Alpha's aura.

Steering him up the stairs, they finally made it to her bedroom, shut the door, and secured it behind her. Her once full and brightly decorated room was now bare and empty of life. A few straggler boxes remained, along with some odds and ends pieces of furniture.

The minute Gabriel heard the lock click into place; he swung around on her. His silver eyes blazing, stoked with fire.

"How could you keep this from me?! How could you not tell me for weeks that you're pregnant?" Gabriel snarled, his chest rising and falling drastically as he tried to contain his anger.

"How did you not figure it out?!" Amelia yelled back, allowing her own disappointment to rise. "I've been throwing up every single day! I can't stand the smell of chicken. Rey refused to shift, and training is so *fucking* exhausting! All the signs were there, and you missed every single one of them!" she was fuming. How dare he be cross with her!

"If you haven't noticed, I've been a bit busy lately!" Gabriel yelled back.

"Too busy to know I'm fucking pregnant?! What a cop-out!" she screamed back. "Have you even spoken to Ren lately?"

"What does he have to do with any of this?" Gabriel spat.

"You, you big dolt! Ren's known the entire time! Your own wolf recognized the change in your mate, and you remained clueless as ever! Christian figured it out before your thick head even grasped the notion!"

Gabriel growled at the mention of another man. His dominant Alpha side was at the forefront of his personality at the moment, and it did not appreciate the mention of another male. "Mine," he snarled.

Amelia jabbed her finger in his face, "See, this is why I was afraid to tell you! Barely five minutes after finding out, and already you're going all caveman on me! Did you stop and think just once how I might be feeling about all of this? We were just starting to get comfortable. We've been together for what? Barely three months?!"

"You said you were on birth control. Or was that a lie too?" Gabriel's voice dripped with mistrust.

His words grated her soul. She couldn't help her reaction.

Amelia struck out at lightning speed, catching him off guard, her fist connecting with his jaw. Her knuckles screamed in protest. Definitely bruised if not bleeding, but the pain was distant. She felt disconnected to the rage building inside of her.

Gabriel's head snapped to the side. Surprise and regret instantly registered on his face as his hand cupped his jaw, already turning a darker shade. His eyes met hers, and she knew he would take back his words if he could. She could feel his remorse. The apology he was desperate to give, but he stopped by the look of hurt so plainly written on her face. Her body language, her sea-green eyes looked at him as she would a stranger.

The man was too quick with his anger and words. He doesn't think before he speaks. He merely spits out the first thing that crawls into his abused, damaged mind, and that usually ends up tied with his abandonment and trust issues. What hurt even worse was that he still didn't trust her.

"How fucking dare you accuse me of such a horrendous thing," she couldn't prevent the hurt that crept in her voice. Her vision blurred with unshed tears. "You've said a lot of fucked up shit to me since we found each other, but to accuse me of this. That was crossing a line. I didn't tell you right away because I didn't know how to process. I have been on birth control since I'm fourteen. It should have worked, but clearly, fate loves to fuck with us."

"I'm sorry, Amelia. I didn't mean it the way it came out. I just-this is a lot," Gabriel said, shaking his head.

"How do you think I feel?"

Gabriel's face softened at her words. Stepping back, his body finally relaxed, his eyes shifting back to their cool tone. "Do you even want a baby?"

Amelia ran her hands through her hair, pulling back the strands that came loose from her braid. She sighed profoundly. Given everything that'd been going on, she barely had a chance to process what was happening with her own body. She was eighteen. What did she know about having a baby? The thought of being a mother, responsible for another life, terrified her.

"I never considered being a mom," she admitted out loud. Amelia turned from him, afraid to encounter his radiant eyes. Frightened to see his reaction to her words. "I told you before. I didn't want to settle down. I never pictured myself with a mate or being your typical female werewolf. Settling down and having a family was *not* something I saw in the cards for me."

Gazing out the window, she observed the warriors in the backyard training. Remembering how just a few brief months ago, that used to be her. Downstairs, with her family, her pack. Kicking ass and taking names.

"But then I met you," she whispered, turning back to confront him. His head rose at her words, meeting her eyes. "The Moon Goddess selected me to be your mate, and I trusted in that. I trusted in the fated bond because you and I, we're one in a billion. Most wolves get to choose their partners. Determine who they spend the rest of their lives with. You and I didn't get that luxury."

Amelia watched as his head hung, afraid of where she was headed. Did he think she was going to reject him? Reject their pup? In some way, she felt she could. He'd definitely caused his fair share of damage. Accusing her of dishonesty, disloyalty, calling her a whore straight to her face.

But had she done any better? She'd been strong-willed and thick-headed through it all. She'd kept her pregnancy a secret for weeks and even went as far as putting their pup in jeopardy just the other night during the rogue attack. What made her any better?

"I choose you, Gabe," his head snapped up, eyes wide. "I may not have planned for any of this, but that doesn't mean I regret the choices that lead me here. This baby," she placed her hands over the small swell of her stomach. "This baby is a part of us. It's you, and it's me."

Amelia watched as his silver eyes, for the first time, melted into pools of gold. He approached her slowly. Each step deliberate and calculated. Time seemed to slow. It was just them, alone in the world. No barriers, no insecurities or doubts. Their hearts laid on the line.

"I never pictured myself as a father. I was a hot-headed kid who did a lot of stupid shit. I should have ended up in prison for most of the crap I pulled. I thought the Army had made me a better man, straightened me out, purged me of my impulses. It wasn't until I met you when I realized just how wrong I was. It's you, Amelia. You make me a better man.

"In the short time I've known you, you've completely changed my world. You've taught me that there's more to being an Alpha, a mate, than all the stereotypical crap us werewolves have to deal with. You're the most persistent, headstrong, infuriating woman I've ever met. But you're also the most courageous, fiercely loyal, and incredibly brave wolf I've ever known. This baby lucky to have you as its mom."

Gabriel laid his hand over hers, rubbing against the growing bud inside. Their pup.

Amelia's eyes glistened with unshed tears. She'd never heard so many words come from him at once. Certainly nothing as sincere or genuine. She couldn't find the words to respond. Didn't know if there was anything to be said that could match all that.

"I love you, Amelia," Gabriel confessed. He rested his hand on the crook of her neck, brushing his thumb along her mark, sending shivers throughout her body. "I know I haven't made any of this easy, and that's my own fault. My insecurities and doubts plagued me when I met you. I was an ass, and I'm sorry."

Amelia blinked up at him. Warm tears slid down her face. Her heart stuttered in her chest. He loved her. He really loved her. Rey was shaking with pride and yearning. The touch of his skin on her mark, his declaration of his feelings, blew her heart wide open.

She should be in mourning. Her focus should be on her father and her pack. The loss of him should be at the forefront of her mind. But it wasn't. All her grief and despair, the cost of losing such a pivotal figure in her life, was shoved to the back of her mind rather forcefully.

Her mind, heart, body, and soul needed her mate like a body required water to survive. Light and dark, unable to thrive without the other. The earth needing the moon's gravitational pull to keep it grounded, the sun to breathe life into every cell. He was her sun and moon, tethering her to a place of stability she never knew she needed.

Amelia pulled him down, his lips meeting hers. This wasn't their familiar kiss of lust and desire. This was something else. Something much deeper. His lips parted beneath her. Their movements slow and full of purpose, taking their time.

It wasn't about the need for skin—the need to satisfy their bodies' basic desires. Amelia needed to quench a thirst much more profoundly. Their mate bond opened, leaving her soul exposed, naked, and bare for him to do with as he will.

His hand tangled in her hair, the other gripping her arm, gathering her body against him. She tasted him. Tasted the feel of his mouth and much more. She could taste his psyche. His mind and body blending into one, and she finally understood. The mate bond was about more than breeding or extending the legacy of wolves, her legacy of Rhea. Their bond was two halves becoming one—a perfectly blended cohesive whole.

Amelia pulled back, her lungs desperate for air. His forehead rested against hers. Their breathing was labored, their hearts beat in harmony. She took in a final deep breath before completely baring her soul.

"I love you, too."

CHAPTER 35

TARGETED

Amelia and Gabriel headed back downstairs. They both agreed that for now it was best to keep her pregnancy a secret. Or as much of a secret as it could be with werewolves constantly hanging around. Now wasn't the time to make such an announcement. With her father's funeral in two days and the entire pack in mourning, it wouldn't be right.

Amelia made Gabriel promise not to go overboard with the protective Alpha garbage. She had enough going on and did not need him hovering over her like she was some fragile doll. She was pregnant, not damaged.

Downstairs, she spotted her brother and future sister-in-law. Their heads bent close to one another, whispering. Amelia couldn't help but smile at the two. She knew they were inevitable. The signals they'd been throwing at each other over the years was nauseating. She was thrilled they were finally together.

Amelia cleared her throat, causing the two love birds to separate. They both stood, having the decency to keep their eyes lowered. Gabriel chuckled beside her, winding his arm around her waist, his fingers brushing her stomach. Amelia couldn't help but smile. Smile at the gesture and how uncomfortable her brother and friend were.

"Can we speak with you in your office, please?" Amelia asked them, motioning with her head back behind them where the office was.

Damon finally met her gaze, regarding her wearily. "Sure," he said, dragging the word out.

Amelia and Gabriel followed behind her twin and Cordelia, making their way to his office. They both passed Damon inside the room as he shut the door behind them. Cordelia stood off to the side, her head hanging. Amelia turned on her brother just as she heard the clicking of the lock.

"Mia, I am so sorry. I didn't know he didn't know. I was so shocked you didn't tell me. We tell each other everything," Damon rambled, rushing his words.

"Like you informed me you were screwing my best friend?" Amelia asked him, eyebrows raised.

Damon's eyes grew wide, looking wildly between his sister and his lover. He tried to produce words, but nothing came out.

"You think I wouldn't be able to smell the two of you on each other. Neither of you has the others mark, but the scent is still there," Amelia gestured between the two of them. "And I couldn't be happier. It took you two long enough."

Amelia couldn't help but chuckle at the stunned look on both of their faces.

"Seriously, Mia, I'm sorry about the baby," Damon said, pleading with her.

Stepping forward, she hugged her brother again, holding on to him tightly. His body instantly molded against hers, embracing her back.

"I don't want to fight with you. We have enough going on as it is. Let's focus on dad for right now, okay?" she asked him, pulling back to find his familiar grin.

"Okay," Damon nodded. "I'm really going to be an Uncle?"

Amelia smiled. "Yes."

"Is that your handy work?" Damon gestured to the bruise along Gabriel's jaw. It was already healing, fading rapidly from a dark purple to yellow but still visible.

Amelia smiled sheepishly while Gabriel rubbed at the soreness. "Yep."

Damon turned to Gabriel; his eyebrow elevated, "Did you deserve it?"

Gabriel glanced towards her, his expression blank until his eyes warmed, and his face saddened, "Yes."

Amelia reached out, gripping his hand in hers, and gave him a reassuring squeeze. They were both hotheads, both unbelievably stubborn and dense, but they were each other's mess.

Damon nodded, accepting his answer before his smile grew, glancing down at her stomach. "Dad would be so proud," he reached up, wiping away the wetness she hadn't realized fell from her eyes. "But you'll always have me."

"I know," she sniffed. No matter how crazy her world got, Damon would always be her constant, her North Star. "Why don't you show me what you've done so far for the funeral."

☾ ☾ ☾

Amelia and Damon devoted the next few hours going over the arrangements. They decided to keep it a closed affair. Not wanting to jeopardize the safety of outside packs, given that the rogues could come back. Damon offered to escort her to their father before the ceremony, but the thought instantly made her want to vomit. She didn't think she could handle seeing him just yet. From what she heard of the fight, his body was extensively damaged.

During their time in the office, arranging their father's ceremony, Amelia was able to look over the eyewitness accounts of the attack. Something was off. She couldn't place her finger on it, but there was a nagging feeling in the back of her mind.

Somehow, no one could smell the rogues before they made it onto the Wandering Moon territory. Damon and her father both were inside the Packhouse when the attack began, making them the last to arrive. By that time, the rogues had already made it through the warriors on patrol and got as far as the Packhouse itself.

She had questions, and Damon described to her everything he could, but she needed to speak to someone on the front lines. Someone who was there from the moment the rogues arrived to the second they left. Her cousin Dominik was one of those qualified people.

Gabriel was busy discussing border patrols and enhanced security needed for the funeral and wake. Providing her the perfect excuse to slip out. She made sure to link Gabriel, letting him know she was leaving. The last thing she needed was a pissed off Alpha charging through the house searching for her.

Out in the hall, she closed the door firmly behind her. They'd be engaged for quite some time, leaving her no reason to rush. Wandering into the commons, she encountered some of her old friends, including Daniel, her ex.

"Mia!" Daniel called her over, looking like he just got off from patrol in gym shorts and no shirt.

"Hey, Danny," Amelia smiled at him, approaching her familiar group.

"Hey, Amelia," Gabby perked at the sight of her cousin, a cosmo in hand.

The hell was she doing, drinking at noon?

"You want some?" Gabby offered, tipping the drink in her direction.

Amelia shook her head. "No, I'm good, thanks. It's a bit early for me," she smiled faintly. The idea of alcohol awakened her nausea.

Gabby shrugged her shoulders, drinking the rest of the liquor with a final swig. "Sorry about your dad, Mia. Really sucks."

"Thanks, Gabby," she tried smiling at her cousin, but it somehow didn't form. She needed to stay on task. "Has anyone seen Dominik?"

"He just left to join the next patrol," Daniel said, jerking his head towards the back door.

"Thanks. I'll see you all later," she barely waved goodbye before running out the back. If she hurried, maybe she could catch him.

Outside, a group of forty warriors were already beginning to strip down. Border patrols were best done in wolf form. Better sense of smell and awareness if the beast was allowed out. She recognized her cousin's familiar hair, standing in the midst of the warriors, already down to his shorts.

"Dom!" Amelia yelled, capturing everyone's attention.

Dominik rose his head, catching sight of her. A slight smile appeared on his face before it fell. He muttered something to the warriors around him, but she was too far to catch it amongst the noise of the other wolves already shifting. He left the group, sending them on their way, and approached her up the back-porch steps.

"Hey, Mia. How are you?" Dominik asked, gesturing for her to take a seat on the porch steps.

Amelia sat down beside him, wrapping her arms around her knees. "I've had better days. How are you? Damon told me you were with the patrol that got attacked."

She examined him up and down, assessing the damage. Nothing obvious was broken, but he did suffer a severe bruise over his ribs and a few bite marks on his arms and legs from what she could see.

"I'm okay. It could have been a lot worse," Dominik shrugged, his eyes remote, filled with the memories of the attack.

It grieved her heart to see him so beaten, so defeated. She couldn't take away the pain of losing their last Alpha, his Uncle. But she could heal him physically.

Laying her hand on his shoulder, his eyes widened, curious to what she was doing. Never before had she shown anyone in her pack what she could do. The time for secrets was over. Secrets get people killed.

Amelia closed her eyes, allowing Rey to mix with her consciousness. She summoned her powers. Collectively, both human and wolf hummed their private tune. It was mellow and graceful, rising and falling with each breath. His injuries were minor compared to others she had healed in the past. She and Damon were always up to no good growing up, so she had plenty of practice. Opening her eyes, she smiled. Finding Dominik completely healed.

Dominik looked himself up and down, his eyes wide with shock. "What the- but how?"

"One of the perks, I guess," Amelia shrugged her shoulders.

"Perks of what?"

"Being a descendant of Rhea."

"We're all descended from Rhea and Ezekial. In some form or another, this whole pack can trace their lineage back to the original pack."

"Yes, but not many are her direct descendants. I am," Amelia could imagine the hundreds of questions churning in his mind. This probably explained a lot of things for him during their time growing up together. But they didn't have time for any of that. If her intuition was right, something was going on, and she had a feeling it had to do with her dreams.

"Look. There's something about last night that doesn't add up. How were the rogues able to get across the border without you scenting them? And why weren't there more deaths? If thirty rogues attacked, by surprise no less, it should have been a massacre. Yet, the only death was my father. Why?"

Dominik merely shook his head, looking clueless. "I don't know, Mia. I swear. I've never seen anything like it. They just rushed us. The wind was blowing right in our faces, but we never caught wind of their scent. They ran right through us but never stopped long enough to cause any significant damage. It was like they weren't after us. The rogues went straight for the Packhouse."

"The Packhouse? But that doesn't make any sense. If they were looking for a fight, then they would have stayed and fought the warriors," Amelia talked it out to herself.

"That was my thought, but they didn't. They ran right through us and went straight for the house. But they never went inside. We were scrambling to get the warriors out and the women and children to safety. But they never touched the helpless. As soon as your dad and brother left the house, the rogues went straight for them," Dominik explained.

"Are you saying they were after my brother and dad? But why? Rogues don't have the thinking capability to pick and choose their victims like that. They're rabid," Amelia felt her head swimming, bile rising to the back of her throat. The image of a rogue lunging for her. Ready to tear her throat out, flashed across her mind.

"That's what we've always believed, yes. But these were different. We tried to form ranks to protect our Alphas, both of them. But there were too many. We managed to kill over ten of them, but as soon as your father fell, they ran."

"They just ran?" Amelia couldn't believe it. "You're making it sound like they were targeting my family."

"That's the way it looked. I don't know how to explain it any other way. But they wanted either Damon or Uncle Thomas dead," Dominik sounded firm in his belief. He was implying that this wasn't accidental. It was a hit.

Dominik's face fell. His blue eyes drooped and shoulders sagged in defeat. It saddened her to see it. Amelia could only imagine. To feel like you failed your pack, your Alpha, was the biggest fear for a warrior. She laid her hand on her cousin's shoulder, squeezing him.

"This was not your fault, Dom. I don't know what's going on here, but it's something bigger than we know. I promise you. I will figure this out. We're not losing anyone else."

"I'm sorry, Mia. I'm sorry I couldn't protect him. There were just too many."

Amelia could feel the sensation building in her stomach and rising up her throat. It was too much. She pushed herself off the deck and ran for the cover of the trees, throwing up in a bush. The acid burned her throat and nose, clutching her stomach as her body spasmed.

A tender hand stroked her back, holding her hair from her face.

"Are you okay?"

She could detect the worry in Dominik's voice, but she was too busy removing the lining of her stomach to answer. The day's tidal wave of emotions was coming out in the form of dry heaving and bile.

"Amelia!"

Great, here comes the overprotective dad. Amelia thought between bouts of hurling.

Amelia could hear Gabriel dismissing Dominik as he got closer. Her cousin was hesitant, but by the look on her mate's face, he wasn't taking no for an answer. Gabriel took Dom's spot, holding her hair and rubbing her back.

She held her finger up, letting him know she was almost done. Her stomach was now empty, and the spasms were starting to lesson. Finally straightening up, she inhaled deeply. The disgusting burning sensation of acid on the back of her tongue nearly produced the same response, but she breathed through it. Repeating the technique a few times, she stood like that for some minutes, quieting the tremors that racked her body. The now hollow pit in her stomach growled at her, informing her she was hungry.

"Pick a side, child! You're hungry, or you're not!" Amelia grumbled loudly to herself, resting her hand on her stomach to quell the now uncomfortable hunger feeling.

Gabriel stepped in front of her, relaxing his hands on her shoulders. Amelia tilted her head against his solid chest. His scent helped calm her chaotic hormones, her traitorous body that couldn't seem to decide what it required. He rubbed his hands up and down her arms, bringing warmth back to her body. She always felt so incredibly fatigued after throwing up. As though she not only threw up the contents of her stomach but all of her energy as well.

"Are you okay?" Gabriel asked softly in her hair, his breath caressing her skin.

She could tell through their bond he was concerned. This was unfamiliar terrain for the both of them but for him; he was on the outside looking in. Unable to comprehend anything that was going on with her body. Hell, she barely had a clue as well.

"I'm okay, just tired," she said against his chest. Her knees felt weak, shaking beneath her weight.

Amelia felt herself being lifted; her feet left the ground. It was probably a good thing. She didn't know how much longer she'd last. Murky clouds obstructed her vision, building and growing like an angry storm, ready to engulf the sea.

"Don't worry, baby. I got you."

CHAPTER 36

DEJA VU

Amelia couldn't remember falling asleep or making it back to their room. Damon had managed to set up a guest suite in her old room, which was comforting to wake up too. For the first night in months, she was able to sleep through the night. Not a single dream or nightmare. It felt wondrous to just sleep.

She had promised Damon she'd sift through some of their family albums tucked away in the attack. Cordelia had the brilliant idea to design a memory board from some of their old pictures. She merely had to find them.

She kind of wished Kelsey was there to help. Her and Cordelia would have gotten along great. They were practically the same person. The two were strikingly similar in personality and crafting abilities. She'd be excellent with helping to sift through all the junk her family had hoarder over the decades.

Cordelia was a traitor. Opting out of aiding her by agreeing to help the cooks in the kitchen. Jerk. So instead, she was torturing Christian. Not giving the man a choice.

She would have preferred Gabriel, but he was out training with the warriors alongside Damon. Working on some of the techniques they'd been teaching the Twilight Moon Pack.

The attic was dusty and poorly lit. Fortunately, there was a boarded window. She ripped the wood planks off to allow natural light and fresh air to filter through. Instantly, the attic didn't feel as cramped or dank.

It took her and Christian a bit to find the boxes they were looking for.

A photo caught her eye; her fingers hovered over the eerily familiar face. Amelia picked up the image near the bottom of the box and brought it closer. She traced the outline of her face, shockingly similar to her own. Even though her father made sure to keep pictures of their mother out so that they would never forget what she looked like, she never thought she'd seen one of her so young.

Her mother looked to be the same age as she was now. Sitting in the bed of an old beat-up pick-up truck. Her long, blonde locks were blowing in the wind. The same full, red lips were pulled into a smile, laughing about something. Amelia wished she could remember her laugh.

It was eerie to see how alike they were. Same hair, eyes, pointed nose, and broad shoulders. She barely remembered much about her mother. The most significant memory she had was her death, which she tried consistently to forget. She couldn't imagine abandoning her child to grow up without her. She'd fight like hell to make sure that would never happen.

"Who's that?"

Amelia startled. Not realizing Christian had moved behind her, looking over her shoulder at the photo.

"Is that you?" Christian asked, tilting his head to the side as he examined the photograph.

"No. It's my mom, Emma."

"Man, you two could be twins."

"Ya, we could."

Christian wasn't mistaken. It was unsettling how much they looked alike. She wondered how she would have aged if she was still alive. Would they still look so similar?

She would never know.

"What's this?" Christian leaned in over her, pulling out a small, black leather book. He flipped open the pages, scanning through them until he reached the end. "Ella, it's your mom's journal."

Amelia jumped up, snatching the book from his hands. She read the date of the last entry; one week before her murder. "Chris, this was right before her death," she whispered. Never knowing her mother journaled.

Skipping back a few pages, she skimmed through the contents of the book. Reading through her mother's written words. In all her life, she didn't think she'd ever read a single thing her mother wrote. Now, there it was, in the palm of her hands. Something she had touched, poured her feelings and thoughts into. She should feel ashamed, feel bad for invading her privacy. But she didn't, not one bit. She was eager to know more about the woman she barely remembered calling mom.

One of the words captured her attention. Emma's handwriting was flawless. Effortlessly written with a careful hand. But as the pages went on, her writing became more unstable, as though she'd been shaking as she jotted down her thoughts.

"Listen to this. *I can't explain it. Thomas thinks I'm paranoid, but I'm not. Someone's been following me. Every time I step out of this house I feel a cold chill creep down my spine. My wolf keeps warning me. My dreams are getting worse, but I don't grasp their meaning,*" Amelia felt a sense of deja vu, her mind reeling. "She was being stalked."

"Maybe she was paranoid. Your dad would have hunted anyone who came near your family," Christian said, reminding her just how territorial wolves really were.

"No, look at her writing, how shaky it is. She's terrified," she said, pointing to some of the more illegible scribbles. "And these are dated weeks before she was killed. She feels like someone's following her, and then a couple of weeks later, she's brutally murdered in our backyard?"

"Coincidence?" Christian asked meekly.

"I don't believe in coincidences," she shook her head. "Plus, if she had dreams as well, then it's definitely not a coincidence. Someone was after my mother, and for some reason, they slaughtered her."

Amelia sat back down on the floor, flipping through the journal.

Everywhere I go, I feel the same chills creep along my skin. Every now and then I can see him. I can only catch a glimpse before he disappears, but I know it's the same man. It's gotten to the point where I no longer take the twins with me when I go out. I could never risk my baby's lives. If this man wanted me, it was best if I was alone. Only one more month before the baby inside me will be born, then she will be safe as well.

Amelia placed her arm around her abdomen. The overwhelming need to protect the life growing inside her overcame her. She had almost forgotten how far along her mother was. The baby girl her mother was carrying was nearly due. Her death took place just a few brief weeks before her due date. But her life was snatched from her before it began.

Flipping to the following page, she read on.

I talked to him. The man who's been following me for months finally had the nerve to cross paths with me. He's lucky I'm so close to my due date. I wanted to tear his heart from his chest, where he stood. He had dark, unsettling eyes and clipped mousy hair. He could have been attractive if not for my instincts screaming at me to run.

The man smelled strange. It definitely wasn't a normal wolf smell. No, instead, he reeked of burnt rubber and gas—a strong diesel smell. Eva, my wolf, was screaming at me to run, but I couldn't move. I wanted to confront the man who'd been stalking me. Who'd made me afraid to leave my house, to be left alone with my children. I wanted him to know I wasn't afraid of him. He couldn't frighten me.

The man had the audacity to introduce himself to me. Michael.

"Michael. Michael," she said aloud, pondering the name. "Why does that sound so familiar?"

"Ella, I'm going to grab a snack. You want something?" Christian called over to her from the door.

"Umm, water and a banana, please," she said absently, refusing to tear her eyes from the journal.

She barely heard Christian leave. Her mind was racing. The smell, the eerie feeling of chills, the man. It all seemed so familiar. She flipped to the next page—the last entry.

The Moon Goddess came to me last night. This time she actually spoke. The dream started the same as the rest. I'm outside. Sometimes it's dark, sometimes it's the middle of the day, but the same wolf comes every time. He's big and scrawny. His fur is a muddy brown color, cropped short to his body. Every time, he attacks me. I try to fight back. This time I managed to mark him, deep cuts down the side of his head.

That's when the Goddess appeared. She said, "Do not ignore my warnings. Your child will die. You will die."

Amelia slammed the journal shut. She threw her hand over her mouth, holding back the vomit that was threatening to appear. The book slipped from her hands onto the floor. She stared at it as if it had developed teeth and bit her.

Those words. Those words were the same ones as her dream the night before. All of her dreams, every single one had been warning her. Her packs were going to be slaughtered. Gabriel was going to die defending them, and somehow, she was going to lose her baby.

And that man. Michael. Her mother described him well. The hair, the eyes, his peculiar smell. In her dream, she said she wounded him.

The cafe! Rey yelled, startling her.

What? What cafe? Amelia asked her, not understanding.

We met Michael, Amelia. That cafe you drove to just outside the Twilight Moon territory. He smelled exactly the same!

Amelia's eyes widened. Michael. The one who freaked her out at the cafe. The one who had three deep and long scars down the side of his head. She shook his hand. Told him her name.

Michael was the one who murdered her mother.

CHAPTER 37

GOLD WHERE THERE'S DIRT

Amelia hadn't left her spot on the attic floor, except to get up and dig through more boxes. So far, she uncovered a total of four journals that belonged to her mother. Emma wasn't the greatest at remembering to journal, so the dates between entries were a bit sporadic, but at least when she did write, she wrote down the more noteworthy things.

Her mother was born in the Lunar Moon Pack, just north of the Wandering Moon in the state of New Hampshire, only a few hours away. But her grandmother, Emma's mother, was a Wandering Moon member. It was through her grandmother that their lineage connected her to Rhea and Ezekial.

Emma made sure to record every story she'd heard when it came to the first fated pair. Some of them sounded like hogwash. Worse than some of the fairytale's humans cooked up, and that's saying something. But others looked promising.

Each firstborn girl is born with a unique wolf. A piece of the Moon Goddess herself. She will contain great power and a strong dominating Alpha aura. Amelia read to herself from one of the journals.

Well, we know at least that much is true. Rey interjected.

Shush. She ignored her wolf and continued to read. *Each firstborn daughter will be granted a fated mate. The Moon Goddess will bless their union with specific abilities. She will be able to heal, foresee the future, and communicate with Goddess through dreams and projections.* Amelia stopped, confused.

"Projections? What are projections?" Amelia spoke aloud, frowning.

I have no idea. Rey shrugged internally.

"You talking to yourself?"

Amelia nearly screamed. Glaring daggers at her brother, who was now laughing hysterically at her expense. She grabbed a journal and flung it at him. It would have struck him too, right in the nose, if he hadn't caught it.

"What are you still doing up here? Dinners almost done. I had to keep Gabriel locked in my office so he wouldn't come tearing up here looking for you," Damon said, absently flipping through the journal now in his hands.

Amelia raised her brow at him in disbelief. "You actually locked Gabriel in your office?"

Damon looked over the journal. A smirk pulled at his lips. "Well, no. But I did convince him not to come up here. I told him I'd persuade you to come down," he looked back down at the journal, his face frowned. "Is this mom's?"

"Yeah. I've found a few of them here," she gestured to the ones in front of her.

"And you don't think that's weird?" Damon asked, his voice insinuating it was.

"Shut up and get over here," she gestured for him to sit down beside her, which he did. "The journal you're holding was the one mom wrote in shortly before she died."

Damon looked back down at the journal in his hands with a new air of curiosity. As though the journal was the most precious thing in the world.

To them, it was.

"Exactly," she said, noting his expression. "Now, in that journal, mom writes about being stalked. Someone was following her around town. She wrote about the way it made her feel, how her wolf yelled at her to run. That's why mom kept her distance from us those last few months she was alive. She knew someone was after her, and she didn't want to put us in harm's way."

"Don't you think if someone were stalking mom, dad would have done something about it?" Damon asked, the tone in voice making it plane he had doubts.

"Mom says she told dad, but he thought it was just pregnancy stress. No one ever saw the man or smelled an intruder, nothing. Does that sound familiar?" Amelia hinted but kept going. "In that journal, mom describes the man. He had the gall to introduce himself to her. His name was Michael. That was a week before her death."

"Michael? We don't know a Michael," Damon thought on it, mulling the name over in his mind.

"Listen, mom described him to a T. From his eye color, hair color, smell, the feeling she got around him. Even her wolf advised her to get the hell away from him. All of it," she said, leading up to the key point. "I met Michael, Damon. I met the man that murdered our mother."

"What?!" Damon asked.

She couldn't help but feel hurt by the disbelief in his voice. Did he really not have any faith in her?

"I'm not kidding, Damon. I met him. He found me in a cafe after I left the Twilight Moon's territory. He approached me and introduced himself. He looks exactly the way mom described."

"Mia, millions of people have brown hair, brown eyes."

"Yeah? Then what about his smell? He smelled exactly like burnt rubber and petrol. He had three long scars down the side of his head, exactly like mom dreamed about. He talked to me about wolves and told me how beautiful I was. He was unbelievably creepy," Amelia said with a shiver, recalling the way ice seemed to crawl down her skin when she shook his hand.

"Does Gabriel know?" Damon asked her.

Directing her gaze down, she played with the hem of her shirt. He just had to bring up her mate. "No. When I met him, I had no idea who he was. Gabriel and I were fighting, and I didn't want to make it worse by bringing up some stranger who gave me the willies."

"You barely met the guy, Mia. It could have been a coincidence."

Amelia slammed the book in her hand down on the hardwood floor. The abrupt noise caused her brother to jolt.

"I am *not* delusional or hormonal or whatever other bullshit you want to pin this on. Dad ignored mom when this was going on, and she ended up dead! All of this," she gestured to the journals, which contained the only clues she'd ever read about containing her history, her powers. "This is real, and I do not see gold where there's dirt. Something really fishy is going on here, and I refuse to believe it's a coincidence!"

"Okay, okay. I believe you," Damon breathed deeply, his own nerves frazzled by his sister's outburst. "What do we do?"

"We keep reading. See if there's anything else in these books that can help us. Mom said she was having dreams. The Moon Goddess was trying to warn her, but she didn't understand what she was supposed to do differently, and she ended up paying for that mistake with her life."

"Have you had any dreams?" Damon asked her sheepishly, afraid of another outburst.

"Yes," she admitted, biting her lower lip. "I've had dreams every night since I mated with Gabriel."

"Mia!"

"Don't yell at me!" Amelia yelled back. "How was I supposed to know they were prophetic?! How was I supposed to know about *any* of this?! No one told me a damn thing! According to mom's journal, every firstborn girl in our family has a fated mate. That would have been nice to know! Once were mated, we get powers to heal, visions, and dreams from the Goddess. No one told me a damn thing! Dad only ever said to keep the healing thing a secret."

"Okay, okay. Fuck," Damon ran his fingers through his hair rather aggressively, tugging at the roots. "What were the dreams about?"

Amelia told him about the dreams, even the variations, the differences she'd experienced between some of them. More specifically, the last one she had where the Goddess warned Amelia in person. Warned her of the pack's death, her mate, and her child.

"Once more I'm going to ask. Have you told Gabriel?"

"What are you, his champion now?" Amelia grumbled.

"Mia," Damon growled.

"He knows most of it. Not the baby part."

"Mia!" Damon yelled again.

"Damon, if you yell my name one more time, I will smack you so hard you'll think your head was no longer attached to your neck," she advised him with a growl of her own.

"This is important shit! You can't keep hiding things from him," Damon said, ignoring her threats.

"I am not hiding things from him. I wasn't ready to tell him about the baby, which is why I left that detail out. But since someone had to spill the beans on me, that's no longer an issue. I'll tell him everything tonight," she promised.

Damon at least had the decency to look ashamed, directing his eyes away from hers. "Look, I really am sorry about that. I was just so excited for you, it just kind of blurted out. I never thought I'd be an Uncle. I was convinced you were going to be a spinster forever."

Amelia chuckled, feigning hurt. "Such a vote of confidence," she smiled at him, enjoying the moment with her twin. "It ended up working out. I was a chicken. I should have told him myself when I first found out. I was just so freaked. I didn't think I'd ever be a mom either. But now that I am …"

She laid her hand against her stomach, imagining what the child might look like. Would it have his square jaw and her pointed nose? Would it be as stubborn as her or as thick-headed as him? A hundred questions ran through her mind of all the possibilities that were currently contained in her growing womb.

"Gabriel told me he loved me," Amelia whispered. Recalling the way he said it, how her heart quite literally skipped a beat in her chest.

"Did you say it back?"

Amelia looked up into her brother's eyes. The same eyes that mirrored her own. The only difference was hers were swimming in unshed tears. "I love him, Damon. I can't lose either of them. I won't."

Damon gathered her against him, cradling her head against his shoulder, rubbing circles in her back. "It's going to be okay. We'll figure this out."

"How?! Even the Goddess said I'd lose them all. My pack, my mate, my baby," she cried against the soft cotton fabric of his shirt.

Damon pulled her face up to look at him, holding her gaze with his own. Ensuring she understood that he meant every word he was about to say.

"Our packs will survive. Gabriel will live, and I would never let anything happen to your baby. That baby you have growing inside of you has the fiercest mom in the world and the most protective father on the planet. Not to mention the Uncle who'd surrender everything for her. We will survive this."

"You said her," Amelia sniffled. "We don't know that."

"Oh, I already know. It's going to be a girl, and she's going to rule the world someday."

Amelia snorted at her brother, pushing herself away from him. She wiped the tears from her face and sighed. "What do we do now?"

"Dad's funeral is tomorrow. That's our priority. We will figure out the rest as soon as the ceremony is over."

Amelia nodded, agreeing with him. Saying goodbye to their father came first. But after that, Michael better find a deep hole to crawl under.

CHAPTER 38

UNTIL WE MEET AGAIN
IN THE STARS

The moon was high in the sky, reaching its apex. The light reflected off its silver face, illuminating the vast woods. There was a gentle breeze billowing through the trees that brushed against her face. The earth was warm beneath her feet. Soft, packed dirt squished between her toes as her feet moved silently through the brush.

Glancing down, she noticed she was dressed in a white dress. The material, sheer and light, floated around her form in the wind. Her unbound hair tickled her face as the air lifted it up and swayed it around her head.

The ground was littered with bodies. Dead wolves and humans, rogue and pack. Stepping over their bodies, already rigid and stiff, set in rigor mortis, she caught sight of a tall, willowy woman.

Her feet carried her faster, leaping over the bodies, ignoring the friends and family she spotted among the dead. Chasing after the woman, she left the deceased behind. The woman stopped just in front of her, causing her to come to a sudden halt. Skidding in the dirt, she caught herself as the Goddess turned her sights on her.

Under the gaze of her violet eyes, her skin prickled with gooseflesh. She could taste the magic in the air that surrounded them. The trees above them froze mid-breeze, as though time stood still before the woman.

"You're the Moon Goddess," Amelia finally said, regaining her voice.

The Goddess nodded her head. Strands of pale gold fell in her eyes, only to be pushed away by an invisible current.

"How can I prevent this? How do I save my pack, my mate, and my child?" she knew she sounded desperate, but in all honesty, she was. Desperate to protect the ones she loved.

"Do not disregard my warnings. Your pack will die. Your mate will die, and you will lose a child," the Goddess warned her.

"But how can I stop it from happening? What can I do?!" Amelia asked, her knees buckling beneath her. Fear gripped her in its vice.

The Goddess turned away, walking farther out of reach. Amelia tried to run, tried to cry out, but the Goddess kept moving farther and farther away.

"Come back!"

☽ ☽ ☽

Amelia jolted awake. Gabriel sat up beside her, woken by her sudden movements.

"Amelia?" Gabriel called to her groggily.

Sweat soaked her shirt, clinging to it like a second skin. Her hair was plastered to her neck and face. The back of her throat was dry and scratchy as though she'd been screaming. Her stomach rolled.

Tossing the covers off, Amelia bolted for the bathroom, making it to the toilet just in time. The cool porcelain felt good against her warm skin as she gripped the bowl of the seat, removing whatever traces of dinner were left in her body. She felt her hair being lifted from her face. A sturdy hand rested on her back like a firm weight.

"Ugh, go away," Amelia tried swatting at him but missed.

"Not a chance. I'm here for you, Darlin."

Amelia sat up off the toilet, flushed the bowl clean, and forced herself to stand. She glared at her mate, her eyebrow raised.

Did he just call us, darling?

He did, Rey confirmed. Her wolf smirked at the pet's name.

"What are we in the wild west?" Amelia asked, wiping her face with a washcloth she found on the bathroom counter, trying to hide the small smirk dancing on her lips.

Gabriel smiled, his face lighting up. "Don't hide your smile from me. You know you like it," he laughed at the face she made, suggesting otherwise. Spreading his fingers through her pale, platinum hair, he pondered. "What about snow?"

"Snow?" Amelia scrunched her brow, watching as he played with her wild mane.

"Your hair is so pale, and your wolf's fur is as white as snow."

Amelia watched as his eyes were fixated on her hair, caressing it between the tips of his fingers. "If anyone's like Snow White, it would be you with your raven hair." She reached up, extending her fingers through his soft locks, hanging in his eyes in a way that had her core humming.

"Snow White's got nothing on you," Gabriel said softly, leaning down to kiss her.

Amelia placed her hand on his face, stopping him short. "Don't even think about kissing me. I haven't even brushed my teeth."

Gabriel chuckled, pulling back. He gripped her wrist before she could pull away, brushing his nose into the tender flesh against her pulse, peppering her with whisper-soft kisses.

Amelia knew exactly what he'd be seeing. Her eyes would resemble large emeralds, filled with lust and desire. He knew exactly how to rile her up, and given the state of her emotions and hormones, it didn't take much.

Gabriel released her suddenly, causing her to whimper from the loss of contact. "Later, Snow. Right now, we need to get cleaned up. It's going to be a long day."

Amelia sighed. He was right. Today she would say goodbye to her father and light his pyre on fire so that his spirit could rest in the stars with the other fallen Alpha's.

☾ ☾ ☾

The day passed by in a blur.

Amelia tried to keep herself busy. Organizing the flower arrangements, helping the Omega's with the place settings for the dinner after the ceremony, setting up tables and chairs outside. It wasn't until she tried to help gather wood for the pyre when Gabriel finally came out, forbidding her from doing any more.

She pouted, forcing her bottom lip out like a lost puppy, but he was right. All she wanted to do was keep her mind busy but exhausting herself wouldn't help anyone. He guided her inside, where she sat down on the couch with a huff, making sure he knew how annoyed she was with him ordering her around.

His annoying self merely laughed, setting one of the couch blankets over her.

"Relax, snowflake. Take a break. The rest of us have it handled."

Amelia glared at him, snatching the nearest thing she could reach. A hardcover book and flung it at his head. He ducked just in time, preventing the egg-sized knot he would have received. The book instead hit the wall across the room, falling to the ground.

"Do not call me snowflake," she growled.

Gabriel leaned down, brushing a kiss against her forehead. "I'm sorry. I won't use it again," he smiled. "Try and relax. The ceremony is in a few hours. You've done enough today. We've got it from here."

☾ ☾ ☾

Up in her bedroom, her dress was already laid out on the bed. She could hear the shower going and could only assume Gabriel was getting ready himself. Luckily, she showered that morning, so all that was left was to put her clothes on and adjust her hair.

Stripping out of her clothes, she pulled on the black lace dress. It was classic in design, hugging her curves with a scoop neck. Her shoulders were left exposed as the dress hung down to her knees. She walked over to her mirror that still hung on her closet door and the stranger she found.

The woman reflected looked tired. Dark circles rimmed her bloodshot eyes. Her hair was frazzled from running around that morning and she couldn't remember the last solid meal she enjoyed. Her appetite was all but gone.

The only reason she was still standing was from the small meals she forced down her throat. If she didn't eat at all, she'd be stuck in the bathroom, dry heaving all day. Her pregnancy did not appreciate it if she left her stomach empty for too long. She'd been surviving off toast, some soup, and water, since learning the news of her father.

Her hands spread over her stomach covering the slight bulge poking out. She honestly had no idea how far along she was. A doctor's visit had not been one of her priorities, but even if she had gotten knocked up their first time, she still shouldn't be showing. That would only mean she was nine weeks at the most and judging from the bump currently showing through her dress, she looked farther along than that.

A brawny, tender hand wrapped around her waist, resting over her lower abdomen, stroking her stomach through the lace of her dress. Amelia leaned back into his sturdy frame. She fastened her eyes as he gathered her against his firm chest.

"You look stunning, Snow," Gabriel whispered in her ear.

Shivers brushed along her skin. Her breath hitched in her throat. She swallowed the hard lump that was forming. A rush of emotion threatened to overcome her.

"Thank you."

"For what?" Gabriel asked, twirling her around to face him.

"For being here. For being so strong and gracious. For just being you. I'm pretty fond of you, you know?"

"Oh, are you?" Gabriel asked, smirking, teasing her. "I guess I'm pretty fond of you too."

Amelia wound her arms around his neck and raised herself up on her toes, giving him a chaste kiss before she laid her head against his shoulder. They stood like that for some time. She'd never felt safer, more secure than in his arms. It terrified her how much she loved the man. Never knowing she was capable of such depth, such attachment.

A knock on her door caused her to raise her head.

"Mia. It's time."

Damon's voice was muffled through the fastened door. Amelia pulled back from him, draping her arms limply at her side.

"I'm coming!" she called back to him.

Out of time, she quickly arranged her hair, twisting it up in a high ponytail. Her hair really did look like snow against the black of her dress. The contrast was startling. It looked as if it had lightened over the last few months.

Gabriel waited for her by the door. His hand stretched out for her. She took it, interlacing their fingers, following his lead down the stairs.

The house was desolate—void of the usual chaos. No pups were running through the house, omega's milling about handling the day to day tasks. No warriors searching endlessly for food. Just still silence.

They walked out the back doors to find well over seven hundred pack members filling the yard. The crowd stretched back to the edges of the forest. Every single one of her father's pack was in attendance. Tears pricked her eyes. Gnawing her lip, she made her way down the porch steps.

The attendees parted the sea for her. Allowing her a direct path to the center of the gathering. In the middle was a large wooden pyre. Her father's body shrouded in white, laid on top. She gasped at the sight, the reality finally crashing down on her.

Gabriel's hands gripped her waist, holding her back against his body, offering her his entire frame for support. Amelia leaned into him as tears spilled down her cheeks. She was unable to avert her gaze away from the body that had once contained her father's fighting spirit, his witty laughter, and his sarcastic remarks. Everything she was, was because of him, and he was gone.

Damon stepped forward, now that she had arrived. Amelia was the last one to show up and the ceremony could start.

"Thank you all for coming," Damon said, his voice ringing out over the soundless clearing. The air was so void of noise, the sound of a pin dropping could be heard.

"I never thought I'd be doing this so soon after taking over as Alpha. I thought I'd be old and gray. I thought my father would be fat, surrounded by his grandchildren, slipping away quietly in his sleep. But the Moon Goddess had other plans for Alpha Thomas. She called him home sooner than any of us could have guessed. Tonight, we say goodbye to our Alpha, our leader. To all of you, he was your Alpha, but he was also your friend, your family."

Damon commanded the attention of hundreds; all eyes focused on him. His voice moved fluidly even though tears were thick on his lashes. Amelia stretched her hand out, feeling Cordelia's familiar, milky skin grasping onto hers.

She pulled Cordelia in closer, using her as an additional lifeline.

"Tonight, we release my father's soul so that he may join the Goddess in the stars, watching over us for the rest of our days. The brighter the star, the greater the Alpha and Alpha Thomas will be one of the brightest. Finally he can join his wife, his fated mate in the afterlife," someone from off to the side handed Damon a large torch, already lit. Red and orange flames licked the air. "Mia?"

Amelia froze at the sound of her name. She stared at her father's body, shrouded in white, hiding the damage inflicted on his body. Letting her hand slip from Cordelia's and pulling out of Gabriel's grasp, she stepped forward. Somehow her feet were able to move, holding her up. Her body didn't feel like her own. It was as if someone else was at the helm, steering her closer to the pyre, closer to her father.

She stopped just before the wood could scratch her skin. Close enough to smell the blood that still clung to his wounds. Close enough to recognize the familiar pack smell that used to cling to him. Maple and tree bark with his own touch of spice from his aftershave.

She gasped, struggling to breathe between sobs. Reaching out, she placed her hand over her father's chest, trying to ignore the irregular shapes she felt beneath the thin cloth.

"Goodbye, Daddy," she cried silently, trying her hardest to hold it all back. "Until we meet again in the stars. Say hi to mom for me."

Damon laid his hand on her shoulder, pulling her back from the pyre before dipping his torch down to the kindling.

The pyre caught fire quickly. The flames reached up, devouring the wood and the body that laid on top. The crimson and orange flames danced in the sky, kissing the blanket of stars.

CHAPTER 39

RESTLESS AND DESPERATE

It was the day of the wake. Most of the pack would be in attendance to celebrate her father's life with lots of food, games, and memories weaved into stories.

Last night was a muddled mess.

After watching her father's soul rise into the sky, she couldn't recall much of what had happened. All she knew was that she was so emotionally and physically exhausted, she spent the remainder of the night in bed with Gabriel. Between bouts of making love and crying, she drained herself to the point of collapse. She knew Gabriel was hesitant to have sex with her. Afraid it wasn't appropriate, but it was the only thing that gave her a moment's release from her bereavement.

They still had no idea why the rogues continued to linger outside the territory or why her father was targeted. She had managed to tell Gabriel the rest of the Goddess's warning. He definitely freaked like she thought he would. But who could blame him? When the Goddess tells you your child will die, it doesn't give you the warm and fuzzys.

It made her sick just thinking about it.

The minute her eyes opened, she felt like death itself. Her eyes were swollen and crusted shut. The back of her throat was parched, as though she drank a glass brimming with sawdust. Her empty stomach despised her, cramping and growling with discomfort, demanding to be fed proper food. But none of that was what concerned her.

From the moment her mind exited sleep and entered consciousness, there was a tight knot deep in her chest. She felt antsy and jittery, jumping at the slightest noise. Rey was pacing back and forth in her mind. Her wolf was restless and agitated as well.

A resounding crash echoed off the walls. Amelia jumped at the sound, glass shattering on impact.

"Relax, it's just a plate," Cordelia said beside her. "Gosh, you've been so jumpy today."

Amelia looked back over her shoulder, and sure enough, one of the teens helping to set the tables dropped one of the plates on the wood floor. Amelia was trying to fold a pile of napkins into cute little pyramids, but was failing miserably. Cordelia had a neat stack piled high before her, while she barely had a dozen completed.

"Are you okay?" asked Cordelia.

"I'm fine," Amelia snapped, a bit harsher than she meant to.

"You don't seem fine. You've been folding the same napkin for the last five minutes," Cordelia nodded to the napkin she had twisted in a ball. Not at all the shape it was supposed to be.

Amelia tossed the napkin down on the table, sighing with frustration. More than anything, she wanted to go for a run. Kill something if she could. Allow Rey to take control and completely lose herself to the beast within, but she couldn't do any of that. The minute she tries to run, she ends up hurling in the bushes. Not to mention shifting is completely off the table for the next several months.

Gabriel was busy with Damon doing manly things outside, like hanging up lights in the trees and setting up the tables and chairs. She'd rather be outside doing physical labor than inside worrying about place settings and whether or not roses go with baby's breath or delphinium. Like any of that even mattered. Her father was dead, and whoever was behind the attacks was getting away with it and probably planning another.

She hadn't realized she'd picked up her glass of water until she heard a cracking sound, her feet suddenly wet. Looking down, she found her hands filled with shards of glass painted red.

"Oh, my God! Mia!" Cordelia shouted, her voice panicked. She grabbed one of the napkins, brushing the glass from her hand, and applied pressure to the cuts in her flesh.

Amelia barely felt any of it. She felt numb and withdrawn. The only thing on her mind was the unsettled feeling she had.

"Amelia!"

The sound of his voice compelled her out of her fog. His tone laced with alarm and concern. Stupid mate bond. Why did he have to feel every single paper cut?

It's not a paper cut. Rey said, interjecting into her thoughts.

Oh, who asked you?!

You need to pay more attention! We can't afford to make any mistakes!

Amelia was startled by her wolf's tone but was distracted from asking what the hell she meant when Gabriel appeared before her eyes, nearly knocking Cordelia on her ass in the process. Real graceful.

"I'm fine. It's no big deal," Amelia tried to wave him off when the pain in her hands began to register.

It hurt. Like a lot.

Gabriel pulled the napkin away from her hands to reveal deep gashes, blood pumping with every beat of her heart. The sight of it had her stomach rolling.

Goodness. Now she can't even stomach the sight of blood. What the hell was this baby doing to her? Trying to make her a pacifist?! Cause that's never going to happen.

"Shit. You're going to need stitches," Gabriel muttered under his breath.

"Oh no, I won't. No one's touching me with a needle," Amelia said firmly. "Damon!"

Her scream startled everyone in the room. She couldn't heal herself, but her twin certainly could. Knives, she didn't mind. But tiny needles sliding under her skin, she had a problem with.

Damon came rushing into the room at the sound of her shrill voice. His eyes were wild and shocked. Glancing down at the state of her hands, he scrunched his brow at her.

"What the hell did you do?" Damon asked, as though he was accusing her of something.

"What, do you think I did this on purpose? A glass broke!" Amelia shot back, shoving her damaged hand in his face. "Help me out here. I've gotten you out of way worse scrapes!"

"Christ, relax. Like I would leave you hanging," Damon grasped her by the arm and hauled her out of the dining hall. Cordelia and Gabriel followed closely behind.

Amelia could feel Gabriel's displeasure with the way Damon was handling her. She smirked at the fact that he felt threatened by her brother. It was cute, in an annoying sort of way.

Once they were safely tucked away in his office, Damon sat her down on the couch, the napkin now officially soaked through. Peeling the fabric away from her wounds, they both looked down at the damage. There were still bits of glass embedded in her skin. The cuts were clean. Straight through tendons and blood vessels.

"We need tweezers to get the glass out," Gabriel said, looking over her shoulder.

Amelia shook her head no.

"No, we don't," Damon said, confirming her head sway.

His eyes were already closed. Amelia followed suit as their song washed over the both of them. She could feel a strange tingling in her palms. Her body fused the skin back together, pushing the shards of glass out of her palm as it knit tendons and flesh. Tiny pings could be heard as the pebbles of glass dropped to the floor.

Amelia opened her eyes to discover her hands completely healed. Blood was now dried on her skin, cracking off as she examined them closer. Not even a scar was left behind.

"That's impressive," Cordelia breathed in awe.

"And convenient," Gabriel added. "Are there any side effects to this wonder twin power?"

"If it's a big job, then we may get tired. Bones and internal injuries take a lot out of us," Damon informed them.

"You have experience with healing internal injuries?" Gabriel asked, his eyebrow raised.

"Don't look at me," Damon raised his hands in surrender, pointing directly at his sister. "It's her fault."

"Really, Snow? Internal Injuries?" Gabriel flashed her an accused look.

"It was like, twice! It was mostly broken bones. The occasional concussion," she shrugged her shoulders. "You think I got as good as I am at fighting by watching Jackie Chan movies? I don't think so."

Gabriel shook his head, massaging his forehead as if he had a headache forming. "You're going to be the death of me."

Amelia winced at his words, lowering her gaze. The restlessness in her chest grew at his remark. She was itching to move, to do something.

"I'm sorry. I didn't mean it like that," Gabriel quickly added, knowing he struck a nerve.

"It's fine. I'm fine. Come on. There's still a lot to be done before the wake," Amelia stood up, ushering them all out of the office.

Cordelia and Damon filed out of the room, but Gabriel lingered behind. He seized her by the waist, pressing her body against his. He concealed his face in the crook of her neck, breathing her in.

Amelia laid her hand on his chest, quieting the tremors that seemed to be vibrating throughout him. "I'm fine, really."

"I'm sorry for making that remark. I didn't mean it like that. Just, sometimes you're so careless. You're worried about losing me, but I couldn't bear to lose you. You're my world, Snow. You know that, don't you?"

Amelia cupped his face in her hands. Her skin was still caked in blood, but neither of them seemed to care. "I'll always be yours. No matter what. I promise you that."

She pulled him down into a slow, deep kiss that grew into something more desperate. The agitation she'd been feeling all day was building inside of her, making her actions bold. Anxiety fueled her blood as she pulled on him harder, gripping his hair by the roots, terrified of letting go.

Amelia bit his lower lip, making him hiss, allowing her better access. She tasted him thoroughly. Their tongues dancing to a rhythm of their own making. One made out of desire, love, and something else that stunk of finality.

They broke away, desperate for air. Her fingers itched to tug him back down. To mount him and mark him all over again. She wanted to cum until it hurt, until they both screamed from release. But now was not the time or place.

Standing on her tippy toes, she kissed him quickly, smiling as she sat back on her heels. "Go," she said, nodding towards the door.

Gabriel gave her one last smirk before disappearing down the hall. Amelia followed shortly after and walked smack dab into a crowd of people mulling about in the Packhouse.

Guests had started to arrive during her healing session. The commons were bursting with bodies. Kids squealing as they ran from their parents, teenagers sneaking booze, and adults ignoring all of it. The uneasy feeling in her chest only grew at the sight of all the people.

Looking out over the heads in the house, she spotted a familiar hair color, one that tended to stick out in a crowd. Amelia thrust her way through the pack, making her way to him.

"Dom!" she called out to be heard over all the chatter.

Dominik looked up, drawing his attention away from a pretty redhead he'd been talking to. Amelia beckoned him to follow her. Turning away, not bothering to see if he'd follow, she paced back the way she came into the empty hall. Dominik was at her back when she turned back around. Smiling at a couple as they passed, Amelia leaned her head in towards her cousin.

"How many are on patrol?" Amelia asked him.

Dominik raised a brow at her, not expecting that to be her line of questioning. "Forty. Why?"

"Double it. Now," Amelia ordered.

"What? Why? Did Damon okay this?" Dominik asked, leaning against the wall.

"I don't have time to consult my brother. I may not be an Alpha but don't test me right now," Amelia was bristling. Her aura slipped from her control as Rey grew in her mind. Their agitation only growing. "Now, double the warriors on the border and make sure each of them is carrying a silver blade of some type. Go!"

Dominik bowed his head in submission, exposing the tender flesh of his neck. Amelia reeled back. She hadn't meant to do that, but whatever got the job done. Dominik immediately left her sights, no doubt going to order more guards to the border.

Just as she was about to join the guests, Christian found her in the hallway.

"Hey, Ella. I've been looking all over for you," Christian paused, taking her in. "What's wrong? You look upset or terrified. Maybe both."

"I have a bad feeling, Chris. I can't explain it. I don't know what it is. But I've been freaking out all day, and it's only getting worse," Amelia said, jigging where she stood.

"Okay, what do you want me to-"

Amelia held her hand up for him to stop.

The sound of wolves snapping their jaws filled her ears. Shadows crept along the walls, menacing and dark, growling in warning. Wild wolves snarled, snapping their jaws in her direction. She smelled the air, pushing past the scent of the pack, her mate, her brother, all of it. It was barely there, but underneath it all, she caught the faintest whiff of petrol.

"Rogues are here," she gasped, her eyes wide.

"Where?" Christian stood up straight, his body alert.

"Everywhere."

CHAPTER 40

STAY SAFE

Damon! Rogues are here! Amelia screamed through her mind link, knowing he was closer to Gabriel than she was.

What?! Where?! I don't smell anything. Damon panicked. A tinge of disbelief was present in his voice.

Move now! Questions later!. Get your ass moving! Amelia ordered him, cutting off the link.

Christian stood in front of her as if he was waiting for her orders.

"Chris, go up to my room. There's a duffle bag under my bed. Grab my knives, all of them. Go!"

Christian went off towards the stairs as she hurried to the commons. Pack members were already getting the mind link and began to usher their families to the safe room. Panic began to overcome the wolves. Children began to cry; kids were seeking their parents lost in the crowd.

Amelia released her aura overall in attendance, immediately quieting the confusion and alarm.

"Everyone listen up. Rogues are coming onto the territory. I need all available warriors outside. The rest of you will begin to head down into the basement to the safe room. Let's move!" she clapped her hands, instantly releasing them all.

Amelia forced her way to the basement door, laying her hand on the scanner, releasing the lock. She opened the door and began ushering in the mothers with pups in their arms, teenagers clinging to their liquor, and elders who would rather be in the thick of it then stuck in a room with a bunch of frightened wolves.

The warriors were saying goodbye to their loved ones before splitting off and joining the rest outside. There were too many pack members here. Too many that could get hurt. The rogues selected the perfect time to strike with all of them in one place.

His scent of cinnamon and apple filled her nose, making her mouth water in response. Gabriel found her in the crowd, pushing through the woman and children to get to her.

"Amelia!" he gripped the back of her neck, holding her out to examine her.

"I'm okay," Amelia assured him.

"How do you know?"

"I received a warning. When I concentrated hard enough, I could smell them," she told him, keeping her eyes set on the stragglers making their way into the basement.

"You have to go down with them. I can't worry about you *and* the pack. Promise me you'll stay safe," Gabriel insisted, placing his hand against her growing bump. "This isn't like last time. There are over sixty rogues out there."

Amelia nodded her head before he kissed her rough and fast, pulling away all too soon and running back outside.

Christian appeared back at her side, her duffle bag in hand. Leaning down, she pulled out a few silver knives, tucking them into her pockets, joining the ones she already had tucked away in her boots and along her belt.

"Take the rest outside. Make sure everyone has a weapon," she pushed the bag back into Christian's arm. But before he could join the other warriors outside, she grabbed him by the shoulder, giving him a quick hug. "Stay safe."

"You too, Ella," he said against her hair.

She watched as he ran out, her attention back to the rest of the pack.

Amelia spotted a middle-aged she-wolf, looking around the house in a panic. She left the basement door open for the others to continue their descent and approached the woman. She recognized her. Another member of the Wandering Moon Pack who had four kids if she remembered correctly.

"Amelia! Thank heavens, it's you. I can't find Jeremiah!" the woman cried out.

Her fear was contagious as it struck a chord deep inside Amelia's chest. "He's your youngest, right? What is he, four?"

The woman bobbed her head, her eyes still searching over the thinning crowd. Three terrified kids clung to her hands and legs.

"Where was he last?" Amelia asked her, trying to keep the woman and pups calm.

"He ran down the hall chasing his ball. He should have been back by now." Tears began to fall down her face, using the back of her hand to wipe them away carelessly.

"I'll go get him. I promise. But I need you to get in the basement with the others. Take your pups, now," Amelia pointed back behind her to the open door. Nearly everyone was already inside.

The woman reluctantly nodded her head, scooping up the smallest child before heading to the safe room.

Amelie turned and made her way to the hall that connected the main house to the single's quarters. She could detect the faint scent of a small child and followed her nose. She ran down the hall, following his smell all the way to the end, into the laundry room. Peeking around the washing machines, she recognized a small toddler cowering in the corner; his head pressed into his knees.

"Hey," she called out to him quietly. "It's Jeremiah, right?"

The boy gradually raised his head, his eyes red and puffy. Poor kid must be terrified. Especially if he heard the mind link. Amelia held her hand out to the child, beckoning him to come forward.

"I'm Amelia, Alpha Damon's sister. Your mom is really worried about you. Why don't we go find her? Yeah?"

The little boy nodded his head slowly before reaching out and taking her hand. Amelia pulled him into her body quickly, lifting him off the ground, and ran back down the hall. The boy concealed his face in the crook of her neck as she sprinted back to the commons. The scent of rogues began to overpower the comforting smell of the pack. They were almost there.

Cordelia was at the door, ushering in the last few bodies. Amelia rushed up to her with Jeremiah in her arms when the sound of snarls reached her ears. She looked over her shoulder out the back door. Her heart raced in her chest.

The decision between pack and family tore at her insides. Fracturing her heart. She made a promise to Gabe, but she also made a promise to her pack, both of them. She'd defend them with her life. She couldn't shift, but she wasn't defenseless either. Maybe this was what the Moon Goddess meant. She had to join the fight. Either way, she couldn't wait on the sidelines. It wasn't who she was.

Turning back to Cordelia, she noted the look on her best friend's face. Tears were already brimming in her eyes, pooling over the sides.

"No, Mia. Don't do this," Cordelia pleaded, begging her friend to stay.

"I'm sorry, Cordie. I have to."

Amelia forced the child into her friend's arms, all the while pushing her through the frame towards the first step, down into the basement. Before she had a chance to realize, Amelia slammed the door closed. Securing it with her biometrics scan.

The sounds of fighting could be heard from inside the now abandoned house. Cups were left half-drunk, food littered the floor from those dropping it in the panic. She produced a knife from out of each of her boots, flipping them expertly in her hands, and walked out the back door.

They fucked with the wrong pack.

CHAPTER 41

LUCK OF THE BLADE

Amelia ran outside.

Most of the warriors had already spread out across the territory to defend all points of entry. But from the sounds she could make out, some had already gotten through.

"Grab whatever weapons you can find!" Amelia yelled at the nearest group, protecting the house and the precious lives hiding inside. "Aim for their throats and heads!"

Amelia ran into the woods towards the closest sounds of fighting. As long as it wasn't anywhere near Gabriel, she'd be okay. He was definitely not going to be happy with her, but the pack's well-being had to come first. She wasn't that far along. Even though she couldn't shift due to possibility of risking the baby's health, she was more than lethal as a human.

She came upon her first fight—two rogues against four warriors. The odds weren't great. The rogues had already managed to wound two of them.

Releasing her first knife, she threw the blade with precision, landing directly between one of the rogue's eyes. The wolf dropped to the floor, dead. Giving the warriors the advantage they needed, taking out the last rogue.

Amelia veered right. The sound of someone screaming out in pain captivated her attention. A teenager, barely old enough to be considered an adult, was in the clutches of a rogue, his arm dangling from its jaws. Moving nimbly, she leaped off the forest floor onto the back of the disgusting beast. Slamming the blade of her knife into the back of its neck, she severed its spinal column.

The wolf collapsed, paralyzed and dying. The jaws released the boy's arm, allowing him to scramble back against a tree. Amelia grabbed the kid by the shoulder, examining the damage. Deep puncture wounds could be seen. The flesh jagged and bleeding profusely. She didn't think he'd lose it, but he could certainly die from blood loss.

Amelia pulled off the belt from her jeans, fastening it around the kid's upper arm as a makeshift tourniquet.

"You need to get back to the Packhouse as quickly as you can. The warriors there will help you," Amelia slapped the kid along the side of the face a few times as he looked ready to faint. "Hey, wake up! You're going to die out here if you stay. Do you understand me?!"

"Yes, ma'am," the boy nodded weakly.

"Good boy," Amelia hauled him up by his shirt and forced him in the direction of the house.

Ripping her blade free from the now-dead wolf, the knife released with a slurp. She pulled out an additional knife from her pocket and ran in the direction of the sounds of fighting.

Amelia sprinted past bodies, already strewn across the forest floor. Some rogues, other's pack. She didn't stop to look at their faces. Stopping would get her killed. She had to keep moving.

Running faster, she pushed past the nausea and the crushing sense of being overrun. There were more rogues than she could count. By her nose, there were well over seventy. If they went strictly by numbers, then yes, the pack overwhelmed the rogues. But rogues were ten times more fatal.

Another fight broke out in front of her. Some of the warriors from the Twilight Pack were taking on four rogues at once. They were doing surprisingly well, but still outgunned. Amelia hurled a knife, flicking her wrist just right, so the blade slipped between the ribs of a rogue. The movement startled the warriors, but they kept their eyes on the fight.

The four pack fighters worked together, herding the beasts into a tight circle, giving Amelia the perfect vantage point. She scaled the nearest tree until she was high enough to drop down in the middle of the rogues. Stabbing her last knife in the side of the head of a wolf, she turned on the next, twisting its neck. The warriors made quick work of the last one.

Amelia bent over, breathing deeply, supporting herself by leaning on her knees. She was going to be sick. The non-stop motion and rush of adrenaline pushed her body to its tipping point.

She ran for the closest bush, eliminating what little she had left in her stomach. All the running, jumping, and climbing was not agreeing with her in the slightest. She felt large hands holding her braid back from falling in her vomit. Amelia wiped her mouth with the back of her hand to find Rick standing behind her.

Amelia couldn't help but smile at the strapping man whose frame resembled that of a bear. He was massive and burly with a bushy head of dark curls but the kindest eyes she'd ever seen.

"Are you okay, Luna?" Rick asked her.

Amelia took in a deep, steadying breath. "I'm good. Are you all okay?" she asked them all before retrieving her knives from the dead wolves.

Rick glanced around at his comrades, not finding any permanent or fatal damage. "We'll survive."

"Great. Now, if you could *not* tell Gabriel you saw me. I'd greatly appreciate it," Amelia said, backing away from the warriors she'd been training with for the last two and a half months.

"Yes, ma'am," Rick nodded, directing the others to follow him in the opposite direction.

Amelia started to run again, this time at a slower pace, her stomach still cramping from the physical exertion, when she felt a burning pain in her side. Like hot knives running across her ribs. Skidding to a halt, she screamed out in pain. Placing her hand on her flank, she lifted her shirt, but there was nothing.

"Gabriel," she gasped.

Mate's hurt! Rey yelled.

"Where is he?"

The pain she was experiencing through their bond was excruciating. It felt as though someone had poured liquid fire into the marrow of her bones. She was convinced her blood was boiling, desperate to spill from a wound that wasn't hers. The idea of what the wound might actually look like nearly made her sick all over again.

West!

Amelia turned in the appropriate direction and began to run at a sprint, her legs pounding into the earth.

The sun was descending rapidly in the west, barely offering any light to guide her way. The full moon rose over the trees, illuminating the forest in a silver hue. The wind picked up, whistling through the leaves above her head.

She could feel their bond growing stronger. He must be close, when a familiar, repulsive smell entered her nose. She halted in place, turning in every direction, trying to place the scent.

Leaves crunched underfoot behind her. She spun around. The man walked out from the shadows, the profile of his face highlighted by the moon. The night on the cusp of twilight. The pearly light made his scars appear even more gruesome than they had in daylight, shining against the matted brown shit he called for hair.

Amelia stood up straighter, trying to ignore the intense pain in her side that belonged to her mate, and confronted the man who was the cause of so much loss in her life.

"Michael."

CHAPTER 42

SIX CENTURY-OLD REJECTION

"You remember me. I'm flattered," Michael snickered.

Amelia tensed her hands, forming tight fists. What she wouldn't give to wipe that smug look off his face, but she had to play this cool. Somehow, the creep was working with the rogues, and that was more important than revenge.

"Why are you here? I don't recall you introducing yourself as a wolf last we met," Amelia said, the coolness of her voice surprised them both.

Keep him talking. You can do this, Amelia. Rey encouraged her.

What if he attacks? The pup-

I'll do my best to protect the pup. Focus on here and now.

"I had to make sure you were who I thought you were," Michael went to walk around her, but Amelia matched him step for step. "You didn't disappoint little rose."

Amelia froze mid-stride, startled by his words. Only her father had ever called her rose since her scent reminded him of a rose—the same as her mother.

"You smell just like her. Did you know that?"

Amelia pulled back her fist.

Not yet! He's goading you. Don't play his game.

Amelia withdrew, lowering her arm. Her blood was boiling. The rage within was barely contained, her body shaking. What she wouldn't give to be able to shift and tear him limb from limb. Instead, she forced herself to calm down. She couldn't butcher him before she obtained answers.

"Why are you doing this? What do you get out of it?" Amelia asked, trying to keep the bitterness out of her voice. She was failing.

"Why, you of course."

"*What*? What could you possibly want with me?"

"You're the daughter of Rhea. A direct descendant of the first mated pair," Michael said as if that explained everything.

"What does that have to do with anything? How do you even know that?" Amelia asked. She knew she was overlooking something. How could he possibly know about her lineage when she barely understood it herself?

"My family has been tracking yours for generations. For hundreds of years, we've been trying to get our hands on one of Rhea's descendants," Michael spat. The venom in his voice shook her core.

"Why? What do you want with us?"

"It was my clan Rhea was supposed to marry into. My line that should have possessed the powers yours do. Rhea was not supposed to marry Ezekial, but the chieftain of *my* clan," he pounded his fist against his chest, causing her to flinch. "But the bitch had the nerve to reject us. Choosing Ezekial over my ancestor."

Amelia swayed her head in confusion. "Wait, I thought Rhea and Ezekial married to stop a war from happening."

Michael laughed. A laugh that would haunt children's nightmares for decades. The laugh crawled over her skin like a snake wrapping around her, choking whatever calm she had left.

"Rhea was already in love with Ezekial. She defied both of their clans, marrying in secret and the Moon Goddess rewarded their betrayal with the fated mate bond. The first werewolf clan."

"Then how did your clan end up as wolves?"

"Well, that's the thing, isn't it? Back then, clans intermarried quite often. After their pack turned, Rhea's sister married my clan's chieftain instead, transferring their power to us. But we were deceived. It was my clan that should have received the Moon Goddesses gift! We're the ones who should have bred her power into our clan. Instead, we've gone practically extinct," Michael was shaking. His wolf must be close to the surface.

"Look, I'm sorry about that. I am, but that doesn't justify what you're doing here. What you're talking about happened over six hundred years ago. No one can know what happened then. They're all dead. Let the past stay in the past," she tried to reason with him, trying to appeal to his humanity. However, given the inky black of his eyes, his humanity was long gone.

"I can't," Michael cocked his head in her direction at a strangely inhuman angle. "You see. I promised my father. Who promised his father before him and so on.

That *we* would make Rhea's descendants pay if we couldn't break them ourselves. We've managed to wipe out most of the females in your line. Waiting for a suitable woman, a sensible woman, to see reason."

"And what reason would that be?"

"Become my mate. Bear my pups. Give my clan the power it deserves, the power it demands," Michael ranted, sounding like a complete and utter loon. He belonged in an insane asylum.

Or put down like the dog he is. Rey added.

Yeah, I like that idea better.

"Your fucking insane if you think I'll turn my back on my mate," Amelia spat at him, her tone full of poison and disgust. The very thought of him touching any part of her body made her want to jump off a bridge.

"I never said it needed to be consensual. Just until you've given me an heir or two, that's all I require," Michael shrugged his shoulders, as though she didn't have many options.

"I'd rather die you sick fuck!" She would never allow herself to be used in such away. She was shaking. Every ounce of her demanded blood, demanded vengeance. Hundreds of versions of his death flew through her mind. All of them gruesome and painful and satisfying.

"That can be arranged," his lips pulled into a smirk that pulled at the scars on the side of his face. The sight made her nearly lose the lining of her stomach, but she bit down on her tongue, keeping it at bay. "Your mother said something similar before I carved her into pieces."

Amelia stopped their little dance. His words shocked her, leaving her frozen, equal to diving into the arctic circle. Her body was numb. She'd been right. It *was* him.

"You fucking bastard!" Amelia screamed, her fingers shifted into claws before she launched herself at him.

Michael wasn't expecting it as she raked the tips of her nails down his face. The man wailed in pain. His right eye slashed open and blind.

Amelia didn't slow down. Punch after punch, she swung for his face, his ribs, his chest, anything she could make contact with. Some of them were direct hits, others he managed to block. She didn't care. She kept swinging. Putting all her anger, her grief, and hatred into every punch.

She loathed this man. Hated him for taking her mother and the baby sister she never got to meet. Hated him for targeting her family for six centuries. For being directly responsible for her father's death and nearly her brothers. Michael deserved the deepest, coldest pits of Hell with his own personal demon to torture him for all of eternity.

Her loathing and fury distracted her. Michael got in a substantial hit to her temple. Stars obstructed her vision. She stumbled back, shaking her head to clear the inky clouds forming. Michael took advantage.

Hands up, Amelia!

Amelia put her fists up just in time to block another hit that would have surely knocked her out. Her vision returned, back to seeing only one of him, she struck out again. His left flank was exposed, his arm hanging lower than it should have been. Faking a hit to his right, she swung with her left. Her knuckles striking the side of his throat.

Barely allowing him a chance to gasp, she spun around hard, kicking him square in the chest. His body soared back until it collided with a tree, crumpling to the ground.

Amelia wanted to finish him. To extinguish his life. Rip his soul from his body and watch as the light faded from his eyes, knowing she ended him. His family was the reason for every brutal murder in hers, every generation that experienced senseless death. And over what? Jealousy?! Some unrequited love?

She moved towards him. Rey came through in her eyes, her claws out and ready to rip his beating heart from his chest when she heard deep growls behind her.

Amelia spun around to find herself confronted with three rogues she hadn't realized circled her. She was so busy with her fight that her rage blinded her to what was going on around her. She allowed herself to be surrounded by savage wolves.

CHAPTER 43

SLIVER OF HOPE

Amelia stood ready, waiting for the wolves to make their move.

Her head was still spinning, pounding with the hit she took. The side Gabriel was injured still throbbed, like a painful itch she couldn't scratch. He had to still be alive. She would know if he wasn't. Their bond would notify her if he was mortally wounded. Would force her to go to his side and heal him.

That sliver of hope is what she clung to.

Her stomach was cramping with discomfort. Exhaustion had her knees shaking, but she locked them. She couldn't afford to be tired, or sick, or whatever other crap issues her body had. Weakness meant death, and she refused to die that day.

The first rogue launched for her throat.

Amelia ducked out of the way. The weight of the wolf brushed the stray hairs back from her face as he sailed over her body. Before she could straighten, she was knocked off her feet by the following wolf. Amelia tucked and flipped her body. Sticks and rocks bit into her skin as she rolled on the forest floor. The third wolf jumped for her. She kicked out with her legs, dispatching it across the small clearing.

The next few minutes were a flurry of fur, teeth, fists, and knees. She barely injured them without her blades, but they were inflicting grievous wounds on her. Scratches ran down her arms. A bite to her shoulder. A claw snagged her just above her eye, causing blood to block half of her vision.

Stupid head wounds bleed like a bitch.

You can do this, Amelia. You have to.

Rey sounded weaker than ever. The effort it took to protect the pup was taking its toll on her. Rey was directing all of her energy into shielding their baby. The early stages of a Were pregnancy were fragile as the pup and wolf spirit bound together.

A sharp, searing pain, ignited down her side as a rogue caught her unawares, running his nails deep into her skin. Blood ran down her side. The scent of it suffocated her.

Amelia was furious. Furious with the ass hole that threatened her pack. Killed her mom and dad. The man that wanted to violate her over some nonsensical bullshit and was using Rogues as his lackeys.

A raging storm brewed within her causing her to see red. Her body began to shake uncontrollably, awakening a deep reserve of unrequited rage. Igniting a violent wave that threatened to obliterate everything and anyone that stood in her way. How dare they threaten her pack, her mate, and most especially her pup! Rey was doing all she could to ensure their pups' survival, but what if it wasn't enough?

The Alpha power that resided deep within her was sparking inside, eager to be set free, to be used for its intended purpose. Amelia arched her back as she released her aura, threatening the rogues that snarled and snapped at the air between them. The rogues instantly whimpered, whining at the authority her aura commanded.

She took a step towards them, making them stagger back, trying to put as much distance between them. Their heads lowered in submission, providing the perfect opening she needed. Pulling out the last of her knives, she ran along the front of the three wolves, slitting their throats open in one swift movement.

Each of the wolves dropped to the floor. Their blood mixed with the dirt of the earth, producing a sludge of mud.

Recovering her breath, the blade slips from her hand onto the floor. The faint scent of petrol filled her nose, but it was too late. The brown wolf was already leaping through the air behind her. Amelia barely had time to twist around. One arm clutched her stomach. The other guarded her face as she closed her eyes, wishing for a swift death. Gabriel's face flashed across her mind.

But no blow came. All she heard was the sound of a collision. Wolf smashing against wolf and then an impact so loud, so deafening, it made her want to gauge her ears until she damaged her eardrums just enough to silence the echoing inside her head.

Amelia fell to her knees as the pain of nearly every bone in her body breaking caused a blood-curdling scream to escape from her mouth. Half of her felt like it had shattered, bones piercing organs into a bloody mess.

An obsidian wolf lay lifeless at the base of the tree beside her. Gabriel received the hit that was meant for her, causing his body to sail into the tree, shattering the entire right side of his frame. He wasn't dead yet, but he was fading fast.

Amelia turned to the brown wolf. Her eyes were dilated and black. No longer human or wolf, but something else entirely. She lunged for him. The scars on his face and the blind eye gave him away. Human fingers were replaced with razor-sharp claws as she slashed at the man with every last bit of vitality she had left.

Michael whimpered beneath her. Her claws sunk into his sides, ravishing every inch of skin she could reach. The coward managed to slip from her grasp, turned tail and ran deep into the woods.

Amelia wanted to follow him. She wanted the sweet taste of revenge, but her path was blocked. Looking around, she found herself surrounded by eight more rogues. Stepping in front of her mate, she crouched low, guarding his body with her own.

Leaning back, she laid a hand over his side. His pulse was weak, barely beating life into his body. She needed to heal him, but with the eight wolves gradually approaching, they were stuck where they were. Helpless. Her heart started to race; panic began to set in. She failed her pack and her mate. Because she failed to act, she'd lose everyone she'd ever loved.

Gabriel's body shivered beneath her touch, reacting to their bond. A small whimper escaped his muzzle, weak and desperate.

Snow, don't.

Gabriel's voice rang in her mind. Every ounce of love, desire, devotion, and fealty, rushed through their bond, overpowering her. She staggered, falling back on her rear. Tears slipped from her eyes, down her cheeks. The man was on death's doors, and still, he was trying to protect her.

The rogues moved closer. Moistening their lips with anticipation.

Amelia confronted them head-on. Her face hard, her lip drawn up in a snarl. A fierce desire to protect overcame her. A pressure began to build in her chest, funneling all of her energy to that one spot. Her aura began to grow around her, shrouding her in a purple mist. All eight rogues lunged for her when she screamed.

She screamed with outrage for her pack. Roared with longing for the man she loved. Howled for the pup, she was determined to see born into this world. But most importantly, she growled with the desperation to survive, releasing a power greater than anything that's ever been seen on the face of the planet.

The rogues turned tail and fled for their lives.

CHAPTER 44

A HOPELESS DREAM

"Help! Someone help!" Amelia screamed into the night.

She scrambled to Gabriel's side. His body shifted back to that of his human, unable to maintain the shift. He was unconscious. His eyes closed. His skin was deathly pale. Blood pooled beneath his body, feeding the earth. Amelia stroked the side of his face, brushing back his velvety, silken hair from his eyes.

"I'm here, baby. I'm here," she told him.

She was nervous to touch him, afraid to make it any worse. From the outside, the damage looked extensive. His exposed flank revealed deep gashes tearing down into his ribs, exposing bones and flesh. She couldn't imagine what the other side looked like. The side that made the near-fatal impact with the tree.

Tree, one. Gabriel, zero.

Branches cracked behind her. Someone was running in her direction. Spinning around on her knee, she extended her hands, not even sure she could defend herself if she wanted to but lowered them when she recognized Christian.

She breathed a sigh of relief; more tears slipped from her eyes. "Thank the Goddess," she breathed a sigh of relief. "It's Gabriel. He's hurt!"

Christian whistled loudly. The sound reverberated through the battle-weary forest. Six more warriors came running, carrying a stretcher between them. Christian wrapped his arms around her, shifting her out of the way. Amelia staggered back, watching as they carefully loaded his helpless form onto the stretcher.

The brief sight she caught of his damaged body caused her to gasp. Spinning into Christians chest, she buried her face in his filth-soaked clothes. How could he survive that? His entire side looked crushed, caved in. No longer human.

Christian grabbed her by her shoulders, causing her to gasp. Her body was finally acknowledging the damage it had received. He pulled her away from him, inspecting her.

Amelia did the same with him, assessing his wounds. He received a few cuts on his face, some bites to his arms. A couple of fractured ribs by the way he winced when she leaned against him and a sprained ankle. Nothing that wouldn't heal.

Her eyes finally moved back up to his, only to find horror in them. His eyes were wide. The goofy grin she loved so much was hanging open, nearly brushing against the floor.

"What's wrong?" Amelia asked him, her brow scrunched. Black spots invaded the edge of her vision, but she ignored it.

"Ella, your pants."

Amelia looked down at what he was gaping at to discover blood running down her legs, staining her jeans red between her thighs. Agonizing cramps constricted her stomach, rejecting the only foreign thing in her body.

Murky clouds consumed her. The blood loss dragged her under into the deep abyss.

☾ ☾ ☾

Dawn could be seen on the horizon. Twilight had drawn to its end, and the sun was rising over the skyline, casting rays of beautiful gold, indigo, and tangerine. The sky danced with renewed purpose and the promise of new beginnings.

Amelia found herself standing in the Twilight Moon territory, at the edge of the lake, in the middle of the training grounds. The water was tranquil—a perfect reflection of the heavens above.

Part of her wanted to touch it, to shatter the dream of absolute silence. The other half of her wanted to believe in the delusion of peaceful serenity and maintain the glasshouse built around her. But life had produced a cynic, and she was no doll.

A willowy figure moved to stand beside her. Her aura was calming to her frazzled nerves, soothing to her aching body, and pacified her troubled mind. The Goddesses aura shimmered around her in hues of violet, the same as her eyes. She could almost reach out and touch it, but she kept her hands secured to her side.

"I tried to warn you," the Goddesses voice sang, brushing over her like a gentle breeze on a warm summer's day.

"You did a crap job of it," Amelia couldn't help the bite to her voice. She wanted to blame the Goddess for her troubles. Blame her mother and father for keeping her in the dark. But mostly, she wanted to condemn herself. "Why couldn't you just tell me what to do? What could I have done differently?"

"You already altered your fate. This was not the ending I saw," the Goddess added frankly.

"That's not an answer to my questions," Amelia sighed with exhaustion, tired of the games.

"I cannot give you all the answers you seek. Some journeys are meant to be explored and discovered in their own time."

"Then, what do I do now? Michael got away."

The Goddess turned, facing her. Amelia responded in kind, meeting her eyes. The Goddesses gaze was staggering. The wolf within her bowed instantly, but the human side was more stubborn, less obedient. Amelia stood her ground before the Goddess.

The woman's lips twitched, almost as if she was about to smile but thought better of it.

"If you stay with your pack, more will die," the goddess stated matter of factly. "You will never bear another child, and your mate will die defending you."

"What?!" Amelia squeaked. "Then what do I do?"

Before the words escaped her lips, the Goddess faded into nothing, leaving her alone on the edge of the lake. The surface was disturbed by a series of ripples.

☾ ☾ ☾

A machine beeping was the first annoying sound that captured her attention. Peeling her eyes open, the light above her was bright and blinding. Blinking slowly, her pupils adjusted to the harsh fluorescent bulbs. Looking around, she found herself in a cramped room with whitewashed walls and medical equipment.

Moving her arm to wipe the sleep from her eyes, something tugged against her skin, causing a sharp pain in the crook of her elbow. Glancing down, she found herself hooked up to an IV machine and heart rate monitor. So that's where the annoying beeping sound was coming from.

She was in the infirmary. Her body felt like a giant bruise. The parts of her body, she could make out were covered in purple and blue splotches, but judging by her breathing difficulty, she was certain she'd broken a few ribs.

Her hand rested on her stomach, brushing against her bump when she finally recalled the blood. The blood that was spreading down her legs. The intense cramping she felt in her abdomen.

Gabriel's deformed body.

She began to squirm against the needle in her arm, ripping it out with her free hand. Her heart rate was accelerating against her ribs, igniting a fresh wave of pain with each beat.

The door to her room opened. A tall doctor walked in with her chart in hand. Dr. Ronald had been her doctor for as long as she could remember. He'd seen her for every shattered bone and fever.

"Relax, Amelia. You need to calm down. Your body has been through a severe trauma, and you need to settle your heart rate," Dr. Ronald ordered her, taking deep calming breaths, encouraging her to repeat.

Fuck that.

"What happened? Where's my brother? Where's Gabriel?" Amelia asked. The noise from the monitor began to beep erratically. The lines on the paper spiking.

"You're in the infirmary. Your brother and mate are here as well," the doctor said calmly.

Amelia could read between the lines.

"What about my baby? What happened to my baby?" Amelia barely whispered, terrified of what he might say.

Dr. Ronald grabbed the small roller chair and dragged it over to sit beside her bed. Her heart dropped at the gesture. That wasn't a good sign. If a doctor had to sit, it was never good news.

Tears pricked the corner of her eyes as she waited for him to tell her the dreaded news. Her actions cost her her child's life.

"You lost a lot of blood, Mia. Christian brought you here fairly quickly, but the process had already begun."

Her breath hitched in her throat, choking back a sob. "I lost the baby?"

"We managed to stop it. But you did lose one of the fetuses, yes."

Amelia froze, her brow scrunched in confusion. "What are you talking about? I don't understand."

Dr. Ronald regarded her curiously, checking through her chart once again before setting it back down in his lap. "Have you seen a doctor yet, concerning your pregnancy?"

"No. I was waiting. I hadn't told Gabriel about the baby until we got here. It's been a bit crazy," Amelia said, her voice completely flat as she tried to work out what he meant. He was expressing words, but none of it made sense.

"You were expecting twins, Mia."

A smile spread on her face before it instantly fell, the weight of his words sinking in. "I *was* carrying twins."

"Yes. We managed to prevent the miscarriage from completely expelling both fetuses. You still have one inside of you. We did a full anatomy scan. You're about eight weeks along, and the remaining fetus is strong with a healthy heartbeat."

Amelia's head fell back against the lumpy pillows of the infirmary bed. Turning her face into the scratchy cotton, tears slipped from her eyes, staining the coarse material.

Perfect silence was not a gift and peaceful serenity was a hopeless dream. Ripples echoed across the lake she considered reality.

CHAPTER 45

DO YOU TRUST ME?

"I really think you should stay in bed, Amelia. Your body is still recovering. You lost a lot of blood. Given the number of gashes and bite marks you suffered, you'll be in a great deal of pain. Unfortunately, I'm unable to give you any pain medication to alleviate it. You just lost-"

Amelia stopped the doctor before he went any farther. "I know exactly what I lost, and I don't have time to lay in bed. I can't afford to sit still while my pack suffers. My mate is hanging on by a thread, and I have no idea what's going on with my brother."

She swung her feet over the edge of the bed, wincing, inhaling sharply, just as her hospital room door opened.

Christian stood at her door. His face riddled with steri-strips. His arms bound in various sized bandages. Amelia identified some of her clothes in his hands. She smiled gratefully at him.

The doctor approached the door and addressed Christian. "Make sure she takes it easy," he said to him before turning back to her. "Do not push yourself too hard. I'm serious, Amelia. Or your body *will* finish what it started."

Amelia nodded solemnly. Christian stepped in the room, closing the door behind the doctor as he left. She tried to stand up from the bed, but her legs buckled beneath her weight. Christian was by her side in a flash, holding her up by her arm.

Everywhere hurt. She was certain there wasn't a single spot left on her body that didn't feel like it hadn't been mauled by a dog or set on fire. Her body felt like it danced with a wrecking ball, and all she wanted to do was crawl back in bed and wallow, but she couldn't. Rey was deeply depressed, feeling like she'd failed. Half of her personality was already down for the count, and Damon and Gabriel couldn't afford for her to drown in her sorrows; mourning the baby she'd never get to meet.

"The doctor's right. You should stay in bed," Christian said, his voice gentle and coaxing.

"You know?" Amelia sounded surprised.

"I was the one who brought you in. I stayed until you were stable and only just left to get you clothes. I knew you wouldn't stay in bed no matter what," Christian explained.

Amelia looked up at his face, and what she saw there hurt. "Don't look at me like that."

"Like what?"

"Like I'm broken."

His face softened, trying to flash her his typical goofy grin, but it failed. "Ella, you just lost a baby. It's okay for you to be sad."

Amelia looked away from him, biting back the tears. She couldn't allow herself to feel it. Not with her mate's life so uncertain. "I can't. Not yet."

Christian nodded soberly.

"I could use your help though," Amelia glanced down at the floor sheepishly, her cheeks reddening. "Help me get my clothes on. I can't bend down for pants or lift my arms."

"Of course."

The tone of his voice made her curious. He wasn't mocking her or smirking with dirty innuendos like he normally would.

"Thanks, Chris."

They spent the next ten minutes getting her dressed. Amelia was naked beneath the hospital gown, and yet Christian seemed completely unphased. He dressed her with a look of disinterested determination. She was thoroughly impressed. He really was a remarkable guy. Not that she ever doubted that.

Her body was worse than she expected. Yes, her skin was one giant bruise, quite literally. But she didn't account for the numerous stitches holding her ribs' skin together or the other various parts of her body that required delicate sutures. She looked like the bride of Frankenstein. With Rey already weak from trying to save the babies, her own healing ability was slowed down to a crawl.

Once she was finally fashioned in leggings and a t-shirt, she sat back against the edge of the bed, utterly exhausted. How could she make it down the hall to Gabriel or Damon when changing clothes had her wanting to sleep for days?

"What's the report?" Amelia finally asked, no longer seeing a reason to put it off.

Christian ran a hand through his hair, mussing it up even more than it was. "We lost twelve wolves; fifteen are critically injured. The rest have minor scrapes."

"And the Wandering Moon wolves?"

"They lost closer to forty warriors. Damon's been seriously injured. They think they might have to amputate his arm."

Amelia swallowed with difficulty, breathing in deeply through her nose. Dr. Ronald barely said a word to her about her brother or her mate, which was suspicious in itself. He must really be worried about her body completing the miscarriage if he didn't even tell her the extent of their injuries.

"And Gabriel?" She asked, terrified to know the answer. He was still alive. That much she knew.

"Gabriel's in a coma," Christian said reluctantly. "They don't think he'll make it through the night."

Amelia bit her lower lip, tears swimming in her eyes. Her heart sank into her stomach, making her nauseous. She wiped absently at the tears slipping down her cheeks. She couldn't lose him. She wouldn't.

"The damage inflicted on his body was extensive. His entire right side was crushed, many of the bones pulverized from the force of the impact. His wolf was out of it for too long, unable to help with the healing. The doctor thinks it's too late. He's bleeding internally."

Her dream came back to her. The Goddess was direct with her words. If she stayed, he'd die, but she didn't say he'd die if she were gone. If she healed him and left, then maybe he'd have a chance.

To protect her pack, her mate, and provide the remaining child a chance at life, she had to leave. Ignoring the Moon Goddess and her dreams was no longer an option.

Amelia straightened herself on the bed. Wiping away the remaining wetness from her skin with indifference. She set her face to an impassive look. If she was going to go through with this, she needed to stay strong and detached.

"I need to see Damon."

Her tone caught Christian off guard. He looked visibly concerned for her. His brow was permanently furrowed. His eyes were blood-shot, making her wonder when he'd last slept. She was sure he was waiting for her to go into hysterics. Strike her fists on the walls until they were bloody and scream at the heavens. Instead, he stood by her side, winding his arm around her waist, and hoisted her off the bed, gripping her tightly against his sturdy frame.

"I can walk, you know," she grumbled.

"No, you can't, now stop being so stubborn. He's just a couple of doors down."

Amelia rolled her eyes but was grateful. Stubbornness aside, she knew full well she wouldn't have been able to make it to her door, let alone down the hall.

Christian walked into a room three doors down, forcing the door open without bothering to knock.

Inside, they found her brother in bed, pale, wrapped from head to toe in bandages. Dominik and Cordelia stood at his side. His sea-green eyes found hers, and moisture instantly penetrated his charming eyes. Christian walked around the side of the bed. Dominik and Cordelia instantly moved out of the way as he set her down on the firm mattress beside her twin.

Damon grasped her hand in his. Her gaze flicked to his right arm. It lay there useless, bandaged, and at his side, unmovable. He squeezed her hand lightly, shifting her attention back to his face.

"I'm so sorry, Mia. I didn't know you weren't down in the basement. If I had known, I would ha-"

"Shh," Amelia wiped the moisture from his skin with the pad of her thumb. Her beautiful brother looked so distraught, shouldering the burden of blame. "This is not your fault. I was the one who made the choice to fight. No one forced me. This is all on me."

"No, it's not. If I'm not allowed to blame myself, then neither are you. Some things are just beyond our control," Damon reinforced his words by squeezing her hand again, holding her gaze.

She looked back to his injury. "What about your arm? How bad is it?"

"It's done, Mia. The damage is considerable. It nearly severed, and there's nothing to attach it to. The blood vessels are too far gone," he shook his head, whether, in denial or disbelief, she wasn't convinced which.

"Nothing's too far gone for us," Amelia whispered, finally squeezing life into his hand.

Damon's eyes shot up to hers. Disbelief frowning his face. "You can't be serious. I won't let you. There's no way. You can barely hold yourself upright, and you want to heal me? Are you nuts?!"

"Stop yelling at me," she hissed at him before turning to the eavesdroppers still lingering in the room. "Can you guys give us a few minutes?"

"Ella, I don't think-" Christian tried to protest.

"You can stand outside the door, but I need a moment alone with my brother," she told them, her face expressing she was completely serious and unyielding. "I'll holler if I need you. Promise."

Each of them reluctantly agreed, dragging their feet out the door until it clicked shut behind them. Swiveling her head back to her brother, she held his eyes firmly, making him squirm under her gaze.

"I am not going to let you suffer longer than you have to, and you are most certainly *not* going to lose an arm. Not on my watch."

"Amelia, you just lost your pup. How are you not a mess right now?" Damon asked her.

"It was twins, Damon," she said under her breath, finally admitting it aloud. "I was carrying twins. I lost one baby, but I still carry one inside me. Healing you can help to heal me too, to give my pup its best chance. Please."

Damon's eyes were swimming again. Not trusting his voice, he nodded.

"Thank you," she sighed in relief. "You ready?"

Damon nodded once again before closing his eyes. Amelia reached across the bed so that she was holding both of his hands before she closed hers as well. They started their familiar tune. Humming the soothing melody between them. Ordinarily their healing spell was quick, and to the point. But the damage here was a bit more extensive. They weaved their song, singing, enticing new tissue to grow. Regenerate old, dead tissue back to life, knitting flesh back together.

Amelia knew it was working when she felt his right hand lightly squeeze hers, and yet they kept going. Feeding off one another, they repaired every cut, every scrape and bruise until they were the picture of perfect health.

After almost an hour, they finally opened their eyes to find one another looking perfectly healthy. Even though she was completely healed, she felt utterly drained. This wasn't even the hard part. Gabriel was next.

Damon sat up higher in his bed. Carefully, he rose his right arm to find it reattached. Raising his elbow, he rotated his shoulder, flexed his hand open and closed, and performed a few other gestures with the arm. They had restored his complete range of motion.

"I'll never get used to this," Damon stared at his arm in amazement, a smile playing on his lips.

"It's probably best that you don't," Amelia said, breaking his bout of joy.

"What do you mean?"

"I need your help, Damon, and what I'm about to ask you to do, you're not going to like. But this is the only way," she knew she sounded cryptic, but she needed him to understand first. "Do you trust me?"

Damon's frown lines creased deeper along his forehead. "Of course I do."

Amelia nodded, not expecting anything different.

"Then, this is what I need..."

CHAPTER 46

VIOLET

Amelia pushed open the door to Gabriel's room.

Walking was still painful. Apparently, even her healing abilities had limitations, and it did not include the aching in her womb. As though she needed another reminder.

Her eyes moved lazily over the room. Hesitant and terrified with what she might find. Finally reaching him, her knees buckled at the sight. Firm arms supported her weak frame as a sob choked her throat, leaving her gasping.

It was worse than anything she could have imagined. From the chest down, white sterile blankets draped over his body. The skin she could see was horribly damaged with blood still crusted in some places. He was hooked up to more machines than she could count. Pumping him full of drugs, keeping his heart pumping and his lungs breathing.

He looked ragged. Nothing like the man she'd gotten to know these last few months. The powerful Alpha of the Twilight Moon pack reduced to a bag of fractured bones.

Amelia hobbled to his side. Her hands stuttered, hesitant to touch him, afraid to make any of it worse. Although, how much worse could it get? The doctors already said he wouldn't survive the night. Nothing was more final than death.

Tears spilled past her eyelashes, running rivers down her face. She'd done more crying in the last few days than she had in her entire life, and she had a feeling it was only the beginning. She needed to be tougher, harder if she was going to go through with what she had planned next. But right now, all she wanted to do was curl up against his side and bury herself in his neck—breath in his scent for what could very well be the last time.

Brushing her fingers against his forehead, she swept the hair from his face, running her hands through his silky locks. Goddess, how she would miss this. Miss his touch. The feel of his hair. The way a single look could leave shivers down her spine. But most of all, she'd miss the man. No matter how infuriating or how bitterly they fought, he was hers, and she was his. Nothing could change that, not even death.

Leaning into him, she swept her lips across his cheek, his forehead, until finally, she met his mouth. She almost expected him to kiss her back, for her touch to elicit some type of response, but there was nothing. Complete and utter stillness. Her heart shattered just a little more.

She traced his face with the tips of her fingers; her touch was feather-soft. If this was their last time, she wanted to memorize every single detail of the man before her. Catalog every flaw she could uncover and store them away for her dreams.

"I don't know if you can hear me," Amelia finally recovered her voice. Though it was cracking and rough, she needed to vocalize what she had to say before she no longer had the chance. "But I need you to do something for me," she licked her lips, hesitating. "Promise me you won't hate me. I'm doing this for us. To keep you alive. To give our child a chance."

The tears flowed more effortlessly, her emotions getting the best of her. She despised this, hated all of it. Hated her powers for enticing some lunatic to hunt her family down, generation after generation. Hated her lineage for providing her a fated mate. Hated the fact that the fated mate she was saddled with was the absolute ideal man for her. The one she presently had to say goodbye to.

"I have to lose you to save you. To save all of us," she shook her head angrily. None of this was fair, least of all for her, but this was the way it had to be. She just prayed to the Goddess that one day he might understand. "I love you, Gabe. With every fiber of my being, I love you." She kissed him one last time before sitting up, wiping the dampness from her face with the backs of her hands.

Damon stood hovering beside her in case she needed the additional support. Neither of them was sure how long she could continue standing, but she would do anything, risk everything to save his life.

"Let's do this," Amelia finally said, clearing her voice. She took in a deep breath, steadying her nerves, calming her body. These were the last tears she'd cry. From that moment on, her pup needed her to be stronger for the both of them.

"I don't know about this, Mia," Damon said, doubt clouding his voice. "The damage. I don't know if we can handle this by ourselves, and I will *not* put your life and your baby at risk."

Amelia whipped her head at her brother, glaring harshly at him. "And I will *not* let him die. I will do this *with* or *without* you, but I *will* heal him. I cannot exist in a world where his heart isn't beating. I won't. I can live with him breathing and hating me. But the minute his heart stops so does mine."

"I get it, but-"

"No, there are no buts. I know you care for Cordie. I hope you love her, and you two find every happiness, but don't pretend to understand this. He's not just my mate; he's my fate. The Moon Goddess created us for each other. There is no one else for me."

"Okay, fine. You're right. I don't understand. But you're not strong enough for this. You can barely stand," he gestured to her body. The way she was holding herself up by leaning against the frame of the bed.

He's right. I don't know if we have what it takes. We could lose our last pup. Rey spoke up. Her wolf sounded miserable, weak, and defeated.

I can't watch him die, Rey. Losing him might actually kill us. It's a risk either way.

I know.

"We're doing this, Damon."

"Then you're going to need help."

Damon and Amelia both snapped towards the door to find Christian standing in the entrance, Dominik just behind him. Cordelia's small frame could be seen as well behind the burly men.

"I can't ask this from any of you. I don't even know if it's possible," Amelia shook her head. This could knock them out for days, weaken their wolves. What if they were attacked again?

"It's a good thing you're not asking," Dominik pushed past Christian to stand on the opposite side of Gabriel's bed. "We believe in you."

Cordelia walked in to stand behind the twins, resting her hands on both of their shoulders. "If transferring a piece of our energy, our wolves, will help save him and lessen the burden on the two of you, then we'll do it."

Christian shut the door behind him, locking it.

Amelia couldn't help but smile. That they'd be willing to risk exhaustion during such uncertain times to help save her mate.

This might work. Rey said.

It will *work.*

"Damon, stand on the other side with Dom. Cordie, go ahead with Damon. Christian, come and stand beside me," Amelia directed.

They each moved around the room, assuming their respective positions. Amelia and Damon stood directly across from each other near Gabriel's head. Christian stood beside her, one arm around her waist if she became faint, the other holding her free hand. Cordelia stood between Damon and Dominik, each holding hands with one another.

"Damon and I will call on our wolves, all of our wolves. All you have to do is relax, don't fight it. You might feel drained or tired. Whatever you do, do not let go. If you feel the urge to follow along with the melody, your wolf might feel compelled, and that's okay. Don't resist," Amelia instructed each of them. Only feeling satisfied as each of them nodded with understanding.

Amelia made eye contact with her twin. His face was as resolved and focused as she felt. This was it.

Here we go. Amelia breathed through their link.

Each of them closed their eyes as Amelia called on the Moon Goddess, the mother of them all. She called on her connection to the spirit of her wolf, of all wolves, and allowed it to fill her. In her mind's eye, she could feel a mist take over—the color of violets.

Amelia began the song of healing, humming softly and slowly. Damon's voice mixed with her own, and soon the five of them were in perfect harmony.

Bones that were once shattered, the damage irreversible, began to reshape and form where they once were. His ribs snapped back; his chest expanded instantly. The damage to his punctured lungs, no longer able to fill on their own, expanded with a deep breath as the holes were plugged and tissue regrew. Every single bone and organ that had been damaged regenerated itself, creating viable tissue that would sustain him for the rest of his days.

Gabriel's body was nearly recovered as they reversed nearly every wound. The one place she left slightly impaired was his mind. He had a major concussion. Allowing some of her power to seep in, she mended him partially, leaving just enough to keep him sleeping for a few more hours. She couldn't risk him waking before she was ready.

Amelia was the first to sever the link. Her hands falling to her sides. The humming echoed in the room as each of them dropped off. Opening her eyes, she encountered a violet mist floating in the air, hovering before her. It was dissipating before her eyes, but the other's gasped at the sight. Violet represented the color of the Moon Goddess, and somehow, she had tapped into that power like never before.

She should feel fatigued. Goddess knows she could sleep for an entire week, but she felt oddly invigorated, empowered almost. Her mate would live, and that fact gave her the final push she needed.

Stepping away from Christian, she squeezed his hand before walking around the bed to her family. She pulled Cordelia into a back-bracing hug, forcing every ounce of love she had into it.

"Thank you, Cordie. For everything," Amelia said into her shoulder. She bit the inside of her lip—no more crying.

Cordelia pulled back, a brilliant white smile plastered on her face. "Of course, Mia. We'd do anything for you."

Amelia turned to Dominik next, giving him a brief hug. "Thanks, Dom."

"Anything for our princess," Dominik said with a smirk.

Amelia swatted his shoulder playfully before turning back to her three friends, her family, and smiled at them all. Knowing it might be the last time she would ever see them. She cleared her throat, trying to remove the lump that was starting to form. "Could you all give me a moment with my brother?"

"Of course," Cordelia smiled, none the wiser as she led Dominik out.

Christian looked back over his shoulder, uncertainty written on his face. Amelia gave him an encouraging smile before he left the room and closed the door.

"You don't have to do this. We can find another way," Damon said behind her, pleading.

She turned to face him. Her twin, her other half. Her partner in crime and her confidant. Damon was her anchor at sea. Even during the wildest of storms, he kept her moored, tethered to sanity. What would she do without him?

"There is no other way. The Moon Goddess was very plain in her warning," she shrugged her shoulders, finally giving in to her fate. "I won't lose this baby. This might be my only chance at being a mother. It's a part of Gabriel and a part of me. I won't give that up. I can't explain it, but I know this baby is important. The Goddess wants me to keep it safe."

Damon seized her by the shoulders, holding her against him. She winded her arms around her brother, not knowing if or when she'd see him again. Shaking her head against his shoulder, she refused to think like that. Damon was the only person she'd keep in contact with. No one else could know where she was. He was the only one who could hold his own against her mate.

"Promise me. You will swear the doctor to secrecy. No one can know about the baby. No one."

"I promise. He won't say a word."

If Gabriel somehow found out she was still pregnant, then her chances of him staying away were slim to none. If he knew she was carrying his child, he would follow her to the ends of the earth, and they'd be right back to where they started. His life in jeopardy and their child's as well.

Gabriel had to believe she miscarried and that she abandoned him. Whether he believed her a coward or a traitor, it didn't matter. It hurt, but it couldn't affect her mission. She had to get as far away from both her packs as she could. Hopefully, Michael and the rogues would follow her, leaving the Twilight and Wandering Moon Packs alone.

Amelia finally pulled away. "I need a car. No one can know I'm leaving."

He nodded his head solemnly. "I know. I'll go grab a set of keys."

Damon left her in the room with her mate. Glancing over her shoulder, she hugged herself. She had never felt more alone in her entire life than at that moment, and it terrified her. Gabriel would be conscious in just a few hours and find his mate had run, abandoning him. She just prayed he wouldn't outright reject her, not knowing what that would do to her wolf or her pup.

Taking one last longing look at her mate, she brushed her lips against his, drowning in the familiar, delicious shivers his touch produced.

"I'm sorry," she whispered against his skin.

Turning to leave, she found Christian standing in the doorway, arms crossed, leaning against the frame. Amelia's heart stuttered in her chest.

"Going somewhere?" Christian asked, tossing a set of keys in his hand.

"What? How?" Amelia stuttered, flabbergasted.

"I convinced Damon to give them to me. You need someone to watch your back. You can't do this alone," Christian said with a final flick of his wrist, catching the keys.

"Yes, I can, and I will. You're not coming, Chris. It's too dangerous," she shook her head adamantly. Who did he think he was? Did her brother receive brain damage? He had to in order to agree to such a hair-brained idea.

"I am not letting you go on the run without backup. You're pregnant, Ella," he hissed the last part, keeping his voice low. "You do not have to do this on your own."

Before she could resist him, he cut her off. "And if you leave without me, I'll tell Gabriel about the baby."

Amelia's jaw dropped to the floor. Her eyes widened. "You wouldn't."

Christian just stood there with that smug look on his face, cocky stance with his hip sticking out, and one eyebrow raised, daring her. She closed her mouth firmly, glaring daggers at him.

"Fine," she snapped. "You can come. But if Michael comes, I'm feeding you to his rogues."

"Deal," Christian straightened up, his goofy grin back. "So, where do we go now?"

"We run."

CHAPTER 47

TAKE CARE OF THE PACK

The drive back to the Twilight Moon territory was longer than she'd have liked.

Damon provided her his mustang, a real power horse, but the drive still took them three hours, breaking every speed limit known to man. Christian drove for her, allowing her time to rest. She managed to get a couple of hours of sleep. Her body desperately needed it.

Her hand rested over her bump. It was still there, but it somehow felt emptier than it did before. She tried to keep her mind off her loss, off the baby she'd never know, but her mind kept wandering in that direction.

The smell of the Twilight Pack filled her. Breathing in the scent, she savored it, locking it away in her memory. The pack had become her home in the short time she lived there. They would be her child's pack, its birthright. Hopefully, one day they could return, but it was up to her to keep its memory alive until then for the both of them.

Christian pulled the Mustang up to the front of the house. Amelia grasped his hand before he could get out.

"We have fifteen minutes before we're out of here. Gabriel could wake up any minute, and if he wakes up before we leave, we're screwed. This'll be over before it begins," she warned him of the possibilities. If they were caught, they'd both be dead. Gabriel's trust in them would be extinguished no matter what they said.

"Got it, pack fast," Christian nodded. "I'll meet you back here in ten."

Amelia smirked, grateful he was coming with her.

They both got out of the car, rushing up the steps and into the house. Not surprisingly, Lena met them as soon as their feet crossed the threshold.

"Luna! Thank the Goddess. You're okay. What are you doing back here? We heard about the attack," Lena said in a rush. Her normally perfect bun was a bit of a mess as if she'd been pulling on her hair with worry.

"I'm okay, thank you, Lena. I came back to get some of my stuff. We might be at the Wandering Moon Pack for a bit longer than expected. A lot of our warriors were injured," she lied through her teeth, surprisingly well. She wasn't sure if she should be proud of that or not, but it would certainly come in handy in the coming months, if not years. "I can't stay long. I have to hurry back, but can I ask a favor? Could you get me some food for the ride back?"

"Oh, of course! Give me five minutes!" Lena cheered, turning away with a bounce in her step as she scurried towards the kitchens.

Amelia went straight up the stairs to her bedroom, closing the door behind her. She rushed inside the closet and grabbed the largest duffel bag she could find. She began stuffing clothes inside, whatever she could fit.

Opening her weapons chest she had crammed in the corner, she flung it open, grasping whatever weapons she could get her hands on. Thank the Goddess wolves were placed in every business known to man, allowing her to carry weapons on aircraft. She knew a guy in the TSA.

Back in the bedroom, she pulled open the drawer of her nightstand. Digging through the few things in there, she grabbed her passport, birth certificate, and whatever other documents she thought she might need. Wherever they were going, they'd need to find someone to make them fake IDs, creating new identities. Whatever would make them harder to track.

Inside the drawer, she caught sight of a pad and paper. Setting her bag down on the floor, she picked up the writing items and scribbled down a quick note. Maybe he'd burn it; maybe he wouldn't. But she couldn't imagine leaving without saying goodbye. A goodbye he could remember.

Leaving the note on the bed, she took one last look around the room. Her eyes drifted to her bookcase. The one he had specifically designed for her. She ran her fingers over the titles until the familiar, worn leather crossed her path. She pulled the book from the shelf and placed it on the top of the clothes in her duffle bag before finally zipping it closed.

One final look back at their bed, she allowed the rush of memories to flood her. Every illicit moan, calling his name in the throes of passion, the scent of his cum mixing with hers. All reminders of just how good she had it with him. She may never have another sexual encounter again, but one thing was certain. Gabriel would be the only man for her.

It wasn't just the sex she'd miss but the man himself. Curling up against him at night for warmth. He never cared how cold her toes were. Waking up to his scent first thing in the morning. The way his hair fell in his eyes when he first woke up. How he always cracked his back stretching, immediately after getting out of bed. She would miss it all.

Closing her bedroom door for the last time, she made her way back down the stairs, Lena and Christian already waiting for her.

"Thank you, Lena. I really appreciate it," Amelia said, handing Christian her bag.

"Of course, anything for you, dear," Lena smiled before leaving them at the door.

"Ready?" Christian asked her. His eyes questioning her if she was sure this was the right thing to do.

Before she could answer him, a shrill voice squeaked behind her.

"Amelia!"

Kelsey. Shit. She didn't know if she could say goodbye to her too.

"I'll meet you in the car," she smiled weakly at Christian before he took their things and left her in the foyer. Flashing her a look of sympathy before he left.

"I was so worried! We heard about the attack! I was so terrified you were hurt or something. We heard the Alpha wasn't doing so well. Is he okay?" Kelsey spewed in a rush, like word vomit.

Somehow, Amelia was able to follow her friend's speech, smiling as she nodded. She'd miss her friend's crazy banter, her wild temper, and colorful voice. She'd never get to show her how to ride her motorbike or train with her again. But at least she'd be alive.

"Yes, Gabriel is okay. He's on the mend," Amelia tried to smile, but it didn't quite reach her eyes.

"Where are you going? Why are you back already?" Kelsey asked, glancing over her shoulder to where Christian waited by the car.

"We're going back to the Wandering Moon Pack. I came back to get some more clothes. Some of our other warriors are still recovering, so we might be there a bit longer than we expected," more lies.

"Oh, great! Let me get my stuff. I'll come with you!" Kelsey bounced, ready to turn and head upstairs before Amelia grabbed her arm.

"No!" reeling herself in, she breathed deeply. "I mean, you can't. We need all of our warriors here in case the rogues come back. Things are a bit chaotic at the Wandering Moon Pack right now, and more people just makes it that much more difficult. I wish you could come, but I really need you here right now. Protect the pack. That's the most important thing."

Amelia squeezed her hands for emphasis, holding her eyes with her own, reinforcing her words.

Kelsey nodded her head, believing every word she said. Amelia ignored the pit in her stomach. Lying was her life now. This was her new norm. Might as well get used to it.

"Okay, I'll stay," Kelsey agreed.

Amelia breathed a sigh of relief before gathering the girl in for a hug. "Thank you, Kelsey," she squeezed a bit tighter than normal. They had become close, on the verge of best friends, like she and Cordelia were. She'd enjoyed spending time with her and would miss her company immensely. "Take care of the pack."

"I will," Kelsey patted her back before finally letting go.

"Bye, Kels."

Amelia turned away before her friend could see her on the verge of tears. No more crying, she promised herself. Biting her cheek, she walked out of the house, down to Christian, and without looking back, they fled their home.

CHAPTER 48

SWEET DENIAL

GABRIEL

His eyes felt like lead, heavy and unmovable. There was a pounding in his head, but otherwise, he felt fine. Good, even. Groaning, he forced his eyes open, blinking hard against the light. Taking in his surroundings, he found himself in the infirmary, surrounded by expensive-looking machines, machines that normally meant death for a wolf.

What happened?

He struggled to sit up, but something pinched his arm, pulling against his skin. Looking down, he found himself hooked up to an IV. He pulled the needle from his arm, flinging it to the side as it dripped saline solution onto the floor.

Physically, he felt healthy, but his head still throbbed. Maybe a concussion? Standing up, out of bed, he discovered a set of clothes on a chair. He pulled off the hospital gown, stepped into a clean pair of pants, and pulled the shirt on.

His muscles felt tense, his body a bit jittery. He wondered how long he'd been unconscious.

The rogues came, but he couldn't remember much after that. He remembered instructing Amelia to go down into the basement. She nodded, agreeing with him before he joined the other warriors outside, but that was it. That was all he remembered.

Gabriel left his room, leaving the sterile equipment behind. Where was his mate? Where was Amelia? Why wasn't she with him when he woke up? That didn't seem like her at all.

He recognized someone familiar wandering the halls of the infirmary. Rick, one of his leading warriors. A big, burly man, who had a fondness for his mate, regarding her as a daughter. But even from the distance he was at, he could see a nasty claw mark down the side of the older man's face, stitched back together and covered in a thick bandage.

"Rick!" Gabriel called out to him. His voice halted the man in his tracks.

"Alpha! Thank the Goddess, you're okay," Rick clapped him on the shoulder when he got close enough, looking him over to ensure he was well. "We didn't think you were going to pull through."

"I'm fine, thanks. What happened?" Gabriel asked him.

Rick informed him of the battle. How many pack members they lost and that he was practically dead, hanging on by a thread. Gabriel asked him about Amelia, but Rick had no clue where she was, only that he recalled seeing her during the battle, fighting off wolves.

Gabriel growled at that bit of news. He explicitly told her to go down into the safe room. To not put herself or their pup at risk. And she agreed! What the hell was she thinking?!

Ren was irritable, pacing, agitated, and worried. There was something he wasn't telling him. Stupid wolf harbored too many secrets protecting their mate.

The next few people he saw down the hall, he asked after Amelia, but no one had seen her. Gabriel began to feel panicked. Where was she? Had something happened?

Finally, Gabriel spotted Damon heading down the hall towards his office.

"Damon!" Gabriel called out, jogging over to him. The movement rattled his brain. "Where is Amelia?! Where's my mate?!"

He knew he was attracting attention, his voice booming throughout the house. His Alpha aura was slipping beyond his control. Damon nodded in the direction of his office and walked away. Gabriel huffed loudly before following the other Alpha. Damon shut the door behind him, gesturing for him to take a seat.

"I don't want to sit, Damon. I want to know where the hell my mate is. What happened? Was she hurt?"

"Amelia was courageous. She saved a lot of our pack, killing at least a dozen wolves on her own. If it hadn't been for her training with your pack and having your warriors here to help, the casualties would have been far greater," Damon told him, maintaining his tone even and void of emotion, which struck Gabriel as odd.

A flitter of nerves overcame him, dancing in his stomach as he fastened eyes with his mate's twin.

"Where is she? I won't ask again," Gabriel snarled.

"Amelia was injured pretty badly. Between fighting and using her Alpha power to get rid of the rogues, trying to protect you. It cost her a lot. She lost a lot of blood," Damon paused, biting his lower lip, just like Amelia does when she's nervous. "She lost the baby."

Gabriel fell back into a seat, his heart breaking in his chest. Ren howled in his mind for the loss of their pup. For the first time since his mother's death, tears swam in his eyes.

"Where's my mate, Damon? Where is she?"

"She's alive. She's the reason you're alive. You wouldn't have survived the night, but she healed you," there was something else he wasn't saying. "She's gone, Gabe. And she's not coming back."

Gabriel stood up suddenly, causing the room around him to spin. He extended a hand out, gripping the arm of the chair to steady himself. "What do you mean she's gone?! Gone where?!"

"I don't know. She just left," Damon said, with a shrug of his shoulders. "She didn't say where she was going, but after seeing you as broken as you were, losing your pup. She didn't want to risk your life anymore."

"What are you talking about? I need my mate!" Gabriel wanted to put his fist through something, to demolish everything in sight. How could she leave?!

"The Moon Goddess warned her that if she stayed, you would die. She's doing this to protect you," Damon said, unreasonably level headed.

"Tell me where she is," Gabriel seized the man by the front of his shirt, elevating him off the ground.

Damon didn't fight back, didn't struggle. He merely relaxed his hands gently over the closed fists tightening on his shirt. "I don't know where she is."

Gabriel lowered him to the ground before spinning around and storming out of his office, slamming the door behind him.

Kaleb! He yelled through the mind link, hoping it would work at such a distance.

Alpha! Are you okay?

I'm fine. He snapped. *Has Amelia been back to the territory?*

She was just here, boss.

What do you mean, just there? Where did she go?

She left about thirty minutes ago. Said she was heading back to the Wandering Moon.

Did she talk to you? What did she say? Was she with anyone? Gabriel fired question after question. None of it was making sense. Why would she do this?

No, sir. I didn't get a chance to speak with her, but Lena and Kelsey did. She said she was there to gather some stuff since you would be there for a few more days. Lena packed her lunch, and they left.

Who's they? He growled.

Christian, sir.

Gabriel spun around, slamming his fist through the nearest wall. His knuckles splintered wood and plaster with a satisfying crunch, but nothing he did could satisfy him now.

Go up to my room. Now! Check her side drawer. See if her passport is there. Gabriel ordered. Giving him a minute. *Did you find it?*

Kaleb hesitated. *I-its gone, sir. There's a note for you on the bed.*

Gabriel collapsed to his knees.

CHAPTER 49

SHE WOLF

AMELIA

Newark Airport was consistently a shit show. One of the most congested airports on the East coast. Luckily, they made it there in record time, purchasing their tickets as soon as they arrived.

Christian had a cousin living in a small pack in northern Italy. The land of pizza and pasta it was. There, they would acquire new identities and credentials. She had no idea what awaited them. What kind of dangers they might face, but she knew she was doing the right thing.

Her heart was back in New York, but her future, her legacy was within her, and she would do anything to see it safely born. Of course, a part of her did doubt herself. Wondering if she understood the Goddess clearly.

Rey wasn't happy about any of it. Her wolf was mourning the child they'd lost, mourning their mate they abandoned, but deep down, she knew it was the only way. Now, their sole priority was their pup. The one thing they had left. Even if they couldn't physically be with their mate, Gabriel lived on in their child.

"Flight 205 is now boarding. Destination, Florence, Italy. Please approach gate 23B."

The intercom announced their flight. Glancing down at the ticket in her hand, she triple checked the correct flight number and gate. Christian slung both of their bags over his shoulders, ushering her towards their place in line.

Amelia rested her hand over her stomach. Overwhelmed with the sudden urge to run. Run back to her mate, back into his arms. Maybe this was a mistake. Maybe they could face this together. What if she couldn't do this without him? Who was she to take his child away, to raise it without him?

Just as she was about to turn around and tell Christian what a horrible mistake they were making, something or rather someone caught her eye.

Off in the corner of the congested airport was a wolf.

The wolf was small, barely a teenager, but she was strong. Amelia could see through her to the blue wall behind, but her silver eyes looked directly at her. It was a vision.

The small pup took tentative steps towards her, allowing her a thorough look. She had silver-white fur with a black stripe down her back. Her silver eyes were easily recognizable and startling. They were exactly like Gabriel's. The wolf nodded her head before disappearing. As though she'd never been there.

Her pup. She saw her pup.

Amelia rubbed her thumb against the top of her bump, smiling. For just a split second, she was overcome with joy and love.

It would all be worth it. It had to.

ACKNOWLEDGMENTS

Shadow of Twilight, began on a whim. Werewolves kept circulating in my mind and I had just finished the second draft of a separate fantasy novel, but I could not rid myself of the idea of Amelia. Thanks to the encouragement of my dear friend, Stefanie, I knocked out the entire first draft in two months. If it weren't for her, being able to bounce off all my crazy ideas, and work out my characters personalities, I'm not sure Amelia and Gabriel would be who they are today. So, thank you so much Stefanie. For always being there for me. For yelling at me, crying with my characters, and supporting me through all my craziness.

I'd also like to thank my family. My parents for their unwavering support. To Derek for supporting me and my hobbies and our four beautiful children who loved the pretty wolves on the covers. To all my family in New Jersey, Brianna, Aunt Denise, and Grandma Donna, thank you for always giving me your honest opinion and for encouraging me.

To the Wattpad community. Without all of you, I'm not sure I would have had the courage to pursue publishing my work. Thank you Holly, you crazy bitch, for keeping it real, Quinny, one of my first real followers and now dear friend, Lacy Sheridan for answering all of my hundreds of questions on the publishing process, and of course Jacqui, for the late night chats and all the smutty convos. And last but not least, I could never forget Ancient, leader of our crazy writing group, for your unfailing, brutal honesty. Without you, I would not be the writer I am today.

Thank you to MiblArt for the stunning covers! You brought my vision to life and I couldn't be happier.

Kathleen, you have supported my writing since day one in high school. Thank you love.

Sam, my British beauty, for crying with my characters and loving my rollercoaster of a novel.

Sarah Schott, for being my off the clock therapist. Thank you for inspiring me to be a better writer.

And to Close, for bringing Amelia to life on my skin.

The story continues…

Read on for a preview of Dusk to Dawn:
Book 2 of Fated Darkness

Coming Soon

All they've done is run. All they've done is prepare for the worst. Amelia is tired, her wolf Rey has almost completely disappeared, leaving them weak and vulnerable. It's been seventeen years. Her daughter Emery has grown into a beautiful, strong wolf, but they've been found again. Amelia doesn't know how much longer she has left.

The mate bond is slowly killing her. It's time to go home, back to their pack where Emery will be safe. Even if she doesn't make it, her daughter has too. Amelia doesn't know if she can survive reuniting with her mate. Has too much time passed? Too much damage been inflicted?

They're coming. It's time for them to run again, but this time they're running home.

Heather Smith has been crafting stories for as long as she could remember. It wasn't until she was fifteen that she wrote her first novel that she had no intentions of publishing. At nineteen she wrote her first completed manuscript that is still a work in progress, but will soon turn into a four-book series.

Currently, she is working on multiple series, all fantasy genre. When she isn't writing about fantastical worlds, she resides in Hudson, Florida with her four children and spends her time attending school events, quilting, and loving on her two Labradors and four ball pythons.

Follow Heather:

Twitter: https://twitter.com/starsascending

Instagram: https://www.instagram.com/heathersmithauthor/

Website: https://www.heathersmithauthor.com